*Shaking
Out the
Dead*

Shaking Out the Dead

K.C. Cholewa

THE
STORY PLANT

The Story Plant
Studio Digital CT, LLC
PO Box 4331
Stamford, CT 06907

Print ISBN-13: 978-1-61188-143-1
E-book ISBN-13: 978-1-61188-144-8

Visit our website at www.TheStoryPlant.com

First Story Plant printing: June 2014

Printed in the United States of America

0 9 8 7 6 5 4 3 2 1

For Sarah and Isa, my goddaughters

Acknowledgments

Thanks to the many friends and enablers who provided editorial assistance, moral support, a sounding board, and hope. Thanks first to my editor, Lou Aronica, whose input and assistance made *Shaking Out the Dead* a better book, and me a better writer. Thanks, too, to Terri Hamilton, the Naked Words Reading series, Caroline Patterson, Tom Harpole, Chris Dorsi, Dave Ames, Edwin Dobb, Judy Klein, Cindy Palmer, Sandy Oitzinger, Hugh Ambrose, Margaret Regan, Ann Regan, Leah Joki, Dennis Small, Robin Rutkowski, Terry Kendrick, Sally Mullen, Kate Mrgudic, the morning crowd at the General Merc, and my parents, Joseph and Joan Cholewa. Thanks to the many books of fiction and nonfiction that instructed and inspired me along the way.

November 1987

I

꙳

Paris was a Montanan without a myth. He didn't ride horses, hunt, fish, or ski. He had never worn a cowboy hat or squinted across the range. Paris was blue-collar bred, and his body was strong — built not by gyms and barbells, but by physical work and car-less, pedestrian life. Behind his eyes there were no big skies, just a duty-bound psyche. His destiny, his purpose, he thought, was to notice. The pretty and the bad. The ugly and the good. See it and let it be. He decided long ago he would not want. He would lighten the burden of the world. Be one less pair of sticky hands.

He pulled the hood of his sweatshirt over his head and tugged the sleeves over his hands. He had gotten off from work at 5:00 a.m. and, despite the chill, wasn't in a hurry. As he walked, his eyes slipped through the landscape. He was intimate with the details. The sidewalk cracks, small graffiti, and low-lit doorways. In the hours before light, the street's subtle decay was not erosion, but the peeling back of veneer to reveal a spirit. Paris worried for this place. He knew, as with all places with souls, there would be those who would come to feed. Their coming caused a prickling in the air, made the molecules quiver.

With a sweatshirt-covered knuckle, he pushed his glasses up the bridge of his nose. He was six feet tall, weighed in at one seventy, and his feet sweated in his boots as he walked through the clean, timeless in-between when night and morning still locked hands, prudently, in a private space beneath the horizon. It was a city in a valley, the mountains in the distance slouching, black silhouettes against the blue-black curve of space. Paris acknowledged creation's glory though it was, in fact, colored sprays of broken glass in an alley, the underpasses, deserted railroad yards, and cars with three flat tires curbed for months that called to him as he made his way home. The mountains didn't need his love. The litter reached to him.

Turning down a dark side street, the earliest of risers still barely stirring behind their dark windows, he headed for Tatum and Geneva's duplex to perform his house-sitting duties. Geneva was in Europe. Tatum was in Chicago because her sister was sick. Four days ago, Tatum had come into the Deluxe, the diner where Paris worked, to tell him she was leaving.

Other than Tatum and Paris, the diner had been empty, an un-bussed table the only sign of recent life. Business would pick up later around eight and then spike again when the bars let out. Then, briefly, the Deluxe would buzz. Paris would serve fried eggs and tuna melts. Customers would toss crumpled napkins onto ketchup-smeared plates. The Deluxe was one of only two choices in the valley for after-hours food. The Deluxe or the Pie House. That was it. All knew in which they belonged. The more criminal the element, the better the bet they chose the Deluxe. Even dangerous people need places to feel safe, and Paris deftly served this demographic. He understood their needs. Being feared is a double-edged sword: you are left alone, but you are watched.

Which is why purple-haired young adults, innocently pierced, patronized the Deluxe, as did aging men with neither wives, children, nor the means nor understanding to purchase the appropriate camouflage that enabled one to blend with the calculable citizenry. The Deluxe gave them a break from being an affront to society. It was a place to be ordinary, simply eating without being perceived as doing so in rebellion against or in contrast to the status quo.

Only rarely did Paris get one of those preening, dark angels — all aggression, looking for fights, and flanked by boy lieutenants. He was glad such types largely hunted elsewhere, but it was not because he feared them. Predatory males had always passed Paris by. He'd heard the stories of other men and boys being chosen, antagonized, beat up, or scared shitless. But Paris was never plucked from the herd and fed to the pack. He liked to think it was because he was an artist. He believed his place outside the social order allowed him to serve his purpose of bearing witness and metabolizing the whole while humbly serving it soup.

But that was not the reason.

Paris was left to his own because he could not be gauged. Was too calm. In control, but not competing for it. Not computing rank. He could have been a simple man who stood for peace, a bodhisattva, a holy man. But just as likely, he could be a motherfucker with a knife in his boot, willing to beat you with a bat 'til your skull broke, if that's what it took.

He wasn't left alone because he was one or the other. He was left alone because other men couldn't tell.

Paris had been surprised to see Tatum coming through the lurid lighting of the bar, through the orange-green flash of keno machines, toward the restaurant in the rear. It was rare for him to see her there, her presence usually just a figment of his imagination. She had slid onto a round stool and slipped a short strand of dark hair behind her ear. The fluorescent lights glared, flattering nobody. Paris stood behind the dulled, but clean, counter in his whites, his demeanor, as usual, disguising his size. Bottles of ketchup, mustard, and Tabasco cluttered the space between them. Paris balanced one bottle of ketchup on another, merging them into one. He did the same with the mustards. The Tabasco, he simply wiped clean.

"My sister's sick," Tatum had said, "maybe dying. I'm not sure."

Paris removed a near empty ketchup from its balance.

"I have to leave," she said. "Warp speed. I'm not sure how long I'll be gone. It's hard to tell what the situation is." She reached into her coat pocket and started pulling keys off a ring. "I'm watching Geneva's apartment. She should be back Thursday night. Could you check in on her cat? Feed him, scoop his box?"

"Yeah," Paris said, "sure." He wiped the rim of the bottle filled with the sludge from others. He shook out his rag and hung it beneath the counter.

"Here's the key to my apartment," Tatum said, sliding a second key toward him. "If I'm gone overly long, maybe you can water the plants?"

Paris looked at the key. Guilt and excitement made his chest and face softly buzz.

"Or you could ask Geneva to do it," Tatum said, "after she gets back."

Paris lifted the keys off the counter.

"I can do it," he said. "You okay?"

Tatum forced a smile, one meant to reassure him.

"I'm fine."

Paris pocketed the keys, grabbed a bus tub, and walked around the end of the counter. He stepped to the dirty table behind Tatum. She spun on her stool, following him with her eyes. The dining room was worn and beaten with time, but not dirt. Paris made sure of that. He paused while loading the tub. He had a question for Tatum but wasn't sure what it was. He turned to face her.

"Yes, Margaret hates me," Tatum said, finding the question for him, "but that doesn't mean we're not close."

Paris flinched inwardly.

"Gotta go," she mouthed.

Paris watched Tatum leave, watched her cross the line between the diner and the bar, the line where the linoleum met the worn, red, cigarette-scarred carpeting. Her coat flared around her, reaching mid-thigh. She turned into a shadow as she opened the door, and the glow of dusk briefly illuminated the space around her, the space she was so adroit at cultivating.

Paris thought about her driving through the night. He thought about the key in his pocket and that he could be alone, again, in Tatum's apartment. He would not snoop, he told himself. Not again.

But first, there was tonight. Near nine, the high school degenerates would arrive, brash and boisterous, throwing food, and paying in piles of change. Around one, after the bars closed, hungry loners would speckle the room eating their solitary meals and delaying going home as best they could. Then, around two, two thirty, the women would begin to arrive, taking extra effort to be natural and not speed through the casino as the bartender, Blair, finished closing up. Maybe just one of the women would come. Sometimes, there were as many as five. Paris knew the Deluxe was a secret among the women of the street. The homeless. The hiding. The shipwrecked. In the wee hours, he doled out soup from the day's vat and served it with the cornbread he made himself when he came on shift. No one ever ordered. No one ever paid. Blair probably knew what was going on, but none of it was ever discussed. Paris knew that to retain the beauty of some things, they must never be named.

2

~

Tatum approached the casket from the back of the room, aware that she was The Sister, the Black Sheep. She didn't know Margaret's friends, but they knew her. Tatum felt their eyes slip from her head to her toes and back up again, their calculators clicking away, adding up details of shoe quality and unpolished nails, trying to penetrate the reality to find the reputation. But reputation is a flat lens. Tatum was there in 3-D. At the front of the room, Tatum sank to the kneeler, folded her hands, and bowed her head.

Piety, even the false kind, works like a repellent. She was left alone.

Tatum had a knack for getting people to leave her alone.

Kneeling, she let her eyes rest on Margaret's face. To Tatum, Margaret's expression from life had carried over smoothly into death: the look of someone who got everything she wanted and resented that it wasn't good enough because it could never include Tatum never being born.

It was that kind of sister-hate.

Tatum was certain that Margaret hated her no less in death than she had in life. In fact, she probably hated her more, and if strong emotions — hate, for example — were powerful enough to wake the dead, Margaret might rise at any moment. As it turned out, single parenthood was not part of the plan for Margaret's grieving husband, Lee. He had sentenced his daughter, Margaret's precious Rachael, to return to Montana with Tatum.

The thought of Margaret's fury with such an arrangement gave Tatum a twinge of discomfort with the corpse. She rose and made her way down the aisle toward the rear of the room, passing between rows of chairs arranged, rather bluntly, for a viewing. She had not packed for a funeral, and so she wore Margaret's black, wool skirt that was cut on the bias and stuck out from Tatum's slim hips like fins.

It did not surprise Tatum that Lee would pawn off his eight-year-old daughter on a woman whom the child was raised to hold in contempt and do so before the child's mother had a chance to *get into* her grave, much less cool in it. Lee was not someone who made sense to her. She didn't know if he was an idiot, but she did believe him to be a liar. Liars' behavior often doesn't make sense and makes them seem like idiots, fake idiots. That's how Lee seemed to Tatum, like a fake idiot.

Tatum didn't know if Margaret's crew of scary friends thought Lee was a fake idiot, but she did know this turning over of the child had been met with wide-scale disapproval, all done in whispers. The disapproval part made sense to Tatum too. She shared their sentiment. But she didn't understand why they seemed to act like it was her fault.

She didn't meet their eyes as she walked between the rows of chairs. She kept her own olive-colored eyes focused on the double doors ahead.

In the hall, mourners from other wakes loitered in twos and threes and moved in and out of restrooms. Tatum made her way toward the front doors and stepped outside to stand in the wet November night.

Humidity. Chicago humidity. November humidity. Her skin loved it, and her hair thickened and curled in it. It was home, yet so different from home in Montana where the dry air chapped hands and left the hair brittle. Tatum hugged herself and watched the flows of traffic pulling away from each other in opposite directions — busy, orderly, all keeping to their side of the yellow lines.

Tatum stepped from beneath the funeral home's awning and looked across the four lanes. She remembered Geneva four years ago dragging her into the empty street in front of their duplex. Geneva had taken hold of Tatum's hand and instructed Tatum to close her eyes.

First, they walked against the flow of traffic. Tatum, with eyes closed, had to admit that she could feel it, the energy resisting them, flowing in the direction traffic moved even though the street was empty. Then, they turned and walked with the traffic's flow, rode its invisible current. It was as though traffic had dug a groove and trained the energy. It ran like a river in its bed.

Tatum considered how much more forceful the flow might be here in the city where the traffic steadily pushed on without rest. So much activity, so many worlds. It made the old couple across the street seem lives away as opposed to feet and yards. Tatum watched them through cracks between passing cars as the old man held both the restaurant door and the umbrella as the bent woman in a rain cap maneuvered her walker inside.

The restaurant's name was Cardella's. It was square and somber, catering, no doubt, to the hungry bereaved. Tatum wished her friend, Paris, were here with her. He'd see it in paint. He'd entitle it *Mourning After*.

Tatum looked up into the haze of light that pooled in the city sky. The mist around her broke a sweat, releasing quick slivers of rain that seemed to step out from the fog and fall. Because she was thinking of Paris, she didn't move for cover. She let the rain slap against her skin the way Paris would. It felt good to do what Paris would do.

But thoughts of one man turned to thoughts of another, and Tatum opened her eyes and stepped back beneath the awning. Loss. Her own didn't rank among such heavy hitters as Margaret losing her life or Rachael losing her mother and home. Tatum had lost a boyfriend. A love. Vincent had dumped her two years ago and then disappeared. She hadn't heard a word from him since. Nothing. She tried to let it go and move on, as they say. She had even thought she was doing it, moving on, but then Vincent would ride in on another thought.

She had talked about it once with Geneva, wrapped in blankets on the patio on a September night. She told Geneva of the way Vincent would swoop into her thoughts. In the moment, Geneva hadn't said much. But the next morning, Tatum found a folded up piece of paper slid under her front door.

"Unrequited love is very stable," it said. It was signed — G.

The next day, graveside, mourners huddled in the crisp, clean cold. The sky was shockingly bright as Margaret was buried in a grove of oaks on her and her husband's six acres west of the city. It was not Tatum's first funeral. Not her first coffin. Cancer had taken her father fairly young and then her mother six years back when Rachael was only two. Wanting to maintain family ties, Tatum had made a point of driving back to Illinois once a year. Margaret would receive her, duty-bound. But by the time Rachael reached kindergarten, she had realized that within the clan she outranked her prodigal aunt. Despite her young years, her snub was most accomplished.

Tatum stood in the inner circle, closest to the coffin, as prayers were offered and roses were placed on the polished mahogany. The minister asked those congregated to join hands. As there was no one to Tatum's right, her hand hung empty at her side. Her left hand, too, hung empty as Rachael had turned away from her toward her father, the fingers of both of her hands curled into his coat pocket.

Tatum wondered what this day might be to Rachael somewhere off in the future, on a late night, years away, when Rachael was grown and lying in a lover's bed, touched and open. In a faraway voice, would she tell him her tale of that first love lost? Would the day still be vivid to her, right down to the feel of the wool of her father's coat beneath her fingers, the cloudless sky, and the notes of the violin turning to her with open hands, about to say something, before dissolving into grace? Or would her story be of cold motherlessness, slippery shadows, and photographs divorced from touch?

Tatum reached toward Rachael's long brown hair but then let her hand fall. Rachael looked over her shoulder as though she had felt the hand creeping toward her. Tatum noticed no flash of hate from Rachael when their eyes met as she had in the past. Just a sweet blank face with a shard of anger cut deep in the back of the eye.

The violinist stretched the final note. It hung in the air, seeming to hold up the mourners, as if when the note ended they would all collapse at once onto the cold autumn ground. But as the note faded and vanished, only hands dropped. Rachael looked away from Tatum, and they stood in new silence.

Lee broke the trance with an escaped sob. Tatum looked to him. He was handsome without character, mid-thirties. He was tall and lean. Though more attractive than a Q-tip, he reminded Tatum of one nonetheless.

The casket was cradled in a sling and lowered by six men holding the sides. When it reached its resting place, the group murmured an *Our Father.* Tatum didn't bother to mouth along. She was listening to Vincent's voice in her head — Vincent, her lost love, grumbling about the cost of the casket and the resources wasted in sending the dead into the earth.

The prayer ended. The minister closed with canned funeral rhetoric and a vague tribute. Too many adjectives, Tatum thought, not enough verbs. She wanted to raise her hand. "How so?" she wanted to say to the minister's assertions about Margaret's goodness. "Give me an example."

There was a collective "amen." Quietly, the group dispersed, hugging separate hugs, sniffling, and moving toward the house for somber conversation and solemn hors d'oeuvres. All very respectful, Tatum supposed. But given how difficult it is to let go of lovers, favorite coats, and old letters, she thought, how in God's name can a spirit break free from its precious body without stomping feet, clapping hands, wailing and raging? *Go, go, go.* We holler and wave and encourage the marathon runner to make it those final yards, to push harder from a strength not physical. Then, at death, we mumble a civil hymn and talk white noise. How's the soul to know in which direction to fly?

At the house, despite being Margaret's closest blood relative other than Rachael, Tatum felt distinctly like an outsider, a slightly unwelcome guest. She ladled herself a glass of punch and plucked a stuffed olive hors d'oeuvre from the buffet spread, a mix of catered food and homemade offerings. She stepped among the people clustered in small groups having quiet conversations. Tatum tried to blend without actually interacting but thought that she might be drawing attention to herself with her persistent pace. So, she sidled up where Lee was talking to one of Margaret's more frightening-looking friends, a step or two back from the conversation. Lee was describing the chosen headstone with its inscription, *Wife and Mother.*

Wife and Mother, Tatum thought, a generic tribute. But critiquing the epitaph, she imagined, would be poor form, so she focused on the stuffed olive she was holding, calculating how to bite it in half without making a mess, until she detected an awkward silence. She looked up. Lee was gone and Margaret's friend was looking at her.

"She deserved to see Rachael grow up," the woman said, obviously repeating herself. What was her name? Marley? She looked like a recipe for pretty gone awry. Every strand of blonde hair was the exact same color. She had blue eyes and symmetrical features. All the right ingredients, and yet, they added up to something else.

"Yes," Tatum stuttered. "But I'm not so sure people get what they deserve, good or bad."

Marley stared at her. Tatum bit her hors d'oeuvre, needing something to do. The half left behind on the toothpick broke and fell toward the floor, Tatum catching most of it in the palm of her hand while still chewing on the half in her mouth. Marley fake smiled at her, said "Excuse me," and walked away.

Tatum found her way to the kitchen to dispose of the olive bits that had fallen to the floor. She washed her hands and slipped away from the gathering to Lee's den. She would rummage through the phone books to keep herself occupied. She'd done this here before and found the phone books in a pile under the same side table she had in the past.

In Montana, six or seven books covered the whole state. Here, it took that many to cover the Chicago suburbs.

She flipped through the phone books, looking through the *G*'s for Vincent's name and number. Vincent Goes Ahead. Though a big family name on the Northern Cheyenne reservation in Montana, "Goes Ahead" would not be a common name in the Midwest. There would not be a list of right name but wrong numbers to call and interview. Tatum looked for Vincent's number whenever she left town, wherever she went. Losing a person to death may not be a cakewalk, but losing one to his life was considerably more complicated. In his final message to her, left on her answering machine, he said he was confused, but she knew better. The confused stay put. It is clarity that provokes us to action.

Tatum sank into the soft leather of the wingback as she turned phone book pages. Clarity and confusion. She knew the difference. With confusion the mind mulls, chews, and frets. It trips and tangles on its own so-called logic. Lots of activity. No movement. With clarity, on the other hand, the thinking is done. It was clarity Tatum felt before ingesting a fistful of pills in a Nebraska motel room ten years back. Clarity she felt before playing chicken with a bullet.

Ah, the drama of youth, she thought, smiling to herself. Her death fantasies had become considerably more tame with age. Her current one featured her dying not by her own hand but of a terminal disease that while not pleasant, of course, would not debilitate her completely until the very end. She would have a party before the fat lady sang, she had decided, a pre-wake kind of thing. Guests would receive a string of raffle tickets as they came through the front door, and at the high point of the evening, she would raffle off her stuff. From her sickbed, she would draw the numbers from a hat. The sofa: 3-6-2. The coffee table: 1-7. Books. Household appliances. The big-ticket items would provide the night's highlight. The car. The boom box. The guests would see the raffle as a perversity, a peverse request but a request of the dying, not to be denied. Secretly, they'd cross their fingers and hope their numbers were lucky.

By the evening's end, only her sickbed and a nightstand would remain. Tatum had shuffled through dead people's belongings. She didn't want it happening to her. She would clean the place out in advance, she decided. There'd be nothing left but maybe a missed safety pin ground into the carpet or an old broom leaning in a corner.

Tatum returned one phone book after another to the pile, once again coming up empty. She didn't know that she would actually call Vincent, even if she did find the number. She certainly didn't know what the hell she'd say.

Then, she stood and wandered in the den reading the spines of books and examining trinkets. She absently wondered what Lee would do with Margaret's things — her clothes and her saved mementos. Though there would be no raffling of Margaret's belongings, at least one item should have been. Rachael. Tatum suspected that Margaret would have been more comforted by a raffle to the general public than her husband's decision.

By the time she emerged from the den, the mourners had dispersed, leaving crumpled napkins and glasses of melting ice. Tatum collected some glasses and dropped them off on the kitchen counter. Margaret's friends filled Tupperware and washed the dishes brought full of microwaveable comfort to swallow and digest along with the immutable facts. Tatum couldn't detect an opening in the kitchen's traffic pattern, a way to jump in with dishtowel or sponge, so she said good night.

Tatum stepped out the front door and looked at the sky. Reluctant reds and golds crushed down into the horizon. It was her time. Vincent always knew that dusk was her moment and would put his arm around her as she gravitated to the window, the porch, wherever she had to go to witness, to see the cars opening their eyes, waking to their true and secret selves. The stars emerging, twinkling with sly. Vincent told her on one of the first nights they were together that she was born with a broken heart, and she believed he knew her for that one line.

What was it? Six months? A year? Before his tenderness turned to a sigh and an exasperated, "Lighten up."

Alas, love is not unconditional. Like all living things, it thrives when conditions are right, withers in a drought or if it is cut off from light.

Tatum sat on the concrete step and looked out at a strip of deep purple squeezed between the darkening sky and horizon. Sunset on the day of Margaret's funeral. Tatum's stomach turned. Sick with grief, she thought, though her eyes stayed dry.

Death. Tragic and unfathomable. Yet, Tatum found in it something satisfying. It was, in many ways, a relief. In every other part of our lives we have options. We make choices, and we get second chances, opportunities to correct choices poorly made. We lose things but know there's the remote possibility of getting them back, finding them in a forgotten drawer or pocket, of seeing them at an airport in Denver or Salt Lake. But not when someone is dead. Dead is done. That person is gone. Nothing you do, no corrective actions or changes of mind or personal transformations will alter that fact. It is final. Something where the only option is to let it be.

3

~

Paris arrived at Tatum and Geneva's duplex and turned the key in the lock of the front door. Inside, there were two more doors, Tatum's on the right, Geneva's on the left. The old brick building was worn but not dilapidated. The crown molding in the hall was dark and heavy; the baseboard, faded and scratched. The hardwood floors were unrestored but far from shabby. There was nothing new and nothing flimsy about any of it.

He tended to his chores at Geneva's first, buying time to see if he could concoct a reason for entering Tatum's apartment, even if just for a second, to breathe in its scent, which was the scent of Tatum. But in fact, it was hardly a smell at all. It was more like the promise of one, or one just missed. Something fresh and wet.

But there would be no reason to enter. Last time he had the key, he had snooped through Tatum's things, all the while skin prickling with the electricity of doing wrong and feeling watched. But God wasn't watching Paris from an unseen place. Paris was watching Tatum. He opened bedroom drawers to untidy piles of clothing. He didn't rifle, but he touched. At her nightstand drawer, he let his fingers shuffle past the flashlight, broken necklace, and Canadian money to the file folder. He lifted a corner of it and, upon seeing the black-and-white photo within, withdrew the folder from the drawer. The picture inside was of Tatum without a top on, a torso shot, her arms reaching behind her as though her hands were clasped at the base of her spine. Her smooth, flat stomach slipped beneath the loose waistline of her Levi's, and her chin tilted to the side. Long strands of hair fell alongside the outer curves of her small, round breasts. Paris had never seen Tatum's hair long.

Whereas "snooping" had felt relatively benign, "finding" had sent an eerie ripple through his body. Victory and guilt: a toxic cocktail. Paris felt it the next time he was with her, and the next, the "violate" in violating her privacy.

But it wasn't only guilt he felt about the pictures. It was jealousy, too. Who was the photographer? Vincent?

At Geneva's, Paris checked the food level in the cat's dish and freshened the water in the small ceramic bowl. He never snooped at Geneva's. There didn't seem to be much need. Her inner world seemed on display. A pleasant background reek of a history of incense and scented candles made one privy to her acceptance of the otherworldly. Paris absently picked up a small statue of Kali, the Hindu goddess. Geneva maintained a healthy population of deities. Buddhas, feathers, a Mother Mary, and pagan figurines sat on window ledges and shelves. Geneva wrote the local alternative paper's version of Dear Abby, Dear Belinda, and a stack of letters sat on her desk. Her responses to the distraught weren't based in psychology, philosophy, or religion. Geneva shot from the hip. Whatever the question asked, the answer was the one already in her head derived from god-knows-what yet applicable to all questions at hand. Geneva thought a lot about a lot of things but never seemed finished with any one thought. She claimed to have a promiscuous mind, a slut of a mind, even. One day she might be in love with one idea, and the next day, in bed with that idea's worst enemy.

Paris put down Kali and turned toward the most distinguishing feature of Geneva's living room, an entire wall of albums, rows and rows, worn and dusty, but with all the integrity of the well-used and well-cared for. He passed them on his way out. In the foyer, he stood facing the door to Tatum's apartment.

Inside, unlike at Geneva's, there would be no trinkets, papers, and collections. If it weren't for the dozen or so plants, Tatum's apartment would be stark. A foam sofa. A coffee table and a secondhand orange chair and ottoman. Nothing hung on the walls, though she did paint one of them a pale, sage green and another displayed a floor-to-ceiling, jagged crack from an earthquake long past. The surrounding mountains rose on active faults. The city sat in a bedrock bowl filled with sediment. Paris had heard it compared to a bowl of pudding. Tap the bowl and the bowl shakes, but the pudding shakes even more.

Though Paris fingered the key in his pocket, he forced himself to turn away. He left the duplex and backtracked toward downtown, thinking about the debt he owed to Tatum. He had looked at the pictures. He had violated her privacy. Stole intimacy. He meant to pay her back.

꩜

Home by 5:45 a.m., Paris descended the steps to his basement apartment beneath a barbershop. He tossed his keys into the ashtray near the door and pulled off his work boots. He stashed them, brown and crumpled, in a closet in the far corner of his apartment. In the bathroom, he turned on the faucet in the tub and washed his feet, scrubbed the bottoms cool, uncrowded the toes and let water pour through their gutters.

Feet cold and clean, he returned to the main room. A bathroom and a main room, that was the extent of his apartment. He thought of the main room as having stations where assigned activities were performed. Not unlike the Stations of the Cross, each spot had its designated theme: Paris Cooks for the Hundredth Time, Paris Stares Out the Window, Paris Draws, Paris Sleeps. More humble than even Tatum's, he had no sofa, just the kitchen table and two aluminum chairs that came with the apartment. His bed was a mattress on the floor.

He went to the stretch of wall that amounted to his kitchen and opened the drawer where he kept his pile of sketches. He reached to the bottom and pulled out a clean sheet. Leaning on the counter, he sketched Tatum's silhouette in the corridor of keno machines and tables that flanked her as she had left the Deluxe. He wasn't drawing seriously. Just doodling. Though, he thought, just maybe, he could finish a picture like this, something done from behind. No eyes for the sketching hand to tangle on. No eyes to break the flow and create that nervous energy that says, *Do the dishes. Take a nap. Jerk off.*

Paris remembered telling Tatum about his trouble with eyes. He had told her, looking at her grimly, as he slid open his kitchen drawer between them revealing the evidence. He had jerked his head a bit to get her to look down. Tentatively, she had reached into the drawer and shuffled through the contents — all the unfinished sketches and ambitious doodles on scraps of envelopes and the backs of flyers. They were portraits, mostly. Customers from the diner. People in the coffee shop. Smokers on stoops.

She had lifted an uneven stack from the drawer and then laid them out on the counter, slowly, one by one. She placed a hand gently on one or the other as her eyes traveled over them and among them as though they referenced each other, like puzzle pieces.

"These are good," she said. She held her chin and nodded. "I'm impressed."

Paris could see she was sincere, but he wasn't looking for reassurance.

"I can't finish any of them," he confessed, pushing his glasses up his nose. "I get working on the eyes, then something creepy happens."

Tatum leaned on her elbows and pulled one sketch closer, then another. She studied the spaces where there was crosshatching or white empty sockets where there should have been irises and pupils. Glimpses through windows of souls.

"Creepy, how?" she said.

Paris stepped away from the drawer and dropped a pouch of grounds into his Mr. Coffee. Tatum leaned on the counter, one foot stacked on the top of the other. In the gray light of the kitchen, in her painter's pants and jean jacket, her silhouette could've been that of a twelve-year-old boy. Her head turned to him, watching him, knowing the wait was part of the answer.

"Here's how it feels," Paris said, filling the coffeemaker with water and throwing the switch. "I'm sitting in a chair. I'm hunched over, and there's just this ink or pencil, these lines appearing." He paused and gathered words. "Then I get to the eyes, and it seems like, to get them right, I have to *become* the person whose eyes I'm drawing." He shot Tatum a look. "Like I have to feel how it is to *be* them. So, as I'm drawing, it starts to feel like I'm . . . changing."

"Changing," she said.

"Transforming?"

Tatum crossed her arms thoughtfully and leaned into the counter with her hip.

"You mean, like turning into a werewolf?" she said.

"Same principle."

"Well, that sounds cool."

"Cool?" Paris said, deadpan. "I take it you missed the movies. Those guys running through the woods trying to escape the moon, scratching at the hair growing in under their shirts."

"Hey," she said, half-laughing, "if you turned into a werewolf, would you still need your glasses? 'Cause that would look weird. Something definitely to avoid."

"Well, we'll never know," Paris said. He was unsure whether she realized the weight of what he was telling her, that what happened when he drew eyes rode a fine line between something sacred and something disturbing. The very stuff of secrets.

"It feels wrong," he said. "It's intimate but one-sided, which makes it creepy and me a creep."

Paris stared absently at the pictures on the counter. Tatum was quiet, but he could feel her watching him. He looked up and met her green eyes. She smiled.

"You know what else I bet is intimate?" she said.

"What's that?"

"Murder," she said, with an evil flick of the eyebrows.

The coffeemaker spit out a gurgle.

"Murder," Paris repeated.

"Well, not drive-by shootings and gun fights, of course," she said, "but those one-on-one stranglings, the bare-handed killings." She mimed a choking, her hands around a neck.

Paris gathered his sketches back into a sloppy pile.

"That's why I'm not a murderer," Tatum said. "Fear of intimacy." She smiled, pleased with herself.

"And why I'm not an artist." Paris dropped the sketches into the drawer. He stepped away and poured them both coffee. He handed Tatum a mug.

"Although," Tatum said, cupping the mug in both hands, "maybe what murderers really suffer from is the combination of the *desire for* intimacy, and the *fear of* it. Murder gives them bang for their buck. Thumbs pressed into the front of the throat, witnessing the shock and fear, revealing the monster that they are — it doesn't get much more personal."

"I suppose it's showing the worst of yourself," Paris said. "At any rate."

"Yeah," Tatum said, "but a murderer is a coward. Wants intimacy without vulnerability." She put down her mug and hopped up onto the counter, sitting near the sink. "Total intimacy," she said, "but no chance of any awkward 'Oh, hi's' when you meet by accident down-town."

"No witnesses," he said.

"Exactly." Tatum lifted her mug and inhaled deeply above it. "You want advice?" she said. "Be a creep. See where it takes you before you write it off. You can always change your mind."

"We're talking about drawing eyes?"

"We're talking about drawing eyes."

It wasn't the first secret Paris had told Tatum, and it wouldn't be the last. He told her secrets over mugs of coffee and over wine drunk from unstemmed glasses. He told her them silently as he idly sketched her, always from behind, on scraps of paper he threw away. He placed his secrets on tables between them like they were things he had found, things he wanted to show her so she could help him determine their value. What did *she* think? What were they worth?

4

Lee packed Rachael's things into Tatum's Toyota. It wasn't everything she owned but enough to imply an extended mourning period for Lee. Rachael's cool silence had evolved since her mother's funeral. For two days straight, she threw tantrums. Tantrums when asked to eat, when told to go to bed. Her tantrums seemed designed to try the nerves of God, forcing Him to spit Margaret back out from the clouds. *"Okay, okay, here she is. Now please, just shut up."*

Tatum could tell that the tantrums had Lee worried that she might reconsider hauling Rachael back to Montana. He kept saying that she shouldn't take it the wrong way.

"'The wrong way?'" Tatum asked him. "What would that be?"

"You know," Lee said, "like she doesn't want to go."

"But she doesn't."

Lee looked at Tatum as though she had injured or insulted him.

But Lee needn't worry his pretty little Q-tip head, Tatum thought. Rachael's tantrums did not trouble her. In fact, she saw them as a healthy sign, a spirit of fight in the face of adversity and evidence that, unlike her mother, Rachael's domestication hadn't completely took. Rachael was in for a rough ride. Her survival would require a strain of the wild. Survival always does.

But the tantrums ended when the packing began. Rachael was silent, smoldering, on the edge of helpless tears. Two of Margaret's friends, Marley and another woman Tatum had met at the funeral, packed Rachael's things. Both were cool toward Tatum and confident that she wasn't qualified for the job. One, then the other, pulled Lee aside for hushed conversations. Tatum pretended not to notice. An hour after the women left, Tatum knocked on Rachael's open bedroom door. Hearing nothing but the TV, she knocked again and then peeked inside.

"Hello?" she said, entering.

Rachael was watching cartoons in her pajamas. She didn't acknowledge Tatum's entrance. Her suitcases, tidily packed just an hour before, had been ripped to ribbons, clothes strewn everywhere.

"I wanted to check in with you about tomorrow," Tatum said. "Do you have any questions?"

No answer.

Tatum sat on the edge of the bed and looked over the undies flung across the little play vanity, the sweaters tossed everywhere. One big corner of a suitcase was crammed in the too small trash basket.

"You don't want to go, I guess."

Nothing.

"I don't blame you," Tatum said. "I know you're sad right now, but your dad is pretty sad, too. He needs some . . . time."

Tatum couldn't bring herself to ask an eight-year-old to be strong for the grown man who was dumping her.

"But more important," Tatum said, "is that you need some things, too."

Tatum smoothed the Disney sheets beneath her hand. The Cinderella story unfolded across the soft cotton. Evil sisters. Glass slippers. A handsome cartoon prince. As a child, what had stood out most to Tatum in *Cinderella* was the carriage turning into a pumpkin at midnight. She thought the consequence of breaking the midnight curfew was to be trapped alive in a pumpkin, in the damp darkness with stringy pumpkin guts and seeds hanging in your face and no dry place to sit, forever and ever after. That's what you get when you break the rules. She was an adult before she realized it was the social faux pas the fairy tale was concerned with, the resulting embarrassment when one's carriage turns out to be nothing but a gourd.

"Look," Tatum said, "I know you don't like me. But when things are real sad, it can be good to get in the car and drive away for awhile."

But Rachael had shut her out. She turned up the television's volume. Tatum touched the image of the fairy godmother and acknowledged herself as an unworthy substitute. No gowns. No princes. No glass slippers. Just a Celica and a spare room. Fortunately, Tatum thought, it wasn't her job to get Rachael to a ball. Rachael didn't need a fairy godmother. She needed a good right-hand man, someone to escort her through hell, drive her to the showdown and be there while she walked her fifteen paces and turned.

"We leave in the morning," Tatum sighed. Not eloquent, not comforting, but all she had.

Then Tatum placed her hands on her knees about to push up and leave when Rachael leapt from the floor and flew at her screaming *no*. She was red-faced, little fists chopping through the air, not belting Tatum, only with the greatest restraint. She stood right in front of Tatum engaged in battle, kicking, punching, every body part scrunched up or flying wildly. It was as though there were an invisible shield between the two of them, like Rachael had been taught not to hit, but boy, if she were allowed, this was what Tatum would be getting.

Tatum was surprised at first and drew herself back. Then, realizing none of the blows were landing, the situation seemed strange and curious. She didn't know why, but she reached through the shield and gave Rachael's chest a little poke.

Rachael stumbled backward, just a step, snapped out of one rage, the next one coming on fast. She grabbed a Barbie off the nightstand, flung it at Tatum, and ran from her own room slamming Tatum inside.

Tatum didn't know to whom, if anyone, she was running. Mommy's dead. Daddy's getting out of Dodge. Rachael was learning that love is not unconditional despite what Mommy said, despite the pretty words in picture books geared to induce child self-esteem. Unconditional love doesn't hold up in a world defined by action because it's something people feel, not something people do. That's what's wrong with it.

Tatum rose from the bed. Hand on the doorknob, she stole a last look at Rachael's room, a little girl's paradise. Tatum knew her apartment had no ruffled shams or lace curtains. No princess phone. When it came right down to it, Tatum doubted she owned anything pink at all.

The following morning, Tatum slid a square package wrapped in a coat into the hatch of her Celica. While Margaret's friends had been packing for Rachael, Tatum had been doing some packing of her own. Discreetly as possible, she had combed the house for what to take for Rachael that she might need as her loss unfolded in a foreign land. She had decided on Margaret's photo albums, and she hadn't asked. She stole them. Her bet was that Lee would never notice. His plans weren't to reminisce. His plans were to move on. Just as Tatum and Rachael were scheduled to leave that day, so was Lee. He was flying out to stay with his brother in Florida. He needed time, he said.

It reminded Tatum of when her ex, Vincent, told her he needed space. She threw away the picante sauce and unused condiments. She took clothes to the Goodwill and scrunched the remaining items into less than half of the closet. She talked less, drew herself inward. But she couldn't get small enough, quiet enough, couldn't hold her breath long enough because Vincent didn't want space, or more space. He wanted the space she occupied. He wanted something else in it.

Tatum suspected Lee felt that way about time. He needed it filled with something new. So just three days after burying Margaret, armed with the irrationality of grief, he was beating feet out of town toward a future unencumbered by the past.

Exiled as she was, Rachael would need the photo albums more, Tatum decided.

Tatum slammed the hatch closed. The moment of truth had arrived. She turned to the front doorway where Rachael had been standing just seconds before, but there was no sign of her. Tatum looked out past the driveway and saw Rachael running as fast as her small feet would carry her across the brown-and-red, leaf-spattered earth.

"Wait," Tatum said, firmly, to Lee. Then she went after Rachael, walking, following at a distance, her breath small ghosts in the morning air. She caught up to Rachael at the grave where Rachael huddled on the ground, looking like a small bundle, forgotten and left behind. Tatum hung back. From her polite distance, she saw Rachael framed by the surrounding trees, a larger one bending over the grave to a smaller one, branches meeting in a finger-touch like Michelangelo's God and Man. Tatum imagined the tree roots creeping to each other beneath Margaret's casket like lovers' hands beneath a table, their brown and gnarled fingers tangling beneath the satin-lined box.

Don't be mad was Tatum's silent message whispered from her mind to the dead.

She approached Rachael from behind. Rachael's white skin answered the morning chill with messy, red blotches.

Then Rachael stood. Tatum tried to gently turn her to leave, but Rachael's feet were bolted to the ground. She stared at the fresh mound of soil that had swallowed her mother. She continued staring, and Tatum wondered how long they would stand there if she didn't assert her adult powers. Who would outlast whom, standing in the cold, knowing that the end of this moment was the end of so much?

Tatum went down on one knee behind her and said as gently as she could, "Rach."

Rachael was still. Tatum knew that Rachael was well aware that she was being evicted and that Tatum was the one escorting her from the premises. Definitely not the fairy godmother with sage advice and a basket of magic, Tatum knew that she was more like the Chinese mothers who tortured their daughters by binding their feet, knowing what it takes to survive in this messy, unfair world. *This is going to hurt,* Tatum told Rachael, silently, in her mind. *It's going to hurt, but you have to do it to survive.*

She reached out to touch the back of Rachael's head, fingertips nearly touching the soft child hair lifted by the breeze, when Rachael bolted.

Rachael ran across the clearing away from the house to where the trees thickened at the border of the woods. Tatum rose from her knee and ran after her. She felt no right to catch her but a responsibility to follow, to make sure she didn't get lost or hurt. Rachael kept running and Tatum followed, keeping up easily. Rachael took fast glances over her shoulder, not oblivious to the fact that she maintained her freedom only by virtue of Tatum's mercy.

Over the pinecones and sticks and morning frost, Rachael ran like a child in a nightmare. Tatum did her best to follow, not chase, but doubted there was a distinguishable difference. Suddenly, Rachael turned, cheeks flush and breath heaving.

"I wish you died instead of my mom," she screamed.

"Of course you do," Tatum said, throwing up her arms. "Duh."

Their eyes crashed in the space between. Rachael was anger and tears and futile indignation.

"So what would you do if your wish came true?" Tatum said, trying. "If God zapped your mom here instead of me. What would you do?" She squatted so she would be Rachael's height. "Huh? How would that be?"

Rachael looked at her, distrustfully.

Tatum did think it would be great. Not because she wanted to die right then and there, but for the magic of it — standing in the forest, making your wish, abracadabra. Rachael's face did not change, but Tatum could feel her wish for the magic, the wish for her own face to melt away and Margaret's to emerge as from a Polaroid.

Tatum went to Rachael and picked her up. She was not light. Rachael turned her head away from Tatum as Tatum knew she would. But she didn't resist. Tatum walked a few feet but Rachael was far too heavy for her to be carrying. She returned her to the ground but kept hold of her hand. Rachael trailed slightly behind but did not wrestle her hand away.

When in it, love seems fused with time. This, Tatum knew, was the problem. It was shocking, always, to discover that they can split paths, that they are two, love and time, and they can turn their backs to each other and follow arcs that pull them farther and farther apart.

The frost was turning from white to clear, and the sun reflected up from the ground. They emerged from the trees. Tatum led Rachael past the grave.

Tatum stood in the *V* between the driver's seat and her open car door under long-fingered clouds feathering across the blue sky. Weather was coming, the road was waiting, and they were an hour behind. Lee buckled Rachael into the passenger's seat of Tatum's car and kissed her temple.

"I love you," Lee said to Rachael, then pressed his lips together and nodded.

Tatum watched his "I love you" hit Rachael like an egg hits a windshield. Splat. Drip. Only the insult reaches the intended victim behind the glass.

"Take care," Tatum said to Lee, across the roof of the car. Kind, quick words. She hoped they excused her from anything more effusive. She swung into the driver's seat and looked sidelong at Rachael. Her expression was flat. Tatum wanted to say something that would let her know that she wasn't in on the bogus "I love you." People should be arrested when they use an "I love you" to cover their crimes, Tatum thought. It devalues it for everybody else.

Tatum turned the key in the ignition and hit the wipers to clean the window. She fake-smiled at Lee, sliding past his Audi parked on the wide drive. He waved sadly, and Tatum thought his pants might burst into flames. Liar. She wondered if he was lying even to himself.

Driving through genteel suburbia, Tatum stole glances at Rachael's profile. Steel, it seemed, was building up behind her doll-like features, giving the impression of maturity. But it was not maturity. It was pain. Sad that one could be mistaken for the other. It made Tatum want to believe, for Rachael's sake, that it was possible that Lee truly did love her, given what love might mean to him.

But no, she decided, as they pulled onto the expressway and drove west. He couldn't love her. Love was not subjective. Love would be unmistakable.

The Celica kept pace with the fast cars zigzagging across lanes to make their exits. City trains rumbled on tracks parallel to the highway. Rachael and Tatum were silent as they left the city and set forth through the flat Midwest. Traffic loosened, and naked trees stood unashamed against the pale sky. Rachael's expression remained flat as the landscape. Tatum suspected, though, that down deep in her psyche where there are no words, molten, rocky notions of love oozed. What it is. What it isn't. Notions that over the years and decades would simmer, rising to the surface in adulthood, cool and hard, as a disdain for love and for the people who claim it as they strap you down and blast you out of their orbits.

Somewhere between Davenport and Des Moines, they stopped for lunch at the Happy Chef. Tatum and Rachael sat in a booth against large windows that looked out to the front bumper of the car. Tatum rested an elbow on the stainless steel ledge while Rachael reviewed the menu. Tatum tried to think up some conversation, a compelling question, too interesting or provoking to be ignored. A soft-fleshed girl with over-plucked brows delivered glasses of ice water and then took their orders. Rachael ordered cooperatively, competently. She handed the menu to the waitress and retreated back into silence. Tatum ordered coffee and then returned to searching the landscape beyond the window, a parking lot, alas, for something to point out or comment upon.

But it was Rachael who broke the silence.

"Where's Nebraska?" she said.

"Montana," Tatum answered, knowing what Rachael meant. "We're going to Montana."

Rachael looked out the window.

"My dad said I was going to Nebraska."

Your dad's a big dumb ass, Tatum thought.

"No," she said, "he meant Montana. I live in Montana."

Rachael's concern was obvious, her tether to what was left of her family in doubt. There had been no doubt for Tatum as to whether she would take custody of Rachael, whether it was for a week, for months, or forever. But now here they were, and Tatum was like any new parent, substitute or not, with a new life brought into the rhythms of her own life, changing it, even steering it, from the start.

The waitress returned with the coffeepot and Rachael's soda. Tatum leaned back as the waitress filled her cup. Rachael did not acknowledge her soda, and when the waitress left, Tatum leaned across the table and touched Rachael's hand.

"Don't worry," Tatum said. "He just used the wrong name. He knows where you'll be. He has my phone number."

Rachael withdrew her hand slowly and wiped the slime of Tatum off on her sleeve.

Tatum knew Rachael's life was reshaping just as her own was, the reality of it sinking in for both at a Happy Chef in Iowa. It was a new world for both of them, but Tatum was aware that she was a volunteer, whereas Rachael, most decidedly, was not.

They were silent again until the waitress returned with Rachael's burger, fries, and soda. Rachael looked down at her food but didn't touch it.

Just as Tatum had poked Rachael back in her bedroom, she reached across the table now and stole a french fry from Rachael's plate. Tatum pointed with the fry.

"It's a good thing we're going to Montana and not Nebraska," she said.

Rachael's eyes followed her french fry to Tatum's mouth.

"Nebraska's a bad deal," she said, munching Rachael's fry. She took a tiny, plastic cup of half & half from the bowl on the table. "Do you know about coffee?" Tatum asked, tearing open the cup and pouring it into her mug.

Rachael said nothing.

"A cup of coffee can pin down a moment in time like a photo on a fridge."

Rachael took the straw from her soda and laid it carefully on her plate, creating a cootie-resistant barrier between the hamburger and contaminated fries.

Tatum tossed the plastic cup aside, picked up her spoon, and stirred.

"In Nebraska . . . " she started.

Rachael stared at her plate. Tatum waited.

"In Nebraska . . . " Tatum said, again.

Tatum kept her voice patient and pleasant. She kept saying "In Nebraska . . . " until Rachael looked up, clearly annoyed.

"In Nebraska," Tatum said, she paused this time for dramatic effect, "I tried to kill myself."

Rachael's face did not change.

"How come you're not dead?" she said. She took the top of the bun off her burger and ate the pickle below.

Tatum thought Rachael starting in on her food was a good sign, so she went on.

"I took a bunch of pills," Tatum said. "I thought they would make me go to sleep and die but instead I just barfed like crazy all night and ended up alive."

Rachael twisted her mouth like she wasn't buying it.

"It's true," Tatum said. "I still remember how cold the bathroom floor was. I lay there all night, throwing up every ten minutes or so. I tried a couple of times to make it to the bed to grab a blanket, but walking made me have to throw up even worse, and I couldn't make it to the bed in time to grab a blanket before I was back with my face in the toilet."

Rachael's brows lifted slightly. The idea of Tatum's face in a toilet seemed to please her.

Tatum sipped from her mug and looked out at the parking lot. She recalled the cool bathroom linoleum and porcelain bowl, the sweating and the not knowing whether she had failed or whether this was what dying was. Her stomach had rung itself out over hours, twisting, it seemed, like a towel, the pressure throwing everything upward, vomiting the vapors of bile when there was nothing else left.

By 4:00 a.m., Tatum had pegged herself for spared. Exhausted. Dehydrated. But not dead. She managed to crawl out of the bathroom and find her way to the bed. She sat on the floor, leaning against the drab, olive-colored spread. Her skin felt stretched tight over her bones. Her own wrists looked to her bird-frail. She had no fat, no fuel. No source from which to draw. Pared down to organs, bones, and a layer of muscle as thin as a sheet, she could feel her heart, a clear vessel that was perfectly empty. It felt transparent. Made of glass. She had struggled up from the floor.

Tatum then left her motel room to find coffee. All she could find, though, was a drop-and-fill vending machine in the hall near the lobby. It was a wonder, she had thought, dropping dimes through the slot, that in a world of lattes, cappuccinos, and breves that such a machine still existed. It was like finding a rack or shackle on a prison wall. A thing we'd decided as a society was no longer humane.

She pressed the rectangular button that no longer lit up. The cup dropped, and the florescent lights in the ceiling hummed. The machine choked and then released a pathetic drizzle of caffeine. For a moment, Tatum wondered if she had succeeded, that she was dead and didn't know it, and that this was hell's lobby.

"Nebraska." Tatum sighed the word aloud in the booth of the Happy Chef.

"If I were dead," Rachael said, "I'd be with my mom."

Tatum looked at Rachael. Her head was cocked in what seemed feigned innocence. Something in Rachael's inflection and expression made Tatum think Rachael was testing waters, being purposely provocative to discover what sort of reaction was available.

"No," Tatum said. "Not if you killed yourself. If you kill yourself, you don't get to see anyone you knew when you were alive."

"Says who?" Rachael said.

"Says the rules."

Then they regarded each other, frankly and stubbornly.

"So, you wouldn't have seen anyone you knew if you died that night," Rachael said.

"I didn't want to see anyone," Tatum said.

5

~

Geneva never left Amsterdam. After mornings spent in her hotel room reading and looking out over white roofs and clotheslines, she'd take the short walk to a bar called Blues. She spent the hours there smoking hash and drinking in the musk of the young, unbathed boy with tight, dark curls — twenty maybe — who tended bar. Lean, he moved with the grace of a girl and the ease of a child, gliding among the tables, gears all well oiled. An incense of hand-rolled cigarettes lightly dusted his new man smell, pleasantly corrupting it. He walked, rag slung over his shoulder, back and forth from the front of the bar to the rear, retrieving dirty glasses from behind pool tables and from oiled mahogany ledges. Geneva imagined a dog sniffing the spot where the young man's foot peeled off the cracked and dirty tiles.

The sun blared over Dam Square, but Geneva parked herself in the bar where it was dark and music videos of American blues artists played in the same loop every afternoon. If she sat there long enough, she could hear Dr. John and Etta James sing "I'd Rather Go Blind" twice. So much for Frankfurt. So much for Versailles. This had been her fifth trip abroad in two years, and now she knew that she was done. At heart, Geneva was not a tourist. She didn't need more vacations. She needed more life.

For the past two weeks, Geneva had been eyeing her reflection in the mirror behind the bar. At sixty-two years old, she knew time was not on her side. She could pass for fifty on a good day, she thought, but nonetheless, she knew her good days were numbered, just as she had known at twenty-six that her smooth skin and gravity-defying features were on loan. While still in her youth and prime, she had chosen to let go of her looks before they left on their own. It's not that she ceased the grooming and upkeep on what God gave her. She was just careful not to count on it.

She intended to be ready for the next stage, too, the next round of loss. When she became an elderly woman — white-haired, shrunken —

she knew she would lose more status, more attention, more "can I help you's?" from store clerks. One doesn't become a ghost overnight. It is a gradual path to a gray blur. Not a potential sex partner. Not a danger. Not likely wearing an enviable pair of boots. People's eyes move on to find something more interesting. There was no one to blame. Geneva thought it might even be biological. We notice what we need to notice — opportunities, threats.

The flight back to Montana was uneventful, just as one wishes a flight to be. Geneva looked through the fogged window of her taxi at the familiar stoplights and intersections. They were unchanged by her absence and, she thought, might say the same of her. But what can we tell from the surface, she thought? Some minds cover more ground on a trip from the sofa to the john than others do on a trip around the world.

She pulled her earphones down around her neck.

"It's the next right," she said to the cabby. "Second duplex on the left."

She repositioned the earphones. Five years ago, she would have never worn earphones in a cab. But now, rudeness and prudence be damned. Geneva remembered how she had shunned the Walkman when it first came out. The walkers, joggers, and cyclists tooling around cut off from a key physical sense struck her as engaged in ill-advised displays of bravado. There are reasons why we don't leave our houses blindfolded or fight with one hand tied behind our backs. Why risk being deaf to the hollered "watch out" and the blaring horn of the brakeless bus careening toward the storefront window?

But Geneva had submitted, been sold, and now, like others, had closed the loop between her mind and her ears. And in that orbit, in the cab, she listened to "Fixing a Hole" by the Beatles. She hoped the song would end just as she arrived at her door. She wanted the soundtrack to her trip to end poetically, cleanly, in a fading track.

It was hard to believe that it was twenty years ago when she'd first heard the song she listened to now. She and her husband, Ralph, had lived in Tucson. She had picked up *Sgt. Pepper's Lonely Heart's Club Band* while record shopping for *Whipped Cream* by Herb Albert and the Tijuana Brass. She had heard the Beatles' pop hits on the radio and on impulse bought their new release. Halfway through the second song — "With a Little Help from My Friends" — she had hauled a kitchen chair into the living room and, for the first time in her life, listened to music. It wasn't background. She wasn't dancing. She sank from the chair to the floor. Lennon's voice was a tuning fork. Inside of her, something vibrated.

She played it for Ralph when he got home. He said, "Pretty weird."

Geneva thought they would divorce for sure. How could they go on when he didn't understand this thing, this thing she didn't understand either, but a thing that for her changed everything?

The following morning, she couldn't get dressed in her own closet. She didn't feel like, nor want to be, the person who had purchased this dress or that bag. Her can of hair spray struck her as ridiculous. The blush she had used every day since seventeen now seemed clownish. Absurd. She sat on the closed toilet lid holding a can of AquaNet and crying.

She stopped cruising cosmetic counters and attending white sales. She crawled through record bins like a roach, her fingertips divining rods. She read the backs of albums, the liner notes, bought bands she had never heard of based on intuition alone or a producer's name she recognized. There are parts of the psyche that are preconscious, floating in limbo, waiting to be charmed from their dark basket by the right string of notes, the right rhythms or chords. A self Geneva didn't know was coaxed to the surface. The Grateful Dead. Blind Faith. Canned Heat. One led to another, loaves and fishes stretching both forward and backward in time. Waylon Jennings. Louis Jordon. Professor Longhair. In '74, she picked up Lou Reed's *Rock 'n' Roll Animal,* and it started all over, a new turn on that same spiral. Iggy Pop. The Modern Lovers.

She was changed, and Ralph didn't seem to mind, which Geneva thought was more than you could say for most husbands. Of course it also might have been that he hadn't noticed.

The cabby hit the wipers and Geneva scrunched her mouth to the side in private thought remembering how, despite her growing music collection, Ralph always chose the music if he was home or the radio station if they were in the car. His favorites were unmemorable songs that would never become Muzak because they were Muzak already. "Krab" for the ears. What really got under her skin, though, was that Ralph thought the music was *them.* Thought when he played it, he was putting on something *they* enjoyed.

But she saw Ralph's pleasure in believing it, and she didn't want, under any circumstances, to diminish Ralph's pleasure. It was not what she signed up for.

The taxi pulled to the curb. She read the meter from the back seat and added a two-dollar tip. She stepped onto the front walk. It was slippery from the sleet. The cab pulled away and "Fixing a Hole" faded out. Geneva snapped off the Walkman and pulled the earphones to her neck. The chill in the air felt more fall than winter, but her fingers felt cold wrapped around the handle of her bag. It was nearly midnight, and the neighbors' windows were dark, all except for Ron's, next door. His light was on, and she could see his bearded profile as he crossed his living room. Ron fought to keep local schools open and fought developers to maintain open space. He put flyers in people's doors offering workshops in recycling and organic gardening. His eyes were quick and intelligent. His belly, soft and paunchy.

Ron brought Geneva snap peas and rhubarb from his garden in the summer and, come winter, occasionally shoveled her walk. He was a retired, revolutionary librarian who claimed the Dewey decimal system should be abolished, that it served only to obstruct the public's access to knowledge. Geneva had asked him once, thinking she was being funny, if he had ever burned Mr. Dewey in effigy. Without missing a beat, Ron told her no but said that in younger, wilder librarian days, he and some librarian comrades had made a Melville Dewey piñata for Cinco de Mayo.

Geneva suspected that Tatum and herself next door in their duplex were a disappointment to Ron. They never showed up for city council meetings or school board elections. Still, he never gave up on them.

Ron's light blinked out and Geneva flinched, just then noticing on his lawn the three deer from the urban herd watching her with minimal interest and zero alarm. Some of them were second and third generation, knowing nothing but city life. They feared no man nor dog. Upon finding one's tulips headless and young trees stripped of bark, they were vermin. But staring back at you through the night and the wet shimmer of November, they were enchantment itself.

Geneva headed up the walk, her steps deliberately slow. The scent of wood smoke, earthy and as comforting as the musk of a young man, snaked invisibly among the trees and houses, the smell speaking to the ancient in her genes. She surveyed the front yard as she stepped. The leaves had matted, and the ground fell sleepy under their brown blanket. Geneva sighed as she felt something inside of her unfurling. A tension she didn't know she was holding began to release. Airplanes, hotels, big cities — she never realized the way they tended to bunch her up in both body and spirit until she reached home. The neighborhood was quiet. Surely, there was traffic and distant train whistles and electrical hums, but the silence underneath it all ran deeper. The silence was what Geneva heard.

At the front door, she checked her mailbox, even though Tatum had been collecting the mail. Then she dug in the outside pocket of her bag for her keys, her fingers seeking their mundane familiarity. She turned the key in the lock and entered the hall between apartments and, by intuition, could tell that Tatum was not home.

She entered her own apartment, closing the door behind her.

Ralph, she thought, as though encountering him, registering his presence. But Ralph had never lived in the duplex. Only Geneva's responsibility for him.

All was as she had left it. Her cluttered desk hadn't straightened itself. A wall of ancient albums on dusty shelves built with one-by-eights and concrete blocks had retained its sooty charm. Geneva dropped her one bag and looked at her blinking answering machine. Everything in the room called her home.

"Voodoo," she called, wondering if the cat was in.

No response.

Geneva went to her answering machine and pulled off her Walkman and set it on the desk. She paused with her finger above the play button. Did she want to know? Did she want to answer the call of duty and administrative function that the blinking light seemed to imply? The thought of it was almost overwhelming. Geneva's mind could readily accommodate reflection on potential cosmic relationships among disparate disciplines, but filling out a form for a supermarket check card was enough to ruin an afternoon.

Get it over with, she thought, and went to hit the button when she noticed the note. It was from Tatum. She had gone to Illinois. Paris was looking after Voodoo. Tatum's sister, Margaret, was sick.

Geneva didn't know Margaret, not firsthand. But she did know that Margaret and her husband and daughter were all the family Tatum had and that cancer hunted Tatum's people with the fierceness of a vendetta. Tatum had told her that Margaret hated her, but claimed she didn't mind. "It's not her fault," Tatum had said, "it's just a family thing."

Geneva dropped the note in the wastepaper basket and turned to the pile of accumulated mail. Geneva sorted, tossing junk into the trash and opening the manila envelope from the *Mountain Messenger*. It was letters for her next column. She answered three letters per week and got paid twenty bucks per. It wasn't that she needed the sixty bucks. It was that she liked being tied to the community in some official capacity on her own terms. Her column was called Belinda's Discount Kissing Booth. It offered camp disguised as advice, or advice disguised as camp. Belinda's true identity was relatively secret.

She pulled a letter from the envelope.

> Dear Belinda,
>
> I am a survivor of childhood abuse. My father was violent, and my mother failed to protect me. I suppose I've gotten over it and on with my life, but I still feel such anger inside. I hear you should forgive not for the sake of those who hurt you, but for yourself. I want to forgive my abusers, but I don't know how. I really don't feel it.
>
> Signed,
> Unforgiving

"'My abusers,'" Geneva said aloud, the expression striking her as strangely humorous. Why not call them 'those jerks'? And forgiveness? She tossed the letter across her desk.

"Can't help you," she said. "I'm post forgiveness."

Geneva had run her laps around the counseling, self-help, and new age track. She was well schooled in the importance of forgiveness to one's spiritual achievement. In her quest to do better on the forgiving front, she had once asked Tatum whether she forgave Margaret and Vincent for the pain they had caused her. Tatum told her that she didn't forgive either one of them because there was nothing to forgive.

"People are who they are," Tatum had said. "They love who they love. A person can't control that. You shouldn't have to apologize for it."

Geneva was not inspired. But still, she tried. She tried to forgive the rude store clerks, bad drivers, and the car salesman who sold her a lemon thirty years and two vehicles past. She tried to forgive her husband for being sick and forgive the loss of a decade as she cared for him, watched his spirit leave his body while some shred of a thing tenacious and meager hung on. What was left to be so stubborn, she wondered? Or was it more an issue of the spirit being somehow snagged, unable to disengage itself?

Five years ago, she had checked him into a nursing home. She tried to forgive herself for institutionalizing him, even though by then he'd been so-called dying for nearly seven years.

Geneva stood beside her desk, lost in the past, disconnected from the physical world. Then, she pulled a pen from a coffee mug and retrieved Unforgiving's letter.

Don't forgive them, she jotted at the bottom of the page, *and feel free to retain the self-righteousness that rises from victimhood. The prevailing knowledge is that forgiveness is really for your benefit and not that of your persecutors. Thus, I would recommend granting them mercy, rather than forgiveness. Mercy will tend to the real objective without sugarcoating the crime.*

She hovered with her pen over the letter for a moment more. Then, she stood straight, tossed the pen across the desk, and unbuttoned her coat.

Geneva turned and walked to her wall of music. First, she checked the turntable to see if Tatum or Paris had listened to anything while she was gone. But it was empty, as she'd left it. She checked the tape deck. The Louis Armstrong compilation she had been playing the morning she left still sat inside. It was a good collection of both early and more mature pieces, including a version of "When You're Smiling" from 1929 with Tommy Dorsey sitting in on trombone.

Geneva snapped the tape deck closed and scanned her album collection, honing in on the B's. She still wanted Beatles and pulled *Hey Jude* from the shelf. Her copy was an import from Uruguay, still in its plastic cover, purchased in 1978. Mint. The back was her favorite picture of the Beatles and the only picture she knew of where Ringo looked downright attractive. She placed the album on the turntable and dropped the needle. She plopped down in her old wingback. A deer hide covered the tattered upholstery where a long-dead cat, Madame Blavastsky, had scratched through to the foam.

Two weeks, thousands of miles, and a couple of grand, she thought to herself while kicking off her leather boots, and I'm back where I started. Must all journeys be so damn metaphoric, she thought? She returned to the same self, the same dissatisfactions, she had been sick of when she left. It made Geneva miss her days of New Age zealotry when she knew that every situation, no matter what it was, was perfectly designed to teach her what she most needed to learn.

I have no business being dissatisfied, she lectured herself inwardly, and began her rote and tired litany of things for which to be grateful. She was healthy. Though not rich, she didn't need to worry about money. She liked her friends. She liked herself. She'd been loved.

Geneva knew Ralph had loved her because she trusted Ralph. However, trusting that Ralph loved her and feeling loved were not one and the same.

She let her head drop against the back of the chair. She knew people wouldn't understand. Current wisdom had it that you should trust yourself. But she knew that voices in one's head are as likely to be liars as messengers of the divine. Trust meant spinning the roulette wheel of life's possibilities. The right answer, the winning number, the truth — make your bet. Ante up. Trust means turning your back to the ticking wheel. You've chosen your number. You believe. There's no peeking over the shoulder. You live with the sounding of the ticking in the background and in the faith that you know where the wheel will stop.

"Hey Jude's" big finish faded. Geneva heard the cat door flap and the soft padding of little paws. Then, "Old Brown Shoe." Voodoo, cool and smelling of wood smoke, leapt into her lap.

"Hey there, sweetie," she said, stroking his back straight through to his tail. He purred with gusto and touched his nose to hers.

Holding Voodoo, Geneva rose from her chair and shuffled over to the turntable. She lifted the needle and skipped to the next song. The needle crackled in a blank groove, then Lennon sang, "Don't Let Me Down." She stepped back and watched the needle ride the vinyl, pressing the cat to her. Voodoo dug his claws into her bosom. A slow, deep sink. An expression of pleasure. Geneva winced but continued to stroke him.

6

It was early evening, and Tatum gripped the wheel with both hands. As Rachael slept, wet November snow shot out from the black of night, splatting against the windshield. Tatum's eyes shifted back and forth between white lines and guardrails as she drove into a pit. She thought of black holes, bellies full of swallowed light. The experts used to say that no light could escape one. But Tatum had read that now they say it might not be true, that tiny particles of light may well be able to escape the black and bottomless vacuum. She had been disappointed by the news, by the loss of absolutism.

A sign for an upcoming exit glowed through the precipitation. Tatum hit the blinker. Normally, she wasn't one to pull over to escape storm, snow, or fog. But not tonight. Things were different, now. She wouldn't try to outrun the dark clouds. She felt a wave of compassion for all the careful parents of the world who mind the speed limit and come to full stops.

She took the exit and picked up drive-thru food. They pulled into the lot of the Cloud 9, a small motel west of the middle of South Dakota. Tatum had stayed there before. It was cheap, simple, and clean. The owner struck her as a retiree who needed some income beyond his social security. He lived in a room behind the check-in desk. A little bell above the door rang when she entered the registration office. He shuffled out, old, tall, and lean, reminding Tatum of an Irish wolfhound.

He handed over a key, and Tatum drove across the gravel lot to the parking space in front of their room. The sleet was wet and cold on their faces as they each dug out from the hatch a small bag to take in for the night.

"Let's eat," Tatum said, hitting the light switch as they entered. The room consisted of a small round table flanked by two well-worn chairs and two double beds separated by a nightstand. The TV sat on a six-drawer dresser. The floor was hard, as though the thin carpet had been glued directly onto a concrete slab. Tatum dropped the bag with the food onto a bed. She found the thermostat, turned up the heat, and joined Rachael sitting cross-legged and opening the bag of food. Rachael had already turned on the TV and found her way to a program taking place in a high school with young actors carrying books and being funny outside of their lockers. Tatum and Rachael opened their sandwiches' wrappers to use as plates.

"I think we should pray," Rachael said.

"Okay," Tatum said. "Good idea." She thought a little dinnertime grace might have been part of Rachael's family dinner routine, good to return to for a small comfort. Tatum put down her chicken sandwich, folded her hands, and gave it her best shot. "Thank you, God, for the food," she started.

"No," Rachael said. "For my mom. Ask God to take care of her."

"Oh," Tatum said. It was a more serious sort of prayer than she had thought. She picked up the remote from the bedspread and clicked off the television set. She searched for words, prayer words. "Dear God," she started but wasn't sure where to go. "God . . . " she started again.

Tatum hadn't prayed since she was not much older than Rachael. By then, she had already recognized that most of what she prayed for never came to pass and figured Mr. Big and Important probably wasn't even listening. She had tried some lesser celestials, saints and virgins, mostly just to insult God, to show him she didn't need him.

"God," Tatum said, "Rachael and I would like you to take care of her mom and my sister." She paused, lost for words again. "Amen," she said. "Please," she added for good measure.

Rachael remained in prayer posture. Not finished, Tatum supposed. Then she blessed herself and picked up her sandwich. She took a bite and then reached for the remote.

"How will we know if He does?" Tatum asked.

"What?"

"How will we know if God takes care of her?"

Rachael stared at Tatum coldly. Then, clearly disgusted, she threw her sandwich at her.

"You ruined it," she spat.

Tatum looked down to her chest. She picked shredded lettuce off her sweater and winged the pickle into the trash.

"Don't be mad," she said. "I'm sorry. I just thought we should define our terms."

Rachael scrambled off the bed and stormed into the bathroom.

Objects thrown, doors slammed. Round two. Tatum hadn't meant to ruin it. The question was dumb, maybe even inappropriate, she thought. But it was sincere. *Take care of* — what did that mean to God? After all, supposedly God was already 'taking care of' everybody, and based on results, Tatum thought, what 'taking care of' someone meant to God might be similar to what it meant to the Mafia.

Tatum got off the bed and went to the bathroom door. She rapped a knuckle on it.

"Rach."

"Take care of my mom in heaven," she heard Rachael say. But her piety seemed exaggerated, an I'll-do-it-myself quality that informed Tatum that the point was no longer to beseech the Lord God, but to let Tatum know how miserably she had failed.

Tatum pressed her back to the bathroom door and slid down until seated on the floor. The praying stopped. Tatum listened for Rachael's breath.

"Are you okay?"

Bam. Rachael kicked the inside of the door. She sounded fit and healthy.

Then Tatum listened to Rachael resume her prayers, asking for favors she would never know had or hadn't been granted. Prayer. It was probably a good sign, Tatum thought. Proactive. Indicating some belief in having power over one's circumstances. Hail Marys and psychic hotlines, they were last ditch efforts to take control, take action, if only to call for help.

She knocked softly on the bathroom door.

"Rachael?" she said. "Hey, Rach, if your mom was here, right now? What do you think she'd be doing?"

No answer. Tatum noticed a bottle opener screwed into the wall across from her and up a few feet. Randomly placed. A considerate thought but weak in execution.

"C'mon Rachael, if we were all on a trip together."

Rachael spoke each word progressively louder.

"My. Mom. Is. Dead."

Then, *bam*, another kick. Tatum felt it through the door.

"I'm just saying 'what if,'" Tatum said. "Pretending might make us feel better."

A second passed. Then, another. Then the bathroom door opened, and Tatum fell back a bit before catching herself. Rachael stepped past without acknowledging her. She went to the motel room door and struggled with the knob. Tatum rose to her feet and followed.

"I want to go home," Rachael said, twisting at the lock.

Tatum reached over her head and flipped the bolt. Rachael walked out into the wind and sleet. Tatum had the room key in her pocket. She reached for their coats.

Outside, Rachael struggled with the door handle of the passenger's side of the car until Tatum came and unlocked it. Then Tatum came around the car and got in the driver's seat. Rachael buckled her seat belt. Tatum considered it but passed. Rachael turned her head to look out the passenger window as though at any moment they might pass prairies, cattle, and mountain ranges. Tatum could see Margaret in Rachael's profile and in the arc of her brow. It reminded her of when she and Margaret were kids in the back seat of the car on the drive home from the Wisconsin Dells after summer weekends late on Sunday nights. Margaret would allow a truce for the sake of comfort, and the two of them would share a grown-up's windbreaker for a cover. Margaret would lean against the cool glass of the window. Tatum would close her eyes against Margaret's arm.

Tatum looked away from Rachael and faced forward. Beyond the windshield, glare from the motel's floodlights illuminated the falling sleet. She felt the hole in the world that was Margaret being dead. She wished that she'd reached her before she died.

Rachael. That was the name Margaret had used in the message on Tatum's machine. "Rachael, it's Margaret," she had said. "I need you to come. I'm sick. It's important." Then, there was a long pause before the machine cut the message, as though Margaret had sat there with the receiver in her hand wondering if there was more to say.

Tatum had called back. She spoke to Lee because Margaret was sleeping. She asked what was going on, but Lee was stingy with the details. She told him that Margaret had called her and that she was on her way. He seemed surprised. Tatum figured Margaret had to be either mortally ill or drugged out of her mind to have made that call. Maybe both.

Drops too sloppy to be hail and too fat to be rain slapped against the windshield. Tatum surveyed the gravel lot. Three cars, counting her own. Not bad for the middle of nowhere. Outside one of the rooms, an orange glow rose and fell as a smoker took in the sleet and the low clouds from beneath the motel's awning. He flicked his cigarette out into the lot. The sky stepped on it wetly. All in all, Tatum thought, the

Cloud 9 wasn't so different from the motel in Nebraska. Somewhat worn, but not seedy. Booked by people who watch the rain.

Tatum briefly imagined that the man outside the motel room was smoking his last cigarette. He would return to his room where a .38 and a bottle of Wild Turkey sat on his nightstand. *Bang.* They would hear it in the middle of the night. It would wake them, jar them from their sleep. Perhaps, in their grogginess, the silent night that followed the shot would fool them. False alarm, they would think. Nothing. They would ease back into their dreams.

Tatum had never told Margaret about the pills in Nebraska. But Margaret did know about that earliest attempt, so long ago in the shadow-cool of the garage. Tatum sniffed, a rueful, private laugh. She hadn't thought about it for some time. She rolled her head to the side to look at Rachael. The shape-shifting of genes made her look like Margaret, then not Margaret, then Margaret again. Rachael's eyes drooped and her head fell forward in sleep then snapped back up to sloppy wakefulness. She blinked slowly.

Tatum reached over to tuck Rachael's coat more tightly around her. For the first time since Rachael could walk, Tatum kissed her head.

The two sat in the cold car pointed at their warm, bland room. Tatum loved the car, being in a car, looking up through a windshield at night, being in-between, which is nowhere. Tatum had lived alone most of her adult life, had worked largely for herself and primarily alone. She used to compile people's data, write reports, organize information and return it to those with a stake in it. She hadn't gone back to it, though, after her bout with cancer. She lived frugally on savings and a modest inheritance from her parents that wouldn't last much longer. It was a life so different from Margaret's. Margaret had it all in the classical sense. She had never tried to kill herself. Yet, Tatum was glad not to be her.

She let her head roll back toward Rachael who slept with rose-colored lips slightly open. She looked peaceful, at last. But then, a shiver jerked her little shoulders, waking her, her eyes opening just for a second before falling back closed. The car was getting colder. Tatum considered starting the engine to warm them up but decided instead to get Rachael back inside.

Tatum took hold of the door handle. She got out and walked to the passenger's side. She unbuckled Rachael, gathered her up, and hauled her back into the room.

Rachael was too tired to resist as Tatum turned back the bed and pulled enough clothes off of her that she would sleep comfortably. Then Tatum turned on the light in the bathroom and cracked the door. The rest of the room was dark. She grabbed the phone book and sat again outside the bathroom door. She opened it to the G's. She looked for Vincent.

But no Goes Aheads were listed.

She closed the phone book and stared at the bottle opener screwed into the wall. She imagined a shrink, a Sigmund Freud type, playing word association. He said, "Motel."

"Suicide," she would reply from the couch.

But Tatum wasn't reminiscing about suicide. She was reminiscing about Margaret. It was happiness Tatum had felt that day when she had turned the barrel of a rifle to her own head. It was a memory she stroked like a cat in her lap.

But she didn't want to think about it. She wanted to tell it. To Paris.

Her heart flickered at the thought of him.

She wanted to tell him the story.

Tatum got up and hauled the phone as far from the bed as she could. She let the call be charged to the room, and she dialed the Deluxe. It was 2:30 a.m. Paris would be there. He would listen without judgment, without defining or nailing down. Labels. Tatum hated them all. They turned lives into case histories. Paris didn't label, not even in his mind. She would not get categorized under it. It would be categorized under her. No more or less weighty than a hundred other things.

7

∿

Blair signaled from the casino for Paris to pick up the phone. Paris walked to the end of the counter to the old, beige rotary with ancient flecks of paint on its cord. The phone was of another time, but it was clean, not greasy or smudged. Paris was the one man over the decades who had taken a sponge to it, thought it worthy of care.

"Hello?"

"Paris?"

"Tatum."

He was pleasantly surprised.

"Where are you?" he asked her.

It was 2:30 a.m. The diner was entering the stillest time of the night. A booth of young stoners were coming off their buzz and readying themselves to go home to their apartments above the downtown shops. Humble dumps, but free of filth and fear. The women would be filtering in soon. The homeless. The politely alcoholic.

"I want to tell you something," Tatum said. "I feel like telling a story."

The stoners pitched their money onto a shared check and moved, tired-eyed, toward the casino and street. The first woman to arrive, tall and acne-scarred, didn't look at them as she passed. She sat down at the stool farthest from the phone, closest to the casino.

"One second," Paris said to Tatum.

Paris let the phone hang from its cord as he ladled a bowl of soup. He pulled a spoon from the silverware rack beneath the counter and grabbed a fistful of crackers wrapped two to a pack. He carried it all to the woman and placed it in front of her. She didn't look up, but the words *thank you* emanated from her, forming in the space around her.

"Tell me," Paris said, returning to the phone.

"I was eleven," Tatum said, her voice disembodied. "I wanted to play with my sister, Margaret, but she wouldn't let me. In true kid sister form, I didn't let up. I whined and begged and loitered in her bedroom doorway. I told her I didn't have anything to do and she said, 'Why don't you kill yourself?'"

Paris watched a second woman come in, his favorite who had told him her name was Linda. Almond-eyed and with stray grays curling wiry in her dark hair, she looked half-something — Indian, Italian, maybe black, or Greek. Her pretty was faded by resignation to a thing that was or a thing that was not. Whichever thing, it either was or wasn't for a long time. She unzipped her windbreaker and took a stool at the counter, in the middle, not in her usual seat at the end closest to the phone. She was not a prostitute of the high-heels and hot-pants sort. She looked as ordinary as her johns. She made certain rounds, kept certain hours in low life places. She was available, and those who needed to know knew. It was clear, somehow, that the money she earned was not her own. She rested her elbows on the counter and folded her hands. She aimed at more than invisibility. It was *nonexistence* she tried to cultivate until Paris was finished.

"So, I go to the garage," Tatum said. "I climbed up on this tool thing and took down my father's hunting rifle. I tried to turn the barrel toward my head. To tell you the truth," she said, "I think I was more *playing* at killing myself than actually going for it. Anyway, the rifle was too long for me to manage, and while struggling with it, it goes off."

She paused. The acne-scarred woman opened a packet of crackers slowly, almost painfully, like a burn unit victim.

"But you lived," Paris said.

"I did. But I also took out the garage window. Anyway, in seconds, the garage door was hauled open. There was my mother and some neighbors. I was on the ground. The rifle was on the ground. My hands were burning. My ears were ringing. Everyone was talking to me. They were making gestures that said, relax, be calm. I couldn't hear a thing. Then I saw Margaret."

Paris knew, then, that Margaret was dead.

"She gave me this look," Tatum said.

Paris could tell it was a good thing, the look.

"She approved?" he said.

"She was impressed," Tatum said. "Then the paramedics came. They examined me and took me to the hospital. Blah, blah, blah. After that, Margaret let me play with her for . . . well, it must have been weeks, but it felt like forever."

This, Paris knew, was the point of the story. The happy ending.

"She died, didn't she?" he said.

Linda's eyes briefly flickered in his direction.

"Yeah."

Paris nodded though Tatum couldn't know.

Paris wondered where Tatum was calling from, but he didn't ask again. She would've answered the first time if she hadn't needed to be only a voice, invisible like his customers. So he let her whisper into his ear without squeezing her into time or space.

"Tell me something, Paris," Tatum said.

"Yes?"

"Tell me anything."

Paris turned toward the phone and stared at the wall's edge. His feet were hot in his boots like they always were. His feet. It was a story he should tell her. One he owed her for looking at the topless pictures. Stink foot. It was his secret. It was no laughing matter.

Hearing more customers, Paris looked over his shoulder. Two more of the women arrived. There were four now in total. The Women of the Deluxe. It was another story he could tell. Another secret.

"You have customers," Tatum said, understanding his silence.

"Yes."

"Then, I thank you for your listening. Perhaps I'll even bid you adieu."

"I'd like that," Paris said.

There was silence for a moment, an implied *adieu*. Paris gave a barely perceptible bow. Tatum hung up first.

Paris put down the receiver and turned just slightly. He looked down the laminate surface of the counter, a white dulled and yellowed. His line of vision included only the curved edge of a bowl of soup, sleeves and hands, and salt and pepper shakers. Paris saw it in paint. As he lifted his eyes, Linda reemerged into existence. She slipped down the counter to her usual stool. A young, tough, but frightened-looking white woman and her cross-eyed Indian friend sat in a booth.

First, Paris poured a cup of coffee for Linda. Then he carried two bowls of soup to the young women in the booth. He moved like a fish through water, returning to the backside of the counter, carrying the stacked dirty plates and the check from where the stoners had been sitting. Paris hated handling money in front of the women. It was the only dimple in the velvet fabric generated in these a.m. hours, the only thing that made him self-conscious with them.

The two younger women in the booth talked in low voices, unintelligent sounding conversation about places and procedures, something vaguely retarded in the rhythms and cadence of their speech. The two stayed for nearly two hours, enduring long silences, unashamed to simply sit in peace. Of the women, only Linda ever verbalized a shy greeting.

Paris performed the side work that he did in the middle of the night. He took the lid off the sunken vat that had held clam chowder for the previous twelve hours. He dipped in the ladle and spun its contents, determining how much was left. The women knew when the soup was gone, just as a dog knows when you've eaten the last bite of your sandwich.

Linda never ate the soup. Her collarbone and thin wrists made Paris believe she was a woman who lived on coffee and cigarettes, though she never reeked. As usual, she was the last to leave. She didn't do business at the Deluxe, though her first time there she did say to Paris, "I'm looking for work, if you need anything done." The service she was offering was unmistakable. Every now and then, before she left, she might ask, "You need anything?"

Paris would smile and shake his head. It made him feel guilty and ridiculous, those nights, for his offering of soup. He knew that on those nights she hadn't made her money elsewhere. She would slide off her stool and walk into the inky night.

The sun bided its time beneath the horizon. Paris had left a spotless kitchen and a balanced drawer for Jerry, the old Vietnam vet who worked the morning shift. Paris passed through the streets on his way to the duplex in the light of lampposts standing proud as trees. Quiet doorways blended with windows and walls in the shadows. Fire escapes crept down brick veneers into benign and potholed alleys. Paris thought about a canvas, a twelve by fourteen, he had in his closet. The artist's task, he knew, was not to reduce the world to two dimensions, but to find the proper detail — the curved spoonful of chowder, the fragile turn of a wrist — the fractal that told the larger story and contained the rest of the dimensions.

Paris had been saving the canvas. Waiting for the perfect idea. His excuse was that canvases were expensive. Not to be wasted.

The canvas had been in his closet for a year.

He reached the library and cut through the park behind it. He passed the concrete water fountain that jutted up from the ground like a squat sentry at the playground's edge. The swing set and slide stood, sleepy as the trees, caught in the half-dreams of hibernation. He wondered if Tatum, like himself, was unable to cross the park without remembering.

It was in this park that Paris had kissed her. That they had kissed.

He stepped past the flat, metal merry-go-round with its silver bars and chronic tilt. The kiss happened the night they'd gone to see a local theater group's production of *Picasso at the Lapin Agile,* a fictional encounter between a young Einstein and a young Picasso. The play had launched for Paris a mild obsession with drawing Einstein. Einstein as a janitor. Einstein shooting craps. Einstein selling snow cones.

It was a summer night, the middle of July, and Paris and Tatum were walking home after the play, cutting through the park as the day's heat dissipated in the thin mountain air. Tatum's throat rose from the scoop of a black tank top. A small, cloth purse just big enough for folded money hung from one shoulder across to the opposite hip. Above them, the sky doled out stars. She looked straight ahead as she told Paris that Einstein tried to save the universe from his own equations. When he calculated the destiny of the world as ending in fire or ice, he did more math, she said, grasped for an equation that would say it wasn't so.

"Did he find one?" Paris asked, stopping at the swing set, partitioned off from the lawn on an island of woodchips.

Tatum pursed her lips and shook her head no.

"Then, we're doomed?"

She nodded, soberly. Then she reached out and fingered a chain link that led down to a leather strap seat. She eyed the swing up and down, considering taking it for a spin. Paris watched her ringless hand, a hand older than her face. When their eyes met, she smiled, as though at an inside joke that had passed between them. Paris felt the kiss pressing at the seams of the moment, a gift apart from them, bigger than they, but theirs to deliver into the world. Paris reached to the side of her face. He leaned in, and their lips touched for only a second, but it was a second that included a Mississippi.

When they pulled gently apart, Tatum dropped her head, staring down at the seat of the swing. Paris could look only at her, his heart banging in his chest, the word 'yes' understood by him for the first time. 'Yes' not as an answer, but as a fact. *Yes.* It surrounded them, suffused them. But he could already see Tatum backing away from it, pretending it was make-believe, a game the wise don't play.

But she had it inside-out. He was certain.

When she spoke, it was with caution. Each word selected carefully.

"Paris," she said, "we're friends. You like me as a friend. That's why you kissed me. But if we were to keep on kissing, tonight and then tomorrow, it would become different. I'd become your girlfriend. All the reasons you wanted to kiss me would go away. People want different things from friends than from girlfriends."

A small pendant earring caught a ray of park light and sparkled. Her eyes were green as a forest.

"I know," she went on, sounding more nervous, "that you're thinking we could be more than friends. But for me, there is no such thing. There is no 'more than'. This is as good as I get. As your girlfriend, I would seem like less, not more. I like that you like me. I don't want to disappoint you. Love doesn't cure us of who we are."

Paris trusted her, so how could he call her wrong?

Her truth swam past him as he stood there in his own. His truth was different from the one she had spoken. His truth was *yes*, but his mind couldn't shuffle the feeling into anything solid or articulate. He only knew the summer cool air and the intimate space of the swing. He followed the kiss and not her words, not his own thoughts. His lips and skin had not served as a barrier. The kiss was sinking into his waters, floating heavily down into the quietest and darkest place, lodging itself in his sands.

Tatum turned away, looking toward the dark lawn and the distant sidewalk. She opened her mouth about to say more but was interrupted. A sudden loud ticking surrounded them. The sprinkler system kicking in. They didn't run. Arcs of spray shot up from the grass surrounding them, spigots jerking in circles and whipping sheets of water across the clean-cut lawn. Paris and Tatum ducked but were safe, out of reach on the woodchips.

Tatum stepped toward Paris but turned profile, grabbing the swing's chains. She sat down on the leather seat and backed it up until she was positioned to push off. She smiled at him weakly. It was a request. Paris thought she was requesting his love but not the risk of losing it.

"I know other stuff about Einstein, too," she said.

"Tell me."

Paris passed through both the park and the memory. He walked toward the duplex in the autumn chill through the northside neighborhoods of the aspiring working class and the liberal professionals. The houses weren't grand, but they were beloved. Matted, raked leaves sat like black puddles on the dark lawns. These leaves were the last round, the round that might not make it into the Dumpsters and compost piles but would sit quiet under the snow until raked up in the spring with ice still clinging to their soggy brownness. The grass beneath would rise greener than the rest.

He walked the blocks, allowing himself the hope that Tatum would be sitting on the front stoop of the duplex. He pretended that she had called him at work from home, choosing to ease back into his company, first just a voice, materializing slowly.

But the stoop was empty.

Love is a demotion. The lover ranks lower than the friend. This is how Paris remembered what Tatum had told him that night in the park. He had decided that, for Tatum, such rankings must have to do with permanence. Those we can keep as opposed to those we can't. Lovers were, undeniably, more slippery, more likely to come and go than were friends. Paris tried to understand her thinking rather than argue against it. He didn't want to frame an argument on love's behalf and risk it being a compelling one that wins her over but, in the end, isn't true. She could be right. He might not hold up under love's mighty scrutiny. When the hope for love outshines its reality, the beloved becomes a disappointment.

And a person can't measure up to an idea, Paris knew. It was apples and oranges.

8

~

Geneva dozed while the cold hands of November pressed against her window. The black sky outside spread its arms, holding back the dawn. Voodoo curved in the soft angle of her knees and hummed, a pleasure engine. The sheets were clean, softly warmed with the heat of but one night's sleep. Geneva had changed them before she left for Amsterdam so they'd be here when she got back, cool and fresh for her first night home.

She hiked the sheet farther up her shoulder and nestled deeper into the pillow. How good it all is, she thought, as the cat stood, stretched, and stepped over her hip to settle again against her belly. Geneva lifted a hand to pet him, a mere flutter of movement, and her mind changed direction like birds in the sky, a moment of love toppled by the fear of loss. A tragic equation of cause and effect.

Her mind flipped through tragic possibilities. Voodoo meeting his end by lethal injection at the vet, a mercy killing, the only recourse to an unrelenting suffering. Or she might find him, little body twisted at the curb, victim of a hit and run. Bad thoughts. Bad. Ill-advised and dangerous. Geneva had heard the warnings. The theories that our thoughts move into the physical world, twisting and shaping outcomes just like in the quantum physics experiments. Balance the bad thoughts with good ones, the gurus counseled, something to even out the bottom line. Voodoo may live another seven years, she told herself, have nine lives.

"Jeez," she said aloud, propping herself to an elbow. How exhausting it is to be happy for just an instant.

Too many ideas camped out in Geneva's noggin. Bad citizens, all of them, they left their litter behind, and they shook down newcomers, forcing all experience to run a gauntlet of comparison, reference, and cross-reference. Life arrived exhausted.

Geneva was well aware that she could crash and burn ecstasy on the rocks of overanalysis. But she didn't believe analysis, itself, was the problem. In fact, she thought it essential to the well-lived life. Just knowing when to stop — that was the rub.

But her thoughts were interrupted. Her ears pricked up to attention. She heard a distinct *click*, a key in a lock. Her own front door opened and closed. The floor creaked beneath footsteps, and the hinges on a cupboard squeaked. There was no stealth, here. Whoever it was thought himself alone.

Then, a voice.

"Breakfast time."

Voodoo sprang off the bed and trotted out of the bedroom.

Paris. Talking to Voodoo. Geneva's heart resumed beating, and her adrenalin slumped off, slightly embarrassed. False alarm.

She got out of bed and put her thin, flannel robe on over her thinner cotton nightshirt. She made her way down the short hall. Quietly.

"Paris?" she said from the kitchen entry.

"Uh-jeez," he said, turning fast and jumping back, holding a bag of cat food. Voodoo startled and made a break for it, leaping across the counter to the living room chair where he arched his back and raised his tail.

Paris held the cat food across his chest with one hand while pushing his glasses up his nose with his other.

"You scared me," he said.

"I'm home."

"I see that," he said. "Tatum asked me . . ."

"I know, I know," she said, waving him off. She looked at the clock above the sink. Five twenty. Voodoo jumped back onto the counter. Geneva picked him up and stroked him.

"Coffee?" she asked.

"That's okay," Paris said. "I'm sorry I woke you. It was still Thursday to me."

"I wasn't sleeping," she said. "I was listening to the ridiculous nonsense in my head. Even when I thought you were a burglar, I was glad for the interruption. So, c'mon, interrupt some more."

"You think the ridiculous nonsense in my head would be much improvement?"

"At least it won't be mine."

Paris put down the cat food and let out a breath.

"I'm really sorry," he said, again.

"Me, too."

Geneva put the cat on the floor. The apartment was dark save for the light on above the stove that served as a night light. Geneva opened a cupboard and retrieved the French press.

"So a sick sister, huh?" she said. "Have you heard anything?"

Paris stepped around the counter and sat on a stool on the living room side, looking in.

"She's dead," he said.

Geneva looked to Paris. She frowned and then pressed the button on the coffee grinder. It was the inverse of a moment of silence but still an acknowledgment of the weight of death. When the grinding stopped, Geneva asked, "How's Tatum?"

"It's hard to say," Paris said. "Shaken, I think, but perfectly calm, too. You know."

Geneva put the teakettle on the stove and then brushed the tiny hairs off the counter between them. Paris watched with his signature expression. Not waiting. Not eager for the next exchange. Just present as a cat. Paris was attractive in a way most young women wouldn't notice, Geneva thought, until another woman saw it first, and then they would kick themselves, knowing they could've had him.

"Cancer?" she asked him, dumping the coffee grounds into the press.

"No," Paris said. "No, thank you. I'll take it black."

Geneva smiled. Then Paris did, too. The two of them were seldom alone. Tatum was the juncture where they met.

"Cancer infests that family," Geneva said. "Passed on like an heirloom."

"I didn't know that."

While the water continued to heat, Geneva went to her record collection. Even in the dark, she could zero in on what she wanted, a row of albums in paper sleeves, no original covers. Ten years ago, the young man who owned the record store she frequented had a flood in his basement. He gave Geneva fifteen albums that had survived the flood intact but with their covers ruined. A purist, he had replaced those too and had given the coverless copies to Geneva. *A*'s, *B*'s, and a few *C*'s. He had alphabetized from the floor up. Some Allman Brothers. Bowie. Camel. Geneva picked an old Camel album, *Flight of the Snow Goose*. Perfect morning music. Jazzy, mellow.

"Cancer took out both of Tatum's parents," Geneva said, dropping the needle.

"I guess I did know that," Paris said. "Do you think Tatum worries?"

"About cancer?" Geneva said, surprised.

"Yeah."

Geneva hesitated. From the sound of his voice, she didn't think he meant did she worry about getting cancer *again*. She did the math with her back to him as she adjusted the volume. She calculated that Tatum had brought Paris around for the first time right when she had finished chemo. Tatum had a cue-ball head at the time and was skin and bones. She looked like a child refugee, a bald young boy. How could Paris not have known? What did he think? That she had just escaped from a concentration camp?

The kettle whistled.

"I honestly don't think she thinks about it much," Geneva said. "She doesn't talk about it, at any rate." Which was true.

Geneva remembered when Tatum told her about the diagnosis. Just two weeks before, Vincent had dumped her, or she had dumped him. Geneva never got the full story. Nonetheless, brokenhearted with a shaky prognosis, Tatum had forged ahead. Mastectomy. Chemo. Geneva had been surprised that Tatum took traditional, prudent steps to beat the cancer. She had expected indifference and self-neglect. She wondered if it wasn't so much a will to live that drove her as it was a determination to be the one to decide whether and when to pull the plug.

Geneva looked at Paris. His brow was drawn, and he stared off to the side in private worry.

"Tatum's okay," Geneva said, pouring the water into the press. "Cancer." She shook her head. "I hear it, and I want to know what did she eat, or breathe? What's the family background? Was she repressed, not dealing with something — anger, resentment, unresolved child-hood issues?"

"Cause and effect," Paris said. "It's pointless to look."

"You think?" Geneva said. "Maybe. I guess I just want to reassure myself that my circumstances are nothing like theirs. I want to kid myself that I'm somehow different and therefore safe." She slowly pushed down the press.

Paris still looked troubled. Geneva pointed a finger at him.

"Don't you dare start worrying about Tatum," she said.

Paris looked taken aback.

"Look," Geneva said, turning to retrieve the mugs. "I once had a cat I absolutely adored. Sure, I adore all my cats, but this one was partic-ularly amazing. Her name was SoHo, and we thought each other was just the bees' knees. Anyway, she got diagnosed with cancer and was given four to six months. After that, every time I looked at her, I saw my own grief instead of the sweet, little creature that she was." Geneva set two ceramic mugs beside the press. One was covered with Egyptian-style hieroglyphs. The other had a ♀ on it. "Tatum's not sick," she said to Paris. "Don't start looking at her as though at any moment she may keel over dead. You may as well worry about asteroids hitting the Earth. They're out there, you know."

"You're scaring me," Paris said.

Geneva smiled, and he smiled back. She poured the coffee.

"Sorry," she said. "I just can't stand any more worrying. It's not you. I'm lecturing myself." She passed Paris the Egyptian mug. "Worrying," Geneva said, "it's largely a woman's disease, you know. An epidemic blocking female enlightenment everywhere."

Paris accepted what she told him. He didn't know anything different.

"Ask me about my trip," Geneva said.

Paris paused, then obeyed.

"How was your trip?" he said with a slight nod.

"Had great soup luck," Geneva said, changing her tone. More upbeat. "Garlic soup from heaven. Tomato bisque to die for."

Paris looked down, and then he made a mock serious face.

"Do you think we make our own soup luck?" he said, looking up.

"Perhaps," she said. "But some of us are just born soup lucky. Perhaps we earned it in a past life."

"Because you shared your soup?"

"Who knows?" she said. "Cause and effect," she repeated his words.

"It's pointless to look."

They saluted each other with their mugs, not quite a toast. Geneva took a sip of coffee but knew she would not finish it. She had drunk it every day in Amsterdam, but it had been a vacation indulgence, more about ceremony than the caffeine. It was served dark and bitter with bread and a hard-boiled egg, the breakfast included in her lodging. But she couldn't live on a regular basis with the low-grade agitation that came with drinking coffee. She thought she needed to know for certain whether any potential heart palpitations were driven by caffeine or some oncoming cardiac disaster.

"I like the music," Paris said.

Geneva liked this about Paris. He always noticed the music.

"Paris," she said, "since you've got the key, could you stop by tomorrow morning too? I need to go see Ralph. I'll be spending the night."

"Sure," he said. "Do you think he realizes you haven't been there for a while?"

Geneva looked past Paris into her living room. Ralph hadn't done so much as mumble her name for nine years. It had been equally long since he had given her that old dog look, a combination of deep love and of being deeply tired.

"You know how they say dogs don't have any sense of time," she said. "They just know you're there or you're not there."

"That's how it is with Ralph?"

Geneva opened her mouth to say yes but knew it wouldn't be true.

"No," she said. She twisted her mouth in thought. "He doesn't know whether or not I'm there. I'm pretty sure."

Outside the windows, it remained dark and would be so for at least another hour. The two were quiet, Paris on the stool, Geneva standing across from him leaning on the counter. Neither searched for the next thing to say. Both of their thoughts drifted privately. Geneva suspected her lecture didn't take and that Paris continued his concern in private. His affection for Tatum was unmistakable. He was so different from Vincent, Tatum's ex-lover and the son of a dear, old friend. Tatum met Vincent because of Geneva, but not through her. She did not set them up, nor would she. Vincent had used Geneva's apartment sometimes when she was out of town or on weekends when she was visiting Ralph. He would leave her small buds of reefer in an empty cookie jar. Geneva was certain he did so at his mother's direction. Vincent's mother was 100 percent Northern Cheyenne and not crazy about white people. Geneva, for some reason, had been granted a special dispensation.

Geneva had watched Vincent grow up. His mother's blood showed in Vincent's eyes and cheekbones, and his nose belonged to his Italian father. The thick, dark hair could've come from either one. Vincent's father was never referred to by name. No love lost. But the resulting offspring, Vincent, hit puberty with sultry looks, a good mind, and a fierce maternal loyalty — a death trap for any girl. To make matters worse, his taste in women tended toward the wounded. A little existential pain made him feel needed. But he expected to be the cure. It was a classic case of can't-have-your-cake-and-eat-it-too. That alone didn't bode well for Tatum, but there was more. The idea of Vincent with a white girl wouldn't sit well with his mother, despite that she now lived in Ventura shacked up with a white seventy-two-year-old California surf bum.

Tatum never stood a chance.

So they split up. Vincent disappeared into his career as an activist in the natural death movement, fighting corporate ownership of the passage to the other side, as he might say. He had published several articles and had even been on a talk show or two.

"Geneva," Paris said, calling her back to the moment. "Back in Europe?"

Geneva looked to him. She was grateful Tatum had brought him around, thrown him into the mix.

"You never knew Vincent, did you?"

"No."

"He entered my mind," Geneva said. "Maybe he's thinking about me."

"Do you like him?" Paris asked.

"Like him?" Geneva said. She looked into Paris's face. His eyes were slightly squinted, almost a wince. She suspected he would prefer she did not like Vincent much.

"He interests me," she said, showing mercy. "Is that the same thing?"

"I'll have to think about that," Paris said.

"Well," Geneva said, "do get back to me."

Paris nodded. He looked into the bottom of his mug. "Thank you," he said and got up to leave.

Geneva lifted her chin, a silent goodbye and you're welcome. Her mind had leeched onto the question she had posed to Paris. Was being interested in someone the same thing as liking him, loving him even, if you're interested enough?

"Good night," Paris said from the door, though it was still-dark morning.

Paris closed the door to Geneva's and faced Tatum's. He had the key. He was glad Geneva was home. It made it easier to stay out. He stared at Tatum's door for only a few seconds before it reminded him of the blank canvas in his closet and he left.

Paris walked with his hands jammed into the pockets of his canvas coat. He had no shadow as he watched the edge of the sidewalk where it met the small patch of grass of the boulevard. Trees tangled above his head until he spilled out of the residential streets and glanced up at the morning moon.

9

~

Rachael heard Tatum say her mother's name. *Margaret.* Aunt Tatum spoke it from a hunkered down place outside the bathroom door in the motel room. Rachael knew the place well. A place where she, too, used to sit. Outside the bathroom door, she'd listen to her mother make bad noises in the shower. Rachael always knew when the noises were coming. She knew because her mother would turn on the TV in the kitchen and walk away. She would suggest a video for Rachael to watch and snap it into the VCR in the family room. She would turn on the radio in the bedroom. Rachael refused, though, to be swallowed by the contrived din of the house. Safer to listen. Better to eavesdrop on the secret. For whatever danger it held, she wouldn't be alone.

"She gave me this look," she heard her Aunt Tatum say into the phone.

Rachael knew the look. She could see her mother's face, a double helix of love and anxiety, a look followed by a hug, too tight. A hug Rachael didn't want.

That was before motel rooms with loud heaters and thin blankets and eating sandwiches off of their wrappers. It was back in the afternoons when autumn-colored leaves hung proudly, seemingly unaware of their fate. They rustled outside the window of her mother's bedroom, where she had retreated, rolled to her side, and forgot about breakfast, laundry, and getting Rachael ready for school.

So Rachael skipped breakfast. She stayed home and collected the leaves as they fell. She brought to her mother the reds and yellows with their edges curling inward like fingertips. She held them by their stems and twirled them in pirouettes while she stood beside the bed. These leaves were the bravest, she told her mother, those unafraid to go first and lead the way.

The weeks slipped by, and Rachael learned to climb cupboards and eat pretzels for breakfast. More leaves fell. They fell in small showers riding together on shared breezes. One evening, when her father got home, he came to the bedroom where Rachael was sitting in the pocket between her mother's arm and torso while they looked at old pictures of great aunts also named Rachael. Her father brought a woman into the bedroom, gray-haired but not too old. The woman told Rachael to call her Miss Geri. Rachael looked to her mother to know whether or not to like her. At first, her mother ignored the woman's presence, not rudely, but as though she couldn't see her at all. Before too long, though, Rachael could sense a silent gratitude, a relief in her mother, and so she ate Miss Geri's food and let her dress her for school.

Miss Geri left late at night, and when she did, Rachael snuck into her mother's bed. In mornings over breakfast, Miss Geri would admonish her playfully, telling her that her mother needed rest.

"Are you afraid to sleep by yourself?" she asked.

Rachael shrugged.

"I promise you," Miss Geri said, "there are no monsters in your closets, and if there were, I'd clean them out." She raised her arm, holding her sponge aloft, demonstrating that she possessed the proper weaponry for the job.

Rachael gave her a half-smile to be polite. She knew the monsters weren't in her closet, and she also knew that they couldn't be fought because they never attack. They watch. They owned you, and it was enough.

When only the stubbornest of leaves remained, holding on to their place in the sky by fragile fingers — seeming, now, the brave ones — Rachael woke up knowing her mother was gone. Rachael sat with the covers wrapped at her waist and stared at the drape of the sheet over her mother's shoulder, waist, and hip. Her hair was messy in back and Rachael thought that she should brush it before Miss Geri arrived. She leaned over her mother's body and directed her voice into her ear. She spoke as though into a dark house she wasn't sure was empty. "Mommy? Mommy?" She shook at her shoulder, but she knew. She also knew that her mother hadn't become a ghost and floated up and away. She was still in there but past a big door, maybe two, hiding down deep.

That's dead too.

When her father came in, Rachael moved back from her mother fast and said, "Now she's dead."

Her father stared at the draped sheet. Then he gathered Rachael off the bed and crushed her to his chest. She felt flat as a shield against him as he squeezed her too tight. She stared over his shoulder into the long hallway that led to the stairway down to the foyer. Her stomach growled for breakfast, and her father's cologne was making her slightly nauseous. His big hand held the back of her head and scrunched her hair.

She struggled from his arms and ran to the master bathroom to get her mother's hairbrush. But once inside, Rachael remembered it was on the nightstand. She turned to leave, but her eye caught a movement in the mirror. She blinked at her reflection, and it blinked back. Still, she didn't trust it. It wasn't her, not who she wanted to be but someone coming for her, to get her, to be her. Her mother hadn't been alone when she cried. A sneaky child was in there with her, and her father too, a ghostly version, whom her mother beat with words like fists, words muffled but not drowned by the shower's drum and patter.

A sudden ringing startled Rachael, and she broke away from the reflection. She ran from the bathroom, past her father, who lifted the phone from its cradle, and down the hall. In her bedroom, she hunkered into the space between the side of her dresser and the wall and let the three sides hold her.

There she sat, alone, hearing no pounding shower, no radio, or television. She covered her ears, but the noise was inside. She tried to be deaf to both worlds, the one inside and out, which created a world without her, one in which she did not exist. When the noise was gone, she felt the static hum around her and pretended she was it. A vibrating nothing.

Then, she realized a thing that had never occurred to her before. All the sounds, all the furniture, the hallways and walls, they existed without her, went on in her absence.

Another ring, but the doorbell now. It was a sound disconnected from meaning, asking nothing of a self that didn't exist. Rachael stayed in her corner and let it ring again. She heard without listening, blended as she was into the invisible fabric of space. Then she heard the clank of the knocker that nobody ever used. The unfamiliarity of the sound focused her attention, called her back into being. Rachael rose from her corner. It made no sense, but she thought, maybe it's Mom. She left her room and crept down the stairs. She approached the front door apprehensively. Even though she wasn't allowed to, she opened it.

"Hey Rachael," Tatum said, stepping in.

Tatum's hair was dark like Rachael's. She wore browns and tans like an explorer, and a black wool ski cap on her head. Rachael knew who she was.

"She's dead," Rachael said.

Tatum looked up the staircase. She took the edge of the door away from Rachael and closed it. She placed her backpack on the floor and led Rachael by the shoulder to the steps and sat down on the second to bottom one. She turned Rachael to face her. She took her hands.

Rachael pulled her hands away.

"I'm sorry," Tatum said, dropping her own hands into her lap but still studying Rachael's face.

Somehow, Tatum's sudden presence did not surprise Rachael. She knew that her mother didn't like her. And she knew, without knowing why or how, that the girl in the mirror was like her.

The sound of a car engine on the long driveway caught both of their attention. Neither moved as they heard someone approach, turn a key in the lock, and enter. It was Miss Geri. She looked down at them, and her face shifted. She knew without asking. Geri frowned sympathetically and touched Rachael's head. Tatum stood and introduced herself.

"I'm Margaret's sister," she said, extending her hand. "Tatum." She paused then, still holding Miss Geri's hand. "I drove all night," she said.

Miss Geri pulled Tatum to her and hugged her even though they had just met. Rachael watched her aunt's eyes shut tight over Miss Geri's shoulder. The hug bothered Rachael, and she was about to tell them to stop when they let go anyway. Geri started up the stairs, and Tatum followed. On the third step, Tatum looked back over her shoulder at Rachael.

"You coming?" she said.

Rachael shook her head no.

Tatum stared at her for another second as though waiting for a change of mind.

"All right," she said and continued up the steps.

In the Cloud 9 motel, Rachael cracked her eyes drowsily. Over the other bed, she could see the top of Tatum's head leaned back against the wall. Tatum sat on the floor near the bathroom. In her half-sleep, Rachael knew what Tatum was doing. She was eavesdropping, listening to secrets.

Rachael's lids fell, and the world was dark. Tatum and Miss Geri ascended the stairs and disappeared on the landing. Rachael stood in her pajamas near the front door on the cool, marble floor. She about-faced and met her own reflection from the top of her head down as far as her shoulders in the entryway mirror. She was pretty. It was fact. She had been a fairy for Halloween, her dress a gauzy and sequined sea foam.

Rachael placed a small palm to the glass. Her stomach rumbled, but it was part of the past, just an echo. She pressed the tip of her nose to the nose beyond the mirror's cool surface. She looked into her own green eyes. Her feet were cold on the marble floor. The chill from the mirror comforted her. Cold like winter water, icy, but not ice.

IO

~

Geneva drove her Saab north past the Scratchgravel Hills, gripping the steering wheel a bit too tight. Earlier that morning, her mood had been foul, her thoughts like an IV dripping resentment into her bloodstream. Jet-lagged, she would have preferred to putter at home. But Ralph had to be her first priority. She hadn't seen him for two weeks. Too long, she was sure, by good society's standards.

Such a difference it is to be driven by responsibility as opposed to desire. She would advise against it, if asked. She knew responsibility could crowd out desire like weeds in the flowerbed. After too many years, you go to the garden to pull. Duty calls. You forget that flowers once grew there. You kneel without question and labor.

But no. She would not think these thoughts. They were not conducive to carrying out gladly the task of the day. Love shrinks on the witness stand. Questioning it did a marriage no good.

The blue of the sky was hot and bright as Geneva took the curves through the canyon, through the cliff walls rising in mudstone layers of red and green. She knew well that she had not been born with the stuff that greases the skids for married life. Acceptance. Amnesia. Marriage required a duck's back. Geneva was born with a porcupine's topography, a back like a pine-covered hillside. Nothing rolled down it, nothing shrugged off. Experience tangled. Words jammed. She'd find the emotional debris, pick it up, dissect it, and smear it on a slide, view it under the power of magnification, all grotesquely large. Making studies of feelings is big business — therapy, talk shows — but Geneva learned the hard way that the scientific mind applied to love instead of test tubes leads not to high fives and by-George-I-think-we've-got-its. Picking through their love in a petri dish, to Ralph, had seemed a lot like looking for problems. And problems are, well, problematic, negative indicators, cause for alarm. And Ralph's alarm led to his anxiety, which led, for Geneva, to frustration. A stray musing or theory on their relationship, she found, inevitably morphed into conflict. There were two speeds: agreement and argument. What she had been seeking was exploration.

It took her years to realize that her mental tinkering was not a quality that had attracted Ralph, as she had believed. Because it was one of her most defining characteristics, it was hard for her to imagine anyone loving her without loving *it*.

But so it was.

For the sake of peace, then, she learned to work quietly in her mental lab.

The roads were clear and the miles added up quickly. Canyon Creek reflected the sky on its way to the Missouri. As she drove, Geneva worked to cast past choices in a more positive light. Was it so bad a lesson to learn to keep the peace? Peace is sought everywhere, marched for by throngs, and she had established it simply by keeping her thoughts to herself. It would be different, of course, had she died in her silence. But she had not. She simply lived in seclusion, mentally speaking, for which there is something to be said. Folks climb mountains to reach monasteries because they're good places to be if you've got a lot to think about. You don't make it in one if you don't.

So you see, I wasn't a doormat, she said silently to some other point of view that lived inside of her. Then she hit the gas pedal hard, hoping to leave her thoughts behind, choking on her dust.

Earlier that morning, when infested with such thoughts, Geneva had taken measures to jar her mind into better thinking, measures not currently available as she hugged the mountain curves. Those who consume drugs, legal or otherwise, are seeking relief. Some want to feel better. Some don't want to feel at all. Then there were those like Geneva, those who were seeking to melt the ice in their minds, having found themselves frozen into one of its frosty corners. It wasn't about feeling better but coming to new conclusions. Optional conclusions. Geneva believed there was a danger in allowing any one opinion to be left alone to run amok in her mind.

So she had retrieved an empty water glass from the kitchen and headed to the bedroom. She grabbed her toiletry bag, still packed, off the pillow and had rummaged, finding her sewing kit readily. She dug out her tiny travel scissors and a sewing needle. Then she reached to the floor for the underpants she had worn home from the airport. She pulled the thick sanitary napkin from the crotch, and she cut into it. She pulled out two sticky chunks of hashish bundled in plastic wrap.

Here in her bedroom, it now seemed a bold move. Were she instead in prison, her assessment would no doubt be different. At the time, though, it seemed neither bold nor stupid. Had it seemed either, she wouldn't have done it. It had felt nothing more than practical. She still had a few ancient buds from Vincent, but Vincent didn't come around much anymore since he and Tatum had split up, not even to see Geneva. He had been her only connection. Packing her Kotex in her hotel room in Amsterdam, Geneva hadn't felt any risk of anyone being interested in the contents of her underpants.

Geneva nicked off a small chunk from the smaller of the two hunks of hash. She stabbed it onto the end of her sewing needle. She pulled a pack of matches from the nightstand's drawer and lit the speared morsel. When it started to smoke, she placed it on her nightstand, covering it with the inverted glass.

"Eva's medicine," Geneva had said, as the glass filled with smoke. That's what Vincent's mother used to call pot. Geneva crouched on the floor beside her nightstand and slid the glass to the edge letting the lip hang just over the side. She sucked the blue curling ribbons of smoke from beneath the glass and slid it back to fill again. Sitting on the bed holding the smoke in her lungs, her thoughts of Vincent turned to thoughts of Tatum. She thought of Tatum's sister getting cut down in the prime of life while Ralph lingered. She exhaled slowly. She remembered a conversation she had with Tatum following Tatum's mastectomy. Tatum had been sitting on the closed lid of the toilet seat while Geneva emptied the plastic drains that caught the blood and fluid from the wound that was once a breast. Tatum hadn't told Geneva that she and Vincent had split up, but it was obvious that he wasn't around.

"What's become of our boy, Vincent?" she had asked Tatum.

Tatum was drugged up pretty good, but not too impaired.

"I bugged him. He left," she said. "Plain and simple."

"Bugged him how?"

"It was a naturally occurring phenomenon," she said. "I don't blame him. I could've shut up more. Reached out more."

"Maybe the talking was the reaching," Geneva said.

Tatum crossed her hands over her collarbone and looked toward the ceiling as Geneva reattached the drains.

"Can a person shut up and still be who they are?" Tatum had asked her. "I mean, if you shut up because you think you're bugging someone, are you being a good person for shutting up, or are you not you anymore?"

Geneva considered her own silence in her marriage as she secured the drains. It had not been a practice she had undertaken unconsciously. She had considered it at length. Had chosen it as a higher path. If talking leads to pain and frustration, is it not a kindness, to oneself at least, to shut one's pie hole?

"All shutting up is not created equal," she finally said. "Women waste a lot of creative energy talking. Maybe we'd be wiser to pursue the intimacy of the apes."

"Would that be the enlightened relationship?" Tatum asked. "Grooming each other and listening to the wind?"

Geneva offered Tatum a steady arm, and Tatum rose slowly from the toilet.

"For me," Geneva told her, "the enlightened relationship would run along the lines of a Wyatt Earp/Doc Holliday kind of bond. But with steamy sex. Friends. Comrades. Equals. Hot sex."

Geneva recalled the conversation as she blew past an ancient pickup truck doing its damnedest to go fifty. The peaks of the Sawtooth Range rose ragged against the western sky. Hot sex. It was the last thing she needed to be thinking about then, and it was the last thing she needed to be thinking about now. She had exacerbated the feeling that morning. Buzzed and turned on by notions of sex between equals, she had gone to the living room, flipping through the playlists in her mind. Marvin Gaye? Al Green? Roberta Flack?

She had surveyed her albums, eyes slowing at the *S*'s and *T*'s. She zeroed in on the band Traffic. She owned two of their albums, the same two anyone who had Traffic albums would have, *Mr. Fantasy* and *Low Spark*. She pulled *Low Spark* from the shelf and let it glide from its sleeve. She placed it on the turntable and skipped to the title track.

The needle hit the groove and from the friction between the two came the sound of piano and sax, coming on, moving in as though approaching from a distance. Geneva had stepped backward away from the turntable. A puttering of bongos, seeming to mind their own business, did their thing, a self-involved rhythm, while the chords of a piano minded the beat. Geneva dropped her robe over the arm of a chair and stood in the middle of the room where the effect from the stereo was best appreciated. There, she raised her arms forward slowly, leading with the backs of her wrists. She let them rise to Frankenstein level and held them there, suspended, shoulders relaxing before she released her arms slowly back to her sides. Reaching up then, out from her hips, she stretched her arms overhead toward the ceiling and then dipped into a hip. The sound was still all sax and chords and bongos as Geneva alternated arms and alternated hips, reaching with one as she dipped with the other. She eased into harmony, into sync, if not with the universe, if not with the voices in her head, then at least with this song. She rolled her shoulders up and back as the vocals broke through.

The stretching, and the hash, did its work on her. She felt her blood in her veins. Body and spirit reintegrated. The combination amounted, for Geneva, to sexuality. Her sense of it.

A mixed blessing, it was, to have that pot stirred.

And now on the road, just remembering her morning, she was horny again. Always a potential side effect of feeling good. Both a gift and a burden.

Geneva arrived at Parkview with only an hour left for visiting. The staff knew her and nodded in greeting. Alone with Ralph in his room, Geneva didn't talk aloud to him the way she knew many family members did to their comatose or catatonic loved ones. But she did try to emanate. She thought at him. She believed it a more effective method of communication given the circumstances.

And she brought him music. She was convinced he liked the Beach Boys, and she put *Pet Sounds* on the CD player she had bought for his room.

Ralph didn't look good, she thought, standing over him as he slept. But do the addled ever? His skin was tragically pasty, his mouth slack. A smother party waiting to happen. *No more disappearing into Europe.* She sent Ralph the telepathic message. Then she fingered his hand, a useless thing. She felt a small storehouse of tears behind her eyes. Nothing that needed to fall, just a stash in the psychic attic.

She looked softly at Ralph in all his frailty. In a way, she supposed, she had always considered him frail, if not of body then of emotional wherewithal. But once she learned to keep her restless mind to herself, he had been endlessly kind. Entirely devoted. She was Geneva. His Gen. He loved her. It was simple.

But the problem with simplicity, for Geneva, was that it couldn't be understood. So she didn't feel his love and nor could she see with her own logic that it was so.

The Beach Boys harmonized. Geneva looked at the picture of her and Ralph on his nightstand. It was of the two of them sitting on a neighbor's deck. It was taken in 1974. In it, Geneva has a great tan — they were real back then and considered healthy. Ralph was wild about tan lines, white breasts and bottoms. Up until last year, the picture had sat on her nightstand at home.

She touched the edge of the frame. Dated as it was, it was still Geneva's favorite picture of them. The sky behind them was blue, and Geneva wore big hoop earrings and an orange scarf tied around her head. Her face is bold and ecstatic. Being a woman then, she thought, was such a blast. A collective, violent awakening.

Her eyes drifted from her own image to Ralph's. Everything looked too big on him. His hair. His ears. His shirt collar. You couldn't tell from the picture, she thought, that he was a good man. But, of course, he was. After all, Geneva had picked him, and she had always had an uncanny ability to weed through a room of men, right down to the one, or the ones, if there were any at all, that were the real deal. Character, or at least its humble beginnings. Potential. Which is not the same thing, however, as having what it takes to actualize potential. The two, one learns, are surprisingly unrelated — a fact she had learned too late.

Geneva looked away from the picture and laid her hand on Ralph's chest and thought about the promise she had made to him. Her word. To love him. I didn't promise to love a memory, she thought. I promised to love a man. Whoever he is. Whoever he might become.

Some marry Democrats who become Republicans. Some marry drunks who become Bible thumpers. Everyone marries a person who becomes an older person. Ralph had become a person with Alzheimer's. What did it mean to love him for who he was right *now*?

Geneva used curiosity the way other people used commitment or hope. Something to hold love's place while it was off-duty, in need of time to itself.

Her hand rose and fell with Ralph's audible breathing. His chest was too thin, and yet, at the same time, paunchy. She thought of how his body had been hers for creature comfort and for moving large objects. He had only asked one thing of her ever: that she trust him.

Geneva didn't like her thoughts. She fiddled with a button of Ralph's pajama top to distract herself and changed the direction her mind was taking. She unbuttoned it and slipped her hand through to the flaky skin below. She contemplated the difference between loving a memory of him and loving the man on the bed before her. She cocked her head, considering it while she undid the rest of his pajama top, pushing it to the sides. Her hand drifted down his sternum to his stomach and over the gray, curly hairs beneath his navel. She had loved his torso in their day, stingy with hair between the pecs but shaping an oval between his lower ribcage stretching down beneath the pants' line. Her eyes traveled with her hand. It had been so long, so long since they were lovers and she could use the bodily drumming between them to drown out her uncomfortable thoughts.

She made small circles with her fingertips on the soft skin above his pajama bottoms. Reaching further down then, she dipped her hand into the pants and patted at the crotch of his adult diaper. The coast was clear. She slipped her hand inside, and idly, she fingered his balls and the limp slug of his dick. As far as she could tell, Ralph hadn't registered a thing. She held his balls, stroking them with her thumb. Despite her intention to remain in the present, memories washed over her. Not weddings and vacations but simple things. Watching him stand in the yard watering a newly seeded dry patch in the lawn. The way he would set the alarm clock at night before going to the bathroom and then, on his way back to bed, he would flick the alarm button back off and on, as though for good luck. Ralph's penis grew meatier. Geneva withdrew her hand, tugging Ralph's dick upward with it.

She stood slowly and looked down at her husband. She considered leaving. She considered checking into her motel room and masturbating. But what she did was place a chair against the door. She returned to the bed and reached to each of Ralph's hips and yanked the diaper downward. There it was, Ralph's dick, with its strange two-tonedness, silky cream on the bottom and a bruise red on top. At attention, he hooked left. Geneva took hold, and Ralph responded, growing firmer.

Then he moaned. The moan was not sexy, was slightly grotesque, even. But Geneva pulled the diaper down past his ankles anyway and then kicked off a shoe and dropped her own drawers, allowing them to hang off one leg. She was sneaking. It made the moment quiver. She remembered the same feeling as she had passed through customs, contraband between her legs, sewn into Kotex. Those who struggle to Be Here Now, she thought, should consider criminal activity. It puts you right there.

She straddled Ralph at the thigh and looked into his face as she kept stroking with her hand, a rhythm she remembered. Ralph's rhythm. Ralph opened his eyes, a glaze of confused pleasure, a physical response that the mind couldn't comprehend.

Geneva eased him inside of her, vulva lips stretching around him, her membranes plumping with rubbery willingness if not dewy welcome. She kept an alert eye on his face, on his slightly opened mouth. It was like mounting a sleeping beast, like she were a woman in a myth, stealing the seed of some creature who might do her harm should he awaken. She reared back and delivered a stroke.

There was no word that she liked. Not *twat*, nor *vagina*. The problem with *pussy*, as a word, was that it didn't age well. Nothing was wrong with sixty-year-old pussy, but the expression "sixty-year-old pussy" was enough to clear a room. Sometimes Geneva had to go with *cunt*. Blunt-edged as it was, at least it sounded like something that might belong to her.

By whatever name, Geneva's drank. She had to close her eyes to the vacancy sign that was Ralph's face. So, eyes closed, she rode him, steadily, returning again to the past, mental images flashing through her mind. Ralph across a room at a party. Watching her. Admiring her. Not understanding her, not at all, but not caring that he didn't understand. Loving all the things he couldn't understand. Ralph's not understanding always made Geneva feel too large, like she had excess hanging over the edges of the marriage, stuff that wouldn't fit. Still, her hips pulled back and fell forward, the rhythm precise and steady. She knew how to get there. She lowered her chest toward his as she moved, increasing the pressure of her press into his pubic bone, in and up, softly grinding.

She waited for the hand, for the sound of her name. *Gen*. But there was nothing. She pressed her palms into Ralph's, ribs sitting up now with her weight on her knees. Geneva pulled herself halfway off of him and paused. She felt a warm rippling through the folds between her legs. When she started back in, it was with short, urgent strokes, mindless of Alzheimer's and nostalgia. She leaned on his hip bones and let the interior friction lead, show her where to go until a focused, hot tingle turned electric and something deeper shuddered, opened and closed. Tears broke loose from the rims of her eyes, orgasm, sometimes a key opening some deep door that has little to do with sex.

She dropped forward. He was still hard. She prayed, again, for the absent-minded gesture, the reflex, some ancient physical knowledge that would lead his hand to the back of her head or the base of her spine. Eyes squeezed shut, she lay on top of him, hope and anticipation dropping from heart to stomach as he shriveled inside of her.

So be it, she thought, and pressed her cheek to Ralph's chest. She had chosen marriage, and she had chosen Ralph. Loving him well, as she had promised, was not among her life's accomplishments. But it was an open-ended intention. A promise without an expiration date. To trust herself, Geneva needed to know that her word meant something. Loving Ralph wasn't about Ralph. It was about her.

The moment was still and good. A near decade of celibacy brought to end. She placed her hand on Ralph's chest about to push up when a stink grabbed her attention then hit her senses full blast as Ralph crapped the bed.

Geneva managed to dismount unscathed, but as she adjusted her pants on her hips, the door to the room cracked open knocking up against the chair Geneva had used to block it.

"Just a minute," she said, straightening herself as best she could in the few moments she had. She moved the chair as the social worker pushed in. She was young with a piercing in her nose, and she eyed Geneva with suspicion. Accident, Geneva reported. Trying to change his diaper, she claimed, the lie bulky and obvious.

Geneva slunk out like a high school slut whose boyfriend's parents had arrived home early. Safely behind the wheel of her Saab, she headed to the Super 8 where she always stayed. Her room was clean and without personality. Geneva sat on the end of the bed across from the mirror and looked at herself and what she had just done. She crossed a line. Violated a taboo. Took a shortcut to feeling alive.

She stood and stepped closer to the mirror. She leaned in. She examined time's work on her face. What she saw in herself was intelligence and a persistent tension that was not unpleasant. A face too interested to be peaceful, but at peace with her unpeacefulness.

The struggle in her marriage, she knew, had been the struggle between two beliefs. Not hers and Ralph's but between two beliefs that resided inside of her. One said, trust your instincts. The other said, trust love.

II

~

All wrinkles are not created equal. Some come from the inside, from the press of wisdom, like ripples on the brain. Margaret's were not of this nature. Hers were imposed from without, from the vandalisms and hit-and-runs that cause one to harden, to brace in preparation for the next blow.

Margaret leaned toward the bathroom mirror and touched a finger to the crow's feet that reached like ice cracking thinly. There was prettiness still but scarred by the ultraviolets of disappointment. She dabbed on cover-up. In truth, the lines were less noticeable than she thought, but still she was correct. The problem of aging is not one of decay but of the peeling back of all facades until your face is your confession.

Her fingertips moved in small circles, rubbing expensive cream into her neck. She watched herself in the mirror as her fingers slowed and came to a stop. Why try? Trying hadn't gotten her far. Not ever. Not with her face. Not with her husband.

Margaret had tried to fix it with Lee. Tried hard. She had tried to fix it by speaking in *I* statements and following the guidance of relationship how-to books. She did what the gurus instructed. She communicated. But if you feel unheard, invisible, and not of consequence, your communicating of those facts only meets the same fate: Unheard. Invisible. Not of consequence.

The relationship gurus had ignored a crucial fact. You can't communicate someone into loving you. Clear and concise articulation of what she needed only insulted Lee. He called it complaining. She always ended up apologizing for the offense, and nothing ever changed.

Eventually, she got sick of apologizing and learned to keep her mouth shut. Behind her sealed lips, the frustration built, was swallowed and came back up, and was swallowed again. It circulated and recirculated in her bloodstream. Frustration mutated into resentment. An overgrown thing, it smothered out other life and seeped beyond the boundary of her skin, a second layer of pain forming around the first. She hated the pain. She hated the hate. When the pressure got to be too much, she would pound her fists against tiles, sob and holler, in the privacy of the shower.

Margaret picked up a wide-toothed comb and guided it through her conditioned shoulder-length hair. She thought about her wedding day, as she still often did, behind the closed bathroom door. She mined the details of it, looking for evidence in that day, some warning or foreshadowing. But the day had arrived in a blue, cloud-puddled sky. The limo stretched. Everything preened. The clouds passed like cherubs, plump and cheery. By the time of the ceremony, the sky blazed. She remembered the gloved hands and lipsticked kisses and passed envelopes and flashing cameras and how that day seemed to her a culmination of so many careful steps, a series of right choices, a sign she had the power to make things right.

That such a supreme sense of certainty can turn out to be wrong is something from which her trust in her own judgment had never recovered. Her resentment was for herself. Her punishment. To teach her a lesson for making such a mistake.

Margaret screwed the lid back on her face cream. She swallowed the tears welling up. Crying was for the shower only, where the tears and curses would be drowned out by the water's rhythms, the spray's hectic drum and patter.

It was time again to move on. For Rachael. It was for Rachael that Margaret tried to conceal her bathroom breakdowns. She didn't want Rachael to hear. Their fates were not to be the same.

And yet, Rachael would flash through her mind as she sat chin to knees as the water fell on her back. Margaret felt Rachael watching, as though from the inside of her own body, as though she crouched in a corner against some interior wall. When pregnant with Rachael, Margaret had read that fetal cells remain in the mother for long after the birth and the mother can still sense the child that once lived within. Now, she wondered if by *long* they meant *forever*.

Margaret moved from the bath to the bedroom. There, she pulled on chestnut wool trousers and an oatmeal-colored sweater, outfitted, as always, beyond reproach and without imagination, which isn't to say that she wasn't well dressed.

She had a doctor's appointment. She wasn't well. She had undergone tests and was going in for the results.

෨

Margaret had known her doctor for years, a middle-aged woman with fading blonde hair bluntly cut. She wore her glasses around her neck on a purple beaded chain, putting them on as she consulted files, pulling them off to view Margaret frankly. Margaret knew that it was bad. Her doctor suggested that she might wish to bring her husband.

She did not.

"Margaret, you're sick," she said. She went on to discuss the C-word. Cancer. She presented treatment options. But the prognosis remained grim.

"I'm going to die," Margaret said.

Her doctor took off her glasses.

"Your cancer is very aggressive. I can't tell you otherwise. But I believe in expecting miracles. It's the only way you'll ever get one."

"How long do I have?" Margaret asked.

The doctor put her glasses back on as though there would be data to consult, but there was not.

"Months," she said. "More or less."

The appointment ended with a "talk to your family and let me know." Margaret gathered her bag and coat and moved to leave. But she stopped and turned before opening the door.

"My husband's having an affair," she said and nodded, acknowledging it as gospel for the first time.

"Do you want to talk?" her doctor asked.

Margaret considered the question and realized that she no longer did.

She did not feel shock. She felt inevitability. A mudslide. An avalanche. A power impossible to fight or resist. At home, she dropped her purse in the closet and went upstairs. She got into bed and never left the house again. She barely left her bed. Margaret would not get a miracle. She didn't want one. She clicked the door firmly closed in hope's face. She bolted it. Hope wouldn't keep her alive. Hope was what killed her. Hope was what had made her believe she could reverse mistakes of the past and lay claim to a life to which she had no right.

Lee was the first person she told she was dying — — Lee, who was having an affair. Intimacy isn't only about pillow talk and whispered dreams. There is an inherent intimacy in betrayal. Betrayal requires intimacy. Can't get by without it.

He was in the bedroom removing his watch and dropping his money clip on the dresser. Margaret still wore the wool trousers and sweater. She sat in bed with the covers at her waist.

"I went to the doctor today," she said. "I'm dying." Her affect was flat. "I'm not going to cook tonight."

She saw him smile at her in the mirror as though he were humoring her.

"Go ahead and order out," he said. "I'm playing racquetball tonight, anyway."

She watched him change for the gym. He didn't believe her. He had often called her "dramatic."

She hunkered back down into her bed and stared blankly at the ceiling. For the first time in her life, Margaret stopped fighting. For something. Against something. It was always something. But she was done. She would not fight for her life. She would not return her doctor's calls. She wouldn't even fight for Rachael's sake. In fact, she decided, Rachael would be better off without her. What did she have to offer her daughter, anyway? Even what I had given her, Margaret thought, wasn't mine to give.

Rachael.

The name was supposed to pass from mother to first daughter. It had been Margaret's aunt's name, not her mother's. But her mother's sister, Aunt Rachael, had only boys and then a hysterectomy. Margaret's mother, and then Margaret herself, had stepped forward to assure the survival of a legacy that had shut them out.

Margaret knew the story well. *She* was supposed to be named Rachael, but her father's mother died a week before she was born, and Margaret was given her name instead. Later in life, Margaret's mother told her that her father's insistence on her name nearly resulted in divorce. Margaret's younger sister was named Rachael instead, but it never suited her because it was not her name. Not her birthright. Margaret knew it deep in her tissue, right from the beginning. She knew looking through the slats of the crib, though she was not more than three, that this baby had something important that was hers. Something related to hope, possibility. Survival, even.

As far as Margaret knew, none of the Rachaels had ever died of cancer. Margaret knew about Rachaels from seven generations back. There was actually a book — small, green, and leather-bound — first put together by a great-great aunt. There was Rachael Elizabeth, the abolitionist. Rachael Jeanne, who taught poor children to read. Rachael

Claire had eight children, "God bless her," six boys and two girls, and every single one of them, even the girls, went to college.

There wasn't a day in Margaret's childhood that she didn't know exactly where that damn book was. And whereas the litany of Rachaels played in her head like an annoying jingle, she knew nothing of any ancestral sister not christened *Rachael.* These invisible daughters were the ones she wondered about as a child, the ones whose stories she needed. These were the daughters whose destinies were tied to her own. Could she have learned from their choices and made her own differently?

Margaret knew that her Aunt Rachael had felt cheated that it was Margaret's mother who would pick up the baton and continue the legacy. But she was somewhat vindicated when Margaret's younger sister, the Rachael of the new generation, turned out slightly substandard. Margaret's aunt probably had her to thank for that, Margaret thought. She had refused to vanish in the shadow of what should have been hers, and she worked hard to make her sister curse her own existence. As the latest Rachael was instructed by her aunt on her pedigree, Margaret had stood by and decided she would not fade into obscurity like so many other sisters of Rachaels. She fed her resentment — and her mother's, long buried — of being born second-string. Margaret and her mother taught this sister in the silent language of family that to be a Rachael was an honor, but an undeserved one. None of them deserved it. And in their house, it may have provided one with a pedestal, but that pedestal was outside the circle at the hearth where mothers and daughters sit together and feel the common bond of genes and gender. Being Rachael came at the price of belonging. Besides, she already belonged to something else. She didn't need them.

When Rachael moved out of the family home, she started going by her middle name, Tatum. When Margaret had a daughter, she claimed what should have been hers all along. No one challenged it.

Tatum's name change had been satisfying, as satisfying as her gun shot in the garage, as satisfying as seeing her through her cracked bedroom door stabbing her own school photograph in the face with a pen. Tatum had rarely come home from college. After a while, though, Margaret felt more like Tatum had gotten away than been run off.

Some are haunted. Others have familiars, serving them, they say, as spirit guides. The invisible presence in Margaret's life was an imagined self. Her life as Rachael. The life she was due. The life meant to be. As Rachael, her husband would not cheat. She would not get cancer.

She would not have had the choices she had made so carefully all turn into wretched errors and worse — wasted, lost time.

Shakespeare was wrong about his rose. A rose by any other name is a rose with its destiny thwarted.

The woman Lee hired had arranged for a doctor to come to the house. So Margaret had morphine now, which took the sharp edge off truths, making them blunter, softer, easier for the mind to hold. Watching Rachael play at the foot of her bed, Margaret weighed her soul, her sins against her virtue. Rachael's naming was an act of spite as well as one of redemption. It was an insurance policy Margaret stole for her at her birth to be there for her always. She was in the Book.

But would it be enough to protect her from her stepmother, a woman Margaret had no doubt would exist? Would Lee have children with her, and would Rachael be demoted to second-class in her own home?

Margaret wasn't happy with the facts, but facts were something she always faced. The gods, perhaps, had been right all along. Margaret was not a Rachael. But her daughter was. Perhaps this was what was meant to be, she thought. Rachael raised by Rachael.

In the gentle morphine glow, Margaret decided she would pick up the bedside phone. Tatum was on the speed dial, #5. Margaret decided it but only stared at the receiver. It was the only way, she told herself. Despite it all, they were sisters. At different times, they had occupied the same womb, and no matter what, there was a sliver of Margaret that came closer than anyone to knowing what it is to be in Tatum's skin. And likewise, no one more than Tatum would know what it is like to be in hers. As with mothers and daughters, sisters possessed cells that spoke to each other, connected, irrespective of time and space. Margaret and Tatum shared a sliver of overlap, and in that overlap, they were the same creature meeting at an organ like Siamese twins. But, sometimes, with Siamese twins, one must die for the other to live.

Margaret had thought *she* was the surviving twin, and Tatum, the ghost.

Guilt hovered over Margaret as she thought of Tatum. But the guilt was no worse than before she got sick. Yes, she had done Tatum harm. Her defense: she was a child. Children are cruel by all accounts, and she had felt her own spirit was at stake. It is survival of the fittest, after all, an inescapable animal instinct. Sometimes, Margaret thought, it hadn't been her doing at all. Their mother was just as responsible. So were all the grandmothers.

Or maybe it was nobody's fault. A family needs a black sheep. The straws are drawn in another realm.

She did not dial.

It was pride. Margaret knew it. But knowing it and being able to put it aside were two different things. Margaret would call Tatum. Just, not yet.

'Not yet' extended forward for days, then weeks. It extended into increased pain and increased morphine. In and out, Margaret floated between underwater dreams and slim cloud islands floating on the black sea sky outside her window. Deep into the night, she would awaken to find Rachael curled up next to her in a pale blue cotton nightgown. Painfully, she would turn over and spoon her daughter. Rachael's skin smelled clean and unburdened. Her soft child limbs gave off an electricity that Margaret had never noticed before. She was growing, blooming, even as she slept. Her sweetness gave Margaret mercy for herself. She had named her daughter well. She had avenged her mother. A noble thing, yes? And was it not an act of love to want her daughter to have what she did not?

She weighed her faults against her virtues. Vengeance. Envy. Margaret counted these among her sins. Hatred. But Lee was not Tatum, and her hatred of him never touched him. You can't hurt someone who doesn't love you. Did the failure lessen the crime? And then, in her favor, she had sacrifice. She never had another child even though she wanted to. She had never told Lee the reason. She would not risk having a second daughter.

Margaret lifted the phone and pressed #5.

Tatum's machine picked up.

"Rachael," Margaret said after the beep, "it's Margaret. I need you to come. I'm sick."

She closed her eyes and rolled her head to the side. When she reopened them, she looked out the window where a silver moon hung, thin and curved, a canoe upended and sinking into the rising float of night clouds. It's poetic, she thought. Poetic justice, that is, for Tatum to raise Rachael. Margaret had honestly loved her sister, but she had hated her more. She had decided early on that Tatum was never to benefit from stealing her destiny, and though it all sounded so silly now, it was where it all started and for whatever reasons never ceased.

She was jerked into wakefulness by the beep of the answering machine cutting her off.

The canoe-moon reemerged from cloudy waters and dropped borrowed light onto the bedspread. With great effort, Margaret reached for the needle of light, to touch moonlight one last time. But as she reached a sharp pain shot through her limbs and torso. It traveled like a wave, not one of water but bad electricity, not like the power that lit up Rachael but something toxic.

The waves became more frequent, like contractions in labor. Her own body was squeezing her out. No more squatters. The building had been condemned.

Clammy cold followed sweat, and she rolled away from Rachael to spare her.

Margaret began to confuse dream and non-dream. Tatum told Margaret that she would take Rachael, she would make sure she remembered her. Tatum told her this as they rode through the night in the back seat of their parents' car. No, Tatum told her that she wouldn't take Rachael. It had something to do with the green leather book. Tatum kept pointing at one of the pages, but Margaret wouldn't look. She stared out of her bedroom window through knuckled branches of autumn trees down to the curved driveway and Rachael running out to the car to be driven to school. Lee walked around the car to the driver's side and fumbled with his keys. Dried leaves puddled on the car's hood. Something in the sudden skitter of them, moved by a wind Margaret couldn't feel, made her recognize that she was one of them, part of the past, mulch.

Margaret woke with a start. Lee looked down at her. He was speaking, but she heard her mother's voice. Her mother told her she loved her best. Or maybe she didn't actually say it, but Margaret knew. Her mother also told her that dying was not heroic. Everyone who had ever wronged her would not get their comeuppance because of it. Her mother laughed.

Margaret laughed too.

Someone leaned in and asked, "What is it?"

But Margaret kept her eyes closed. She felt Tatum's car coming toward her, following the curve of space. Just as she always felt Rachael nestled somewhere inside, Tatum was there too. Like the pit of a peach, she sat inside of her, and Margaret grew firm and ripe around her. Margaret gave birth to Tatum, and because she did, Margaret would always feel her. Tatum had left behind straggler cells and a hard center that was not her own.

Margaret willed herself to turn over but could not budge. She tried to move just an arm and was able to make it happen. It creaked back behind her until she touched the thin cotton that wrapped the tiny furnace.

Rachael.

Was it night again, already?

Margaret had heard we come into this world alone and we leave it alone too. But that was backward, she thought. Her mother's body brought her here and her daughter's walked her to the edge and reached for her with sweet arms as she vanished. It was the time between she had been alone.

∿

12

A pale strip of light glowed between the drawn drapes. While Rachael took her turn in the bathroom, Tatum dressed quickly to avoid Rachael catching her naked and a breast short of a pair. She figured she was monster enough.

Tatum flipped her hair over to towel dry it thinking that the next time she and Rachael went to bed, they would be in Montana, under her blankets and under her roof. Tomorrow morning, Rachael would sit at her table. Tatum wondered what they would have to say to each other, day after day after day.

When she flipped back over, Rachael's reflection was in the mirror sitting on the bed behind her.

"Yikes."

Tatum looked over her shoulder to assure herself Rachael existed in the flesh. Rachael sat on her hands. Her eyes were large. She looked hung over.

"What's on your mind?" Tatum asked.

Rachael's eyes moved slowly from her own reflection to Tatum's.

"How am I going to go to school?" she said.

"You can go to school where I live, or you can take a break if you want."

"How will I get back — when my Dad's better?"

"I'll drive you," Tatum said. "If that would take too long, we'll take an airplane."

Rachael's eyes returned to her own reflection. Tatum hoped this was all a good sign, figuring out the logistics of being stuck with her aunt rather than working on an escape.

"I knew she was going to die," Rachael said.

Tatum joined Rachael at the bottom of the bed.

"I wish I had known. She didn't tell me."

"She didn't tell anyone," Rachael said. "Just me."

Tatum doubted she was telling the truth. It didn't sound like Margaret.

"She must have trusted you very much," Tatum said.

"She did."

Their eyes met in the mirror, again. It was an interesting contrast to the night before, Tatum thought, perhaps a new experiment in coping. She considered placing a hand on Rachael's knee but didn't want to push the moment. Rachael was talking. Tatum decided to let it be enough. She half-smiled at Rachael in the mirror and then stood and gathered their things, piling their bags in the chair nearest the door.

The car hummed beneath the pigeon-gray sky. The speedometer climbed toward 80 as they cut through the flat South Dakota landscape. Leaves from unseen trees skittered across the highway, small migrations hustling toward the safety of a ditch. Rachael seemed in a trance. Tatum wanted to snap her fingers in front of her face, walk her around the block, or throw her into a cold shower.

"Have you noticed the leaves?" Tatum said.

Rachael lifted her eyes enough to see over the dashboard.

"When's the last time you saw a tree?"

Rachael looked out her side window. Bored? Looking for trees?

"It's strange," Tatum said. "Don't you think?"

Rachael turned from the window and looked at her aunt. Tatum smiled. Rachael did not smile back. Her expression was still flat, a shield inserted between the world and some inner sanctum. Such shields, Tatum knew, were dangerous. Over time they start playing tricks on your mind. You start mistaking it for yourself. One begins to protect the shield rather than the other way around.

"Rachael," Tatum said, "do you want to talk about your mom, or want me to? I could tell you a story about when we were kids."

Rachael kept her face averted. She mumbled something under her breath.

"What?" Tatum said. "I couldn't hear you."

Rachael turned and faced her.

"I said, 'no thank you.'"

By noon, sloppy ice dollops of rain smacked the windshield like bugs. Great gusts of wind shoved the Celica, but it bounced back and held its ground. The roads were empty. Tatum's car buzzed along under the black blanket of sky. Weather-wise, it appeared that the going might get tough, so Tatum pulled off the highway at an exit that promised a Genuine Cowboy Town so that she could take a break before a potential stretch of white-knuckling it.

But the sign had lied. Beyond the Sinclair dinosaur at the exit was a short main drag. The road was dirt, and the sidewalks were wood and raised off the street, boardwalk-style. Beyond the stores' front doors (some painted to look like swinging ones) were pharmacies, beauty salons, hardware, and feed shops. The whole place looked closed and deserted, but it was just an ordinary town, quiet, behind a cowboy veneer. Tatum reached the end of the main drag that ended abruptly in a field. She pulled into the last parking slot on the block and got out to stretch.

"Guess I better hitch up the car," she said, pretending to tie it like a horse, trying to get into the spirit of things.

They stepped up onto the boardwalk. The dime store had an ancient children's ride in front of it. An elephant, a pony, and a fish were dressed in circus regalia, saddled and ready to spin in a small circle.

"How do you think a fish made it into the circus?" Tatum asked Rachael.

The silence that followed was promising. Rachael didn't answer, but Tatum thought she was considering the question. Acknowledging absurdity is one of the first steps toward healing.

"Want to take a spin?" she offered Rachael.

Rachael looked at Tatum and rolled her eyes.

Tatum didn't care. She wanted to see it in action, hear what little ditty it might play. She dug in her pocket for change. A dime slipped from her hand as she dropped the change into the slot. As she bent to retrieve it, she thought of Paris. He always bothered to pick up stray change from a sidewalk. It wasn't because he was cheap. It was because he was unwilling to ignore its value.

The ride cranked into action. Surprisingly, the ditty was a circus-y version of "Both Sides Now." Tatum would've put her money on "When the Saints Go Marching In."

"Rock on," Tatum said, watching it turn.

Rachael refused to be charmed. She walked away, past the ride to the edge of the raised boardwalk. She looked out onto a knapweed-infested field, dead and broken, in the November chill.

Tatum stared at the back of Rachael's head as the elephant, fish, and pony paraded in circles. She was still thinking of Paris and found herself seeing the image of Rachael before her through his eyes: A child's silhouette framed on three sides by the wooden walk, the awning above, and the side of the building. The coat open and askew on her shoulders. The kiddy ride in the foreground. The dead field in the distance. But Tatum knew that Paris would see her in the frame too. He would look at the person looking, see Tatum seeing Rachael. And, if he ever wanted to, he would be able to see Rachael seeing Tatum as well.

A sudden discomfort brought Tatum's hand to her neck. She rubbed at it, unconsciously. Paris would see her through Rachael's eyes. Through the family eye.

Families can reduce a person, sum one up in reference to a single bad day in grade school, or excellent grades in math. The athlete. The smart one. The sensitive one (spoken with a sneer). And, of course, the black sheep. It was bad enough having the family idea of her living in her own head, Tatum thought, but at least there, it could remain secret.

She turned away from the view in an effort to turn away from the thought and noticed the pay phone near the dime store's door. She walked to it, grateful for the opportunity to refocus her anxiety. She zeroed in on the phone book and started flipping through. She hit the G's. Two Godwin's. A Goe. A Goebel and a Goedker.

Then, Goes Ahead. First name, Vincent.

The task had been performed as routinely as checking one's lottery numbers. Always expecting. Never expecting.

It won't be him, Tatum thought. This was Indian country. There must be other Vincent Goes Aheads. She lifted the receiver. She dropped the found dime in the slot and followed it with more change from her pocket. She dialed the number from the book. Her palms were warm. Would she get a machine, she wondered? Hear his voice? Was it even the right Vincent?

The ring was long, drawn out. It rang again, and Tatum's throat tightened. She stood with her forehead against the phone, eyes closed. Tatum wondered if Vincent could feel her coming. If the hair on his neck was standing up and a voice was whispering to him "Don't answer." She huddled close to the phone and closed her eyes, increasing the intimacy between herself and the ring. *Don't do this*, a voice inside of her said.

13

~

Paris felt rich. One pocket jangled with quarters from tips from the diner. In the other pocket was a new box of Lemonheads just purchased at the convenience store. It was his night off. It was dusk, and he was doing his laundry — blue jeans and white T-shirts, a dozen white socks, some whose bottoms were stained an oily brown. The laundromat was on his block. He slipped his quarters into the slot, attentive to the cool surface and rough edging of each. Paris loved quarters. Loved their aesthetic. The big fish in the humble pond. King in a world of small change.

His clothes didn't need him to watch them spin, so he headed back to his apartment to wait out the cycle. Besides, Paris felt the itch in his fingers. He could draw. Maybe even paint. He had a sense of glorious achievement, and he hit the sidewalk optimistic. He took the concrete steps to his apartment door two at a time. Inside, he tossed his keys into the ashtray and went straight for the drawer that held his paper and pens. He paused before it, hand on the knob, and thought maybe he should eat something first. He sidestepped to the refrigerator and opened it. After several seconds of staring at the condiments he said, "Geesh. What am I doing?" He pushed the door closed. "Just open the fucking drawer."

Paris yanked it open. He reached into the middle and withdrew a random pile that he scattered on the counter. The Einstein Era. Sketches of wild hair and a bulbous nose. Eyeless, all of them. Some pictures had the blank space for eyes gouged out by a frustrated pen. He remembered the point at which he had become unnerved. He knew the challenge was to draw the hidden thing, make visible what the subject tried to hide. Einstein's genius made it hard for him to fit into the smaller world of most minds. Paris could feel it. The result was not arrogance but loneliness, a squatter in the eye that conducted itself like the homeless, deflecting attention.

Flipping over an Einstein, Paris set in on some fast, loose sketching. He started with a torso, the ridges of the rib cage barely visible beneath a thin layer of skin. He sketched the breasts he remembered from the picture, small and well shaped. He reached the top of the piece of paper too soon. Only half of a head would fit. Fine. It meant no room for the eyes.

Paris examined his sketch, tapping the end of his pen against the counter. He thought about the canvas slid up against the wall inside of his closet. Was it time?

He left the kitchen and crossed the room. He hauled the canvas from the closet. Leaning it against the wall, he sat down cross-legged before it. He knew its language and waited for it to speak. It would speak in clues at first, doled out slowly. A red smear. A blue-black arc. A beginning pressed against some inner seam. The moment grew fat, poised to pierce the dimensions. To be. To be. To be.

The streetlights outside were flickering, coming on. They spilled through the guardrail above the steps and cast the palest of light onto the basement apartment's floor. Paris was drawn to it. At first, it was just the streaks on the floor that drew his attention. But soon he had abandoned the canvas to follow the light to its source from the street above. From his window, he watched the flickering lamp glow purposelessly like a morning moon. He stood there imagining showing Tatum the painting he had not painted.

Piece by piece, the moment broke up like a cloud. Want. It had contaminated the moment. Dissolved it. Paris wanted to paint. He wanted Tatum. But all he did was stand there in what he did not and had not. A pocket full of quarters and a new box of Lemonheads. Just minutes ago, he had had it all.

He turned from the window and wandered back to the canvas. He kicked at the edge of it, not hard, but toppling it nonetheless. His laundry, he knew, sat in a lump in the bottom of the machine. He didn't care. He stood there until his feet snuck up on him, hot in his boots.

He left the apartment and finished his laundry. Back home, he washed his feet before matching up socks on his kitchen table, partnering them based on stain and wear. As he rolled them, he worried about how long he'd gone without physical contact. Without sex. He worried it warped him in some fundamental way. Unhandled babies fail to thrive. Films from grade school showed rhesus monkey babies, deprived of touch, despondent in their cages, clinging to cloth-covered pads for comfort.

T-shirts and underwear neatly piled on the table, Paris tried to find contentment in that each sock had found a mate. No strays or escapees. He stepped away from his laundry to check the kicked canvas for damage. It had survived. He returned it to the closet, an act of defeat. Retreating to his mattress, he flopped down, pulled off his glasses, and dropped them to the floor. He curled around a limp and deflated pillow. Thoughts he rarely permitted slipped through cracks into his consciousness. He didn't want to be alone forever. He didn't want to be alone now.

A tear made a break for it, slipped out the corner of his eye, surprising him.

"God, you pussy," he whispered, wiping it away.

He rolled onto his back and covered his face with his pillow, trying to smother the want and need. Then a vision came to him. There was a half bottle of Chablis in the door of his refrigerator. He tossed the pillow aside and felt around alongside his mattress for his glasses. In the kitchen, he poured the wine into a glass with a Chicago Cubs logo on it. In his mind, he relived kissing Tatum in the park. He held the memory in his hands, hoping for a psychometry, a resurrection of feeling.

His thoughts flickered. Park lights. Shadows. The night he kissed Tatum and the angles made by the playground equipment and the hush of the summer leaves in an imperceptible breeze. He didn't walk Tatum home that night. He never did. They split paths where it made sense, her heading into the dark hominess of neighborhoods, Paris heading toward the soft glow of downtown. Tatum's key turned under starlight. Paris's turned at the bottom of concrete stairs in the blue-white illumination and faint hum of an imposter moon.

Quarters and Lemonheads. He had been so rich.

Paris stared blankly at his cabinets. Cheap particleboard. Ugly plastic knobs. It was like a reflex then. No forethought. He reared back with his arm and whipped his glass at the cabinets. It shattered, splattering the cheap wood and floor.

The adrenaline receded as quickly as it had spiked. Still, he forced himself not to move to clean the mess. Instead, he imagined himself tossing the place, hitting walls with chairs and upending the table and his mattress. He imagined himself living among the rubble for days, stepping around the debris to reach the bathroom.

But that was not who Paris was.

He pushed his glasses up his nose and ran his hand through his hair. Then he bent over and grabbed the plastic garbage can from under the sink. He cleaned the floor and the cabinets thoroughly. He finished by running his hand over the surfaces, feeling for stickiness and missed shards.

Holding the garbage can in one hand, he stared at the counter where his drawings were scattered. With one arm, he swept the Einstein era into the trash. Then he roughly opened the drawer, pulled out the rest of the sketches, and jammed them into the can. When the drawer was empty, he slapped it closed with an open hand.

The metal lid of the Dumpster behind his building clanged shut. Paris stood there with his emptied can, thinking about Tatum's phone call to him, the hunkered down sound of her voice. He thought about how sometimes when he was telling a story and she was excited to interject, she would raise her hand. Paris would stop his story and look around the room. "Tatum," he'd then say, calling on her with a quick point of the finger.

What could love be to her, he wondered, if not that?

The sound of soft laughter fluttered down from a fire escape above the alley. He looked up. Above the buildings, clouds dusted the sky, but the stars were not intimidated.

He was going to do it, he decided. He was going to try again.

Don't do this, a voice inside of him said.

He pretended not to hear.

14

~

One more ring, Tatum thought, huddled against the pay phone. Then she turned her head to look down the boardwalk toward where Rachael stood. Rachael's eyes were darting from the car, down the boardwalk, toward the street. Tatum could tell she was looking for her.

"Rachael," Tatum called out to her, still holding the receiver.

Rachael's eyes snapped in her direction. Her chest began to rise and fall quickly as if up until then she had been holding her breath. Her cheeks were red from the cold, and her eyes were stocked with tears, not falling, but beading in the rims. Tatum fumbled the phone back onto the hook.

"What's wrong?" she said, walking down the boardwalk to Rachael.

"Where'd you go?" Rachael's voice was full of accusation.

"I was right here," Tatum said. "Right there." She pointed back toward the phone. "I was trying to call someone. What's wrong?"

"I want to go home," Rachael said, and her tears broke the surface, spilling out.

"I know, I know," Tatum said.

"Was that my dad? Did you tell him to come get me?"

Tatum squatted to meet Rachael at eye level. She couldn't tell whether Rachael was afraid she was getting dumped or hopeful that the cavalry had been called.

"It wasn't your dad," Tatum said. "I was calling some stupid guy I used to know."

Rachael looked distrustful.

"Honest," Tatum told her. "He used to be my boyfriend, and I found his phone number in the phone book. I'm glad you stopped me."

"Your boyfriend?" Rachael said.

"Yes," Tatum said. "He dumped me." She figured it had pleased Rachael to know she had spent a night with her face in the toilet. Perhaps her having had her heart flushed down one would make her downright giddy.

Rachael's voice quavered.

"What did he say?" Tears clung to her lashes.

"He didn't answer the phone."

"I mean, what did he say when he dumped you?"

A gust of wind made the buildings creak. Tatum reached over and hiked Rachael's coat higher up onto her shoulders.

"He said he loved me but wasn't *in* love with me," she told her. "I think it was just too hard."

"What was too hard?"

"It was too hard to love me."

Rachael looked away and started to shiver. The wind had quieted but was only resting. A wet freeze was descending, a hint at the nature of the coming storm. Tatum could feel the temperature dropping.

"Does anybody love you?" Rachael asked, eyes averted.

The question was frank. Rude, by adult standards. But Tatum understood where Rachael was coming from. She needed to know. If their fates were to be bound, she would need the straight story.

"I'm not sure," Tatum told her truthfully. She thought about parents, boyfriends, Vincent. She gave her most optimistic answer. "I think there are people who must have loved me, but that maybe it was in a way that I don't understand."

"Like when that guy said it but then didn't want to be with you?"

Tatum started to laugh, at herself, but swallowed it quickly when it occurred to her that Rachael wasn't asking about her or Vincent. This was about Rachael, herself. It was about her father.

"You're easy to love," Tatum said.

She looked at Rachael's profile — Margaret's profile — staring out onto the dirt street. The wind whipped back up and whistled down the boardwalk now, carrying shards of ice. It stung, but they didn't move. Rachael was lost in calculations. One's own unlovability and another's inability to love can be so difficult to tell apart.

The wind bit hard on their ears. Tatum reached forward and pulled Rachael's coat together in the front. She knew she loved her. She loved Rachael like she loved Margaret. From whatever proximity allowed. She loved them because she wanted to. Because she wanted to feel love.

"I'm going to hug you," Tatum said.

Rachael looked up at her, anger in her wet eyes. Tatum pulled her close. She held her and rubbed her arms to warm her. Then she pushed back slightly and pressed her forehead to Rachael's. Together, they hung like a tear, awaiting a blink, awaiting release.

Rachael pulled away and looked at Tatum, her eyes full of hurt now, raw, without questions or blame.

"If you're sad, feel sad," Tatum said. "If you're empty, feel empty. Whatever it is, Rachael, just feel it. Feeling full of love and happiness isn't so different from feeling full of anything else. Even full of nothing. Full is full."

A gust of wind whacked them. They steadied themselves against one another. Tatum could feel Rachael calming, comforted, and numbed by the cold.

February

15

～

Geneva sat, elbows to knees, head in hands. She had awakened to a dread and a pit in her stomach. She lifted the pillow beside her on the sofa and placed it in her lap. She smoothed the face of it. There, embroidered, was the Serenity Prayer.

> God grant me the serenity
> to accept the things I cannot change;
> courage to change the things I can;
> and the wisdom to know the difference.

The Serenity Prayer, she thought, flipping the pillow over. So smug. What did it know of life?

The pillow had been a gift from Ralph, given for no occasion, decades ago. She had pushed away the wrappings, and her heart had sunk. Ralph was asking her not to struggle. She could see that. He was asking her to be other than she was.

Perhaps, she considered, she'd have been wise to heed his wishes. Become someone else. For indeed, what had she made of herself? Was she no better than a frat boy on a drunken sorority girl? Had she lost her antennae for right and wrong? Would not an alarm have gone off in her heart, in her gut, if her actions had caused Ralph distress? What could she say to a judge in her own defense? *Your Honor, he had a boner. A boner! Do you have any idea how long it had been . . . ?*

Geneva recalled getting the evil eye from the social worker. It hadn't crossed her mind to deny the escapade when the nursing home called, and now she had been asked to refrain from visiting until the board could discuss the matter. Apparently, she had been determined a danger by the new staff social worker who had found in Geneva her first victim. Or rather, her first perpetrator. She had put certain phrases delicately, but threateningly, to Geneva. "Elder abuse." "Spousal rape."

Geneva lifted the pillow to her forehead as though she could block the view of the scene unfolding in her mind. Heads of thinning hair and pasty complexions. A room with a history of committees, agendas, and strategic planning. Bland coffee and supermarket baked goods. Budgets would be discussed. Personnel, too. Then, a cleared throat and a nervous shuffling as they turned their attention to geriatric sex.

Geneva moaned into the pillow. I'm a monster, she thought. But the fact, itself, was less distressing to her than the idea of a room full of others coming to the same conclusion. After all, self-scrutiny had always been her forte. Both subject *and* object. But now, she was what the world had been to her. She was a resident of the petri dish. She was smeared on a slide. She tapped the pillow against her forehead several times. On the last tap, she held it there, eyes squeezed closed behind it.

This feeling has got to go, she thought. Her internal needle was stuck, she knew, covering the same ground, over and over. She tossed the pillow to the side and stood. She approached her wall of albums, knowing it was in there somewhere. The song, songs, or side of an album that could meet her as an emotional equal, a force, that she hoped on this day would prevail. She gravitated to a worn, blue sleeve and pulled it from its tight spot on the shelf. *It's A Beautiful Day.* It was the name of the album and the band. The vinyl was old school, thick and heavy. Its claim to fame was the song, "White Bird," but like the pillow, Geneva preferred it B-side up. She knew that Tatum and Rachael were not home, and so she cranked the volume high.

The music was meaty. A trip classic from the '60s, rock and roll crossed with snake charmers and hookahs. It stood on its own, drugs or no. Geneva liked to think of it as the music on a comet's Walkman as it hurtled through the vastness of space. She paced to the front windows and held back a drape. The sun was invisible, having risen behind a bank of thick, gray clouds. Maybe, she thought, her anxiety wasn't about the board. It was simply due to being unable to visit Ralph. Maybe he anchored her more than she knew.

She tested the idea, but it didn't ring true.

Stray flakes drifted past the window. Geneva's mind hummed, trying to calculate the distance between how she felt and how she wanted to feel. But there is no distance, she thought, because there's no such thing as space. Then, she remembered it was time, not space, that was the collective illusion. But the error had come in handy. It reminded her that worrying was also the symptom of an illusion, the mistaken notion that one's distress had utilitarian purpose, that it might mitigate the impact of a potential incoming blow. The problem was not the problem. The worrying about it was. She had no problem to solve, she told herself, no action to take regarding Ralph. Not on this morning, anyway, and not in this instant.

The thought was a breadcrumb. She tried to follow it. A gray quiet built within her, reflecting the sky outside. It was not joy, but it was calm. She took the moment, and when an even better thought graced her, she was determined to seize upon it with tiger paws.

She turned from the window, less paralyzed than she had been upon waking. She went to her bedroom to dress, choosing pink cashmere — acknowledging winter while invoking spring — and the black cords that she liked for their incongruency with her age. *It was a miracle*, she mentally informed the universe, shuffling her hair into place, that through the disease and the drugs Ralph's pecker was able to break through for a howdy-do. She would not let the board rewrite her history. The moment had been hers, not theirs, and the moment had been Ralph's, for whatever it might have been to him.

"Take that," she said to the mirror, in defiance of some judgment she sensed in the great Out There. She insisted on happiness. It was an insult to suffering, she knew, but she was making the choice. Happiness isn't found. It is won.

At 10 a.m., she left the duplex, stepping out into snow that tumbled from the sky like confetti. From beneath cashmere and wool, Geneva found the soft cold easy to absorb. There was no reason to brace. She walked, listening to the quiet carried down from the sky. She watched flakes snag on pine needles and wink out on the pavement. It was Saturday, and as she emerged from the residential neighborhood and headed downtown, the streets grew more energized, but not with the determined pace of necessity that governed the week. Next, next, next softened ever so slightly, giving way to now, now, now, just a breath here and a moment there.

Geneva stepped past the storefronts, the copy shop, Hoagieville. She smiled at the sign for the Chairman of the Board, an extreme sports shop. Not all boards were out to get her. She passed the doorway and the two young men who stood in it.

"It's gonna puke," one of them said excitedly.

"No, man," the other said, more reserved. "It's gonna rain."

Geneva stole a sidelong glance at the young men. She liked the way this new crop were dressing, drooping pants and flat ski caps that came down to their eyebrows. They were shepherds of evolution, bringing the surfboard in from the sea and taking it to the snow-covered mountains. She secretly blessed them as she passed and their efforts to keep the groove alive.

To them, however, she was invisible, she knew. A middle-aged woman, at best. An old lady, at worst. Irrelevant, certainly. But still, the fact of them brought her pleasure, memories of crops of yester-years, the greasers, hippies, and punks. She felt a smile make a break for it. She liked the way it looked on her reflection in the window of the Made in Montana store. She remembered, as a young woman, that she had never doubted her wiles. She had not been a beauty. It was just that of all the things in the world to do, attracting a man never seemed to be one of the more difficult.

Up ahead, she noticed Tatum's car pulling to the curb. Their timing was perfect. The plan was to rendezvous outside the Grounds. From there, Tatum was off to run errands. She would be picking up the birthday cake for tomorrow's celebration. Geneva's birthday was two days ago. Rachael's was tomorrow. Rachael and Geneva would wait in the coffee shop, doing their homework. Rachael had a school assignment. Geneva had a column due.

Rachael got out from the passenger's side and looked up the sidewalk. She didn't wave but did continue to look as Geneva approached. It was a greeting of sorts.

Geneva wasn't sure what she thought of Rachael. A shell-shocked little creature, she had seemed at first, arriving late in the night some three months back. Tatum told her the story. The dead mother. The father not up to the task. Geneva could never admit it outside of the privacy of her own mind, but at first, she was not thrilled with the arrival of a child into her world. She had already navigated the world of mothers as a childless woman while in her twenties and thirties. She remembered it as a world of women who either imagined her life as joyless or resented her freedom. They all seemed to believe there was a depth of love of which Geneva was incapable as it was a skill acquired exclusively through breeding.

Geneva thought they were wrong. She thought it was a skill some needed to have children in order to learn.

"Ready to get some work done?" she said, looking down at Rachael.

Rachael held a notebook. She looked up but didn't answer. Still, Geneva knew that Rachael, even if she didn't actually like Geneva, approved of her. She seemed to think they shared a secret, as though the two of them were allies, that they knew something about Tatum but were too polite to speak it.

Tatum stepped up onto the curb.

"Any word?" she said, referring to the board meeting being held as they spoke.

"None yet."

Tatum nodded.

"Well, I'll see everybody in about an hour." Tatum touched Rachael's shoulder before stepping back into the street. "Be productive," she called over the roof of the car. Then she swung into the driver's seat, hit the engine, and pulled away.

Geneva looked down at Rachael.

"Let's get at it."

Inside the coffee shop, it was soft light, warmth, and Saturday bustle. The music was reggae. No one could complain. Coats and mufflers and hats and gloves feathered booths like nests. Geneva beelined it for a newly opened booth, knowing it wouldn't last.

The coffee shop, the Grounds, was an institution. It had endured for twenty-five years, surviving economic upswings, bear markets, hairstyles, cultural upheavals, smoking, and nonsmoking. Through it all, it remained itself. Summer upon summer, dirty feet padded over the wood plank floors. Winter upon winter, shivering regulars tromped in, geared up in their Nepalese, cold-weather wear. But the clientele was not a tidy row of paper dolls. Professionals and hippies. Retirees and teenagers. Fringes of different orbits warmed their hands against their mugs while the rich scent of a fresh grind rose toward the tin ceiling. Customers and employees alike argued politics, religion, and Belinda's column — all subjects inappropriate at the dinner table.

Geneva and Rachael slid into the wooden booth, one on each side.

"What's the homework assignment?" Geneva asked, pulling off her own coat.

"I have to write about what I might be when I grow up. Like what job."

"What are you thinking of?"

"I don't know. Maybe a photographer."

"Not bad," Geneva said. "I was interested in that for a while."

A girl of maybe twenty appeared at their booth. Rachael, her coat still zipped to the neck, looked up at her.

"Hot chocolate?" Geneva said to Rachael.

Rachael nodded.

"Two hot chocolates."

"Redemption Song" strummed through the old speakers propped up on the loft above the counter. Geneva watched the girl walk away, long underwear poking out from her long, hemp skirt, her bare feet stuffed into Birkenstocks. The service might be quick. It might be slow. You might have to remind the staff of your order. It didn't matter. In fact, Geneva thought it was adaptive, kept the mainstream at bay and protected a critical ecosystem, one of the tide pools where life begins.

"Well," Geneva said to Rachael, "I don't like any of the letters I've gotten, so I need to write a column. I think I'm just going to go on a rant."

"What's a rant?" Rachael asked, seeming only half-interested.

"It's a lecture to the world. A spirited one."

The answer seemed to satisfy Rachael, or failed to interest her. She reached up and unzipped her coat.

"Maybe I'll write about some other job," she said.

"Well," Geneva said, "there's lots out there."

Geneva knew she probably wouldn't be a lot of help in this area. Though she'd had several jobs and fleeting careers, she was never truly bonded to the workforce. She was always competent at what she did, but her competence far outweighed her interest.

"Your Aunt Tatum used to be a technical writer. Paris is a cook."

"What about Vincent?" Rachael asked.

Geneva raised her brows. She was aware of Rachael's interest in Vincent. Tatum had told her that when she tried to engage Rachael in conversations about her dead mother or her father, Rachael was non-responsive. But Vincent she was always eager to discuss. Where was Vincent now? Why, again, did he leave? What she seemed to be after, Tatum told Geneva, was the fatal flaw, the accident to avoid if you're to keep those you love from blinking out of existence.

"Vincent's job," Geneva told Rachael, choosing words carefully, "is to help people who want to practice certain traditions and values."

"That's a job?"

The hot chocolates arrived and were placed before them. They were beautiful, topped with whipped cream and chocolate shavings. The warmth from the mugs drew their hands. Geneva bought some time on the subject by fiddling with her drink. She spooned whipped cream into her mouth and mixed the rest down into the chocolate. Given the circumstances that had brought Rachael into her life, Geneva found it difficult to discern whether talk of funerals and death was a good or bad idea.

"Sometimes when people die," Geneva said, "they want to have special kinds of funerals or ceremonies. Vincent tries to help them make it happen the way they want."

It made him sound like a funeral director instead of an outlaw.

Rachael stuck her own spoon into the whipped cream. Geneva watched her for clues as to where she might want, or need, the conversation to go.

"I don't think I'd do that as a job," she said.

A neutral close to the subject, Geneva thought. Fine.

"Maybe you should do a brainstorm," Geneva suggested. "Make a list of all the jobs you can think of and then decide the one you want to write about."

"We're supposed to write about the one we want to be when we grow up."

"Just write about whatever one sounds interesting to you," Geneva said. "Pretend it's what you want to be. They'll never know."

Rachael twisted her mouth like Geneva didn't understand the rules. She opened her notebook as though settling it that Geneva would be no help. Geneva followed suit, pulling her yellow legal pad in front of her. *What shall Belinda say?* But in searching her own mind, all she could find was dread about the board convening at Parkview Homes. The fear of arrest rippled through her, but then, she thought, if they were going to press legal charges, they would've done so already. Wouldn't they? Parkview was a private institution, and it cost an arm and leg. Perhaps, they didn't want the publicity.

Geneva briefly considered using her column as a forum on the whole affair. But she wasn't certain that the world would be with her. Clearly, quite a few had already seen things quite differently than she did. Why take the shame public? Why take on a scarlet letter, a *P* emblazoned on her breast? *P* for Predator. Perpetrator. Perhaps, she could use her column to plea for a reduced charge, a scarlet *H* for Humper.

She mulled, pen poised. Rachael also sat with her pencil at the ready, but her eyes cruised the room.

"Ralph was a financial planner," Geneva volunteered.

Rachael looked at her, and Geneva could see the words *financial planner* bounce right off her forehead. Such words did not belong in a third-grade world.

"Sorry," Geneva said.

She let her own eyes drift over Rachael's head and over the back of the booth. Unexpectedly, she caught the eye of a man at the counter who had clearly been observing her. Large and gray-haired, he nodded when her eyes landed on his. A jolt went through her, and she let the corners of her mouth lift in greeting.

She was not invisible. The boys in the storefront had been blind.

She looked back down to the blank page and her ringless left hand flat on the table. Her wedding band, it had never been a standard feature. It had come on and off throughout her marriage without a lot of fuss. Ralph never made an issue of it. Geneva had told him that the only way of it not being a big deal, whether or not it was on, was to never get in the habit of always, or never, wearing it. Geneva was wary of investing inanimate objects with power — not because she thought the power was imagined, but because she knew it came to be real. She didn't want to have to assess, every day, whether or not she had it in her to bear the symbol's weight.

She flexed the back of her hand as though there were a ring to view. The skin was chapped, the days of smooth hands long behind her. In her right hand, she held her pen, cigarette-style, between her first and middle fingers. Unconsciously, she began to tap it, one end and then the other, on the table.

But thoughts of the wedding band were thoughts of Ralph, and thoughts of Ralph were thoughts of Parkview Home. She sighed and Rachael looked out from under her brow. Geneva smiled weakly, communicating, she hoped, nothing more than writer's block. The board would scold her, she told herself, put her on probation, pacify the social worker, and get it swept neatly under a rug. Wouldn't they? They would form a committee and create a policy. The Geneva Clause, or the G-clause, perhaps, for short.

It all seemed so unfair.

She looked at Rachael across the table. She imagined her saying, "You want to talk about unfair?" Nonetheless, the "No fairs" and "Why me's?" had seized her. She recalled Paris once saying that it was pointless to look for cause and effect. Yet here she was. It was irresistible, the question, "Why?"

She repositioned the pen properly in her hand.

Two kinds of people believe everything happens for a reason, she wrote. *One kind believes that the reasons reveal themselves in the future. The other kind believes that the reasons lie in the past.*

16

Tatum stood in the camera section of Osco Drugs. The film display took up an entire wall with nearly identical packages. She withdrew from her coat pocket the slip of paper on which Geneva had written down the kind of film she was to buy. Tatum knew nothing of photography, cameras, and their accouterments. Her only camera had been a pocket Instamatic, circa seventh grade. The logistics of accumulating snapshots, for her, was simply too overwhelming, too complicated. Better to live the undocumented life.

Not so for Rachael. Before dropping her off at the coffee shop, she and Tatum had taken a walk around Spring Meadow Lake. The lake was, in fact, an old gravel pit filled with groundwater that seeped up from the beds of sand and rubble below. But nature had adopted it as one of her own. In the spring, frogs and ducks took up residency. Cottonwoods crowded the shore and willows wept in the surrounding fields of timothy, wheatgrass, and mountain brome. But it was winter, and all the busyness slept.

Still, the lake hosted couples on quiet winter strolls and ice fishermen dropping their lines for bass and trout. The pictures Rachael took there were not of the naked trees or the distant slouching mountains. They were of reeds, stripped of color, standing broken in the frozen shallows. In the back of the park on the wood plank bridge, she had looked down through the railing at a big-mouthed bass slipping by in the water beneath the ice. She aimed her camera and snapped.

"What do you think that fish is thinking?" Tatum had asked her.

"He's not thinking anything."

"Not enough brains?"

"No," Rachael said. "He's dreaming."

Wishful thinking, Tatum had thought, that it was all a dream and that with the thaw, one would wake to the world, intact and unharmed. She stood beside Rachael, watching the fish disappear beneath the bridge. "I'll never leave you" — that's what Tatum wanted to say to her.

But she didn't. She wanted Rachael to feel safe, but more, she wanted Rachael to trust her. Pianos do fall from the sky. Tatum would hate for one to make her out to be a liar.

Tatum found the package with the words that matched the ones on her slip of paper. She chose wrapping paper from a different aisle and then paid at the counter. The camera had been Rachael's Christmas present. It had been Geneva's idea. Back in December, Tatum had told her that Rachael had asked for copies of all the photographs in the family albums she had stolen for her. Geneva suggested that getting Rachael a camera might give her a "medium" for figuring out that time hadn't stopped, that memories were still accumulating. The idea proved to be inspired. Rachael carried the camera everywhere. She always wanted doubles of her prints. Tatum understood why she'd want backups of things that could be forever lost.

Next stop, the bakery.

Tatum pointed the car toward the historical district at the base of the north slope where downtown ended and the foothills began their ascent. The bakery was tucked in a small strip of brick buildings that originally served as hostelry for prospectors. Above the shops, small subdivisions slithered up the mountain's face, each resenting the next as one climbed higher than the one before, bulldozing their hearts' desire in the effort to inhabit it more fully. Tatum parked the car in front of Sweetie Pies and Cakes. New, white flakes fell on the old stacked snow clinging to the shade and northern walls. It was February, short and sweet. Winter, and no one expected it to be anything else.

A bell rang above the door as she entered. Bonnie Raitt sang on the radio. The shifted lintel above the archway that led back to the ovens revealed the valley's history of tremors, subtle and not so subtle alike. The display case, on the other hand, was thoroughly modern, featuring confections, bundt cakes, and truffles made fresh that morning. In the corner of the bottom shelf was a small cluster of Valentine's Day items on sale half-price. The stale sentiment made them look older than they were. Unappetizing, they conjured images of lonely people eating heart-shaped discount cookies in the eerie glow of late-night TV.

A woman emerged from the back room. Her face was young, but her hair was gray, long, thick, and pulled back in a ponytail. She took Tatum's name and disappeared again. Tatum's gaze drifted back to the discounted treats. She fought the urge to rescue them. She forced herself to look away.

Cupcakes are not tragic. Her impulse to rescue them was just the sort of thing that had driven Vincent away. "Don't do what sad people do and you won't be sad," he used to say. At first, she had admired his stance. She had tried to adopt it, but it wasn't a philosophy she could maintain. Besides, she wanted to speak her melancholy. It was a place she knew, part of her, and she wanted to share it with him, like one's hometown.

"Why do you do this to yourself?" he would say. "It's frightening."

"Frightening? Why?"

"It's not prudent to care about someone more than they care about themselves," he said. "Never do it."

Tatum had tried to ring the South Dakota listing for Vincent when she and Rachael had arrived back in Montana, but the voice that answered said no one was there by that name. Maybe it had been an old listing. Maybe Vincent had lent his name to a friend with an unpaid bill so he could get reconnected. Vincent would do that. Tatum had asked the man if he knew anyone by Vincent's name, but he hung up.

Sometimes Tatum wondered if Vincent knew she was out there, hunting him down. Did he find himself looking over his shoulder, feeling her rifling through phone books and interrogating phone operators? Perhaps he told people, "If a woman calls here looking for me. . ."

The woman with the gray ponytail returned with a white square box. She opened it for Tatum's inspection. The frosting was yellow, pink, and lime green. The cake said, "Happy Birthday" in cursive writing beside a number nine made of roses.

Tatum paid in cash. She placed the cake carefully on the back seat of the car and headed back toward the coffee shop. She hesitated at the intersection. The coffee shop was a right turn, but Tatum turned left, heading back to the duplex, deciding to take the opportunity to call Lee and remind him his daughter's birthday was tomorrow. Lee was not completely neglectful. He did call, just not often enough. He didn't realize, Tatum thought, that a desired thing too long denied can become the enemy.

Tatum parked at the curb and carried the cake inside. She left it on the kitchen table while making space in the refrigerator. She shuffled juice boxes, milk, and hot dogs. When she turned to get the cake, she found herself staring into the living room. Two pairs of Rachael's shoes were kicked off by the door. Paris's wool hat sat beside two of Rachael's barrettes on the trunk Tatum used as a coffee table. The items made her smile and look forward to tomorrow's party.

Paris. Due to logistics alone, she had seen less of him lately, and the time they had together often included Rachael. Tatum had never experienced missing him before. She had anticipated but never longed. No need to want what is there. She smiled quizzically at the new sense of urgency in her when they were together, a wish to rush, to hurry and close some gap, to do with touch in an hour what it took days and weeks to say. The urgency unnerved her, and she found herself overcompensating. Backing off. She didn't want to make him uncomfortable.

She wedged the cake into the refrigerator then walked to the coffee table. She picked up Paris's hat, brought it to her face, and brushed the coarse wool gently against her lips. Then she put down the hat, trading it for a barrette, which she opened and closed. She picked up the other one and wondered what would have happened had she killed herself in that garage or hotel room. What would've become of Rachael? Or would that one change have shifted reality significantly enough that Margaret would have never died?

Tatum took the barrettes and carried them down the hall to Rachael's bedroom, the room that used to be her office. Now, she did have pink in her home. The bedspread. The curtains. Rachael had grown in the short time she had been there, and there were clothes to buy as well. Tatum knew it was time to consider getting back into the workforce, though she had been surprised when Lee sent her two thousand dollars. She had to force herself to see it as good and not as hush money or a bribe.

Her eyes drifted through Rachael's room, taking note of the two stacks of photo albums under the dresser. One stack consisted of the ones Tatum had stolen for her. The other stack was the new albums for Rachael's new pictures. Rachael filled these new ones quietly, secretly, politely declining invitations to share the contents. Tatum placed the barrettes on the dresser and sat down on the floor with her back against the bed, facing the underneath of the dresser. She knew which pile was which, which were Rachael's secret ones and which were the stolen ones. She considered peeking at the secret ones but instead pulled one of the stolen ones randomly from the pile and opened it.

The first picture was of Margaret, profile, holding a piece of cardboard that said "seven weeks." Tatum turned the pages through a progression of Margaret's pregnancy with Rachael. The last pages were hospital shots. It was remarkable, Tatum thought, how women always do look beautiful in such pictures, their hair matted down with sweat and their eyes heavy with exhaustion. Margaret was no exception. Tatum had been surprised that Margaret chose to name her daughter Rachael. "You don't mind, do you?" Tatum's mother had said to her on the phone. The strange thing was that while she didn't mind, she did still feel that she should have been asked first, as though something had been taken from her, and it was hers, whether she wanted it or not.

Tatum touched the picture of Margaret looking down into her newborn swaddled bundle.

"I guess I won in the end," she mumbled. But the words were barely out of her mouth when the hair on the back of her neck bristled. A shame-fueled heat broke out behind her face.

I won? she thought. What the hell's that supposed to mean?

Tatum snapped the album closed and crammed it back into its pile. She got up off the floor. She hurried down the hall, feeling polluted by her own thoughts. She grabbed her keys off the counter and made for the door, forgetting to call Lee.

In the car, she hit the gas. She fled as though from a crime. She turned on her wipers as the snow came at the windshield in loose droves, rushing at her, then disappearing.

17

~

The background bustle of the coffee shop moved to the pulse of the offbeat syncopation and upstroke strumming of Bob Marley and the Wailers, giving rise to a collective groove. The hum of voices and the hum of thought laid down tracks. Rehashings of the night before. Pointless conversations serving no purpose but to hear the sound of another's voice meeting with one's own, spinning what nonsense one could from found threads of thought. Rachael and Geneva sat in their booth making their contribution. Rachael dawdled over a list of professions while Geneva reworked the words on her yellow pad:

> Two kinds of people believe things happen for a reason. One kind believes you must look to the past to discover those reasons. Find the causes to explain the effects. The other kind believes the reasons are found in the future. Events occur to propel us down paths we do not in the present understand.

Geneva considered her thesis. To which group should she pledge allegiance? Looking to the past, the cause in her situation would be her own behavior. Hump your veggie husband, and you'll pay the piper. But what if her situation was not the effect but the cause, the precursor to the unforeseen? The latter, Geneva thought, had the distinctly better ring.

"You know what rationalization is?" she asked Rachael.

Rachael looked up from her page.

"It's trying to convince yourself of something," Geneva said. "But at the same time, you kind of know it isn't true."

"Like lying, but pretending you're not?"

Geneva laughed.

"Is there any other way to lie?"

Rachael returned to her own page while Geneva considered rationalization. Was it a lie, or simply psychological opportunism, finding the philosophy that casts one in her best light and adopting it as her own? Why not choose that which offers salvation? The religions all knew it. Salvation sells.

But then, she thought, what is a philosophy, or religion for that matter, but a frame, illuminating some data while discounting other. Turn the frame cockeyed, and one's god or theory collapses. They're all just lenses, she thought. Looking through them, you can frame your world but not create it. *That* required a different tool altogether.

Geneva thought she was onto something. She positioned her pen. But then, on the right side of her body, the surface of her skin began to tingle as something not material pressed up against her like breath. Her eyes lifted to meet the presence.

"May I?"

It was the man Geneva had made eye contact with earlier. Broad-chested and over six feet tall, he wore Carharts, no belt, and a black T-shirt. He smelled, at once, of flesh-heat and winter. His hair was gray and neatly cut. His beard, salt and pepper.

"Just for a second," he said, sitting down sideways on the edge of the booth on Rachael's side. His body language was of a temporary sit down, no intention of intruding.

Geneva instinctively calculated his age. Fifty-eight? Seventy? Rachael sucked in her lower lip and looked at him.

"You're Belinda?" he said to Geneva. He looked like a giant beside Rachael.

"Guilty."

He gave a brief nod as though he had confirmed something with himself. He pulled the latest *Messenger* out from under his arm.

"I like what you wrote this week," he said, dropping it onto the table.

Geneva didn't need to refresh her memory. She hadn't considered it her best work. Not even original. Someone had written, *how does one get past envy?* She had replied: *See your good as tied up with theirs.*

"You could save the world with that one," he said.

"Ah, but who listens?" Geneva shrugged.

"You haven't spent a lot of time twiddling your thumbs, have you?"

Geneva laughed, embarrassed and flattered by the question. She spoke in her best Belinda voice.

"One person's thumb twiddling is another's search for enlighten-ment."

His blue eyes sparkled, but it was the least of their charm. The sparkle was icing. The cake was experience and the source of the light.

"I like what you think about," he said.

He placed a large, calloused hand flat on the table between them.

"Anyway," he said. He took a sidelong glance at Rachael.

"Granddaughter?"

Geneva hesitated, realizing that he was flirting. He had found a reason not to leave.

"She's . . ." Geneva stumbled on the words. "This is a friend of mine." She withheld Rachael's name for prudence's sake. You never know for sure who the ax murderers are. "I'm Geneva," she said, willing to take the hit herself.

"John."

He extended a hand across the table. Geneva met it with a single squeeze. It was rough and seemed, somehow, to need tasting to appreciate. Her mouth watered.

"What are you working on?" John asked Rachael.

Rachael was quiet for a second and Geneva thought maybe shy.

"Homework," Geneva said, but then Rachael jumped in, as though to prove she could speak for herself.

"I have to tell my teacher what I want to be when I grow up."

"I see," he said. He perused her list from his side view. "Can I write down a suggestion?"

Rachael let him take her pencil and notebook. He was a lefty and wrapped his arm across the page. He finished and slid it back to her. Rachael read it and made a face. Geneva leaned over and read it upside-down. It said, "quite a character."

"A noble goal," Geneva said.

"Well, Belinda," he said, getting ready to move on. "I mean, Geneva."

Geneva sensed a "wait" fumbling around inside of her, some reason that would reel him back to the table, but there was none. She looked over her shoulder as he walked to the back of the coffee shop. He stole a look over his shoulder, too, busting her.

Geneva turned back around. Her senses felt shuffled. Rachael raised her brows.

"What?" Geneva said.

But Tatum suddenly slid into the booth on Rachael's side. She put an arm around her. Rachael tolerated it.

"Got your birthday cake," she said. "Yours, too," she said to Geneva. She had brought with her the scent of the cold, just as John had. Geneva had never noticed before how the cold works like a perfume, mixing uniquely with each body's chemistry.

"It's getting wetter out," Tatum said. "How's the homework going?" she said to Rachael.

Rachael leaned back, away from her notebook.

"Photographer, cook," Tatum said, reading the list. "Helping dead people?" She looked at Rachael, then Geneva.

"We were talking about people's jobs. Yours, Paris's," Geneva said. "We talked about Vincent's."

"Oh," Tatum said. "Well, don't forget Paris is an artist too. Not just a cook." Then, she squinted at the notebook, "'Quite a character'?" she said, pointing to the strange handwriting.

"We got some outside help," Geneva said.

"That's what I want to be," Tatum said.

Rachael shut her notebook.

"I think I'm just going to say I want to be a veterinarian."

Geneva sent them on their way, refusing a ride. She was glad to see them go. She checked over her shoulder again, but John was gone. There was a back door. He must've left through the alley. She drank the last of her chocolate, cold now, and doodled on the corner of her pad the same daisy that she'd been doodling since childhood. That man, John, had perked up something in her that she hadn't had perked in a while. But now, she felt a malaise creeping back in. She recognized the malaise as a lamenting of the perklessness it had forced her to admit.

Desire. Buddha said to forsake it. But Geneva begged to differ. Desire drove the planets and all of evolution. The universe, she knew, expands for the same reason people do. Desire. The desire for more. To be more.

She gathered her things, put on her coat, and paid at the register. Wet snow fell on her as she made her way back through the downtown. As she passed the Chairman of the Board, she considered the likely verdict of the Board of Parkview Homes. They would seek a solution, not justice. She made her prediction: monitored visits. A slap on the wrist to a horny old lady. A bone thrown to the social worker who was indeed just doing her job.

But the thought slowed Geneva's steps. She had assumed she would endure the sentence and do what one must for those she loves. But if that's what her future held, she found the steps suddenly harder to take. She came to an awkward stop on the sidewalk in front of a pawnshop with a used drum kit in the front window.

Move, she told herself but found her legs uncooperative. She knew she could insist, force one foot in front of the other, but she found herself reluctant to override their judgment. Weariness washed over her. She gazed through the pawnshop window and her heart skipped when she noticed a gray head, mistaking it, for just a moment, for John.

She forced herself forward. She continued to walk, but slowly. The rain-like snow fell on her face and lashes, unsure of what it wanted to be, resisting the choice. Geneva looked up into it, squinting as it came down upon her. She wondered which way it would tip.

18

~

Paris scowled, something he rarely did. He was looking forward to seeing Tatum but dreading it, too. Desire had hijacked the good. The good was no longer good enough. Shadows came and went on the melting snow as he passed beneath the trees on his way to the party. Wind chimes tinged softly, barely disturbed by a movement of the air. Loosened snow slipped from branches, and gutters dripped. The afternoon was unusually warm. El Niño pushed the mercury into the fifties. Bad news for the snow pack, but good news for a winter barbecue.

As he walked, Paris recalled what Tatum had asked of him when she returned from her sister's funeral. The scene had not unfolded as he had dreamed. He had imagined her, rumpled and road-weary, showing up at his door unannounced in her khaki coat. He would know by the look in her eye. Death. Loss. Mortality. It would've burned away trivial fears and doubts born of prudence and cleared the way for a new kiss, one that, this time, would take.

But she did not show up at his door. She called and asked him to meet her at the Grounds. She introduced him to Rachael over coffee and hot chocolate. When Rachael went to the counter for napkins, Tatum leaned in with a quick explanation of a runaway father and uncertainty as to whether the situation was temporary or permanent. Her forehead wrinkled above olive-colored eyes.

"I've got a kid now," she said. "You will still be my friend?"

That is what she had asked of him. To be her friend. Not to try to kiss her again. Not to put his hand out for more.

"Of course," he had said.

Quietly, he kicked himself. It was his lesson to learn, over and over. Stop wishing, willing, and wanting.

It was not religion that drove his aversion to desire. Not Buddhism with its well-known indictment of desire as the root of all suffering. For Paris, the aversion was an ancient one, born in childhood. After so many years, it was no longer a decision but a pattern of the psyche and a habit of the heart. It had served a purpose once. It had helped him flee the guidance counselors and standardized tests that kept telling him to want more, to be more. It had helped him slip through the arms of his mother, single and full of frustrated dreams for him. He had run from encouragement and the debt it seemed to him to imply. He did not want to stand, back to a wall, measuring himself against some mark he was supposed to reach, wondering every day whether he was up or down.

Besides, it seemed to him that love and desire could never share the same moment. Though often mistaken for each other, they were, in fact, mutually exclusive. To want and to have were separate experiences.

He turned up the walk of the duplex carrying the pan of cornbread he had made the night before at work. He opened the front door and entered the foyer. Cautiously, he rapped his knuckles on Tatum's door as he pushed it open.

Tatum poked her head out of the kitchen.

"Hey," she said. "I'm just cutting up a few vegetables. Everyone's out back."

She wore a cream-colored cable sweater and a long, lavender skirt made of a rough and heavy cotton. She turned and headed back into the kitchen. Paris followed, watching the silhouette of her hips. He slid into one of the chairs at the tiny kitchen table and pushed aside Tatum's black gloves and hat to make room for the cornbread. Tatum's back was to him. She stood at the sink over a colander of portabellas.

"Tatum," he said.

"Yes?"

He wished she had answered, "Paris" like she used to. Sometimes, it had been all they said, the entirety of an exchange. "Tatum." "Paris." They would remark on the fact of each other, and it was enough. But Tatum had pulled back from him. Maybe it was Rachael. Maybe it was that she could sense he wanted more. He wasn't sure.

"I've been thinking about something," he said.

"What's that?" She turned off the faucet.

He had been thinking of Tatum while serving his 2 a.m. patrons, the women. He'd been wondering why Linda, who to him always looked hungry, would never accept his soup. The question formulated in the night. He had decided to bring it to Tatum, lay it before her, and see if they could talk like they used to.

He cleared his throat.

"If a person was told hunger was love," he said, "do you think she would choose not to eat, or not to love?"

Tatum's head came up. She wiped her hands on a towel that hung on the oven handle. She spoke each word carefully. "If a person was told hunger equals love," she repeated.

"Would she choose not to eat?" Paris said.

"So she'd feel love."

"Or would she choose not to love?"

"So she wouldn't feel hungry." Tatum leaned with her back to the sink. "What you're asking," she said, "is that if you learn that love hurts, will you avoid love? I think the answer is yes."

"Yeah," Paris said. "But I think there's another side to it. Would it also be that if you learned love hurts, will something not feel like love unless it hurts?"

Paris sensed a bristling in her, an ever so slight backing away from the moment.

"Talk about a lose-lose," she said. She pulled a cutting board down from its nail.

Paris swallowed the silence that followed. In the past, he would've let the question sit with her, trusting gaps in the conversation to be contemplation. But silences that once were full now felt strained, like something was missing.

The kiss was missing.

"I brought cornbread," he said to fill the hole.

Tatum looked over her shoulder and smiled.

The urge pressed on him, as it had more often of late, to tell Tatum he saw the topless picture. Betrayal requires intimacy, and its fact might close the distance, if even for a moment.

"How's Rachael?" he said instead.

Tatum patted down the mushrooms with a paper towel.

"'How's Rachael?'" she said, repeating the question to herself. "Let's put it this way, given the choice, I'd hope she would choose not to love."

Paris noticed her freeze. She then shook her head, as though disappointed with herself.

"I don't mean that," she said. "It's just that Lee hasn't called yet. I hope he remembers to call today."

Paris pressed his lips together and nodded.

"What did you get her for her birthday?" he asked.

"Film, some picture frames, a set of maracas."

"Maracas?"

"Not good?"

"No. It's good. I think it's fine."

Tatum drew a knife from the block and placed it on the cutting board. Paris reached for her again with words.

"How's all the mother-stuff coming along?" he asked.

Tatum dumped the mushrooms onto the cutting board.

"I'm not a mother," she said. "No one, certainly not Rachael, is under the impression that I am. But it's good." She paused, holding the knife. "Weird, too."

"Weird how?"

"Well," she said, proceeding to slice, "it's like I'm responsible for my moods now. I need to be something other than I am for someone else, which feels . . . dishonest? And yet, the right thing to do." She put down the knife and dumped the mushrooms into a bowl. "Sometimes, I think I should just be myself and hope that's the best example. But shouldn't I be trying to make things better? At the same time, though, I have no illusions that I have the power to fix the thing that's been broken." She laughed. "How's that for an answer?"

The front door creaked open, and Geneva's cat, Voodoo, pushed through, tail in the air and walking high on his toes. He made his way to the kitchen, confident of a warm reception. He leapt onto Paris's lap.

"So, you're wondering if you should pretend everything's okay for Rachael's sake," Paris said.

"Right."

"Maybe everything is okay."

"Now you sound like Geneva."

Paris stroked Voodoo's back. Tatum poured salad dressing over the mushrooms and tossed them.

"You know," she said, "Vincent once said something like, it's dangerous to want to affect someone's life. It gives that person too much power."

Paris furrowed his brow.

"*Dangerous*," he said, as though this were the key word. "Dangerous for whom?"

"For the person trying to do the affecting," she said. "Anyway, if my job is to try to help her feel better, which means different than she does, I'm completely inadequate for the job. I've never tried to change my own feelings. How would I know how to change someone else's?"

Paris pursed his lips.

"So you just let her be sad?" he said.

"Sometimes," she said. "Probably most of the time. Is that bad?"

"I don't know if there's a right and a wrong."

"But there's better and worse."

Paris considered Rachael. She had exactly what he wanted: Tatum. And Tatum was concerned that she wasn't enough.

Voodoo leapt from his lap. Tatum looked over her shoulder and saw Paris's inward focus.

"What is it?" she said.

Paris hesitated. He drew himself up in the chair and took a deep breath.

"I threw away all my drawings," he said.

Tatum stopped her work at the sink. She turned to face him. She crossed her arms over her chest.

Paris put up a hand as if to say it's not important. Not the point.

"It was months ago," he said. "The point is, sometimes I find my attention on the drawer. I've even opened it and looked inside. I haven't started using it for something else. I don't know," he said. "What I think I'm trying to say is, for some reason, things that aren't there are sometimes treated as more important than things that are."

Tatum continued to look at him with concern.

"Like Rachael's parents, for her," he said. He poked with one finger the foil that covered the cornbread. "Maybe, for you, like Vincent."

The comment hit some brake, brought the room to a standstill. Paris knew he had been obtuse, but he hadn't done it on purpose. He had been trying to say too many things at once. He wanted her to know of his own difficulty appreciating what they had together instead of wishing for more. But it was also true that he wanted her to know: Vincent was gone, but he was right here.

The moment could tip either way. The distinction between hope and fear is a fine one. If you fall to the side of hope, you keep falling. That's the attraction of fear. With fear, you get to land.

"You think I spend more time thinking about Vincent than paying attention to Rachael?" Tatum said, landing squarely. "I don't."

Paris was surprised at the meaning she took from it. Apparently, him in that role, Vincent's role, could not even occur to her.

"That's not what I meant," he said. "I don't think that."

Tatum turned her back to him and busied herself with cleaning up.

"I don't think that," Paris repeated.

He picked up his cornbread and headed down the hall for the back door. His heart banged in his chest. *You idiot, you idiot,* he repeated in his head. At the back door, he paused with his hand on the knob. His mind scrambled for a buoy, something solid to take hold of. Simple things. His job. His apartment. The women that crept to his counter as if out from parallel universes. The world belonged to itself. Not to him. *Let it be.*

But he turned to go back to the kitchen not knowing why. He took two steps and ran smack into Tatum coming around the corner.

"I'm freaking," she said.

"Me, too."

"Are we good?" Tatum asked. "I need us to be good."

"We're good."

There had been the one kiss in the park, but no others. Though they were friends, they had not been the sort that hugged in their comings and goings. Each other's presence, not body, had been each other's comfort. They looked at each other, relieved, but still frightened. It was not clear what arrived where first, but Paris's free arm wrapped around Tatum while he held the cornbread in the other. Tatum's forehead rested on his shoulder. Then they stepped apart, weak smiles all around.

"I'll be right out," Tatum said, looking at the ground. She turned and returned to the kitchen.

Let it be, Paris counseled himself to keep from following her back up the hall. *Let it be good.*

He stepped through the back door, and eyes turned to meet him in greeting. Geneva was starting up the gas grill. Her neighbor, Ron, the old librarian, was just breaking through the hedge, wearing a yellow fleece pullover and carrying a ceramic tray. Rachael stomped on a thin sheet of ice, freeing the water beneath. Paris placed the cornbread on the card table and took a seat on the steps he had just come down, a twin to the steps that led to the patio from Geneva's back door.

Rachael hadn't raised her head, but even so, Paris could see the shard cut deep in Rachael's eyes. She was not like him. She was at home in her hunger. She wanted and knew she deserved what she wanted. That she didn't have it was an error of cosmic proportion.

"Happy Birthdays," Paris said to Rachael and Geneva. "How's nine compared to eight?" he asked Rachael.

Rachael didn't look up from the puddle.

"I don't know," she said. "It's my first day."

19

"We're all related," Geneva said, waving the copper-headed brush in the air. "Trees, plants, dogs, cats, you, me. We all evolved from microbes."

The yard was south facing and made the most of the sun. Geneva and Rachael prepared for the barbecue in a percussion of melt dropping from windowsills, rooftops, and gutters. The snowdrifts against the garage grew soft and hollow as the snowline in the tiered flowerbeds retreated. The scent of mud rose up from beneath winter's clean, fresh breath. Rachael poured sunflower seeds into a cupped hand made of stone that hung by fine chain links from a thumb-sized jut off the trunk of the apple tree. Geneva had been scraping the grill and rhapsodizing, caught up in spring's false alarm.

"What's a microbe?" Rachael said, hauling the bag of seed back to the tiny patio.

"The microbe," Geneva said, "is the mother of us all."

Rachael stashed the seed in an old, metal milk box.

"At the beginning of time," Geneva said, "our time, anyway, microbes floated in ancient oceans. Everything evolved from microbes."

"What did they look like?"

"Microbes?"

Geneva thought for a second, not knowing the answer for sure. Rachael pressed lightly with a pointed toe on a fragile film of ice where a small puddle had formed in a dip of the bricks in the patio. Bubbles jostled beneath the ice's surface.

"Well," Geneva said, "you or I couldn't see them with our eyes. We'd need a microscope."

"Do they look like bugs?"

"Not really," Geneva said. "More like a flower, I think. No faces or butts."

Rachael scrunched her brow.

"How'd they know where they were going?"

"Well, they weren't going anywhere," Geneva said. "They just floated around, and that was good enough."

Rachael imagined the flower creatures, spinning and drifting. She considered what costume a kid might wear to be one. She idly spun slow circles and decided on her color. Seafoam.

"Know what a fish calls planet Earth?" Geneva said.

"What?"

"Planet Water. It's all perspective."

Paris came through Tatum's back door just as Ron cut through the hedge carrying a blue ceramic platter. Rachael stopped spinning and stomped on the ice sheet. The cold water penetrated the exterior of her boot but stopped short of her skin. Paris. Vincent. Her father. Rachael put them together in her mind. But she knew Paris was different. He wanted to be here. Rachael wasn't sure but thought maybe it meant that he was less important.

Geneva, Paris, and Ron greeted one another. Geneva admired the blue ceramic plate laden with cut red and yellow peppers and broccoli florets that Ron had carried through the hedge. He said he made the plate himself. That he had taken a class.

"Everything's organic," he said, as he placed the tray on the card table.

"Wonderful," Geneva said. "Even the yellow peppers? They must have cost an arm and a leg."

"Seven eighty-nine a pound."

Rachael, again, spun in place, floated in an imaginary sea. She was more restrained than before, arms closer to her sides, chin closer to the chest. She tried to make it look as though she were examining the ground and not that she was imagining herself a flower, drifting without intent. The cool air around her was water, and it rippled through her petals. She stole a peek from beneath her brow. Paris was watching. Rachael thought he pretended to be drifting too, but that really, he was swimming. They were both on the Planet Water. In it.

"I once bought an organic cabbage at Earth's Bounty," Geneva said, hand on a hip, pointing with the copper brush. "Four dollars and ninety-nine cents. For one little head of cabbage. I ate it to the core."

"Well, it's worth it to me," Ron said. "I never shop for produce at the regular supermarket, not since being fooled by a peach." He turned to Rachael. "So, you're the birthday girl."

"Geneva too," Rachael said. She liked Ron well enough. When he looked at her, he smiled like she proved his point. "How could you get fooled by a peach?"

Ron folded his arms across his chest, glad to be asked. His legs were planted widely, in the at-ease position.

"Like I said, I don't buy fruit at the supermarket," he said, "but there were these peaches. Gorgeous, humped beauties. I bought six. They had a little give but weren't quite there. So I left them in a brown paper bag for two days, and next I looked, brown spots. They were heading south. So I cut into one. Hard as a rock right below the first inch of give. Not a speck of flavor. Fooled by a peach." He said it as though it were both unbelievable and unforgivable.

"Seduced by a mirage," Geneva said, turning knobs on the gas grill. "But even when the senses are fooled, the body never is. Can't extract nutrition from cardboard."

"Gave me cause to pause," Ron said. "Shouldn't our animal instincts protect us from impostors?"

Flames kicked up from the grill. Geneva adjusted the heat.

"First the peaches," Paris said, deadpan, from where he sat on the steps, "next it'll be the cantaloupes."

"No joke," Ron said, shaking his head.

Tatum emerged through her back door carrying the mushrooms in one hand and a bowl of chips in the other. She wore her hat and gloves.

"For all we know," Geneva was saying, "we may have all eaten our last good peach and not even know it."

"And you call me negative," Tatum said as she came down the stairs.

Rachael noticed that as her aunt stepped past Paris, he extended one finger from where his hand rested on his knee to touch the fabric of her skirt as it rustled past. He never looked up.

"Look at all the colors," Tatum said to Rachael, referring to the red and yellow peppers and the green of the broccoli florets, all assembled on the blue ceramic platter. "Why don't you get your camera?" she said. "This could be a good picture."

Rachael's camera sat on the table among the plates of food. She came over and picked it up but did not take a picture. Tatum pulled up a plastic lawn chair and took a seat. Rachael took a chip from the bowl.

"What are they teaching you in school these days?" Ron asked Rachael.

"Multiplying," she said. "What we want to be when we grow up. State things, like the state bird and state tree."

"The state tree," Ron said. "The P-pine. Nothing like it."

"It's the Ponderosa Pine," Rachael said.

"They were darn near fireproof," Ron said, rocking back and forth on his heels. "Their canopies are so high brushfires never touched them. Then we decided to protect them by putting out fires that needed to burn. We ended up with a lot of fuel on the ground. Little trees. Fuses. They took the fire right up to the canopy and the dry needles. They called it 'managing' the forests," he said with a laugh. "Now, when the state burns, it burns hot and fast. Did they tell you about that?" he asked Rachael.

She shook her head no. "The grizzly bear is the state animal," she said.

"We've managed to get rid of most of them too," he said. He looked up through the barren branches, letting his eyes slide across the baby blue sky. "We've taken so much from this place," he said. "Trees, gold, silver, minerals, coal, wildlife. There are places I look at, and all I can see is the beauty that's gone. Clear cuts. Subdivisions."

"And yet, there's so much beauty left," Geneva said, not wanting to go too far down that road.

"True," Ron said. "But it's hard to watch what you love disappear."

An awkward silence followed.

Tatum reached out and touched Rachael's fingers.

"You cold?" she said.

"Aw, hell," Ron said.

"I've got hot apple cider," Geneva said, abandoning the grill. She pointed a finger at each of them. "Yes, yes, yes?" she said, getting a count.

"Do you need another sweater?" Tatum said to Rachael.

"I can get it," Rachael said as she climbed the steps to their back door.

Her bedroom was at the rear of the duplex, and having failed to close the solid door, she listened to the adult conversation drifting in through the screen. She looked through her bedroom window at Tatum sitting beside the table. She couldn't see Paris, but she could see Ron's back, his gray hair messy above his pullover. She heard Geneva next door. Music starting up and spilling through the walls. A woman's voice and a piano. "*. . . And I think to myself, what a wonderful world.*"

Rachael aimed her camera through the window at Tatum and clicked.

Geneva reemerged into the yard carrying a tray of mugs with steam rising into the air. She slid the tray onto the table

"I think living in a beautiful place inoculates one against runaway consumerism," she said. "It satisfies. It's un-American."

"Beauty is a tourist attraction," Paris said from the steps.

Tatum looked in the direction of Paris's voice. Rachael watched from the window. She could see that her aunt was more than listening to Paris. She was looking at him and thinking secret thoughts.

Then Tatum looked up to the window and caught Rachael watching her. She neither smiled nor waved. Rachael could tell she was thinking secret thoughts about her, just like she had when she had looked at Paris. Rachael turned away from the window, put down her camera, put on a sweater, and rejoined the party.

The group then stood around the card table, skewering vegetables, scallops, and small chunks of chicken. The afternoon wore on, full of aimless talk punctuated with expressions of amazement at and gratitude for the warmth of the day. Geneva placed skewers on the grill. During cracks in the conversation when silence snuck in, glances and small smiles were exchanged in recognition of the thin layer of melancholy shimmering at the edges of the afternoon, making it all the sweeter.

The sun slanted too soon. The thin mountain atmosphere fought futilely to hold the heat. They would eat the cake inside. Rachael went in while the grown-ups cleaned up. In the kitchen, she pulled a glass from the dish rack and placed it on the table. She retrieved the half-gallon carton of milk from the refrigerator. It was one of the things that was different here, like calling adults by first names. Her mother didn't let her pour from the carton unless she was in the kitchen too. The milk poured smooth and formed a perfect, white surface, white as snow.

The previous weekend, when the snow was new, Rachael and Tatum had walked the six blocks to the north hills to watch the dogs crisscrossing over the sparkling fresh blanket. Owners trailed leisurely behind with leashes bunched up in mittened fists.

"What do you think new snow smells like?" her aunt had asked her. "Do you think it smells like the sky?"

Rachael had watched the dogs burrowing through the drifts. They looked back at her now and then, staring out from frosty muzzles. Her aunt had started spinning slow circles, arms extended, looking up at the sky.

"My sister loved new snow," she told Rachael. "She'd get mad at me if I tromped through it first."

At some point, Aunt Tatum's stories had stopped being about "your mother" and were instead about "my sister." Tatum's sister was a child, not unlike Rachael herself.

The phone rang in the background of Rachael's thoughts. But she was remembering new snow and how back at home when a fresh blanket fell, she was allowed to play only on the side of the house with the fewest windows so her mother could look out at smooth, white perfection. The phone continued to ring, intruding upon Rachael's thoughts. She had never answered her aunt's phone before, but she stepped toward it and tentatively picked up.

"Hello?" she said.

Silence.

Then, a hesitant "Is Tatum there?"

It wasn't her father. It was Vincent. She was sure of it.

"Hello?" he said again.

Rachael held the phone in one hand, her milk in the other. She hung there until she heard a click and the line go dead. She replaced it on its cradle.

But she didn't step away. She watched the phone, waiting for it to ring again. Outside the window, she heard the drip of icicles, slowed down from earlier that afternoon as the ice firmed up as the temperature fell. Rachael thought of the dogs with their frost-dusted backs leaving belly trenches in the surface of the snow yet somehow not ruining it. Then the phone rang again. Rachael let it ring. She turned her back to it.

Rachael stood in the kitchen, holding her glass and listening to the ringing. The sound both soothed and stirred her, like the sensation of hiding while hearing someone search for you. Your name is called. You hear your own breathing. They cannot see you but are reaching out with antennae. So it's more than your body that you have to hide. The game played in Rachael's head. An unnamed He was looking for her. But whoever it was that was looking, she thought, he would have to wonder where she was, what happened to her, and be worried.

The back door opened, and the sound of music and voices drifted in. Tatum's head was cocked as she entered the kitchen, carrying dirty plates and empty platters.

"Did I hear the phone?" she said.

Rachael looked to the phone, but it was silent. Just a moment ago, it had felt good to let it ring and walk away. But now she felt a slow, creeping panic. She had made a mistake, though she couldn't name exactly what it was. But she knew she made Him go away. She flushed, the inward terror clear on her face, and her glass slipped through her fingers, crashing on the linoleum.

Tatum jumped back when the milk and glass splattered.

"Oh no," Tatum said, "what's wrong?"

Large, curved pieces of glass sat sharp edges up on the floor. The back screen door opened and fell closed. Paris came up behind Tatum, looking over her shoulder at the mess.

Rachael looked at the lightning bolt of milk across the blue linoleum.

Tatum's brow was a question mark. Her hands were full.

Paris picked up the broom and dustpan to his right by the fridge and stepped between them.

"May I?" he said.

20

༄

Paris stood alone in the yard, looking over the fence and into the sky. The trees reached above the rooftops with gnarled, beggar's hands against a background of mountains drenched in purple winter dusk. In a canvas, there is a dimple, an implied horizon, no more illusory than the one before him shape-shifting in the changing light. He knew there was nothing there. The Earth, after all, is round. To ride into the sunset is to never arrive. It is to forever chase a lie.

Paris thought of his sketches decomposing in a landfill as he gathered the last of the glasses from the earlier meal. They chinked together in a cluster as he grasped them with his fingers. He carried them up Tatum's back steps.

Inside, Rachael was already asleep in her bed, having started to run a temperature. Tatum washed dishes and stacked them in a rack. The sounds of chores, the scrubbing and clinking, was pleasant to Paris, reassuring. He put down the glasses and took a seat at the kitchen table. The coffeemaker spit and gurgled. Tatum knew Paris had to go to work soon. She wiped her hands on the kitchen towel and poured Paris a mug. They retired to the living room.

Paris seated himself on the sofa, and Tatum sat on the orange chair, putting her feet up on the ottoman. On the trunk Tatum used as a coffee table sat the film and the maracas she had given Rachael and the birdhouse from Geneva. The barrettes had been put away, but Paris's hat remained. Paris picked up a maraca. He held it with two hands and shook it once. He turned it over in his hands like it were an artifact.

"You know," he said, "I've always felt sorry for the leader of a conga line. He gets the 'Hey, dude, saw you last night, cha-cha-cha.'"

Tatum smiled and rolled her head to look in his direction.

"But the leader of a conga line is not the instigator," Paris said. "It's the number two person in the line who started it. Conga lines start when the second person in line grabs the first person's hips. After that, it's out of the leader's control. No control over the length of line or the behavior of the people in it."

"Some leaders are chosen by the people."

"The next morning," Paris said, returning the maraca to the trunk, "no one remembers who was second in line. No one remembers who started it. Only who led it."

"Was there an incident, Paris? Something you want to tell me about?"

"No," he said. "Just being philosophical."

They were trying to return to normal, get past the tension of earlier that afternoon, and create new moments to usurp the old.

Tatum pushed the film with a socked foot.

"It's a mysterious thing," she said, pulling a fleece throw from the back of the chair across her body, holding it under her chin. "Rachael loves taking pictures and filling her photo albums. She asked me to make copies of all these old pictures she has of Margaret and Lee. I wonder if she's mingling them with ones from now, trying to merge the past and present. Whatever she's doing, it's top secret. She won't show me. And she does it with the focus of a priest. Isn't it funny how kids have secret worlds, entire universes of purpose we know nothing about? Do you have a secret world, Paris? You don't have to tell me about it, since it's secret and all, just tell me if it exists."

"A secret world?" Paris said. "Not just secrets or secret thoughts, but a whole world?"

Tatum waited.

"Sometimes I feel like my whole life is a secret world," he said.

"Secret from everybody?"

Paris wasn't sure.

"I remember when I realized that secrets were possible," he said.

"What do you mean?"

"Well, I think, for a while, during childhood, I thought everyone knew what I thought. That we were all thinking the same thing, but it was taboo to talk about a lot of it. I thought there was a great conspiracy to pretend certain things weren't real."

"But that's not how it was?"

Paris adjusted his glasses at the corner.

"No," he said. "Something that happened at school showed me that everyone doesn't know everything. That I, alone, might know something, or maybe just me and another person. Everyone isn't pretending not to know. They genuinely don't."

"What happened?"

Paris leaned forward, hunching over his mug, which he held with two hands.

"I wasn't a popular kid or a geek kid, either," he said. "I was more of an invisible kid. But this other guy who rode the bus, Warren, he had the curse, and he was the morning target of one of the biggest thugs in my grade school. Bruce. Me and Warren were in second grade. Bruce was in like fifth. Every morning, Bruce stole Warren's lunch and ate it right in front of him on the way to school. I watched it for almost a year. Warren was so hungry every afternoon, he was passing out. Some days I acted like my mom gave me stuff I hated, and I gave it to him. I had to be careful, though. I couldn't risk being his friend. I felt bad for him, but I had to survive, myself. Besides, there was something kind of weird and gross about him."

"Seems like most guys named Bruce turn out to be bullies who steal lunches from guys named Warren," Tatum said.

Paris sipped from his mug and adjusted his glasses.

"I had this parakeet," he said. "Elvis. One morning I woke up, pulled the sheet off his cage, and he was lying there dead in the bottom. I told my mother I was going to bury him, but I didn't. I went into the yard and crammed him into my pocket. When my mom was in the bathroom, I pressed him between two pieces of white bread and packed him into a lunch sack. That day, when I got on the bus, fast as I could, I grabbed Warren's lunch and dropped this other bag into his lap. He looked at me strange but didn't have time to think because Bruce was boarding too."

"Wow," Tatum said, seeing it coming together. "What a plan."

"So, I'm sitting like three rows back from Warren. I'm as nervous as if I were wired with explosives. The whole world felt so different. Vivid. It felt like everyone in the world had to know, had to see it on my face. Anyway, new day, same story. Bruce steals Warren's lunch and sits a row in front of him, like he always did, so the poor kid had to watch him eat his food."

"Bruce ate Elvis."

"He tore the plastic wrap off like he did every day. See, I had to count on him doing it like he always did. He had his eye on Warren, you know, 'Ha, ha, I'm eating your sandwich, whatcha gonna do about it.' — God I hated him. Well, he was true to form that morning. He takes a bite, and right away, he's spitting and jumping out of his seat. When he sees what he bit into, the idea of it makes him even sicker than the bite, and he mini-pukes on the spot. 'You're dead, you're dead, you little fucker,' he says, puke dribbling off his lip."

"Whoa," Tatum said.

"He beat the shit out of Warren later that day, but he never stole his lunch again. Plus, the story got around. Warren was kind of an everyman's hero for a while. We never said anything about it."

"And that's how you learned about secrets."

Paris nodded. He put his mug back down on the trunk.

"It was both good and bad," he said. "I mean, on one hand, I learned I could have secrets separate from what anyone else in the world knew. But, it also meant," he paused, "it also meant, I don't know, like we weren't all in it together."

He looked at Tatum. She closed her eyes and let her head fall against the back of the chair. A branch from the ficus arced above her, and a small smile played on her lips. If it were any other woman, Paris might believe there was an invitation in her demeanor, an acceptance, or even encouragement, of an advance. He found himself wanting to give her more. Feed the sweet space she seemed to be inhabiting.

"Paris."

"Tatum."

"I'm sorry about earlier."

"Me too."

She raised her head from the back of the chair and looked at him. "I've been thinking about what you said."

Paris shook his head like he didn't remember.

"About what's not there mattering more than what is."

Paris blinked and tried to hope for nothing.

"I probably spend too much time thinking about what I could never be for Rachael instead of thinking about what I could be doing for her."

Rachael. It was about Rachael.

"How can I better help her, Paris? What do you think I should do for her?"

Something in Paris closed, quietly.

"I mean," Tatum said, "you can love someone, but really, what does that do for them?" She leaned forward and picked up the same maraca Paris had been fiddling with. "It never raised anyone from the dead," she said. "In fact, people say you can love someone to death, but never that you can love someone to life."

Paris didn't want to think about love's utility. About what it could do *for* anybody. *For.* The word made him edgy.

He stood, abruptly. Tatum looked up.

"Paris?"

He ran a hand over his head. What could she do *for* Rachael? What could he do *for* her? It was a mark on a wall. Something to achieve.

Paris looked at Tatum. Anger was not familiar to him, and he lacked the experience to navigate its expression.

"I think I have to go," he said.

"Work?" Tatum said, knowing that wasn't it. "What's wrong? Oh, no."

"I, I'm sorry," Paris said, "I . . ."

"Paris, I'm sorry."

"No," he said, closing his eyes. He did not want her to apologize. He didn't want her to feel wrong.

"No, you're right," Tatum said. She rapped the maraca against her forehead. "Ack. This is what I do. I ruin shit. I'm an idiot. Please don't be mad at me."

"No." Paris grimaced and shook his head. "You don't ruin shit." *I'll die if I made you feel that way* — Paris didn't say the words. He would not make her feelings responsible for his. "I have to go."

Tatum huddled down deeper beneath the throw, gripping it beneath her chin.

Paris walked fast down the street. He was blind to the night, so it let him be and looked away as he passed. What did he want? Nothing, he insisted. But then, what was it that made his head hurt and chest tighten? Was it just as Tatum didn't know what to do for Rachael, he didn't know what to do for her? What act would elicit the desired response?

"For" — that was the problem. *For* destroyed people. If you're doing something "for" someone, and it doesn't work, well, then it means somebody failed somebody. Somebody didn't do the right thing or somebody didn't react right.

Paris did not want to be there *for* Tatum. He wanted to be there *with* her.

~

21

"I can take care of myself."

Tatum whispered it. She whispered it twice.

"I can take care of myself. I can take care of myself." She said it faster and faster and rocked with its rhythms. "I can take care of myself." It was an incantation.

Sitting on the kitchen floor, still wrapped in the fleece blanket, she pulled her knees to her chest and rocked like an autistic child. She tried to drown out thoughts of Paris. If she didn't, she feared her heart would explode.

Good things get fucked up, she thought, as she rocked. I'm the constant. Tatum knew it was a fact that she drove people away, and what drove them away was not temper or cruelty, not a nasty habit or violation of hygiene or courtesy. It's just me, she thought. I'm just better appreciated from a distance. A few arms' length, and she found she could engage and deflect at once. Move in too close, and the jig was up. Next thing that poor soul knew, misery had descended upon him, and whatever it was she did, Tatum thought, he needed her to stop doing it. And what that "it" was that she needed to stop doing, best she could figure, was being herself.

It made her wonder if her soul was surrounded by a moat, troll infested. Something repellent in the path of the space where she wanted someone to enter.

Either that, she thought, or I am the moat. The troll.

"I'm okay," she whispered. "I'm okay."

She rocked and used the mantra to drum out other thoughts, the calculating of failures that spit out sums she didn't want to face. Margaret's presence in it all revealed itself slowly, appearing, casually, among the psyche's rubble as though it had been there all along. Tatum did not sense Margaret as a ghost, but as an understanding, a sense that she too had known about the moat. Not Tatum's moat, but one of her own. Tatum wondered how she did it, had a life, had a family.

How did she keep the planets in balance, generate enough magnetism, enough attraction, to draw loved ones in, but not so far that they'd meet the trolls?

Trolls.

Trolls were the problem. Ugly and hopeful. They know they're fundamentally unlovable, and yet they ache for love. A tragic combination.

The panic slowly eased. It always did. Pathetic though it was to be reduced to a puddle on her kitchen floor, she found herself noticing that suicide hadn't even crossed her mind. Not even recreationally. Unless, of course, the noticing that she hadn't considered it counted against her.

With such thoughts, she slowly shifted into her second self, the one that could carry on and perform life's mundane tasks. She rose from the floor. She turned off lights and locked the front door. She picked up Paris's mug from the coffee table and put it in the sink. She headed down the hall, past Rachael's room, to turn off the back porch light and lock the door.

Through the glass window in the door, she noticed Geneva in the yard opening the lid of the grill. Tatum still had the fleece throw wrapped around her shoulders, and she pulled it tighter around and stepped outside. The cold felt fresh hitting her face and nostrils.

"Whatcha doing?" she said.

Geneva reached into the grill and then turned around holding up a shish kabob, forgotten and left behind.

"I knew it," Geneva said, laying it down on the small, attached shelf. She wore a berry-colored parka, and her pajama bottoms were stuffed into snow boots. "I saw it in my mind," she said. "I was puttering about, doing other things, and suddenly there it was, a floating image. Isn't that odd?'

Tatum smiled and hiked the blanket up farther.

"How's the sick girl?" Geneva asked.

"Sleeping."

"The father ever call?"

"I don't think so," Tatum said, "unless we missed it. Did you hear from Parkview Homes?"

The question reminded Geneva of what precisely she had set out to forget. Yes, the director of Parkview Homes had called. No decision had been made. A committee had been assigned and was having a phone conference the following day. On the phone, the director had been sympathetic and apologized that the process was taking so long. Geneva had hung up full of an irritation she endured for an hour before taking a hit off her stash.

"The director would like the situation to go away," Geneva said. "But he needs to validate the social worker who's pushing this."

"Validate her concerns, or validate her?"

"Number two."

"In more ways than one."

Geneva laughed.

"Well, yes and no," she said, trying to be fair. "Reverse the sexes. Old geezer climbs on his veggie wife and humps 'til the cows come home. Cause for concern?"

"But the sexes weren't reversed."

"True," Geneva said. "Equal and fair are not one in the same. But that's a concept far too sophisticated for the world's glut of literalists."

"I'm sorry."

Geneva shrugged a whatcha-gonna-do shrug. The hash had tweaked her perspective, and she wasn't interested, at the moment, in indulging any feelings of victimhood. Some took drugs to escape reality. Others took them to escape lies, melt the neurological barriers that allow for self-deception. The result was clarity, which is why drugs are dangerous. Delusions or the loss of them — either can flip a person out. And, just minutes before, some rather unflattering clarity had descended upon Geneva.

Being banned from Ralph was no burden. She couldn't deny it. In fact, she felt off the hook. She did not miss Ralph, nor did she believe that Ralph missed her. She was unable to conceal from herself that her impulse toward him was not one of desire but responsibility alone. Was it inevitable? Just as tadpoles become frogs and acorns oaks, must love make its journey from desire to duty?

That's where she had been when the shish kabob appeared to her.

A soft wind kicked up, creating a hush out of nothing.

"Paris is in love with you," Geneva said, switching gears, redirecting the focus to someone else's complications.

Geneva's words sent an electrical current running through Tatum's torso, into her legs, and down to her feet. It was a feeling similar to being caught in a lie. She pulled the throw up over her head like a hood. It flashed through her mind that maybe Paris was wrong. Secrets weren't so secret. Was it the cosmic membranes that were thinner than imagined, or just the duplex walls?

"Why are you saying that?"

"Because you already know it," Geneva said. "I don't think I'm giving anything away."

"But why now? Why are you telling me that now?"

Geneva cocked her head. "Something happened?" she said.

Tatum sat down on her steps and told Geneva about the encounters between her and Paris, both at the start and end of the day. She told her about the misunderstandings that had newly cropped up in their interactions, the new and unwelcome awkwardness.

"I miss him so much," Tatum said. "Sometimes even when I'm with him. It's just so weird that you would say that tonight, right in the wake of all this."

They were quiet for a moment. Wet light sparkled in the yard as the snow re-stiffened. Above them, the sky was blue-black. Stars pierced the night, not objects, but action. Light hauling ass. Geneva picked up the shish kabob.

"We were guided here tonight, brought together by the shish kabob," she said in the voice of a campy prophet. "It wanted us to review the lesson of the Tree of Life."

"And what's that?" Tatum said, half-laughing.

Geneva replaced the shriveled oracle on the shelf beside the grill and closed its lid.

"Energy flows and takes form," Geneva said. "Energy flows into form and fills it. Eventually, the form gets filled to capacity. When it can no longer hold the energy, it has to break, free the energy, until it takes form again. This is the lesson."

Tatum curled her toes against the cold.

"Are you channeling a shish kabob?" she asked.

"If the form fights for its life," Geneva said, "tries to hold itself together under the pressure, it breaks violently. Or it begins to atrophy. It leaks to death."

"In English."

Geneva looked at Tatum. Tatum looked back.

"Change or die," Geneva said. "Your relationship with Paris has to change or it's going to combust or dribble away."

Tatum looked away, then up at the sky.

"That stinks," she said. "Nothing's forever, huh?"

"Not even nothing."

"If you're right," Tatum said, "about Paris's feelings, I feel bad for him. He's in for a big disappointment. I'm impossible to love."

Geneva rolled her eyes.

"'I'm impossible to love.'" She echoed Tatum's words, somewhat derisively.

"You know, Geneva" — Tatum's voice was tight with irritation — "I get a little tired of this bullshit that says we all have value and worth. You know who says that? People with value and worth. You know why they say it? So they don't have to look at the reality of the lives of the people who don't have it."

"An oppressed people," Geneva said.

"Fuck you," Tatum said, but without energy. She stood and turned to go inside.

"Wait," Geneva said.

Tatum turned, wearily.

"You don't have value to have, you have it to give. You value. The only way you cannot have value is if you don't value anything."

Tatum dropped into a hip and crossed her arms over her chest, tightening the blanket. "If a person is too hard to love," she said, "no little saying or little philosophies can change that."

"Then what's the flaw in Paris that he loves the likes of you?"

"This isn't about Paris."

Geneva turned away, waving a hand in the air.

"I've got some bad news," she said, moving back to the grill. "If you feel unworthy of love, you're probably not feeling worthy *to* love, either. I hate to break it to you, sister, but you're probably withholding love from people who are aching for it."

"I love people."

"Sure," Geneva said, "but is your love making the great journey? For love to get out, you risk some coming in." She picked up the shriveled shish kabob. "Ever read Faulkner?"

"Probably," Tatum said, "in school. I think I read the one with a retarded guy in it."

"*The Sound and the Fury*," Geneva said. "I was thinking of *As I Lay Dying*. The mother character in the story says that children violated her aloneness. They tore open what was meant to be shut and protected. Something like that."

Tatum hugged herself. She looked into the yard. "You think that's what's happening to me?"

"Trust the shish kabob," Geneva said. Then she waved good night and headed for her steps, shish kabob in hand.

"Geneva."

She stopped.

"Geneva," Tatum said. "Paris kissed me once."

"Did you kiss him back?"

Tatum thought for a minute. She had honestly never considered it. "I think I did."

Geneva stayed quiet.

"If it doesn't work out," Tatum said, "I could lose him forever."

"We lose everybody anyway," Geneva said. "To death. To busyness. To the failure to make the effort. That's why you just have to love them, love them, love them. No matter what."

"Unconditional love, huh?"

"I don't think of it that way," Geneva said. "I just think of it as love. Why qualify love?" Geneva finished climbing her stairs. "Good night," she said, "and good luck." She slipped through her door. Her porch light went dark.

Tatum looked at the sky, black and silver. The stars above were not immortal. The space in which they hung was not eternal. Big bangs come, and worlds collapse. Nothing is forever. Not even nothing.

Inside, Tatum peeked at Rachael asleep in her bed. The tough hand life had dealt her did not yet show up in her face. She looked innocent. Unruined. Tatum considered Geneva's proposition that feeling unworthy of love entailed withholding it, that there was no such thing as one-way traffic when it came to the heart. If that were so, Tatum figured her love had probably been as useful to Rachael as her dead mother's. Something guaranteed, but existing on the other side of an invisible barrier. Love that's there, but not *here*. Tatum's body accepted the truth of it. The biochemistry of regret kicked in and took shape. She felt guilt.

Revelation is not necessarily ecstatic. Rarely is it the turning point that its reputation suggests. Revelation is merely an option. A flashing arrow, perhaps, but not a destination. Tatum pressed her hand to

Rachael's forehead, checking for fever. She was warm but in a good way.

Tatum left the bedroom door cracked, put on her p.j.'s, and paced the living room. She stared at her coffee table, empty seeming, without Paris's hat.

Paris.

The moment you realize you've waited too long, you worry it might be too late.

She would call him. First thing in the morning. They would see each other, and she would tell him everything, though, she had no idea what "everything" was. She would tell him she missed him. She could start there.

In the bathroom, she brushed her teeth, trying to imagine what words she would say. She looked at herself in the mirror, ready to rehearse. But nothing came to her but memories, the past throwing up a sand storm. The kiss in the park. Margaret's funeral. Motel rooms. Tatum forced her focus through the haze of it and made eye contact with her own reflection. She had managed to land squarely in the moment, apart from the memories and tomorrow. Green eyes met green eyes. Then, in one fell swoop, like ripping off a Band-Aid, she pulled her top off over her head. She looked at the gash, the angry searing where a breast used to be. Not once had she mourned it. The scar had given shape and form to a thing already there, something embedded that had finally and simply risen to the surface. Never had its violence shocked her.

But she thought of Paris now. She stood behind his eyes to see. For the first time, she looked at it.

22

A fluorescent light above the counter buzzed. Paris looked up and watched it sputter. None of the customers took particular notice. Not the two Goth girls, looking young and vulnerable, despite their black makeup and practiced vacant stares. The couple in the corner failed to notice too. They focused on their newspaper and tried to resign themselves to each other's failings. The meth-head at the counter picked at his doughnut, never looking up.

It was business as usual, as Paris liked. Routine is dismissed by most as the daily grind. But Paris found it good and holy. Spring, summer, fall, winter. Over and over. The planet never wearied of it and wished for more.

Besides, Paris had had plenty of business-not-as-usual for one day. Too much unspoken and misspoken. He hated the sense of a boundary, invisible but solid, between him and Tatum, like Plexiglas in the ether. They had tried to act as though it wasn't there. Maybe the acting was the problem, Paris thought, but what else is there to do? Bang on his side watching her bang on hers? Is it that one couldn't get out or couldn't get in?

The meth-head abandoned his doughnut. It looked as though it had been pecked by birds. Paris opened the vat and stirred the soup, thinking about the women who would straggle in later. The soup was *for* them. He would be here *with* them. Then he came around the counter to sweep beneath the stools and noticed Blair, the bartender, in the casino talking to one of the Deluxe's owners. The owners were two brothers who had inherited the place from their father, a former Butte miner with a prosthetic hand. The father's grit, however, had skipped a generation. His boys were effeminate without being gay. Their faces were pointed, and they looked both craven and mean at the same time. Their edicts flowed through Blair to Paris, even though Blair wasn't Paris's supervisor. Blair and Paris were more like separate rulers of neighboring kingdoms. It was a chain of communication, not of command. Blair shot Paris a look over the brother's shoulder. Paris didn't like it. It nipped at the heels of a fragile well-being he was struggling to cultivate in cleanliness and routine.

Paris cleared the meth-head's plate and rang up the seventy-five cents due and dropped the three cent tip into his apron pocket. He continued to work efficiently, as he always did, boss or no boss looking on. The Deluxe's owners were not bright but knew enough to largely leave Paris be, recognizing, if not appreciating, a bargain employee when they saw one. The brother waved to Paris from the casino before leaving. Paris nodded in response, all business.

Blair and Paris met at their kingdoms' boundaries, where bright light met neon haze. Both wore white T-shirts and jeans. Paris's cook's apron was wrapped around and tied in front. Blair had a rag thrown over a shoulder.

"Gary says they're selling the building," Blair said. "Thinks they can sell it for office space."

Paris frowned.

"He didn't leave a copy of the want ads," Blair said, "but it's coming."

"Shit," Paris said.

"No shit," Blair responded.

An old cowboy stepped past them into the diner. Blair and Paris turned away from each other as duty called.

The cowboy ordered off the breakfast menu. Paris started a fresh pot of coffee and flipped hash browns. Axioms jangled in his head: Was the news about the diner the proverbial second shoe? First, disconnect with Tatum. Now this. Had, indeed, the other shoe dropped? Or was the governing theory the theory of threes, that bad tidings were packaged like blind mice and little pigs. If this were the case, there was more to come. It was just a matter of time.

The cowboy ate his eggs and potatoes. He came and went quietly, leaving a modest tip. The couple left too, the man placing his hand on the small of the woman's back as they slipped through the casino. The Goth girls enlisted Paris's help to figure out their check. They paid, and Paris was alone.

He cleared the dirty dishes and wiped down the tables.

Paris worked. He tried to insist that all was well. But his feet told the truth, hot and nervous, and deadly, no doubt, when he would peel off his socks in the dawn.

Linda arrived at 2:20 a.m. with the retarded girls in tow. Paris took the girls bowls of soup and fistfuls of crackers. He poured Linda coffee.

"Soup's good tonight," he said to her, pleased there was so much of it.

But Linda made a face and shook her head no.

Paris went into the kitchen to run a load of dishes. He kept an ear open to the dining room should more of the women arrive. Through the cook's window, he saw a dishwater blonde in a man's coat he hadn't seen in weeks slide into the booth in the corner. Her B.O. was acidic, but it clung to her, leaving most of the diner unscathed. Paris was sympathetic, and he took her soup without asking and poured her coffee too.

If the worst were to come to pass and the Deluxe closed its doors, he thought as he returned the coffeepot to the burner, he would never say anything about it to the women. Let the doors one day be locked, he decided. Let it be heard of by word of mouth. Let it disappear as it once appeared out of nothing into nothing.

He collected the napkin holders and was restocking them behind the counter when he felt the foreign presence enter the room. Actually, what he felt, at first, was the antennae of Linda and the retarded girls going up, reaching and assessing threat vs. opportunity. Paris looked up. Two Indian dudes slid onto stools at the counter. It was perfectly normal. It was completely wrong. An invasion on sacred ground. The retarded girls watched them warily. Paris dropped menus in front of them and set them up with utensils.

At 8 p.m., Paris would've liked them. One wore a western shirt with a zigzag pattern in purples and reds and a bolo tie with a bear. He had long hair and a cowboy hat. The other one had a clean-shaven look. Smooth skin. Short hair. A plain, white dress shirt with blue jeans. Their vibes were good ones.

The men both ordered burgers.

Paris dropped the patties on the grill and smooshed them down with the spatula. He listened to their conversation through the hiss of the meat.

"His old lady wrapped him in silk," Bolo Tie said. "Then, she wrapped him in a tarp and duct taped it."

"That'll do," said White Shirt.

"She says the silk will protect his 'vibration' — it's a New Age thing. Little Mickey and Amos packed him in the truck. Too bad it's been warm, eh?"

White Shirt nodded. "I can't drive my truck anywhere anymore," he said. "Not off the rez."

Paris served their burgers slightly rare.

The men ate in silence for a time, following up bites of burgers with fistfuls of chips. Paris didn't make eye contact with Linda or any of the other women, feeling somehow responsible for the intrusion.

"I didn't know Buster at all until the cancer," Bolo Tie said through his chewing. "I guess like overnight he got hooked in with the traditional stuff. Started carrying rocks, smudging. He got real particular about funeral arrangements."

"Sounds like he came to his senses."

Bolo Tie pushed his dish away, tossing his napkin onto it. Paris approached to clear it.

"Hey, Vincent, by the way," Bolo Tie said, "Frankie wants to talk to you before we move Buster."

Paris's eyes darted toward the man in the white shirt.

"Yeah, that's cool," Vincent said, "as long as I'm on the road by the day after tomorrow."

"I told them."

It wasn't hard to piece together. This was Vincent. The Vincent. Paris wasn't sure if he wanted to hurry them along or keep them there to study him more closely.

"I got some people to see tomorrow," Vincent said. "Some stuff to do."

Paris wrote up their check, tore it off his pad, and placed it in front of them.

"Thanks, man," Vincent said, reaching into his back pocket for his wallet. "I got it," he said to his friend.

Paris looked in Linda's direction, and her eye caught his. He could see what she saw. Him, unnerved. Paris hovered at the counter, performing fake chores. He wiped clean surfaces and checked freshly refilled condiments. Linda stole glances. The two men leaned on their elbows and worked their teeth with toothpicks. Paris cleared Vincent's plate. Vincent gave the pile of check and cash a shove in Paris's direction.

"Keep it, man," he said.

The tip cleared 20 percent.

The two men slipped off their stools and motioned a thank-you to Paris as they left. Paris watched Vincent go. He cut a tall, lean figure. He was taller than Paris, but only barely so. Paris suspected he was a man without camouflage. No powers of invisibility. But Paris couldn't deny it. Vincent had it going on. Cool.

"Friends of yours?" Linda said, interrupting his thoughts.

"Friend of a friend," Paris said, "I think."

"Friend of a friend, but not your friend."

"Something like that."

Paris watched the men slip out the casino and into the night. When his attention returned to the room, heat rose in his face, recognizing the humility of the diner. Dingy counters. Bug-filled lights. Carpet in the casino you wouldn't want to think about. The place was worn down and worn out. Those who claimed it were only able to do so because of its undesirability. For some reason, it reminded him of something Tatum had said earlier, about love being useless, unable to change a thing and unable to raise the dead. Perhaps, like the Deluxe, love was a humble dump, not the great force it was rumored to be. Perhaps it was even as humble as Paris himself. But Paris dismissed the thought quickly. It was a possibility he could not allow. He needed something mightier than himself on his side.

Then, feeling eyes upon him, he looked down the length of the counter. Linda. Their eyes met, and he felt the impulse to tell her all of it. But there she sat, half-invisible, knowing when a person wanted different. Different than what he had. Different than the moment. When a man needed to be someone other than himself.

The other women had already left, having slipped out while Vincent and his friend were eating. Paris never said a word. At least, he was pretty sure he didn't. So he didn't know how it happened, why it happened, that Linda stood and stepped behind the counter, took his hand, and led him into the kitchen.

Inside the janitor's closet, Linda pressed him into a corner between the wall and some shelving. Paris didn't resist, and he watched through the cracked closet door and through the cook's window a sliver of the doorway between the casino and dining room. Linda went for his belt and said, "It's forty bucks," as she dropped to one knee. Paris was half-hard, rubbery. Linda stuck him into her mouth and sucked him firm. One hand on the shelving, the other on the wall, Paris braced himself. He looked down briefly at the part in Linda's hair and the few wiry grays that grew from her crown, and then he looked back through the cracked closet door. He bit on his lower lip and fought to keep his eyes from closing. He caught himself rocking a bit but kept his hands off of her head. The thought of the forty dollars that he couldn't really afford crossed his mind but quickly disappeared. His mind followed his body now, away from the afternoon, away from the Deluxe, away from Vincent and his people to see tomorrow.

Pressure focused in his groin and grew excruciating. It was deprivation, time, and blank canvases. Desire sharpened to a point. He saw an image of Tatum in his mind. The picture of her breasts. The smallness of the nipples. The curved half-moons above her ribcage. The draw of her throat. Her tits. Linda was no longer a prostitute but a woman, just not the woman who she was.

Then Linda paused, mouth drawn up and hesitating at the bulb of Paris's dick. When she resumed, it was with slower strokes, calculated, it seemed to Paris, the knowing clear that it was better to work 'em up and back 'em off, work 'em up and back 'em off, than to find yourself in a prolonged, frenetic frontal assault on your face. The comfort of the neck and jaw, it seemed, took precedence over expediency.

Paris realized his eyes had closed. He cracked them and checked the coast. Still clear. Linda's new rhythms backed the heat up from his groin into his chest. It had to go somewhere. It was briefly more diffused but not diminished. When she picked up speed again, the sensations all refocused, dropping downward, bigger and with more force than before. Then Paris was with only himself, his body turned to rock, his dick and every other muscle. His jaw tightened. His toes gripped the floor through his boots. One hand dropped to the side of Linda's head and returned to the wall just as quickly. Then his head dropped back, and he burst, gulping in reverse. He rocked and shuddered, softly buckling, the small of his back gently banging against the wall behind him.

Linda, still on a knee, wiped her face on her sleeve. Paris hiked up his pants and zipped them. Linda stood. She was almost as tall as he was. She gave him a "well, that's that" smile. Paris looked at the lines outside her eyes curved downward along the outside of her cheek. She was not hard. She was not bitter. And she was not Tatum.

I love somebody, Paris suddenly wanted to tell her to turn the lie he had told himself into the truth.

He reached into his back pocket for his wallet and handed her two twenties.

Linda left the closet. She walked around the counter and past her coffee mug, grabbing her coat on the way out through the casino into the dark morning. Blair walked past the entrance to the diner with a towel in his hand, looking in, knowing something but unsure what.

Paris ran his hand through his hair, discomfort quietly overcoming him. He adjusted his glasses and did the math. Disconnect from Tatum. The Deluxe, closing. Vincent. Linda.

Not three, but four.

Had it started all over, he wondered? Were there now two more to go?

Snow was falling when Paris finished his shift. The sidewalks were slick with black ice, and the new snow added to the treachery. He cut down an alley that he normally didn't take. The pavement there would be broken. Rougher. Easier to traverse. Besides, why not do something different? They say missing a bus can change a fate.

He passed the alley's metal Dumpsters with their slanted lids. He walked over the potholed asphalt. How different did he want his fate to be, he wondered? Was for everything to be the same again the different thing he wanted? It had been a discomfort with which he was comfortable, a dissatisfaction with which he was satisfied enough. But how one *feels* about the truth is not the truth itself. The truth was the discomfort and the dissatisfaction. The truth is always there underneath. And the underneath goes on, layer beneath layer, on and on forever, truths pushed up, one by one, by heat and pressure.

There was no wind. The snow fell straight to the earth, orderly, too wet to float, but dragged by its own soggy weight. He had lied Linda into being Tatum. But sex was still sex. The blowjob had left Paris feeling slightly wetter inside. Released. But into what and whether he wanted to be there, he did not know. Sex breaks spells. Bad ones and good ones alike.

He reached his building and took the concrete stairs to his door. He stood in the spotlight dropped onto him as though he had a monologue to deliver. As he turned his key, the light was blocked, then freed again, crossed by a mysterious presence. Paris looked up, but it was gone.

He opened the door, and the phone rang. He stepped over the envelope that had been slipped beneath his door and picked up on the second ring.

"Hello?

"Paris? It's Tatum."

23

≈

Hans Mood was closing in on retirement. Dealing with geriatric sex-capades had not been part of his plan. He had been the director of Parkview Homes for seventeen years and hoped for nothing more or less than to coast through his final months, be gracious at his retirement party, and drive off with a gift watch and certificate of appreciation sitting on the passenger's seat as he went forth into a life of tying flies and raising llamas.

The problem was, he knew, the makeup of the Board of Directors. The craziest member, Mrs. Doncy Feldspar, also had the most time on her hands — a lethal combination for any board. Then there was the new social worker, Alice, with the short blonde hair and the tiny nose piercing. He had misread her in her interview. He took her for an artsy type with a full life outside the Home. She would, he thought, have the quirky sense of humor that best suited those working in nursing facilities. But no. She was a zealot. She had gone over his head and sent letters to the board members. She and Mrs. Feldspar were gaining energy from each other's momentum. They had stumbled upon a sin and, without much else to do, had made it their mission to punish it. Heroes and saviors worried Hans. They needed victims. They needed villains. They caused trouble everywhere.

The other members of the board were too passive to put up any resistance. Some were mildly concerned about a lawsuit being brought forward on behalf of the resident, potentially by their own employee. Hans was beginning to be a bit concerned himself. Real problems can be born of the made-up ones.

He opened the file and picked up the phone. He sighed and collected himself. Principle. Those who placed it above peace were self-absorbed, he thought, and lacking a proper sense of prioritization.

He called Geneva. He asked her to understand that elder abuse does occur and even though he did not believe she had done anything wrong, rules exist to protect the vulnerable. He told her the committee had proposed a probation. Supervised visits for four months followed by a reassessment.

"'Proposed'?" she said.

Hans cleared his throat. "Decided, I suppose."

"If you don't think I did anything wrong, why the probation?" Geneva asked.

"As I said, we have rules to protect the vulnerable . . ."

"Do you think I'm a threat to my husband?" she said.

Hans hesitated. He told the truth.

"No, I do not."

"If I'm not a threat, then the probation isn't for Ralph's protection but to slap my, well, let's just say wrist. Have I characterized this accurately?"

Hans ran a hand over thinning hair. He didn't want to delay retirement for the sake of following through with a lawsuit. He didn't want to stick around for an additional six months following the resolution of the lawsuit to assure he left Parkview in ship shape.

Geneva didn't wait for an answer.

"I'll consider your offer," she said. "Your 'proposal.' My lawyer will get back to you."

Both hung up their respective phones and retreated to their separate worlds.

Hans sighed at the picture on his desk — the muzzle of a llama affectionately poking over a fence between the smiling faces of him and his wife.

In fact, Geneva didn't have a lawyer and didn't want one. She hoped it wouldn't come to that. After hanging up, she returned to sorting through the letters she had picked up from the *Mountain Messenger* yesterday afternoon. Preoccupied, she read them with less patience than usual. Trouble with bosses, parents, and lovers. Same old. If she were a good woman, she knew, she would be grabbing her coat, probation or no, and enduring the social worker scribbling in the corner as she sat faithfully beside her husband's bed pumping in the Beach Boys and sending telepathic messages. But Geneva was not a good woman, she knew. A good person, yes. A good woman, no.

Besides, at the moment, she couldn't go anywhere. Rachael was sleeping on her sofa. Tatum had shuffled her across the hall this morning. Rachael was feeling better, but yesterday's fever earned her a pass on school. Tatum had invited Paris to come over that morning, and they needed privacy. Geneva hoped for Tatum and Paris. In a way, she also felt sorry for them that it had come to this. Love is a crapshoot. The house always takes its cut.

So Rachael had climbed onto her sofa, and Geneva covered her with a blanket and returned to her task. It crossed Geneva's mind that neither of them had received a call from her "man" on her birthday. No husband. No father. Sometimes Geneva forgot that Rachael's father wasn't dead too.

Geneva lifted the next envelope from the pile. The outside of it read "To Belinda." No mailing address. No return address. Geneva flipped the envelope over. It must have been dropped off at the paper, someone saving on the stamp. She slit it at the side. She slipped from it a torn sheet from a blue legal pad. It said:

> This morning, I met a woman in a coffee shop with
> her young friend. I'd like to invite her to dinner, but I
> don't know her last name or how to reach her. I cook
> a mean venison stew. Spicy.
>
> John

Geneva placed the letter on her desk. A thrill snaked its way up from her toes. She stared at the piece of paper, remembering his voice. He had called her Gen-eva, not Ginneva like most people did. The entirety of him came back to her. The giant hand. The dusty, cold-weather smell. The promise of a serious tool belt.

"I want to watch TV."

Geneva returned to earth. It was as though she had been lifted by a sudden wind and then gently placed back down.

"Can't help you," she said to Rachael without turning to face her. But it was a lie. She did have a television. She kept it in a closet in her bedroom. Caged. Inconvenient.

"Why don't you guys get TV's?" Rachael said with exasperation.

"They are extremely rude," Geneva said. "They talk when no one's listening. And they suck your life force." Geneva spun in her chair to face Rachael, who looked bored and rumpled. "What if I returned you to your aunt without a life force. How would I explain that?"

Rachael rolled her eyes.

"Can't you afford a TV?"

"I can afford one," Geneva said. She opened her top drawer and placed the blue sheet inside. She looked at the phone number listed after his signature. "But one has to be careful about acquiring new things," she said, closing the drawer, slowly, regrettably.

"Why?"

"You get a nice chair," Geneva said, "and it makes you realize you need a new sofa." She got up and walked to the wingback. She leaned on the back of it. "You get a fancy house, and you need dishes to go with it. Keeping up with the Joneses is one thing," she said. "Having to keep up with your own sofa is to live under an oppressive regime. It takes up too much mental space," she said, tapping the side of her head. "You want a nice life, surround yourself with nice things. It's a reasonable strategy. But, eventually, even your friends will come to match your sofa."

"So?"

"Well, nice is nice," Geneva said. She went to Rachael, leaned in, and felt her head. "But my interests lie elsewhere."

"Where?"

Rachael's temperature felt fine. Geneva sat down at the opposite end of the couch.

"I prefer an *interesting* life to a nice one."

"So why don't you get an interesting sofa?"

Geneva pointed a finger at Rachael. "Clever girl," she said. "I would if I could find one." She grabbed one of Rachael's feet and started rubbing it. "But searching for an interesting sofa doesn't seem like an interesting thing to do. Know why I rented to your Aunt Tatum?"

"No."

"I thought she'd be interesting."

"Am I interesting?"

"Fascinating," Geneva said.

Geneva propped up the pillows and leaned against the opposite arm of the sofa, facing Rachael. The drapery was closed behind them, and the gas heat rose through the vent in a hush.

"How 'bout Paris?"

Geneva nodded. "Also interesting." Voodoo jumped up and walked back and forth between them, receiving well wishes. "I bet your mom was an interesting person," Geneva said.

Rachael's face didn't change. She petted Voodoo.

"Yes," she said. "Vincent didn't think Aunt Tatum was very interesting. Did he?"

Geneva sighed. Those who leave have so much power. Being longed for is much more glamorous than being counted on. It was a strange reversal that those present become invisible and those not there loom larger than life. She looked at Rachael. Her face was a mask of mock innocence. Geneva wasn't going for it.

"Your mother didn't like Tatum," she said. "And maybe you were taught she wasn't a good person. But she is."

Rachael's brows lifted slightly.

"Then why did he leave?" she said.

"Who?"

"Vincent."

"Rachael," she said, hoping to make a grown-up point to a very little person. "When I'm with you, I want to be with you because I like you. Not because I want a feeling. There's a big difference. Vincent wanted a feeling, not a person. So he needed Tatum to be different so he could keep the feeling. But it's important that we're loved for who we are. Don't you think?"

Rachael shrugged. Geneva pushed away her foot, stood, and walked over to her albums.

"How did he want her to be different?" Rachael asked.

Geneva selected the *Greatest Hits of Gladys Knight and the Pips.* She slipped it from its sleeve. "Here's a strange thing about love," she said. She looked over her shoulder and gave Rachael the once-over. "I think you're old enough to know." She held the album by the edges, between her palms, and placed it on the turntable. "When you love someone, you want to be your best self for them. But if that person can't love your worst self too, you tend to hate them for it."

Geneva skipped the first track to get right to "Midnight Train to Georgia." She adjusted the volume. She held out her hands to Rachael, inviting her to join her.

"C'mon," she said.

Rachael threw off the blanket and joined her in the middle of the room.

"Follow me," Geneva said as she lifted her arms above her head, reaching up. She swayed like a tree, back and forth to the music. Rachael followed suit.

"Moving is important," Geneva told her. "Greases the gears." Her hips joined the effort.

Rachael seemed open to it and swayed along, watching Geneva and trying out the moves. Geneva decided to take the opportunity to lobby on Tatum's behalf.

"What I think is fascinating about you," she said to Rachael, "is that I think you have a very strong center." She made a fist in front of her heart. "I think you're smart and funny too."

Always best to first gain your target's trust. Get your opinion valued. Flattery works well for this purpose.

"I think your Aunt Tatum's interesting because I think she's secretly happy. I think it's interesting that she keeps it secret."

Rachael seemed to take this in as she continued to dance. She took a liberty with Geneva's moves and added a spin, smiling when she came back around.

"I don't think so," she said.

"I know it doesn't seem so," Geneva said, "that's why I say 'secretly.'"

"She tried to kill herself."

Geneva's head jerked back slightly. She stopped dancing. Rachael didn't.

"What are you talking about?"

"In a motel room."

Geneva thought it best to keep moving, to keep the conversation moving as well. She rolled her shoulders.

"What makes you say that?"

"She told me."

"Who told you?"

"Aunt Tatum."

What was she thinking?

"What did she tell you?"

"That she was in a motel and took a bunch of pills."

Jesus Christ.

Geneva wasn't sure what to say.

"I think it was because of Vincent," Rachael said, very sophisticated.

"I don't know what to say," Geneva said, trying to conceal her shock. "I'll have to ask her about it. I'm betting it was a mistake. A bad judgment call." It was not that it had happened, of course, that was the shock. It was that she had told an eight-year-old with a dead mother. Geneva shook her head. "Dang," she said.

"Midnight Train to Georgia" ended. "I've Got to Use My Imagination" was starting, all beat and brass. It was a song they had danced to before.

"Told you," Rachael said as she bobbed her head from side to side. Then, she exaggerated it, bobbing like an idiot.

Geneva recognized it for what it was. A victory dance. But victory, in the long run, is better for the spirit than defeat. Self-righteousness, despite its accompanying problems, trumps despair when it comes to psychic survival. So, Geneva thought, it was not to be discouraged. She danced along.

"Will you play that fish in the sea song next?" Rachael asked.

Geneva loved a request. It forgave a million sins. She held up a finger and walked over to her albums. She let Gladys continue to sing while she hunted for "Too Many Fish in the Sea" by the Marvelettes. It was on a compilation album, so she dropped to a knee to look past the Z's where she kept compilations and opera.

Behind Geneva, Rachael shifted back and forth from the waist. She tried turning her wrists above her head in the way she had seen Geneva do it. It had looked exotic and ethereal but too difficult to try while being watched. Doing the move made her think of her birthday gift, the maracas. She decided to try to surprise Geneva by getting them.

She crept quietly to the door, any sounds of her movements concealed by the music. She cracked the door, keeping an eye on Geneva. She moved to sneak into the hall and stepped right into a man's legs.

He wore blue jeans and just a jean jacket over his white shirt even though it was winter. His hair was jet black. She knew him from the pictures.

"Hey," he said, clearly surprised to see her, "is Geneva home?"

Rachael slipped past him and across the hall. She reached Tatum's front door and looked back over her shoulder. It was Vincent.

24

~

Paris showered off the grease and sweat of the night. He washed his feet and tried to scrub the cling of his encounter in the janitor's closet from his body. Tatum had asked him to come over after work. He was at her door by 8 a.m.

Her appearance surprised him. He expected sweats, rumpled hair. Tatum in the morning. But she was dressed, groomed even, in tighter jeans than she usually wore and a blue corduroy shirt. She looked nervous and lovely. The energy around her brimmed with a quality that flooded Paris with hope. But, in the split second it took after opening the door, it seemed that Tatum had assessed him too. She cocked her head and squinted. Sex clings to a person. Shower or no. Paris could tell that she sensed something but couldn't put her finger on it.

Inside, Paris walked two steps behind her into the living room. Then, she turned suddenly.

"I had all this stuff to say," she said. She looked puzzled. "But it all seems stupid now. I had some weird idea."

"Tell me your weird idea," he said, not wanting what it was to slip away.

Tatum bit her lower lip. She shook her head.

"Please," he said.

"All right," she said. "Here goes." Her voice sounded uncertain, as though at any moment she might change her mind. "I was talking to Geneva last night, after everyone left." She paused. "I was thinking..." She sighed and looked at the floor. "Look, this may all seem dumb, but I'm sorry. I'm sorry about last summer when you kissed me — when we kissed each other — in the park. Look, I was afraid. I...I ruin things like that. I don't why, but it's so. But I want you to know, I...I... You're..."

She shook her head again.

"It was a good kiss," Paris said.

Tatum closed her eyes.

"It was a good kiss," she said.

Her eyes remained closed. She was wrapped inside of herself. But Paris could feel what she was saying. He stepped toward her and placed his hands on her arms. Her eyes opened, green pools. He was welcomed in. Paris pushed down all that had come before, held its head beneath the surface. The pictures. Linda. Vincent. Everything. He kissed Tatum. He pressed his lips to hers as he pressed on the past, kissing Tatum until history stopped kicking and floated to the bottom.

Their lips came apart. Tatum released a heavy breath. She looked at the floor.

"This is a big can of worms," she said. "You need to know." She looked back up and into his eyes. "I'm cursed. I have to stay under the radar of God to get away with a thing like this."

"A thing like what?"

"Something that feels like this. Good."

"I'll help you," Paris said.

Tatum shook her head. She half-laughed.

"Thanks, but I'm beyond help."

"I mean, I'll help you stay under the radar of God. I'm good at that."

Tatum bowed her head.

"You're killing me, Paris."

He moved in to kiss her again. He placed his hands gently on the sides of her face. He could feel her wanting him, fighting her own resistance. First, a touch of the lips, and then tongues just barely flashing past each other. Then they parted just inches. Tatum ran a hand down his coat sleeve then took his hand in hers, intertwining their fingers.

Paris pushed back her hair.

"You have no idea," she said, not looking at him, "how it can come to be with me. It's not pretty."

"Stop," Paris said. "You want to confess sins right now. Issue warnings. Fine. I'll start. Here's what you should know."

Tatum looked up and took a deep breath, ready for anything, revelations of the deepest failings.

"My feet," he said.

She half-laughed and then drew in her brows.

"Your feet?"

Paris took her hands.

"It's not like a birthmark, or a scar," he said. "People can find beauty in ugly things. Smell isn't like that."

"What are you talking about?"

"Stink foot."

"Stink foot?" She laughed.

"Don't laugh. I wish it was funny, but it's not. It started during adolescence, the way stinks do. It was a handicap. I couldn't even jerk off successfully. That's how serious this is. I'd be imagining some girl," he said, "imagining her in a park or the back seat of a car. We'd be going at it as could only happen in my dreams, and, and I'd lose focus. I'd start wondering, how'd I get my pants off without taking off my shoes? How could I be having sex if I *did* take off my shoes? I lost many an erection to logistics."

"It's that bad?"

Paris only stared to convey the severity of the stink.

"Part of me wants to tell you to let me smell for myself," she said jokingly, "but part of me believes you and is scared."

"My mother had sour feet," Paris said.

"So, it's genetic."

"She used to get them scraped."

"Can't scrape off the stink, huh?"

He shook his head no, then looked at her sheepishly.

"How much can a man with stinky feet expect from this life?"

Tatum looked about to cry. Happy tears. An intolerable happiness. She squeezed her eyes closed. Paris moved in to kiss her again. Mouths opened. Limbs weakened. Taste and smell and touch transported them back in time to a place free from context and identity, a time of unfiltered pleasure.

They pulled away from each other for the thrill of anticipating coming back together again. Tatum looked rapturous. Vulnerable. Then Paris noticed something inside of her retreat.

"No," he said.

She stepped backward.

"I have to tell you something."

Paris panicked inwardly. The image of Vincent leaving the Deluxe bubbled up, not drowned, after all.

Tatum's forehead wrinkled with a thought.

"Something to show you, anyway," she said.

Then she reached toward the top button of her blue corduroy shirt. Her fingers paused there, a protective gesture. Then she unbuttoned the top button and continued down.

Paris's breath shortened. His eyes followed her fingers.

"I see your stink foot," she said, unclasping the front of the bra beneath. "And I raise you this."

Tatum opened one side of the blouse and bra to reveal the red and puckered seam.

Though Paris hadn't expected it, he was not surprised. His eyes fell on her rib cage and traced the length of the scar. He saw what was there, not what wasn't. He knew why she had the pictures taken, regardless of who had taken them.

He felt Tatum's eyes on his own, trying to calculate his reaction.

"Talk about a damper on fantasies, huh?" she said.

"You're beautiful," Paris choked out, and he looked away.

It's a stupid world, he thought. Men made it stupid for women. They made a world where she couldn't see that he felt like he needed to rip out of his own skin to be close enough to her. Her broken fingernails. Her fine wrinkles and moist eyes. Her scar. There was nothing missing, nothing not enough or nothing too much, just everything that she was.

Tatum pulled her shirt around her.

"Paris?" she said.

He looked up. His eyes were brimmed with tears.

"It's bad, huh?" she said.

Paris reached for her, and she reached forward too, their fingers intertwining, catching one another. They stood and pressed into each other. Paris didn't want her to think he was crying for her, feeling sorry for her, but he didn't know what to say.

Hands locked, he stretched both their arms out to the sides and up over their heads.

"You're beautiful," he said again. There was an ache in his voice, the truth coming out painfully like it was something dislodged from inside.

"Paris," Tatum said. She pushed him back, let go his hands, and shook him by the shoulders. "Heed me. You're going to find out. The thing will happen. You'll need to shut me out in order to endure me. I don't know what you think I've got, but it isn't there. You will fool me too, because I want to believe. I'll want to believe what you see in me is real. But you'll find out that it's not. Then I'll see that it's not. That's my worst secret. The best of me is an illusion. I've got nothing."

"'Sometimes nothing is a real cool hand,'" Paris said.

Tatum buried her forehead in his shoulder. He pushed her away and placed his palm on her throat. He let it drift down between the undone buttons of the blouse and bra, savoring each inch of skin.

"I feel like I'm jumping down a rabbit hole." She laughed nervously.

Paris's eyes lingered on her collarbones, then he met her eyes.

"We are," he said.

Paris pushed the shirt and bra slightly off her shoulders just as the front door opened.

Rachael saw it. Despite Paris's tight proximity, despite that Tatum had closed her shirt fast and turned her back to the door. Rachael saw the carved out place on Tatum's chest. She saw the damage.

Still hurriedly buttoning up, Tatum turned to face Rachael. Rachael backed out through the door. She stood in the hall for a moment before Geneva's door flew open.

"Rachael," Geneva said, relieved.

Rachael hurried past her. She elbowed past the man she knew was Vincent and ran down the hall and slammed herself in Geneva's bathroom. She latched the door with the metal hook.

Inside the bathroom, Rachael stared in the mirror. The girl looking back was the one who had been there the day her mother died, invoked into being, brought in by ghosts and secret damage. Rachael knew about both. She knew about bathrooms too. Things happened in them. Ghosts frequented them. She looked away from the mirror to the door she herself had latched. Illogically, she felt locked in. Trapped. She looked back to the mirror.

"I hate you," she said, and she slapped at the reflection with her palm.

"Rachael," Tatum said, from outside the door.

Rachael knew it was just her own reflection she looked at, but at the same time, it was someone else. The girl she once was was vanishing. She watched her lower lip quiver. Why did she have to be there? Why did she have to be the girl in the mirror? Why couldn't she be someone that things didn't happen to?

She backed away from the mirror and looked around the room as though for an escape. She pushed away the heavy curtain at the window that looked to the side of the house. The snow outside was ugly.

Melted and refrozen. Messed by footprints. Paris's. Tatum's. Geneva's. Her own. Rachael tried to remember the unblemished humps of whiteness she once viewed outside her own living room. She tried to force the mirage.

But she could not see it.

"No," she said, and she slapped at the image outside the window. The duplex was old, as was the pane of glass. Triangles of frost grew in its corners. "Go away," she said, and she slapped it again, harder and with both hands, a firm blow, and the window cracked with a fast, sharp *tissshh*. Small chunks of glass beneath the base of her hand separated from the rest.

Outside the bathroom, Paris watched from Geneva's front door as Vincent pushed Tatum aside, grabbed the knob, and turned it hard while hitting the door with his shoulder. The lock snapped easily as wood fibers popped and splintered. Geneva was first in.

Vincent backed away from the bathroom.

Rachael stood beside the window with tiny shards of glass at her feet. She looked frightened and surprised.

"Gimme," Geneva said, reaching for her hand.

Rachael stood frozen. Tatum looked from over Geneva's shoulder. The cold air from the outside leaked in.

Geneva and Tatum examined Rachael's hand and arm. It didn't seem too bad. No great shard had cut her wrist, just small pin pricks of blood and some glistening sharp slivers on the base of her hand.

"We need tweezers," Geneva said, opening the medicine cabinet.

"C'mon," Tatum said, lifting Rachael up over any broken glass and then leading her into the living room.

Vincent had joined Paris at the door. Paris could see that Vincent didn't recognize him.

"Hey," Vincent said to him.

"Hey."

Tatum made eye contact with neither Paris nor Vincent. Her focus was on Rachael, out of necessity.

I should have told her he was here, Paris thought, watching, wondering if she still would have kissed him.

Tatum put Rachael onto a stool at the counter.

"You okay?" Paris asked Rachael.

Paris wished in that moment that he were a useful man, one who could make a pane of glass appear from a basement and head to the bathroom and provide concrete and silent assistance. He wanted to say something, do something, to assert himself in the clan. Vincent had done his part. Now, it was his turn.

But what?

Geneva appeared, armed with alcohol and tweezers. She traced a gentle finger over Rachael's hand, seeking out sharp edges. She plucked, and Rachael winced.

"Ouch," Paris said.

"I'll catch up later," Vincent said to Geneva.

"Do," Geneva said.

"I'll call you," he said to Tatum. "And you be careful," he said to Rachael.

Paris got a nod.

Then Vincent was gone. The hole he left behind made Paris recognize how much space he had taken up.

"We're pretty accommodating of crazy around here," Geneva said to Rachael, "but this is not okay."

Rachael looked over Geneva's shoulder at Paris.

"That was Vincent," she said to him.

"I know."

Tatum looked at Paris. He shrugged.

"Well," Geneva said, "a few little cuts. You must have your mother's luck."

It had just come out, a blurted inside joke directed at Tatum, a sarcastic snipe at her bungled suicide attempt. But Geneva realized her mistake immediately.

"Your aunt's luck," she said, experiencing a suicidal impulse of her own.

No one liked the silence in the room.

"Weebles wobble but they don't fall down," Tatum said to fill the air.

Geneva tweezed a shard and dropped it onto the counter.

"I thought we were going to do some dancing," she said to Rachael, trying to get things back on track. "What the heck happened?"

"Rachael saw my scar," Tatum said. "Did it freak you out?" she said to Rachael.

"No."

"Is it why you hit the window?"

Tatum and Geneva clustered tight around Rachael. Geneva raised Rachael's chin so they could search for an answer in her eyes.

Rachael could tell that they weren't angry about the window. They didn't want a good explanation for her behavior. They wanted her reason. They didn't want to know why on earth anyone would put their hand through a window, but why would *she*.

What could she tell them? That there was no floating in ancient seas? There were backs and fronts and forwards and backwards? That her aunt had missing pieces and the snow was messy and the girl in the mirror watched? The music still played in Geneva's apartment, and it worked in Rachael, vibrating, dislodging the icebound. A wall she had built within herself thinned to a membrane, and something large passed through it. A deep swallow in reverse. Secrets, escaping.

"I want to go home," she said, and the tears flowed.

"She wants to go home," Tatum said to Paris in the hall between apartments.

"Is that even a possibility?"

"I don't know. It seems like the kind of thing you shouldn't have to ask for." Tatum shook her head. "What did we do?"

"What do you mean?"

"I mean," she kept her voice hushed, "we start making out and windows break and the past crawls out of the gutter."

Paris felt the fear washing over her. It was contagious.

"I should get back in," she said.

Just then, the front door to the duplex opened, and a UPS man slid a box along the floor to Tatum's door. She glanced over at the return address. Lee.

"Speak of the devil," she said. "I guess the birthday gift has arrived. You don't think these are signs, do you?"

"Only if they're good ones," Paris said.

Tatum turned to go into Geneva's.

"Boy, I think we'd be hard pressed to read 'em as good."

Paris grabbed her arm.

"Then we don't need no stinkin' signs." He said it with a Mexican accent.

He pulled her to him. He kissed her briefly, but deeply, a kiss meant to reinforce, to drive away past lies and past mistakes, and to protect them from omens.

Paris walked home, head down into a strong midmorning wind. Above, cloud banks came together, traveling en masse, migrating southeast, eating the blue sky like locusts. Wind chimes rang like warnings, unwittingly attracting the attention of spirits. Paris crammed his hands into his pockets. His boots hit the pavement, one step after the other. A cat with a tattered ear peered out from behind a car tire. Its meow had a question mark as he passed by. The trees reached for the wind while Paris wrestled with his thoughts. Omens he could handle. Karma would handle him.

Not twelve hours ago, Vincent sat at his counter, and Linda kneeled in his kitchen's janitor's closet. The Deluxe was closing. He told Tatum secrets but did not confess the truths he owed her. Vincent. The pictures. Paris worried that their kiss this morning could go the way of their kiss in the park. His steps sped up to keep pace with his anxiety, and he failed to greet the half-melted snowman with a magpie standing on its sunken, buttoned chest. His whole way home, he ignored the crushed cups. A lost mitten tried to flag him down, dirty, palm open to the sky.

But he was blind to them.

"Fucking Vincent." He said it out loud. Vincent was going to call her. That's what he had said. What did he want? Why was he here?

Paris took the stairs down to his apartment. As he entered, he picked up the envelope on the floor he had stepped over earlier. He sat at his table and opened it at the side. The message was official, typed, and brief.

He was being evicted.

He placed the letter on the table. He sat elbows to knees, hands folded, head hung.

Don't take it personally. That's karma's message. It's physics. Nothing more.

He closed his eyes. He breathed deeply, seeking traces of Tatum's scent, a scent you could chase but never quite catch, left behind on his clothing. He held her scar in his heart. His hands burned with envy.

Vincent had never seen it. This, Paris somehow knew. The scar was the dividing line between the two of them, and Paris loved it for that fact. He conjured the image of Tatum's torso, the asymmetry, and press of her ribs from beneath her skin. His eyes opened slowly and were drawn by the black gap beneath the closet door. Inside were his paints. His charcoals. His canvas.

He felt a blaze in his chest. He didn't move from his chair. The stillness around him shimmered, and he thought that, perhaps, want was merely hope, made to feel unworthy.

25

Tatum led Rachael back to their own apartment, blocking with her body the view of the UPS box in the hall. She decided to keep quiet that it was from Lee until she was certain there was a gift in there and that it wasn't just a shipment of odds and ends that would make it look like he was clearing a space for a home gym.

Inside, Rachael stood in the middle of the living room, looking lost.

"Do you want to talk about it?" Tatum said.

Rachael blinked as though not registering the question.

"Vincent?" she said.

Tatum did not mean Vincent. She meant the scar, the missing breast.

"Vincent came to see Geneva," Tatum said. A fact she, herself, had registered.

"He said he was going to call you."

Tatum was about to say, *I don't want him to call*, but it caught on the inside of her lips. It was a new thought. A new idea. Was it true?

She approached Rachael and sat down on the coffee table, the trunk, to be eye level with her.

"You know," Tatum said, "I do want him to call. But you know why?"

"Why?"

"Because I want to tell him not to call again."

Tatum wasn't sure what she said was true, but it felt good to say it.

Rachael looked up at her. Her eyes were intelligent. She understood Tatum's meaning. There's power in rejecting the one who rejects you.

"Rachael," Tatum said, unsure of what she would say next. "I'm so sorry for everything that's happened to you. I know you don't want to be here. But you know, I'm happy you are. At first, I thought I could help you learn how to be sad and have it be okay. But I can't now. Because now that you're here, I don't feel sad, myself, anymore."

Rachael looked at the ground.

"It feels so good to have you in my life," Tatum said, "that it makes me think I want Paris in my life more too." Tatum swallowed. "Did you see Paris and me kissing each other?"

"Yes."

"Does that bother you?"

"No," she said but didn't sound certain.

"Should we talk about the scar?" Tatum said.

Rachael said nothing.

"Want to see it? It's scarier, I think, if you see it and look away fast than it is if you look closely."

"Okay."

Tatum unbuttoned her shirt, keeping it closed. When it was undone, she looked Rachael solidly in the eye.

"Ready?" she said.

Rachael nodded.

Tatum opened one side of her blouse and bra, revealing the gash. She looked down at it. She ran her finger along the tight seam.

"Here's where they sewed me back up after cutting away the bad stuff." She avoided the word *cancer*. Too scary. Too never-over. "It doesn't hurt at all. You can touch it if you want, but you don't have to."

Rachael came forward. She reached up and touched the skin, puckered like pressed, old lady lips.

"The scar is worse than it could've been, but I didn't do all the stuff that would help it go away."

Rachael pulled her hand away but continued to look.

"Why not?"

"I think I wanted it. This may sound weird, but I think I like it, even though I know other people might find it ugly."

Tatum thought enough was probably enough, and she rebuttoned her shirt.

"What do you think?" she said.

"So you're better now?"

"Gold, baby. Good as gold."

"I have to go to the bathroom," Rachael said.

"Be nice to the windows."

Tatum followed Rachael as far as the kitchen. Rachael continued down the hall, and Tatum quickly slipped into the hall to retrieve the box. She brought it to the kitchen counter and pulled a knife from the block with an ear out for Rachael. She slit the tape down the center of the top of the package. Let there be a present, she thought, opening the flaps. From down the hall, she could hear the sound of Rachael peeing. She had left the bathroom door open, something she hadn't done before. Tatum figured she didn't want to be alone. She smiled, touched. Strange, the things that make you feel needed. She pushed aside a brown piece of packing paper to an expertly wrapped gift. Phew. She lifted it out and placed it on the counter. It was as appetizing as a cake. She reached into the box for the second item and pulled out a green, leather-bound book.

It took a second for it to register. Tatum hadn't seen it in years, a decade at least. The volume was thinner than she remembered. Somehow, she had exaggerated its size in her mind to match the distain in which she held it. The Book of Rachaels. She hated the thing. She didn't know what it might mean to Rachael, or whether it would remind her of her mother, for better or for worse. Tatum tossed it onto the counter like it burned in her hands.

"Ugh," she hollered. "Goddamn it."

Rachael had flushed the toilet and now stood before the mirror. She pushed the bathroom door slightly more closed but not completely. She hiked up her T-shirt and looked at her own chest, flat like Tatum's, but without the lightning strike on the right. She had been imagining a scar there, just as she might imagine a Halloween costume, when she heard her aunt holler. She pulled down her shirt and spun away from the mirror as though caught at something she shouldn't be doing. She stood frozen in the bathroom, afraid.

"I'm okay," Tatum hollered down the hall. "Sorry. Uh, spider," she said.

Rachael crept into the kitchen.

"It crawled out of the box. Spiders, ew," Tatum said. "Hey, look what your dad sent." She put a hand on top of the gift.

Rachael moved toward it tentatively. She reached up and placed a hand on either side but then let her hands fall back to her sides.

"Aren't you going to open it?"

Rachael reached toward the counter again but this time toward the green book. She slid it to the edge and took it in both hands.

"Oh, yeah," Tatum said. "That came, too."

"I'm in this," Rachael said.

"Me, too."

Rachael's head whipped around.

"No, you're not."

"'Fraid so."

"This is the book for the Rachaels."

Tatum took the book from her and flipped to the last filled page, only about a third of the way through. Rachael's entry included just a few details of her birth. Her baby picture was tucked inside four plastic corners later to be supplemented by adult shots. Tatum flipped through the blank pages that followed, those reserved for the future Rachaels, and found what she was looking for. A loose baby picture. She flipped back to the entry before Rachael's.

"Rachael T. The *T* is for Tatum. That's me." She held the picture next to the name. "No one ever told you that?"

Rachael took the book. She turned back a page or two looking at the entries. She stepped away from Tatum and turned her back to her.

Then Rachael closed the book and slipped it back onto the counter. She touched the colored wrapping of her gift. She turned to face her aunt.

"My middle name is Mallory," she said.

May

≈

26

The weight of the sky grew. The sun climbed behind the gray wall of it. Midmorning, it spit out a rock. Then another, and another. The hail spilled onto the earth, rattling, pounding the sidewalk and nicking at the windows as it battered its way through the neighborhood. Paint jobs suffered flesh wounds. The tulips broke under heavy fire. From behind windows, nervous homeowners with bad roofs peeked. They crossed their fingers and exchanged hopeful looks. Maybe this would be it, the storm mighty enough to merit an insurance claim. With luck, there'd be money left over for lawn furniture.

Paris and Tatum, Geneva, and Ron watched the sudden downpour from inside Geneva's apartment. The hail bounced off the hood of Tatum's car and off of Paris's mattress, which was strapped to the roof of the car under a tarp. The winter had been mild; the spring, cold and erratic. A deep freeze had hit at the end of March. Flurries had emerged from sunlit April mists. And now, May first brought a hailstorm, straight from the apocalypse.

Geneva played no music, but the hail made for a constant *click, click,* with the occasional burst that rattled like spilled marbles. Paris looked out the window from over Geneva's shoulder. Tatum stood just to his side, slightly behind him. Tatum and Paris had slept together four times. Socially, they still behaved as friends. But anyone within twenty paces could feel the tug and pull between them. Paris's joy was deep as he stood there. In that moment, four people silent in a room listening to a hailstorm seemed all he'd ever wanted.

"I tasted hail, once," Ron said, and three heads turned to him. "Bitter. Sooty."

It seemed the sign the sky had been waiting for. Magic words, stumbled upon, accidentally. The hail ceased. Just a few more nuggets fell, randomly, as they dislodged themselves from clouds.

"I can see how ancient people would think a storm was an angry spirit passing through," Tatum said.

"Maybe not even angry," Geneva said, "just mighty and reckless."

Twigs and leaves, casualties, littered the sidewalks. The four picked up where they had left off when the hail had chased them from their work. Geneva swept the rocks of ice from the walk while Paris and Ron negotiated the mattress off the roof of the car. Tatum pulled a box, the only box, of Paris's clothing from the back seat. Rachael was in school today, but yesterday, she had helped with the moving of most of Paris's things into the basement of the duplex. The diner hadn't closed yet, but Paris had been evicted from his downtown apartment. He needed just a month or two to save up enough for a first and last months' rent and damage deposit. So he moved out of one basement and into another. Both had daylight windows. But this one also had a space heater and upstairs privileges at Tatum's.

Paris and Ron maneuvered the mattress up the walk. Tatum held the front door. It had been her intention to help Paris carry it, but Ron had waved her off. He walked backward now, watching the ground over his shoulder. He shifted his way through the open door. Paris's eyes met Tatum's as he passed. Each smiled and looked away.

But they hadn't been falling effortlessly into love. In fact, Paris never fell at all. It was where he had started, and so he continued to float there while Tatum treaded love's waters, struggling to keep her head above the surface, slapping and kicking with arms and legs.

In Paris's old apartment, after the first time they had sex, Paris had asked her, "Would you freak if I said I loved you?"

Tatum dragged his thin sheet up over her head.

"Would you believe it?" he asked.

"La-la-la-la-la," Tatum said, loudly.

Paris tugged the sheet off her face.

"You don't believe me?"

She rolled her head in his direction. "I believe you," she said. "But I know the me you love may not be the me I am." She sat up, pulling the sheet to her neck. "Someday, you might be disappointed that I'm not all you thought. You'll be the one who was wrong, but I'll be the one you're disappointed with."

"That's not true," Paris said. "I'll always . . ."

Tatum held up a hand to interrupt him.

"Don't 'always' or 'never' me, Paris," she said. "People lie without meaning to. You don't want it happening to you."

Then Tatum turned and placed her feet on the floor. She dressed, quietly. Paris pulled on his jeans but remained barefoot. He wondered for how long she would be gone.

Over the next several days, Paris called her once per day. When her machine beeped, he would sit silent at the other end of the line, enough time for the heart to speak and no more. He would hang up as though parting company with her. He let go reluctantly.

It took six days to receive her breathless call.

"Paris? Can 1 . . . " she said.

"Come over."

It had been less awkward. More abandon. Afterward, Tatum lay on her stomach with her head on her forearm.

"I'm a danger to myself and others," she said.

"Who isn't?" Paris said, rolling over and kissing from the base of her spine to the base of her skull.

When she left that time, he didn't hear from her for four days. Paris imagined her sitting in her orange chair, one hand nervously toying with the nearby leaf of the ficus. She would chew on her bottom lip. Her mind would be up the road, calculating risks and outcomes. She would rise from her chair and watch the sun set, as she liked to do. It would feel to her like defeat when she showed up unannounced at his front door at the bottom of the concrete stairs. Paris led her in and took her to his mattress. He kissed her and then disappeared into the bathroom. He turned on the tub, washed his feet with cool water, and then returned to the bed, feet pink and clean.

They made love. Quietly and slowly. Afterward, Paris hovered above her, leaning on his elbows. His hair hung forward.

"I can't help it," he said. "I do love you."

Tatum squished her eyes closed then rolled out from under him and sat on the edge of the mattress. Paris picked up his glasses from the floor and sat up too.

"You're going to disappear again," he said.

"Don't love me, please," she said, reaching for her pants. "I won't be able to take it when you don't some day."

"I don't think I can not love you as a favor," Paris said. "If you don't want it, that's different, and I accept it."

"No," she said, snapping up her shirt from the floor as she stood. "I do want it. I just can't afford it."

"You don't love me."

"Stop it," she said, throwing her shirt at him. "That's not fair. If anyone's..."

She stopped and buried her face in her hands. Paris gathered up her shirt as a ransom.

"If anyone's what?" he said.

Tatum sat back down.

"I can't believe what almost came out of my mouth," she said. She turned and looked at Paris. "I almost said, 'If anyone's not loved, it's me.'"

"Turf, huh?" Paris said, sitting beside her. He ran a hand down her bony spine.

Tatum flopped backward on the mattress.

"I am so fucked up," she said.

Paris bent over her and kissed her forehead. They made love for the fourth time.

Geneva waited in the basement with a stack of blankets and a set of flannel sheets piled in her arms as Paris and Ron maneuvered the mattress down the stairs. They tipped it onto the rug Geneva had unrolled to carve a room out from the larger space.

"I have sheets," Paris said, seeing Geneva standing there.

"These will be better," she said.

"Done with me?" Ron asked.

"Thanks, man," Paris said.

They shook hands, and Ron headed up.

Geneva put the blankets to the side and tossed the pillowcases to Tatum, who had followed them down. Tatum worked Paris's skinny pillows into them.

"Your sheets have completed their service," Geneva said. "Let them retire. These," she said, shaking the sheet out over the mattress, "need a life. Purpose and meaning. They've been sequestered too long in a cedar chest."

She tucked in the edges while Tatum and Paris passed energy back and forth above her, a silent conversation in which she was not included.

They would make love for the fifth time shortly.

Paris and Tatum's newfound passion was hard on Geneva. She was happy for them, but the energy between the two of them was so taut that it made her realize her separateness from it. She left them, climbing the stairs and returning to her apartment. She was heading for Parkview Home later in the day. Ralph had been put on breathing and feeding tubes, and Geneva couldn't help but wonder if his decline was due in part to her absence. So, she had accepted the sentence: monitored visits. Ralph rebounded enough to get off the machines, but the Home had asked Geneva to sign a Do Not Resuscitate order, a DNR. Signing it, of course, was the right thing to do. But what she wanted to do was storm into Mr. Hans Mood's office and declare with great indignation, *You think signing a DNR for my husband would be advisable? Hear me well: I'll sue if every effort is not made to ensure his well-being. I'll get the Right to Life involved. If he's got one cell left quivering, damn it, you help it quiver.*

Such had been her petty dreams of vengeance. Instead, she had signed and been surprised by the onset of anxiety that accompanied the very real possibility that Ralph's days were numbered.

She would leave for Parkview in the afternoon. Right now, she just wanted a bath. She went to her bedroom and kicked off her shoes in front of the dresser. She pulled off her earrings and flipped open her jewelry box. On top sat the old, blue, folded piece of legal pad paper. She lifted it between a finger and her thumb. It was the note she had received from John inviting her to dinner. Unanswered, it had taken up residency in her jewelry box. She knew it belonged in a garbage can, cast into the realm of "what if?" Wistfulness, she could allow herself, but not the suspense of indecision. Her lack of response *was* the decision, she thought, lying to herself. The note was just a souvenir.

Geneva did not see herself as having chosen a man, Ralph over John, per se, but instead as having chosen a path. It was a path she chose long ago. Committed love. Seeing a thing through to the end in order to know what one can only know by taking the whole road. There was knowledge at the end of it. There had to be. So she would not indulge thoughts of sacrifice or martyrdom. She would not make Ralph a burden. People aren't high maintenance. Love is.

She refolded the note and returned it to the box. She picked up the envelope beside it and checked the contents. Inside were three joints that Vincent had brought her on his last pass through town. Several hours after Rachael put her hand through the window, Vincent had called, and Geneva met him for burgers and shakes at a greasy spoon. They had caught up quickly. Geneva noticed he didn't ask the identity of Paris, despite that Tatum's blouse hadn't been buttoned quite right. Vincent shared his successes — an article had been picked up by the *Utne Reader*. He shared his troubles — fines, harassment. He told her of his plans. He and a friend were starting a business making simple, plain, pine coffins and marketing them to yuppies. He was studying composting human remains, though he knew the country, neither Indian country nor the U.S. of A., wasn't quite ready for the idea.

Vincent was an interesting man. Geneva enjoyed his good looks and charm. No woman could compete with him when it came to holding his own interest. Geneva identified and thus couldn't condemn him for arrogance. He was a good kid. A good man. He had called his mother's old friend and made sure she had a small stash of weed. He had taken her out for lunch. He had risked running into an old girlfriend to do it.

Geneva removed one of the joints from the envelope. She frowned at it but took it with her into the bathroom. She sat down on the closed lid of the toilet. Through the heating vent, she heard sporadic sighs and throaty gulps of air. She struck a match and was about to light up when she had second thoughts. Did she need her mind any more open than it already was? Few understand the open mind. It's not all "yeah, whatever, that's cool" because it accommodates all the opposing arguments and the judgmental voices too. The open mind is not laid back and groovy. It stretches and stretches, works to accommodate more and more. Geneva figured her mind had stretch marks, and she really wasn't in a mood to reconsider hard-won choices or see anything from a new perspective. She didn't even want to acknowledge her choices as choices. They were decisions. Done deals. If God were truly benevolent, she thought, returning to her bedroom and placing the joint back in the envelope, he would have given Adam and Eve *freedom*, and not free will. Free will was the call to choose, but not to create.

Choices. She was fed up with them. Yes or no. This or that. Duality, it was such a bore. Free will says, sure, eat the apple, but do and you'll pay. That didn't sound so "free" to her. Free*dom*, on the other hand, says eat the apple if you must. It will lead to something different than not eating the apple, but see what you get and go forth from there. Free will had a distinct undercurrent of right and wrong, reward and punishment, that freedom was, well, free of.

She slipped out of her clothes and into her robe. Returning to the bathroom, she pushed back the shower curtain. Through the heating vent came the sound of muffled laughter. It made her think of John. She would've asked God for a sign — *should I call?* — if she hadn't just questioned his almighty judgment.

Stop looking for answers, she told herself, turning on the water in the tub, drowning out the laughter. As the tub filled, she thought about the sayings, axioms, and pithy quotes pasted on her refrigerator and written on fragments of envelopes and napkins, tossed into drawers and kept for unknown reasons. She had more answers than questions. No wonder she wrote an advice column. The imbalance between the two, she thought, just went to demonstrate that there weren't any answers, or rather, there were dozens, hundreds, millions. They just didn't necessarily match up with any particular questions.

She slipped out of her robe and into the tub, settling into the warm water. What could it mean, she wondered, that she was a person who had accumulated more answers than questions?

But she decided not to answer. It would only contribute to the problem.

27

～

Tatum's hips balanced at the edge of the mattress. Paris knelt on the floor between her legs and kissed with a warm and open mouth. His tongue lashed out. It dragged, slick and gritty. His hand slid up Tatum's stomach to her breast, up the curve of it until he pressed her nipple between his thumb and the knuckle of his index finger. She caught her breath. Her pelvis softly tilted, then tipped. Paris's other hand stretched across the flat side of her chest, fingers curling inward, slowly, as though he could fold her scar into his palm.

Tatum was present as a drip on a faucet. The tension stretched her. Orgasm, when it came, was not coming down. It was a pumping, a diffusing, a spreading out like waves, creating space as it pushed outward. It served only to raise the stakes. She wanted more.

Paris leaned back on his heels and wiped his chin on his shoulder. Still fully clothed, he stood and headed up the basement stairs. Tatum turned to her side and pressed her legs together to still the hum. The bathtub turned on above.

Dragging the sheet across her body, Tatum slid up the mattress and propped herself on an elbow. Faint light from the window wells cast a green hue across the well-swept concrete floor and the walls with boxes two and three deep. Few of the boxes were hers, yet she zeroed in on her modest stack. Just a couple of months back, she had puttered among them, nervous and anxious, as though she were stashing a body. But it wasn't a body. It was a book. The Book of Rachaels. At the time of the stashing, there had been no plan for Paris to be moving in. The basement was still the domain of the past. A desert for personal items. Exile.

Tatum's eyes settled on the green leather spine just visible over the box's edge. The past loves crashing the present's party.

"So, we meet again," Tatum said, and then she rolled onto her back.

Upstairs, the water shut off.

Tatum heard Paris before she saw him, and she sat up. He hit the bottom of the steps and came to the end of the mattress. His feet were bare. Tatum felt tempted to kiss one, the top of it at least. Kiss the monster. He pulled his shirt over his head, and it caught on his glasses, tangling for a second. Tatum pushed away the sheet and came to the edge of the bed on her knees. She kissed at Paris's softly muscled chest and placed a hand on the pale circle of hair surrounding his navel. Paris pushed her backward and came down, one knee at a time, between her legs.

Tatum wrapped her legs around his hips. He pressed her arms over her head and held her wrists with one hand as he braced his body with the other. Torso grazed torso. And then it was all heat and steel and velvet.

They had stolen the moment, like new lovers do. A pocket of time that is what it is. Not part of the great march toward something else, not one of seven plates to keep spinning. Stealing moments draws the attention of grace, serves as a lure, and so she too was tangled in the arms and legs and entwined fingers. They lingered on the mattress, the three of them, insulting the self-importance of time.

When duty did call at last, they dressed in a satisfied silence. Outside, Tatum sat on the stoop, watching Paris behind the wheel of her car acquainting himself with the controls. She felt turned inside out, cool air reaching long closed-up places. The iron-gray sky above was splitting open to reveal ragged, blue portals, and the trees seemed to sigh as though washed clean. They had taken a beating from the hail, but it was somehow all good, the ordeal having left them ravaged and refreshed.

"Wow," Tatum said, wrapping herself in her own arms. Sex between her and Vincent had become so tragic in the end that she had forgotten this post-coital purged feeling. Vincent had always gotten her off, but in those last months, it seemed more something he did to assure himself of the kind of lover he was than a drive that had to do with her. She orgasmed to avoid insulting him.

Paris pulled away from the curb. Tatum watched him go, thinking about the fact that Vincent had never called like he said he would the day he had showed up at Geneva's. In fact, Tatum had begun to wonder if Vincent had ever even said it. She didn't want him back, she felt sure of that, but the possibility that he might want her was an attractive one. She had hoped to reject him, look him over like a table of trinkets, wrinkle her nose, and shake her head no.

She placed her hands on her knees and stood. "Do you have to bring a problem everywhere you go?" she remembered Vincent saying on more than one occasion.

Perhaps he had a point, she thought. After all, she had been happily humming along with big plans for a big day, and now she had gone and polluted it with thoughts of him.

She went inside determined to get herself back on track. The itch to return to the workforce had been growing, and she even felt up to giving her oncologist a call. She was ready to follow through with the mammograms and health care plans discussed years ago. She felt alive. She wanted to stay that way.

The first step was to dig up her address book. She knew where it was, dumped in a junk drawer under the kitchen counter. It was the bottom one, and she squatted down to open it. She pulled miscellaneous instructions and never-mailed warranties from the top of the mess. She knelt down to shuffle through the rubble. Duct tape. Napkin holders. Sunblock. String. She pushed around the debris until she spotted her old address book. But then reaching for it, she noticed a picture frame peeking out from beneath. She knew the frame and remembered what had been in it when she had tossed it into the drawer. The picture had been of Vincent. She pushed aside the address book and pulled out the frame. It was empty. She flipped it over. It was intact. Not broken. She looked back into the drawer. She pushed aside an opened pack of batteries, a Christmas ornament, and a trivet. She dug through the drawer, looking for Vincent.

28

The hailstorm had left a kind of afterglow in its wake. Small splotches of sky peeked through the cloud coverage, and the grass seemed to illuminate itself from within. Paris thought of Tatum's eyes as he drove, a green so different than the grass, which was both pale and bright at once. Tatum's eyes were green like a swamp, a green pulled under water to stand in muddy bottoms.

Paris drove to his old apartment and parked out front. As he came around the car, a passing woman lifted her eyes to him and smiled. She was no girl. She was a woman, with tiny laugh lines at the corner of the eye that looked out from beneath her beret. Her loose black pants billowed slightly, rustling the Chinese symbols that climbed the outside seams. He smiled back and watched her pass. Her satchel strap cut her back in half along the diagonal. She was happy. Paris could feel it because he felt it as well. Like a million bucks. Maybe two.

The woman on the street was just the latest of many. Not just women but people. People had been noticing him. The women in the diner squinted softly and stole sidelong glances. Blair did double takes. It was a foreign experience for Paris, drawing attention. But even strangers on the street found their eyes drifting in his direction, choosing him from the littered world, from the people, storefronts, and traffic, choosing him above even their own thoughts. Perhaps, he was their thoughts. The thing they'd been looking for. Not him. *It.* The *it* he now had. The *it* everybody wants.

He bounded down his steps and opened the door he had left unlocked. His apartment was nearly empty now. Other than the contents of his closet, only a dank smell and a beat-up industrial ambiance remained. Paris crossed the room, wondering what its future was. Mailroom? Storage room? He imagined it filled with rows of metal shelving, office supplies, stacked and organized. Bodies would move in and out of the space. But would anyone ever see how at night the streetlight cut through the railing above and spilled across the tiled floor? It was no different than moonlight on water. It lifted one from the press of schedule and duty and made you remember, *this is your life*, and you feel the joy, the melancholy, or the sadness that comes from the recognition. It doesn't really matter what you feel. It's just good to feel it. It's good to know.

It had been the invisibility of the apartment that had endeared it to Paris. The way it blended unobtrusively into the world, it may as well not be at all. And now, they were finished with each other. Eventually, everything becomes the past. A fact that is a comfort when your life is in the sewer. Less so, when you're walking on air. Recognizing the impermanence of things set off a cautious voice in Paris's mind. *With or without her, you will be fine*, it said. *One's happiness is not dependent on anything outside oneself.*

Paris gently kicked an empty box toward his closet, smirking at the voice. It spoke from some well-laundered world where business cards were exchanged. It spoke from black words on a white page, books concerned with love's health, bearing white-coated advice. Paris knew what the clinician did not: his life would be damaged without Tatum. Ruined, even. Simple as that. He didn't need to believe otherwise for the comfort of knowing he could go on should he lose her. More than wanting to feel safe, he wanted to feel *this*.

At his closet, he went down, one knee at a time. He reached into its deep corner and pulled out his canvas. He leaned it in the door jam and found himself wanting to stare into it. But he forced his attention to the task at hand. He pulled the empty box he had kicked over toward him. He tossed into it boots and tennis shoes. He hadn't packed them earlier because he didn't want them in the car with Tatum and Ron. Even if he had duct-taped the box closed, he hadn't been certain that the stink wouldn't seep through before they reached the duplex. Footwear packed, he opened a shoebox of bank statements and bills and other official documents. As he tossed the contents between two piles, one to keep and one to trash, the canvas kept drawing his attention. Like the dead hounds a psychic, spirits called to Paris out from grainy, white surfaces. Incoherent murmurs reached him, a thing existing, awaiting invocation. When he finished his sorting, he turned his attention to the final corner of the closet. One last box. His paints, brushes, and charcoal.

He placed the box on his lap and looked again into the canvas. The thing was still there, trying to focus itself. A tight spray of lines. This was what he saw first. The corner of an eye? The woman from the street? The tilt in his neck unconsciously adjusted as he became the thing, felt it moving up from inside of him even as it moved out from the canvas. But then, as it came into focus, Paris found himself pulling away. It wasn't the woman from the street. It was Linda.

Linda's absence had been weighing on him. She hadn't appeared in the diner, not since that night in the janitor's closet. He had pretended that night that she was Tatum, and hours later, Tatum had called him to her. Paris wondered if it was some strange magic and worked both ways. If he kissed Tatum and thought of Linda, would Tatum disappear?

Paris jerked himself backward, farther from the canvas. It was a stupid thought. He didn't even want to kiss Tatum and think of Linda, but now here it was, like someone saying no matter what you do, don't think of an elephant.

"Shut up, shut up, shut up," Paris said aloud, trying to drown the idea in inner noise.

He tossed both the box and the canvas back into the closet. He didn't want Linda in the canvas. He didn't want anybody in it. He gathered up the pile for the Dumpster and shoved it to the middle of the room. He shredded old bank statements by hand and told himself that he would be taking his art supplies to the trash too. His life was not going to be about something that wasn't happening or wasn't there. An empty stool. A door not knocked on. A blank canvas. He had plenty of something. He would not obsess about nothing.

When he finished the shredding, he gathered the debris. He turned his back, though, on the canvas and shoebox of supplies. He went to the Dumpster without them. He would not throw them away nor would he take them with him, he decided. He would leave them to their own fate.

Paris packed the last boxes into the car and paused before closing his front door for the last time. Only the aluminum kitchen table and chairs that were there when he moved in and the art supplies shoved back into the closet remained. Paris would not miss this place, he thought, because it had been good. Complete. And now they parted at their crossroad. He sighed and closed the door. He climbed the steps to the street.

Outside, the sky was gaining ground, breaking through the clouds by a force of sheer will. On the sidewalks, people walked with slightly upturned faces, and above the quaint downtown skyline, the mountains reached and stretched, snow-tipped and too old for preferences.

Paris drove slowly, under the speed limit, and took a convoluted route through downtown. His eyes scanned the sidewalks. He was looking for Linda, even though he had never seen her in daylight before. In the illogic of spells and magic he told himself that if he saw Linda, the curse he had accidentally placed on himself would be broken.

Pulling past the Deluxe, Paris slowed the car even more and looked out his window. Then, at the next intersection, he took a hard right and came back around the block. He had never gone into the Deluxe in the daytime, not since turning in his application. But he had to look. Maybe Linda's disappearance was nothing more than a change in schedule.

He parked the car and left the noon hour light behind as he slipped into the casino.

Life under a rock is self-satisfied. Left to their own affairs, the crawlies and the beetles beneath go about their business. They chop wood and carry water in the sludge and muck with satisfaction. There is no low self-esteem. No one is ugly in the land of slime. But if you lift that rock on a sunny morning, to the prying eyes, the scene is a ghoul fest, creepy and unclean. Such was the Deluxe during the day.

Paris walked through the stale beer and cigarette reek of the casino to the diner. The diner was empty except for Jerry, the Vietnam vet who worked the day shift. He stood behind Paris's counter, smoking and staring into the distance. Jerry, Paris, Blair, and a daytime bartender named Betty were all the employees left at the Deluxe. The other rats had deserted the sinking ship. These four were the most reliable of the bunch and were each offered a five-hundred-dollar bonus if they stayed on until closing.

"What's up?" Jerry asked in his gravelly voice.

Paris gave the diner the once-over.

"I lost something," he said to Jerry, and Jerry didn't ask what.

Paris stepped behind the counter and back into the kitchen. He bent over and looked beneath cabinets in order to appear authentic. Then he stepped into the janitor's closet and stood there for a moment as though feeling Linda's presence in the past might reveal where she was in the present. He saw her almond eyes looking up into his from on her knees before him. A flush of shame overcame him. But he fought back.

He had helped her. Given her what *she* needed, money, and not the silly soup he always wanted to give. It was about time.

He didn't hear Jerry come back into the kitchen.

"Any luck?" he heard him call.

"Yeah," Paris said, stepping out from the closet.

Paris slipped back out through the casino, raising a hand in greeting to Betty as he passed. He returned to Tatum's car. Everything was fine, he told himself. No Linda. Which means he found nothing. "Nothing" can't be figured out or solved. "Nothing" isn't even there.

29

As they had walked to school, Tatum pointed out to Rachael the dead leaves that managed to hang onto the trees all winter long and now into spring, blocking the new growth. Rachael knew Tatum was happy because today Paris would finish moving into the basement. Two blocks before the school, Tatum stopped, as Rachael had requested during the very first week, and Rachael proceeded alone under a sky whose pockets were loaded with rocks.

But Rachael did not proceed alone. Not really. Her aunt didn't know it, but in the side pocket of her backpack was the Vincent she had cut from a photograph she had found in a junk drawer in the kitchen. She liked holding the paper doll in her hand, and she liked to look at it. It gave her a feeling, the tingle thrill of theft.

The tingle thrill helped remake her. The first day she carried him, Rachael told another girl that her name was really Mallory. Not Rachael. Mallory is what her mother called her before she died.

This information, the dead mother, ended up serving as a field of gravity. A small group of girls were drawn to her, finding definition and purpose in including her. They found security in their juxtaposition to her, their own mothers' existences reassured in contrast. Rachael told them her father was an Indian. She showed them a picture.

And it was so that Rachael awakened from her shock with a mix of truths and lies, enough of each to support the other. Too much of either and the scales would tip, disrupting nature's developmental edicts. She learned multiplication and grammar. She made friends. The mind performs miracles. Once split against itself, it survives by finding balance.

When Rachael reached the chain-linked boundary of the school-yard, she didn't turn to wave at Tatum, though she knew she was still there. She walked through the gate knowing the watcher would change. Tatum would disappear, but other eyes would turn upon her. She was noticed. Always noticed. By teachers. By girls. By nine-year-old boys.

Even those who gave her a wide berth couldn't help but be distracted, if just for a moment, when her presence registered. It wasn't just that she was pretty, although that was certainly part of it. It was the vacuum that accompanied her and made her a larger presence. A motherless space. A fatherless space. Nature abhorred it. People wanted it filled.

Barely in the schoolyard, she was flanked by three small girls.

"Rachael," the first hollered.

"Mallory," said another to the first, asserting her greater intimacy.

They circled her and chattered their way across the playground, stopping short of the steps to the school, the turf of the reigning posse of fifth-grade girls. The younger girls stood close enough to the older ones for association, distant enough to demure. One of the fifth grade girls was the older sister to one of Rachael's friends, Claudia. They were a family of sisters, five of them, Claudia being the youngest. Claudia spoke fast and frequently. She was always slightly disheveled — messy hair, jacket askew on her shoulders — by her efforts to keep up. She brought worldly news from the future to her friends.

The information, like Rachael herself, both attracted and repelled, was seductive and dangerous. The latest news had to do with a thing called a *period*. Yesterday, Claudia had explained that when you're almost a teenager, if you're a girl, you start bleeding out your — and she made a gesture close to her body, a pointing downward toward her crotch.

But the girls didn't swallow the information whole. It wouldn't be the first time Claudia's sister and her friends had passed on misinformation to the younger girls in order to shame them later for believing it. But another of Rachael's group, who also had an older sister, had investigated on their behalf. It was true, she reported to them. Her sister told her that the fat girls would get it first.

"That's what the machines in the bathroom are about," she said.

The school bell rang, and the older girls disappeared through the doors. The younger ones held back for a moment before following.

The news of the bleeding, which seemed to be true, was something Rachael had never heard of before. But it did not shock or frighten her. It was just another given dropped before her with the others, dealt out like cards. For the rest of that day, when she went to the bathroom, each time that she dropped her underpants, she checked them for evidence. Drops of blood, or a river? She didn't know which to expect. She furtively checked her desk chair when she stood, on watch for a red pool, even though she was not the fattest girl.

30

Tatum emptied the kitchen drawer once, put it all back in and emptied it again. Nothing. It wasn't there. Rachael took the picture of Vincent. She must have. There was no other explanation. But why? Tatum went to Rachael's bedroom and eyed her secret photo albums from the doorway. There was no Keep Out sign. She had never been told not to peek. But Tatum couldn't quite kid herself into thinking that what she wanted to do wouldn't be wrong. Invade Rachael's privacy, and they would live a lie. This, Tatum knew. If she looked and didn't tell, she would condemn herself to pretending.

But she wanted to find it. It was the only picture she had of Vincent, and the empty frame had set off a craving. Tatum needed to see it and know that it still existed. Besides, Tatum told herself, what Rachael did with it might reveal critical information that she, as Rachael's guardian, should know.

Tatum entered Rachael's bedroom armed with her excuse. She squatted before the dresser and fingered the old photo albums, the ones whose contents she knew, the ones full of Margaret. The past. Tatum sat back on her heels and looked at the stack of the newer ones, the secret ones.

Vincent. What could be Rachael's reason for wanting him? Tatum knew her own reasons. It was the psychic press of incompletion. The interrupted pattern. She would've left him as soon as she was sure he didn't really love her. But he became sure of it first. She then thought of Paris and wished she hadn't. They were different men.

But she was the same.

Her thoughts and the old photo albums made Tatum feel deflated by the past. It made her remember what is. But "remembering what is" is impossible. It is oxymoronic. "Remembering what is" casts a spell that plays with time. It invokes the past back into being.

Tatum walked away from Rachael's photo albums, leaving them undisturbed. Her thoughts continued to mold her, though, seemingly from the outside, shaping her to old dimensions, a size uncomfortable and yet right-feeling. Her heart for the day's agenda was lost, and she returned to the kitchen and its floor littered with the drawer's contents. She picked up the duct tape, napkin holders, and trivet and tossed them back into the open drawer. She looked at her address book and tried to re-summon her ambition. She lifted it from the drawer and realized a pen was stuck inside, marking a page. The page didn't interest her, but the pen did. She let it roll from the book into her hand and then held it like a knife ready to stab. She remembered Margaret's funeral and the grave marker Lee had chosen for her. *Wife and Mother*.

Some things are written in stone. The only way to fix some things is to destroy them. She readjusted the pen in her hand and with the other hand rubbed at the flat side of her chest.

She wouldn't let it win. Vincent. The past. Anything in the way of what could be. Symbolic gestures have power. This, Geneva had told her. They ground the intentions in the physical world and instruct the subconscious in terms it can understand.

She had an idea.

Tatum left her apartment. At the bottom of the basement stairs, she took in the center of the room, Paris's bed — the present, maybe even the future — carved out from the stored debris. Tatum climbed to the box where the Book of Rachaels sat on the top. She opened it to her own name and the block of space that followed, the insult, a blank salute to her unworthiness, recognized by even her own mother. Tatum would add Margaret to the Book of Rachaels. She would add her mother too. She would fix the book by destroying it.

Her heart pounded in her chest. She thought of Margaret and her mother and tried to bring into focus the thing to say. But memories of others are inevitably memories of ourselves, reminding our cells of who we used to be, for better and for worse. Hope might be plucky, but history had weight, and it wasn't afraid to throw it around.

Memories gathered to watch her, their doubting eyes making her nervous. Hope sat in the middle of the basement space without her. She observed it from her place on the periphery, knee-deep in boxes and history, holding a pen above a page. The longer Tatum failed to bring the thing to say into focus, the more time other voices had to whisper in her ear.

Hope, the voices said, like happiness, is not dependable. Hope is a rug that can be pulled out from under you at the whim of others with greater claims to it. Hopelessness was the greater refuge. Harder to snatch away. That's why others abandon the depressed. They resent that they can't control their feelings, rip away the despair with the ease with which they could topple joy.

Or so the voices said.

The voices whispered in her subconscious, but the message reached her conscious mind. What she was doing was taboo. In fact, she realized that technically the Book wasn't even hers to change. It belonged to Rachael.

"Goddamnit," she hollered, tossing the Book back into the box, the holler and the thud drowning out the sound of the door opening above.

Paris had parked in front of the duplex. Eager to leave behind the haunted canvases and empty stools, he grabbed his box of shoes and headed up the walk. Barely into the foyer, though, he heard Tatum holler from the basement. He dropped his box and ran down the stairs. Reaching the bottom, he looked to his left. Tatum stood among the boxes, holding a pen, looking guilty and surprised.

"Hey," he said, seeing her unharmed.

Tatum closed her eyes.

"What's wrong?" Paris said.

But Tatum just stood there.

Paris spoke softly. "Excuse me," he said, "but your invisibility shield is malfunctioning."

Tatum smiled, weakly. She opened her eyes.

"I'm sorry," she said. "I was looking for some old junk. I wasn't thinking. I'm in your space."

Paris motioned at the house above them. "Actually," he said, "I'm in yours."

Tatum climbed over the boxes. When she reached him, Paris asked her, "Are you okay?"

"Yeah. I'm fine."

But lies weigh less than the truth. That's how another detects them, by some internal psychic scale. Density and texture reveal them, not a person's knowledge of the facts. Paris considered whether to press her.

As though she could sense the coming questions, Tatum reached for his hand to stop their progress. Paris leaned in and kissed her, a dishonest kiss, one to hide in, one for her to hide in.

"Tired?" she said when they pulled apart.

He hadn't slept since before last night's shift. He nodded.

"Sleep," she said, and she turned to go up the stairs, checking once over her shoulder as she left. At the top, she closed the basement door, but Paris could still feel her anxiety. He was no stranger to it. It held a threat. Reasons to run.

He went to the edge of his mattress, sat down, and untied the laces of his boots. Tatum wasn't fine, and he wished she hadn't lied to him, not because it insulted him or made him feel betrayed, but because he wanted to know her. But then he was no one to talk. He hadn't exactly shared the last hours of his life with her either. Lucky for him that with lies of omission, there was nothing to weigh. Still, he worried. Lies multiply. They have to to survive. Like cancer, they build an alternative world that ends up killing the host world, taking it down with it.

Paris remembered the box he had abandoned upstairs, and he retied his boots. He stood and moved toward the steps. But the spot where he had seen Tatum held a gravitational pull. Was she trying to clear out something she didn't want him to find? Did she sense his past crimes and was being proactive? Paris sighed. Perhaps he could atone for the past, he thought, by not rifling, again, through Tatum's belongings. He could be a better man.

And yet, there was an "on the other hand" that attracted him. Don't we all want our secrets known? Want our diaries read by eyes that fall in love with us for knowing the bone cold truth? In fact, Paris thought, love doesn't make us respect each other's secrets, it drives us to unravel them, one by one, at any cost.

Doesn't it?

31

~

Outside the valley, the sky loosened, clouds merely puddling where they once were sea. Geneva didn't gun it like she used to. The speed limit was plenty, so she let the speedometer creep just a few numbers above it, enough to stay in the flow. Not the flow of real traffic, the traveling cars and pickups, but the flow that was there underneath it all, invisible and rushing between yellow lines. No point in resisting and moving more slowly to acknowledge rules and regulations of which flow took no notice. No point in pushing either, trying to outrun it or beat it home. She knew the flow travels, always, at the optimal velocity. That's why it's called the flow.

As she approached the highway exit, she gently pressed the brake. New and delicate growth peppered the close-cropped side of the road. Geneva cultivated her mindset as she drove the final stretch to Parkview Homes. Patience without waiting — that was the objective. To wait was to operate in violation of the flow's dictates. Signing a Do Not Resuscitate order had set up a pending. But it was a pending that must be ignored. Ralph had a flow of his own, and it was to be respected. Her job, Geneva thought, was not to check her watch, but to stand by and witness and not allow him to die alone in the company of people whose only interest in him was his safety.

She reached with her right hand to her purse and opened the flap, double-checking to see that she had remembered the tape she had made for Ralph. *"And I think to myself, what a wonderful world..."* It would suit the day perfectly. Geneva had recorded version after version of "What a Wonderful World." She had opened the tape with Louis Armstrong and closed with an instrumental by Charlie Byrd. In between, she included Ray Charles, Eddy Arnold, Glen Campbell, and Ruth Brown, to name a few.

She hadn't listened to it through before snapping it out of the deck that morning, but she had checked all the transitions between songs, and they were clean. She didn't put it in the car's tape deck because she wanted to hear it for the first time with Ralph, in his room, the context for which it was designed. She was curious as to whether it would come off as a study of a song or just be repetitive and irritating. If the former, good for her and good for Ralph. If it turned out to be the latter, too bad for the social worker who served as Ralph's guardian.

Geneva parked in the lot but remained in the car. The gray clouds above had dissolved to little more than streaks and smears, mere scuff marks on a blue sky. She took a deep breath and looked through her window toward the old stone building. It had once been the Masonic Home serving the old and infirm of the order and their wives. But as the old geezers advanced toward extinction, it was primarily their wives who had taken up residency there. But the real estate was worth a mint. It's hard to win a fight in which you don't get a vote. Sorry ladies. The Masons sold it, and the facility changed hands. The wives were out. The doors were thrown open. Geneva was first in line. The grounds were beautiful. The cost, significant.

Masons or no, the community was a small and closed one, the kind where everyone in it knows everything. So Geneva tried to take her cue from Hester Prynne and wear her so-called sin without shame. She opened the car door. As she approached the front of the building, she gathered herself, lifting her ribs from her pelvis, letting her head reach up from her neck. She mined herself for height, claiming each fraction of an inch. She would meet squarely the gaze of anyone who cared to stare.

She signed in and made her way to the intensive care wing. Outside Ralph's door, Geneva met Vernita — Ralph's guardian, her babysitter. Vernita was a frumpy, middle-aged Native American woman with a bad perm and dark framed glasses. If Vernita had a judgment, if she were on one side or another in the case of the humpstress of Parkview, Geneva couldn't tell.

Vernita followed Geneva into the room and took the chair farthest from the bed. The circumstances were not intimate, as was the point. Under surveillance, Geneva felt as though she floated slightly outside the surface of her own skin, watching herself be watched. Though in the past she had preferred telepathic communication to talking aloud to Ralph, now it seemed uncaring, as though the silence were evidence against her. So, she kept up a blameless patter.

"Ralph," she said in greeting and then paused at the dresser to snap the tape into the deck. She hit the play button, and Louis started to sing. The volume was modest, but still, the music organized the room, said how it's going to be. Geneva took slow steps toward the bed stand where she put down her purse. From its outside pocket, she withdrew a crystal on a fishing line she had brought along to hang in the window. She dropped it into the palm of her hand and then bent over and planted a kiss on Ralph's forehead. Then, she stood there staring at him, turning over in her mind for amusement's sake the question as to how far she could go before Vernita blew the whistle. Could she lick his cheek? Suck his earlobe?

She walked around the foot of the bed. Approaching the window, she withdrew a hook with a screw bottom from her coat pocket. She pushed the screw's pointy end into the top of the window frame. She waited for Vernita to try to stop her. Second demerit for violation of Parkview property. But, as Geneva's back was to her, she didn't even know if Vernita were watching.

Three more hard twists and the screw was in tight. Geneva looped the end of the fishing line and hung the crystal. The sun was positioned perfectly. Dozens of dots — red, purple, gold, and green — jiggled into being, spraying light across her cheeks and shoulders and down the front of her coat. Beyond the window, the lawn was a mix of new green and raked dirt. Geneva looked out to the paths paved for wheelchair access to nooks with park benches and bridges with guardrails. Slightly farther out was a small grove of Russian Olives surrounding a small pond. Geneva used to wheel Ralph to it before the time came when he would become completely disoriented if he left the building. Then, even if he left his room. His fear made him dangerous. Fear tends to do that.

She turned from the window.

"1967," she said, moving toward the bed as Louis's version ended and Ruth Brown's began. "It was written in 1967." She removed her coat and placed it on the back of the chair. "George Weiss and Bob Thiele wrote it. Weiss wrote a ton of hits. Elvis. Ella. Sinatra. All the greats sang Weiss."

Had Ralph been conscious, he would have rolled his eyes and smiled, so gracious to endure her chitchat.

"Thiele had his own radio show when he was just fourteen," she said. "Jazz."

The dots of light swayed slightly as the crystal turned, rolling right then slightly left. They danced across the bedspread. Geneva listened to Vernita listening, trying to discern whether she was tuned into the music or to the drone of her own thoughts.

"Know who recommended Ruth Brown to Atlantic?" Geneva said. "Duke Ellington. Ruth put Atlantic on the map."

Glen Campbell was next. The break between was a nanosecond longer than Geneva thought perfect.

She knew nothing of Glen Campell's version, other than that it was. So there was no patter of trivia or regurgitation of old liner notes, nothing to conceal from herself her true thoughts: conversations with Ralph had greatly improved with his Alzheimer's. No reactions for her to react to. No opinions about what she had to say that were really opinions about what it meant about *her* that she would have such an opinion. Ralph's conversational style was often that of the politician's. Skip addressing the argument. Undermine the credibility of the arguer. It was a sensational diversion. Content never survives the strategy. Yet, she had never given up hope, not really, that it might change. It took Alzheimer's to cure her of that hope. Well, maybe not cure, but it had forced a refocusing of it. The hope for change became the hope for answers. There was a reason she had chosen Ralph. A reason it had felt so right. The reason simply had not yet revealed itself. But it would. It just took patience.

Patience. The virtue that was its own reward. Not that different, really, from having a high pain threshold.

A quick knock on the door preceded its opening. An aide, a young man, arrived with a cart. For a brief second, in his eyes and smirk, Geneva believed she detected herself in his mind, naked and wrinkled-ass, riding Ralph into the sunset. On the bright side, it was probably the first time in a decade plus that a man had undressed her with his eyes.

She stood slowly and stared at him like she were wearing her birthday suit and that it was his good fortune to see. He averted his eyes.

"Let me step out," she said, and she flipped her coat from the back of her chair. She snapped off the tape deck as she left, disappointed she wouldn't hear the tape from start to finish as a whole.

In the hall, she paused to pull on her coat. A nurse she knew well acknowledged her with a mere chin nod and then averted her eyes. Being watched and avoided amounted to the same thing. She would rise to the occasion of it but couldn't deny that she cared. Being misunderstood is to not be known. Existing only to oneself grows tiring.

Geneva turned to head for the front door when a young woman emerged from the next room. She had short blonde hair and a tiny piercing in her nose. She carried a clipboard and wore a name badge.

The girl flinched when her eyes met Geneva's. It was Alice. The social worker. She did not seem to imagine Geneva naked.

Geneva adjusted her coat on her shoulders.

"Boo," she said flatly.

Alice looked beyond Geneva's shoulder for an escape. Open warfare was not her forte.

"We obviously know who each other are," Alice said nervously.

"*Is*," Geneva said. "Who each other *is*."

Alice steadied herself, focusing for battle.

"I'm sure your intentions weren't to do harm," Alice said, her words clipped, like she was in a hurry. "But my responsibility isn't your intentions. It's the resident's experience."

"And my husband's experience was what?" Geneva said, in a voice darn near a purr. "How do you know he wasn't fully lucid, calling out 'Give it to me, mamma'?"

"If that were the case," Alice said, "you should have submitted that information to the board. It would have been of interest to his doctor, too, I'm sure."

"What are you," Geneva said, "twenty-four, twenty-five?"

"I don't see that it's relevant."

Geneva crossed her arms over her chest.

"You have no idea all that you don't know," she said.

"I'm sorry you feel that way," Alice said.

"You have not been authorized to apologize on behalf of my feelings."

Alice readjusted the clipboard on her hip. She was younger than Tatum, Geneva could see. Younger than Paris. She was right-on from head to toe, from haircut to sensible and cruelty-free footwear. She was a righter of wrongs; the meter of justice. The terrible grays of experience had yet to tarnish her absolutism.

"I have extensive training in geriatric, psychiatric matters," Alice said. "My master's thesis. . ."

Geneva burst out with a laugh, interrupting her.

"I'm sorry you. . ." Alice said and then stopped herself.

"Have you ever considered 'I'm sorry *I*'?" Geneva said.

"I have nothing to apologize for."

"And yet, you keep saying sorry."

"Excuse me," Alice said. "I have rounds."

Their eyes locked, but as Geneva looked, the fight drained from her. The girl knew nothing, but how could she know otherwise? Her youth, the piercing, the clothes — they misinformed. She wasn't righteous. She was self-righteous. She stood not for justice but for control. Geneva believed in heroes, revolutionaries, and fighters of the good fight. But that's not what she had here. Alice was a person whose power in life would come from red pens and a deftness with bureaucratic processes. In other words, she had no power. How, Geneva wondered, had she ended up in battle with such an inferior opponent?

"Move," Geneva said, without energy, as Alice stood between her and the lobby. The idea of stepping around Alice did not occur to her.

Alice moved. Geneva left the building. She stood on the front steps and grunted a laugh. The sun was blasting. The sky, screaming. The day was hollering, *hallelujah*. In Montana, spring days are rare. April snow could turn to rain, and rain might piss from the sky through June. The Memorial Day weekend could feature wet and sloppy snow. Sometimes, spring showed up for a day or two in February, then another two in May. A Tuesday and Wednesday, perhaps. But then, by Thursday, the thermometer might snake up to ninety and within weeks turn everything brown and bring on yet another taxing fire season. But, nonetheless, today, here it was. The rarity. The gorgeous spring day.

Geneva walked down the steps, into the spring day but not able to be part of it. She crammed her hands into her pockets. Nurses and aides and administrative staff took their breaks walking the asphalt paths. A lone visitor pushed her loved one in a wheel chair, pausing to feel his hands for coolness or warmth and adjusting blankets accordingly. Geneva pointed herself in the direction of the pond and the Russian Olives. Annoyances, large and small, came between her and the afternoon's glory.

It wasn't just Alice. Unfair though it was, she found herself blaming Ralph too for her current slew of irritations. She thought the thought she tried hard not to think: she wanted Ralph to die. She wanted him dead retroactively. She wanted the wisdom, the gift, that was the product of commitment. The lesson. She wanted it all realized. Commitment, she knew, from the outside, can look like martyrdom, or even laziness. But for her it was about trust. She had to trust her own judgment. There was a reason for her choices, and she wanted the reason revealed because then it would be over.

She would be free to think about something else.

Soft human sounds traveled on the air. Two employees in polyester pants and shapeless sweaters speed-walked by, arms pumping, the low, gravelly sound of workplace gossip passing back and forth between them. Geneva felt the over-the-shoulder glance as they passed and heard the shift in volume and tone. *That's her.* She didn't hear the words, but she didn't need to.

An unexpected sniffle snuck up on her. She blinked back a few tears. Tears because she had tried and her best wasn't good enough.

The sun is on my face, she told herself, arguing with the tears.

She looked up into the screaming sky and tried to open herself to it. Be as wide. Be as true. But the dark question crept in her heart: did she not love Ralph, or did she not know how to love? Who was the problem, the subject or object?

Of all her damned questions, it was damnedest. Ralph had loved her, this she knew. But he had not been interested in her. This, she felt. As for her, perhaps it hadn't been Ralph whom she had been interested in all these years. Perhaps, what she was interested in was love.

A handful of barn swallows appeared in the sky before her, dipping into view, zigzagging on the hunt. They were the first of the season, and Geneva stopped to watch the aerial ballet. They swooped and rose with grace, never gliding, never at rest in the sky. They flew over her head, and she turned to watch them, about-facing back the way she'd come. The air around her collected the warmth of the sun. Ralph's sponge bath, no doubt, was over.

She brought her eyes back to the earth. The home sat before her on the landscape, heavy and solid, looking to her like a glamorous prison. She wanted to be released. Geneva headed back to the choices she had made, but she stopped when she reached the bottom of the steps to the building. They looked to her like Everest, a great effort to climb. Back to her chaperone. Back to her shame. Back to the world that had shrunk and defined her. Back.

Back at Ralph's room, Vernita was waiting outside, armed, as Alice had been, with a loaded clipboard.

Geneva hit the play button as she walked toward the bed. She flopped into the chair. She tried to shut her mind and hear only the song. *I see trees of green, red roses, too. . .* Ray Charles was singing. A blind man. And yet, she was not moved. "Moved" and mad can't share the same spot. Mad digs in too deep for movement, and Geneva was mad. Mad at Ralph. And mad at Alice for reminding her of it. What might she have done in this world had she not been wasting her creativity, turning her psyche into a pretzel, trying to love right, trying to make her love right?

She was mad at all of it, and she was mad at being mad on a day the earth was singing.

The sun had traveled and no longer hit the crystal. Ralph's lower lip protruded farther than his top one, ever so slightly, the mildest of pouts. Geneva thought of younger days when she would lay in the crook of his arm and run a moistened index finger over the swell of it. The memory made her push air through her nose. At the time, she was young and had no idea of the size of the gulf between what he wanted of her and what she had to give. And she had no idea of the nature of the burden of being with one who wanted not too much, but too little.

When the tape ended, Geneva stood. She would not be checking into the nearby Super 8. She was going home.

Geneva pushed hard on the gas pedal. The speedometer pressed forward. She vacillated between self-righteousness and self-doubt and found them equally crippling. A hunger for a life without Ralph, without all the questions about him, about them, about love, overcame her. She slapped the steering wheel with her hand. Her breath grew shallow, and the skin on her face seemed to tighten. She wanted it all done, processed, sewn up, and digested. Whoever she would be when it was all over, she wanted to be right now. She leaned over her steering wheel and let a good, solid scream rip. Her Saab tore down the highway. The flow, Geneva thought, could kiss her ass.

But the flow, alas, misunderstood. It thought she said, "Kick."

The wail of a siren hit her ears, and cherries appeared in the rearview. Geneva cursed and hit the blinker. Pulling to the shoulder, she reached to the glove compartment for the proper I.D.'s. She watched the officer approach in her side-view mirror. Standard issue cop: leather jacket, long legs, and mirrored sunglasses. She rolled down the window. He took her license and registration.

"Do you know how fast you were going?" he said.

Geneva looked at her reflection in his sunglasses.

"Ninety?" she said frankly. "Ninety-five?"

"In a . . . " he said.

Young authorities, Geneva thought, with their guns and their clipboards. She knew what he meant. She knew the right answer. *In a seventy-five zone. Sir.*

"In a . . . " he repeated.

Geneva looked up at the cop but saw only herself where his eyes should be, and without a shred of false innocence, she answered, "In a twenty-year-old Saab."

32

～

Tatum had let Paris sleep for three hours, and then they went to pick up Rachael from school. They took the car as the day had become glorious and, after collecting her, drove to Spring Meadow Lake under a sky as blue as cornflowers and giant, white cruise ship clouds.

Rachael walked several paces in front of them on a path soft with spring melt. Tatum watched her move through the landscape, small and self-contained, not bursting from seams like the spring growth that surrounded them. It lacked empathy, Tatum thought, spring. Fall and winter were sympathetic. There for you. Dead leaves and abandoned nests said *me, too — you are not alone*. Spring, on the other hand, was a collective celebration. You could opt in, or you could opt out. But no one was stopping the party to try to convince you to come.

"Spring," Tatum said. "You can't help but love it, but it just doesn't offer comfort the way fall and winter do. Ever notice that?"

The blue bunch wheatgrass was already greening. Cottonwoods lined the shore. Bulrushes and cattails clustered in pockets in the shallow water just ahead.

"It seems perfect," Paris said.

They rounded a bend, catching up to Rachael, who had paused at the bridge to look out over the railing. As they flanked her, she switched to look over the other side.

"What's on your mind, Rach?" Tatum said, turning and leaning back to the railing.

Rachael didn't turn.

"Nothing," she said.

"So you've reached enlightenment?" Tatum said. "Calmed the mind into a nirvana of silence?"

Rachael looked over her shoulder. "What?"

"It's a joke."

Rachael made a face. She didn't get it and didn't seem in the mood to try.

Tatum turned back to Paris. She curled her hands over the wooden railing, and Paris covered one of her hands with his own. Tatum looked into his profile, at the sandy hair, the full lips. He was an easy fit in the natural world, at home among the tree trunks, reeds, and sky. He was like the surface of the water, too, penetrable yet indivisible. You could break the surface, but he remained intact, and it was you who found yourself surrounded.

Paris turned to face her. As their eyes met, a sense of dissolving overcame Tatum, dissolving into Paris as though she could experience him from the inside out. It felt half like merging, half like ceasing to exist. Both had a powerful attraction.

"What's in your mind?" Paris asked in a voice just above a whisper.

"Nirvana," she said.

Paris pulled her toward him. He kissed her on the lips. She pulled away and looked down.

"What?" Paris said.

"Earlier," Tatum said, "in the basement, I wasn't looking for anything. Remember that book I told you about? The book my family keeps with all the women named Rachael in it?"

"Yeah."

"Lee sent it several months ago. It's in the basement. I was going to write in it. I was going to change it," she said. "Write about Margaret. Make it a different kind of book."

"But you didn't?"

"No. I couldn't. I was unable."

He looked at her quizzically.

Tatum shrugged. "Writer's block, I guess."

Paris reached toward her and plucked a dandelion seed from where it had landed in her hair.

"I'm sorry I faked with you," Tatum said. She didn't want to say "lied."

Paris went to touch her cheek, but she turned before his hand could reach her. She stepped past him, crooking her neck to see up the path.

"Where's Rachael?" she said.

Paris turned and looked over his shoulder.

"Rachael," Tatum called.

Rachael had left the path, walking into the brush, under the giant willow, down the embankment, and toward the water. *Nirvana*. She whispered the word and liked the way it felt in her mouth. She thought it would make a pretty name, good for a turtle. Wearing the chucka boots her aunt had bought her, she climbed slowly down a small hump near the shoreline to where the ground was muddier.

Above, she heard the sound of Tatum's voice. She heard her mention the Book of Rachaels, a book where everybody in it was dead except Aunt Tatum and herself. The sound of her mother's name also distinguished itself from above. Her mother was in heaven, Rachael knew, but she could no longer imagine it. Heaven was a place she couldn't locate, not even in her mind. Heaven seemed farther than the moon, past the sky, which was never-ending. It was nowhere. Heaven was nowhere, and that's where her mother was. Nowhere. And yet, her cut-out shape, a hole in the fabric of the Universe, remained.

Rachael stepped out onto a thumb-shaped jutting that extended into the lake some thirteen feet. One foot then the other fell on progressively squishier ground. She thought of her mother but not in heaven. She thought of her in the bathroom behind the closed door. She imagined that the cancer made blood drip from her and wash down the drain when she cried in the shower, blood like the girls at school had talked about. Rachael reached the tip of the jutting and looked down at the smooth and algae-filled water at her feet. She wondered if Aunt Tatum bled in the shower too. Or if she did when she was sick. Rachael knew secret feelings were felt in bathrooms. When you came back out, no one was supposed to know.

She then squatted where the mud turned to water. She looked over her shoulder. Furtively, she stuck a finger down her pants. She withdrew it and examined it for blood.

"Rachael?"

Startled, she jumped up and turned, folding the finger back into her palm and tucking it behind her back. Her aunt stood in the arch of the willow.

"Whatcha doing?" Tatum said, side-stepping down the slope.

Rachael's cheeks flushed scarlet, and she took a step backward, her foot landing squarely in the water.

"No," she cried out, lifting the soggy boot and keeping the guilty finger hidden.

"What's going on?" Tatum asked. "What do you have? Did you find something?" She extended a hand to help Rachael out of the muck.

Rachael took a second step back, her other boot now soaked too.

Tatum's hand then dropped to her side. She blinked.

"Rachael," she said, "what's behind your back? Is it Vincent's picture? Do you have Vincent's picture?"

Rachael's little mouth opened. Then Tatum extended her hand again to help. But Rachael twisted to avoid it, jerked herself too hard, and lost balance. She went down sideways, her head slapping against a granite slab jutting up from the cold, shallow water. Tatum lunged forward, stepped into the water, and jerked Rachael up by the arm.

"Omigod," Tatum said, pulling her to dry ground and kneeling before her. She tried to separate the wet hair from a cut.

Rachael weakly shoved at Tatum's hand. She reached for the spot of impact and felt a wave of confused grogginess. It didn't register yet as pain, but the cold shook her.

"Stop," Tatum said, pushing away her hand. "Let me see."

"No," Rachael said, and she pushed away Tatum's hands long enough to bring her own fingers to her temple. As she touched it, she noticed Tatum's fingers, the blood on them. She looked down at her own fingers, and her face went white.

"I know. I know," Tatum said, reaching for her wrists. "It's okay. It's okay."

Rachael pulled away.

"C'mon," Tatum said firmly, taking hold of a wrist.

"No," Rachael said, struggling loose but losing balance in the process.

Tatum grabbed her arm, keeping her upright.

"Let go," Rachael hollered. "I want my mom."

"She's not here," Tatum said. "I am."

Rachael screamed in Tatum's face, a primate's threat, and then she lashed out, her fingernails dragging across Tatum's cheeks.

Tatum let go of her and put her hand to the side of her own face. Rachael looked as shocked as Tatum, and then she was suddenly lifted up and over Tatum's head. It was Paris. He held Rachael, her back to his chest. At first, she writhed and kicked with her heels at his knees and thighs. Then came the tears. He hiked her up once, flipping her chest to face his own.

"C'mon," he said as he headed back up the embankment and toward the car, walking at a brisk pace. Tatum trotted behind him.

"Paris, stop it," Tatum said.

But he kept walking.

"Paris," Tatum hollered.

But Paris didn't stop.

"We have to go to the hospital," he said.

At the car, Tatum fumbled with the keys. She climbed behind the wheel, and Paris got into the back with Rachael. Tatum peeled out of the gravel lot. She stole glances in the rearview mirror as she drove. Rachael was whimpering now, but her tears weren't the tears of protest like those near the water when Paris had first carried her off. Paris pressed his hand to Rachael's temple. He held her whole body tightly, Tatum could tell. The thigh Rachael sat upon and the chest against which she rested were firm, yet soft, like the earth beneath the grass. Rachael was not trying to wrestle away.

"Don't let her fall asleep," Tatum said, though it didn't seem likely.

The knee beneath Rachael jiggled. Rough fingertips touched her cheek. Tatum was outside the circle.

Tatum wanted to blame Vincent. But she was the one who had brought him up, who had gone looking for him again. She didn't understand why she saw him by the water in the guilty blush of Rachael's cheeks and the hidden hand behind her back. Tears fought to the surface, rimmed Tatum's eyes, and plopped onto her lap. Her mouth twisted, and she sniffed, and her vision blurred. She looked into the rearview and met Paris's eyes, then she looked away in shame. She sniffled and wiped her nose with her hand.

She was relieved to reach the hospital's lot.

"Go," she said. She needed them gone.

"It's okay," Paris said to Tatum, touching her shoulder. He carried Rachael from the car and through the sliding doors without looking back.

In the car, Tatum wiped at her cheeks with the heel of her hand. She struggled to get ahold of herself. She was tired of herself. Very tired of herself. But there was no one else to be.

Rachael received two stitches, but it was Tatum who looked the worst for wear. She didn't make it into the hospital until all was said and done. She dealt with the front desk, providing the information she could and promising to bring in insurance information later. Back at the duplex, Rachael slept. Her cheeks were white against the pale green pillowcase. Low, southern light came through the drapes. Paris and Tatum stood beside the bed.

"Thank you," Tatum said softly.

"I'm sorry," Paris said.

Tatum's brow drew together.

"For what?"

"I've never known you to cry," he said. "I wanted to be there."

Tatum sighed.

"I'm the one who screwed up," she said. "Not you. Don't be sorry."

"I'm not really apologizing," Paris said. "I'm sorry I wasn't there like, you know, as in I regret I wasn't there. I've never seen you cry like that."

"What, you wanted to watch?"

"I wanted to be with that part of you."

Tatum looked at Paris. He shrugged, and Tatum's breath caught in her chest. Could she believe it? That he wanted to be with that part of her? Her heart pushed out energy toward him, but she had to look away. She moved toward Rachael instead. She climbed onto the bed and lay on top of the spread, scooting up beside Rachael as close as she could be without actually touching her.

Paris seated himself at the end of the mattress and placed a hand on Tatum's ankle. Though calm on the outside, he was still shaken by what had happened at the water's edge. He had seen Rachael's fingernails catch Tatum's cheek and after that, a bright, white light exploded inside of him. Next thing he knew, he was in the back seat of Tatum's car with Rachael in his lap with no recollection of how he got there.

Then, at the hospital, he had carried Rachael from the car and through the sliding doors, struggling not to look back to where the woman he loved was crying and the man who loved her was walking away. If he looked back, he would never make it through the door.

Paris wanted to climb into the bed on the other side and make a circle with Tatum that held Rachael safe in the center. But he stayed where he was, watching them. The two seemed far away and separate, even from each other. It made Paris want to say their names, to see their eyes open, and pull them all to a single shared space.

"Paris," Tatum said, breaking his revelry. "You should get out and save yourself while you can."

"No," was all he could think of to say.

Then he slid up the mattress and lay beside Tatum. He kept his knees bent and boots hanging off the edge of the bed, trying to be mindful of the spread while protecting them all from the greater evil of his exposed feet.

Tatum reached up with a tentative hand and placed it on Rachael's shoulder.

"Tell me something," she said to Paris.

He could tell she wanted him to say something that would take her away from the voices in her head. She wanted him to carve out a new space for them to occupy, wrap them in a story where it all had already happened and led them here, however indirectly, to each other.

"Paris?"

He didn't want to let her down.

"I have a secret," he said. "Want to hear?"

Tatum answered with a bend of her knees that he could feel as her feet pressed to his shins.

"It's about the diner. Around two a.m. . . .," he began.

It was a story he had once been saving, a perfect story, before he had ruined it in the janitor's closet. Paris told Tatum about the women, about the soup and the quiet of the night. Paris told her that he had tried to draw the women, but he could never draw their eyes.

Then, he was quiet. Lies of omission weigh nothing, but they carve out perceptible holes, and the hole in his story, to his mind, was gaping. No Linda. Nothing. Like she was never there. He reached his arm across Tatum, but with his will, he cast a broader wing of protection. Across Tatum. Across Rachael. Across the Deluxe and a wider world, a sea of uplifted eyes wanting only to be noticed, to be seen. His lie had carved an empty space into the room. He tried to fill it with a promise.

Be a man.

The words formed clearly in his head, and the hairs on the back of his neck prickled. This was what it meant to be a man. To possess not with a clenched hand, but to *be* possessed by a promise. A promise to protect. In declaring them as his, he realized, he became theirs.

It was an oath.

It was love.

33

~

Geneva held her speeding ticket, slightly crushed, in the hand support-
ing the bottom of her purse as she dug out her key. The scent hit her
first, heady and dusty, and then the snatch of color caught her eye.
Purple and white lilacs crammed into a jelly jar sat beside her door.
She turned the lock and dropped her purse and unused overnight bag
onto the floor inside. Then she returned to the hall and picked up the
flowers. She carried them, and the speeding ticket, inside to her desk.
She lifted the folded note from the bouquet. It simply said, " — J."

Geneva lowered herself into her chair. The day did not slip away.
The bad mood and the bouquet. It was a staring contest.

Then the bad mood spoke.

Ralph. She had never blamed him for anything. But then today,
driving home, some inner switch got thrown. Geneva found herself blaming Ralph for an "it all" she didn't know she had in her. Her
resentment festered. She let it pump through her veins. Defensiveness
locked up her jaw and tightened her lips despite her knowing that
such rigidity trapped one inside rather than protected one from what
could come from without. She also realized that the reason she hadn't
blamed Ralph all these years wasn't due to her love or her personal
virtue. It was about control. If she blamed Ralph, it meant the problem lay elsewhere, outside of herself. Whereas if it were *her* fault, *her*
responsibility, it was hers to change. And the only person she needed
to count on was herself.

But no more. From now on, she decided, it wasn't her fault. Nothing was. Ralph, the social worker, the cop — they were the problem.

She looked at the lilacs. They offered no opinion. Geneva reached
toward the speeding ticket and turned it face down on the desk.

Then, she closed her eyes to make both disappear in search of
some inner silence. But the dusty, heady lilac scent was persistent and
seemed able to reach inside of her with soft tendrils. Her body drew a
sudden fast breath, reaching for more, an act separate from her will.

The exhale was slow, and almost complete, when there was a soft rapping at her door.

Geneva opened her eyes.

"Hello?" Tatum's voice.

Geneva closed her eyes again. Despite her affection for Tatum, she was in no mood for handwringing, melancholy or gloom, or at least not someone else's. She didn't want to say words or think thoughts or manage herself in any way in relation to what someone else might want or need.

Another knock on the door.

It was a roll of the dice. Geneva hoped for the best. She sighed heavily and said, "Come in."

The sound of Geneva's arrival, doors opening and closing, had wakened Tatum, who had been dozing across the hall. Paris was gone. Tatum peeked over the top of Rachael, who slept beside her, and looked at the clock. 7:30 p.m. Paris must have gone to work. Tatum remembered that Geneva said that she would be gone for the night and wondered what had happened, why she was home.

So she had slipped from the bed and out of her apartment, leaving the door ajar, and rapped a knuckle on Geneva's door.

Geneva answered after the second knock. Tatum stepped inside. Her eyes were drawn immediately to the jar of lilacs on the desk.

"Oo," she said. "Pretty."

Geneva looked at the flowers and nodded in agreement.

"Where'd you get them?" she said. She stuck her face into the blooms.

Geneva fingered the note that accompanied the flowers.

"I met him at the coffee shop," she said. "In passing. He doesn't know I'm married."

"In-ter-est-ing," Tatum said, enunciating each syllable.

Geneva pushed the note away, picked up another slip of paper, and gave it a wave.

"Got a ticket," she said.

"For what?"

"Speeding."

"How fast?"

"Ninety-five."

"In a what?"

"In a Saab," Geneva said, for the second time that day.

"Sounds like you're a fast woman on all fronts." Tatum crossed the room and flopped down on the sofa. "So who is he? What's he like? Why are you home?"

Geneva didn't answer right away. Then, she looked at the bouquet like it was the flowers, as opposed to the man, that she was about to describe." He's attractive," she said but then corrected herself. "Handsome, in a soft and rugged way. He seems like a thinking man."

"Gosh," Tatum said, "and the downside is?"

Geneva shot her a look.

"No one would blame you," Tatum said.

"Well, it's not about 'no one' — whoever that is. It's not about 'everyone' either. Just me."

"You'd feel guilty?"

"I'd feel like a liar," Geneva said. She tossed her speeding ticket across the desk.

Tatum wondered if Geneva meant she'd be lying to Ralph, or the new guy. She was about to ask for clarification, but Geneva spoke first.

"Even Rachael knows that rationalization is just lying to yourself."

Tatum didn't understand how Geneva would be lying to herself and was about to pursue it, but again Geneva spoke first.

"Tell me," she said, pulling off her coat and deliberately redirecting the conversation, "how was your day?"

The diversion worked. Tatum told Geneva about the day's premiere drama, Rachael's fall and the trip to the hospital. She left out the part where she had sat crying in the car while Paris took care of Rachael.

"You should have seen Paris and Rachael on the way home," Tatum said, remembering the two of them in the back seat, Paris's arm around Rachael, Rachael's cheek on his arm. "I think Rachael fell in love with Paris."

"Who wouldn't fall in love with Paris?" Geneva said, offhandedly.

Geneva's words entered Tatum like they were something she hadn't meant to swallow. *Who wouldn't fall in love with Paris?* The idea tasted of metal. It unnerved her, that she could be one of millions. *Who wouldn't fall in love with Paris?* She hadn't realized it. Paris definitely didn't realize it. She rose from the sofa and walked to the window. She knew for a fact that no one would ever ask who wouldn't fall in love with her.

"I think Rachael stole a picture of Vincent," Tatum said, with her back to Geneva.

Geneva reached up and clicked on the floor lamp beside the desk.

"Paris really took the lead today," Tatum continued. "Taking care of Rachael. Maybe that male energy is something she needs. Maybe that's why she took Vincent's picture."

"Did you consider asking her why she took it?" Geneva said.

Geneva's voice sounded oddly testy.

"I have," Tatum said, turning to face her. Then she corrected herself. "No. I asked her *if* she took it. That's when everything went weird." Tatum crossed her arms over her chest. She dropped her head and shook it. "She needs her father."

Geneva stood and wandered toward the kitchen.

"I've really tried my best," Tatum said, "but I don't know. I just. You know, the truth is, I never even went in the hospital. Paris did. I sat in the car. . ."

"Stop," Geneva said. She was standing behind her kitchen counter.

Tatum looked up.

But Geneva just stood there, fingertips on the countertop. Her eyes were closed. She didn't move. She didn't seem able to.

The silence made Tatum anxious.

"Can I just ask you one thing?" Tatum said softly.

"What's that?" Geneva said.

Tatum's voice wavered.

"I have to call Lee," she said. "Insurance stuff. But I was thinking I should tell him maybe that Rachael needs him. I failed today in a way that scares me."

"Do what you need to do," Geneva said.

"I don't know if it's what I need to do," Tatum said, taking a step toward the kitchen. "I just think Rachael. . ."

"Have you asked Rachael what she wants in terms of her father?" Geneva said, stopping Tatum's steps with her voice.

"I was thinking I shouldn't ask until I know I can deliver. That I should line him up first."

"What she wants has nothing to do with what you can deliver," Geneva said. "Her answer to the question would be clarifying, perhaps for both of you."

"Well, yeah," Tatum said, "but why get her all full of hope for something she can't have?"

"The point," Geneva said, "would be that she wants it. Admitting it. Knowing it."

Tatum could feel Geneva's frustration, and it confused her. It forged a convergence of feelings that combined made Tatum feel like she was something collapsing from the center.

"What did I do?" she said.

"Rachael's been great for you," Geneva said. "Paris adores you. You're acting like . . . like some kind of reverse-Rumpelstiltskin, spinning gold into shit."

Tatum's body cooled from the surface of her skin down to her core. She hadn't seen it coming. Not from Geneva. Paris, maybe. Rachael, all in time. But Geneva? Time was up?

The humiliation was always greater when it came as a surprise.

Geneva's face shifted as her attention was drawn over Tatum's shoulder.

"Rachael," Geneva said.

Tatum turned.

"Rough day?" Geneva said.

Rachael stood in the doorway, a bandage covering her right temple. She shrugged as though rough days were the norm.

"Come let me see that," Geneva said.

Rachael walked to the kitchen. Geneva pushed back Rachael's hair and examined the bandage.

"Dang, dang, dang," she said and then shuffled Rachael's hair back into place.

Rachael looked up at Geneva like she was waiting for her to tell some truth lurking in the moment. Geneva felt Tatum, too, standing there in hurt and confusion, exerting a pull, wanting comfort.

But Geneva did not want to be there for them. She didn't want to be *there*, in that place of hand-wringing and need, worry and questions. She had flowers on her desk and a speeding ticket. She had a husband who wouldn't die. She thought that it was more than enough.

"I had a rough day too," she said.

Their voices had been quiet. Rachael had been sleepy. But still, she had heard. Not word for word, but key phrases and names. She filled in blanks not knowing they were blanks, creating sums from disparate facts. They knew she stole the picture. Tatum was calling her father.

Her father. He was as shadowy as her mother. The difference was that he always had been. She and her mother had been one unit, and he had been another. Together they made their family. But without her mother, there was no unit. No family, and the not-there of it scared her. To imagine her father taking her away was like to imagine disappearing.

Back in Tatum's apartment, Rachael left the kitchen where her aunt was preparing a supper of soup and grilled cheese sandwiches. In her bedroom, Rachael unzipped her backpack's side pocket and checked on Vincent. She pulled him out and tucked him up her shirt sleeve. She slipped quietly from her room.

Spinning gold into shit. Tatum tried to remember the story. Rumpelstiltskin was a nasty troll, she recalled. He spun straw into gold on behalf of some girl who pretended she was the one spinning it. She had to promise her firstborn in return for the favor. The girl got out of it somehow, though, pulled off some kind of double-cross.

Tatum flipped the sandwiches in the frying pan. Rachael appeared and slid into one of the chairs at the small table. Tatum spatula-ed the sandwiches onto plates, slid on an oven mitt, and poured the soup into bowls. She laid out the humble meal. They sat across from each other. Rachael's bandage made a bulge above her brow.

"I blew it today," Tatum said. "And I'm sorry."

"It's okay," Rachael said, not looking up.

"I know how much you wish she were here."

"But she's not here," Rachael said.

Tatum looked down and saw two tears plop onto her plate.

"I'm sorry." She blotted the tears with a paper napkin. "I'm just a crybaby today. I miss Margaret, I guess," she blurted, not knowing the words were coming. It was the truth, though. Her missing of Margaret was a missing that stretched back in time to long before her death. It was a missing of Geneva too, unfolding forward into the future.

The snowball was rolling. Tatum knew she couldn't do this. Not in front of Rachael.

She sniffled and bucked up.

"How's your head feeling?" she asked.

"The doctor said I was going to have a scar."

Their eyes reached across the table for each other's. Tatum wanted Rachael to know she would not be like her.

"It'll be a little one," Tatum told her. "People will have to look real close to see."

Geneva stood in her kitchen. History, she decided, repeats itself not because we forget, but because we keep remembering, chewing and reviewing, mindlessly re-invoking. Something had to change. She wanted something different than what she had, and so she knew she had to do different. Think different. Be different. She was tired of being a control freak who knew that the only thing she could control was herself. So she decided to start with that. She would disavow her history of taking responsibility. Blame was to be the new name of the game. She did not feel good about the way she had spoken to Tatum, but she decided not to feel good about Tatum instead.

What else? She leaned on the kitchen counter, refusing to budge, not until she could make an original move. She blocked habitual thoughts and waited. And waited.

The mind can be quieted, but the senses don't sleep. The heady scent of lilacs snuck up again and licked at her. She involuntarily lifted her eyes to them, and it was as though a needle had dropped in a groove. She heard in her mind the distinctive opening guitar riff. The song was "Beast of Burden." The band, the Rolling Stones.

She let the music play in her head. It took a verse for her to dislodge herself, to stand up straight and follow the path from her kitchen to her bedroom, where she retrieved the phone number from her jewelry box. Sitting on her bed, she dialed it, and when John answered, she said, "I want to accept your dinner invitation because I need to know how I'd feel when I got there."

There was a pause. Then an audible shifting.

"I understand your motives," he said.

Geneva believed that he did.

"How 'bout tomorrow night?" he said.

"That would be fine."

"Are you a woman who will eat a pork chop?"

"I am."

"Six-thirty, seven?"

"That sounds good."

There was a spot of silence.

"Thank you for the lilacs," Geneva said.

John gave her directions, and then they said their good-byes and hung up their respective phones.

Geneva sat there until a slow smile spread across her face. She rose from the bed and headed for the stereo. Her glass had been half-full for some time. But now, she wanted to pour that half down the drain. They say something is better than nothing, but Geneva did not think it was true. Sometimes, nothing *is* better than something. With nothing, there's no thing to judge as inadequate. There's no disappointment. Some glasses are only half-full because that's all there is of the beverage. No sense in asking the bartender for more. An empty glass at least holds the potential of being filled to the top with that which one desires.

Geneva dropped the needle on *Some Girls*. *I want to be happy*, she thought, *and I don't give a damn how I get there.*

34

Dirt and dead flies cut the glare of the florescent lights. Paris moved from table to table sorting the sugar packets from the Equals in their caddies. By the feel and texture of the night, by the weight of the casino up front, the balance of bodies and sound, Paris could calculate the hour. The women should be arriving before long. Paris refused to look at the clock, however, and tried not to think of the progression of the hours, one day turning to the next. To distract himself, he purposefully filled his head with numbers. He added up his wages over two months, then three. He added them to the five-hundred-dollar bonus he was promised if he stayed until closing. Then he counted back the hours to when he was in Tatum's bed, telling her about the women from the diner. In the telling, the number of facts he had omitted was one. Linda. He left out her entire existence, and the story suffered for it. He wanted to tell Tatum all of it, even what happened in the janitor's closet. But he found it to be a weighty recognition that now, what choices he made for himself happened to Tatum as well. Even retroactively. Love, it seemed, dragged the past forward into the moment and the moment into the future by the promises implied. Perhaps by its nature, love was sticky.

Having sorted all the blue packets from the white, Paris returned to the backside of the counter. There were no orders to fill or tables to clear. Undirected, his mind spit up another fact he had conveniently omitted when he told Tatum about the women of the Deluxe: Vincent had been there once in the diner among them.

The lies of omission were stacking up.

He grabbed the push broom and headed for the cooler. His eyes skimmed the metal shelves as he swept. How many days would the crate of tomatoes last, or the bin of sliced onions? He struggled to add up things other than lies. He bent to push the debris into a dustpan, and a carton shaped like a pizza box caught his eye. "Cheesecake" was stamped plainly on the side. Jerry had told Paris that the Deluxe was out of cheesecake and that they weren't supposed to restock. It had already been dropped from the menu.

Cheesecake reminded Paris of regular cake, and regular cake reminded him of birthday cake. The jig was up. He could no longer drown out the fact of the new day. His birthday. A date he tried to forget from year to year. It wasn't a fear of aging. It was an exercise, just as some people did crossword puzzles or refused calculators in order to keep their minds sharp. Paris was training his brain. He figured if he could forget his birthday, he could forget anything. Then, if anything really terrible ever happened, he would know he could bury it in his own mind until it was no more. Knowing one's birthday was sometimes necessary, he knew, but need be, he could always look it up. Some years, he had forgotten splendidly. Other years, like this one, it refused to be repressed.

Paris put the broom to the side and extracted the box from the shelf. He left the cooler and placed the box on the cutting board. Sliced up, the cheesecake would be eight good-sized pieces.

He turned a large knife one way and then the other, creating wheel spokes across the yellow surface. The lightest reflex of a smile lifted the corners of his mouth. He had told Tatum about his ambition to forget his birthday. It was shortly after they had met. It had been her own birthday, and she had come over with a bottle of wine. They drank it from juice glasses Paris had purchased at the Salvation Army. Birthdays were the subject de jour, and Tatum had asked him, casually as could be, "When's yours?" — a perfectly sensible question.

"I'm trying to see if I can forget," he had told her, though he hadn't known her long. "I want to see if it's possible."

"That would be hard," she had said. She didn't say "How weird." She didn't even ask why. It was a feat. She could see that.

"You just gotta not think about it," he told her. "When someone asks," — he put his fingers on his temples and closed his eyes — "you just make a lot of noise inside. Drown out the answer. Yell, 'I don't know, I don't know' inside your head."

"Interesting skill to cultivate," she said. She swirled the red wine in the bottom of the cheap glass. "I'm scared to death of forgetting," she said. "I feel like you have to remember everything in order not to make the same mistakes over and over."

Paris spatula-ed slices of cheesecake onto small plates. He would appease his birthday this year. Make it an offering so it would recede back into his subconscious without a struggle.

He carried five plates at once toward the dining room, two in each hand and one resting in the crook of his left elbow. As he approached the swinging door beside the cook's window, he sensed a new body in the room beyond. He frowned, unhappy he had neither heard nor sensed someone enter. He stepped out from the kitchen loaded down with cheesecake, and she was there at the end of the counter.

Linda.

Words caught in his throat.

"What's the occasion?" she said.

Her hair was somewhat rumpled. She looked tired, but then, she always had. Paris unloaded all but one of the plates on the work space behind the counter. He extended the last one in her direction.

"My birthday," he said. He told the truth.

Linda waved off the plate.

"Well, happy, happy," she said. She reached into her coat pocket and pulled out several crumbled singles. "I'd like some soup," she said, "if you've got it."

Both the request and crumpled singles caught Paris off guard. She did not make eye contact, almost as though her having the money embarrassed them both.

Just then, the two retarded girls passed through the doorway and slid into a booth. An older woman with a dry drunk's twitch tailed the girls and seated herself in the corner. Paris poured coffee for Linda — the old habit — and then picked up three slices of cheesecake and took them to the other women. They accepted it without question. Then he filled a bowl of soup for Linda and delivered it with packaged saltines. As he placed it before her, she looked down at her hands, which she took turns with, one rubbing the other. The first wave of relief upon seeing her had blinded him to what he now saw. Her facade had melted. He had known it was a facade but had believed it was sadness below and not what he now saw. Fear.

The retarded girls talked in a low murmur. Paris ladled soup for them and for the older woman and dropped it at their respective booths. Back behind the counter, he pulled plastic wrap from its roll to cover the remaining slices of cheesecake. He stole a sidelong glance at Linda. He hoped her fear was not related to his own past bad judgment. She lifted her eyes and returned his gaze. For a moment, it seemed like she had something to say, but then her face went white.

In a single movement, she was up and over the counter, banging her knee, and spilling her coffee. She bit her bottom lip and crouched low, hop-limping her way into the kitchen. Paris dropped the plastic wrap and moved swiftly toward where she had been seated. Instinctively, he dumped her soup and spoon into the bus pan and wiped away all traces of her. The retards watched with wide eyes. The older woman kept her eyes averted.

Paris turned to face the doorway. A man stood there, arms puffed slightly at his sides. Paris assessed him quickly: Sober. Clean. Wound up tight. Weak and violent, a bad combination in a man for all women, children, and small animals. The man's eyes darted through the room, landing on each woman in succession and then to Paris, who was hanging up his rag.

Paris thought the man might turn and leave, not finding among them what he was looking for. But no such luck. He took a seat at the counter, sitting sideways on the stool. He ordered only a Coke. A bad sign. A Coke is an excuse. It's putting money in a meter. Buying a place to park.

The retarded girls focused on their soup and did not speak. Paris sat on the stool behind the counter that Jerry used during the day. Rarely did Paris sit at work, but he did so now, a sentry in the corner. Paris felt the man sizing him up, but he kept his own eyes unfocused on the space before him. But it was to no avail. Paris had lost his invisibility.

The man bought twenty tense minutes with his Coke. Paris wanted to go back into the kitchen and check on Linda, but he didn't want to leave the man unattended. He wondered what the man's relationship was to Linda. Pimp? Husband? Boyfriend? Some combination? He felt certain the retarded girls knew. The threat he posed was not that of the unknown.

Finally, the man stood and dumped change from his pocket onto the check. But instead of heading for the casino and exit, he turned and approached the retarded girls' booth. He looked back and forth between them.

"Where the fuck is she?" he said softly, but with menace.

Paris slid off the stool and came to lean with both hands on the counter. "Hey, hey, hey," he said. His biceps peeked out from his white T-shirt sleeves.

The man turned around.

Paris pointed downward at the top of the counter. "Bring it here," he said.

"I'm looking for my wife," he said, his back now to the girls.

"Which of you is married to this guy?" Paris said to the retarded girls. They looked back at him with blank faces. Then they looked at each other, and the white one seemed about to speak. Paris was relieved the man spoke first.

"This isn't your business," he said to Paris.

Paris lifted a hand and waved him closer to the counter, away from the women. Then, he leaned forward, looked him in the eye, and spoke softly.

"Those girls," Paris said, "they don't know anything."

"They know plenty."

"What's she look like?" Paris said. "If she shows up here, I'll tell her you're looking for her."

Paris forced himself to hold the man's eyes. Still, he could sense the woman in the corner booth trembling. This was not what she was told to expect. The man's eyes couldn't quite hold Paris's and made small movements back and forth as ideas and strategies unfolded and crashed against the wall of possibilities. There was no getting past Paris, he must have decided, because he backed away from the counter and pointed at him.

"Fuck you," he said.

Paris placed his hands on his apron-clad hips.

"Fuck me," he said, as though in total agreement.

The man pursed his lips and bobbed his head in three short, tight nods. Blair met him when he reached the casino and escorted him to the front door.

Paris came out from behind the counter and watched him go. Then he turned to the retarded girls. The cross-eyed Indian one said, "He's bad."

"He's gone," Paris said. Then he went back behind the counter and wiped him away with a rag. He pocketed the eight-cent tip. The dining room exhaled, and Paris went to the kitchen to look for Linda.

His eyes panned the room, the floors and the counters and sinks. He stepped toward the janitor's closet and crooked his neck, looking inside. Nothing. He moved toward the rear of the kitchen and checked the cooler. She was not inside, wrapped in her own arms, shivering. Paris then pushed on the metal bar, opening the heavy back door that led to the Dumpsters. A motion detector light ticked on above him. The alley cut through the purple night like a river, the cracked brick buildings rising up on each side like carved out canyon walls. Paris looked both ways. Angled light reached the Dumpsters, potholes, and fire escapes. But Paris saw her nowhere. The motion light ticked back off, detecting nothing either. Linda was gone. Paris hoped her small fistful of singles wasn't all the money she had.

The image of Linda clutching her dollars made Paris's hands tingle. He curled his fingers to his palms as though he, too, could feel the soft, kneaded texture of the bills. He stepped back inside the kitchen, pulling the door closed behind him.

But Linda didn't need to be drawn. She needed money.

Paris looked at the carton from the cheesecake, still on the work counter. He was going to give Linda his five-hundred-dollar bonus, he decided, to help her get to somewhere where she didn't need to hide. He had the money in savings from his last paycheck. He would give her that and cover the loss with the bonus. He would right past wrongs. He would be a man. If he were going to remember his birthday this year, this would be his birthday present. To himself.

He returned to the dining room just as the women were emerging from their booths to walk back into the dark.

"Tell her to come back," he said to the retarded girls, and they stopped and turned. The Indian one said, "Okay," and they continued out through the casino.

Paris cleaned up after them all. He loaded the dishwasher and then lined up doughnuts like neatly fallen dominoes on an orange Rubbermaid tray. He did what he knew how to do. He worked.

Light pressed against the dark sky. Blossoms that had survived the hail glowed. The first birds chirped, waking the others. Paris walked the cracked sidewalks until he reached the duplex. He crept downstairs and sat on the edge of his mattress with his work boots still on, contemplating the logistics of his feet. He liked to wash them first thing after work, but he didn't want to wake Tatum and Rachael. If he set his feet free, without washing them, the basement would be contaminated, and if Tatum came down later, she would be exposed. He realized he no longer had a deep corner closet where he could stash his offending footwear. He scanned the room for nooks and crannies. He stood to take a tour. He pushed through his own boxes and thought of the box he had left behind, the one with his paints and charcoals. He thought of Linda, and again, there was the tingling in his hands.

He continued shuffling through the rummage that surrounded the rug Geneva had unrolled for him. He made his way to Tatum's cluster, the place where he had surprised her earlier. He reached down and picked up a green leather book from the top of a box. It looked old. Expensive. Permanent, like a Bible.

He forgot his feet and took the book back to his mattress and sat with it on his lap. He opened the cover and turned the pages slowly. He knew Tatum's Rachael story, but he'd never seen the book. The old pictures were interesting, but the narratives beside them did not impress him much. A pen marked the page where Tatum belonged, and there was a blank space where her picture should have been. He touched the space with his fingers. He picked up the pen that was tucked into the seam of the book. Where Tatum's picture should have been, he started to sketch. It was an irresistible impulse, and he didn't pause to question it.

He sketched out her torso. He drew the scar. A place cut open. A place sealed closed. He drew a breast, a simple curve of specificity. Paris stayed with the moment. Then he hogged the space beyond that allotted to Tatum, his drawing reaching down, claiming much of Rachael's space below it and encompassing her baby picture. At first, the motion of his hands, the focus, and the appearance of lines, curves, and shading served to ease a tension that stretched across his shoulders and neck. It was an overdue exhale, moving out measuredly. But as the birds outside above the window wells worked themselves into a frenzy, an anxiety beset him, causing him to adjust and readjust his shoulders as he worked, as though he couldn't get them to sit quite right on his body. He felt pressure as he worked on Tatum's eyes. A pressure to act. To escape. His feet steamed.

The arrival of the day cast a green glow throughout the basement. Paris closed the book's cover. He flopped backward on his mattress, fully clothed. He had done it again. Violated her space. Yet, as he lay there, he seemed to grow lighter, as though he were not guilty at all and was, in fact, absolved.

Facts are products of evidence, and evidence exists only in the past. So facts are products of the past. Making decisions based on them, and using them to predict the future, is to look into an old-news crystal ball. When a choice is made based on the facts, and then made again and again, a layered reality is created. Fact stacked on fact. Past stacked on past.

There is fact, and there is hope. Choices are rooted in one or the other. Tatum knew this. She'd chosen different paths at different times. She'd hung in there out of hope. She'd split, knowing the facts. Sometimes, she just four-wheeled it, left both paths, and tossed pills down her throat. Maybe it didn't really matter which path she chose? So far, they had all led to the same place.

Outside her kitchen window, a black-capped chickadee sang its two-note song. Tatum lifted her head in the direction of the sound. She hadn't slept. Hadn't even been to bed. She paced the kitchen in her stocking feet, carrying the slip of paper with Lee's phone number on it. She needed to call him to get insurance information for the hospital. But for Rachael's sake, she knew she needed to ask for more. The world to which she had brought Rachael could crumble beneath her. Paris might not be there next time to stop the blood and tears. And Tatum knew that her own shame, if not Geneva's exasperation, would dig an ever-widening gulf between the two doors across the hall from each other. Rachael could well end up collateral damage. She needed insurance in more ways than one.

Tatum fingered the piece of paper. The phone number was for Lee's answering service. He was in New Jersey currently, setting up a satellite office for his company. Something to do with pharmaceuticals. He was two hours ahead, and she thought she might catch him before he went to work. She would get nowhere with a lecture, she knew, or anything with even a whiff of criticism. He had to be seduced, flattered. She fanned herself with the phone number, considering what to say. She looked into her living room and noted the wilting plants, signs of her neglect, reminding her of the to-do list that never got done. Track down old work contacts. Schedule a mammogram. Why did uphill tend to be a battle while downhill tended to snowball? Momentum and the laws of physics had a way of taking sides.

She picked up the phone and dialed Lee's number. She left her message.

"There's been a little accident. Everything is fine. Two little stitches is all. I just need some insurance information for the hospital." Tatum hesitated. "Lee," she said, "try to see yourself through Rachael's eyes. You're important to her. Why don't you give her a call and check up on her? I think it would help. Okay. Thanks."

It was the best, and least, she could do. A sorry commentary that the two were one and the same.

She hung up the phone. There was still an hour, maybe two, before Rachael woke. Tatum went to her own bedroom and lay down on top of the bedspread. She closed her eyes. Hope and fact. She felt she was stuck between the two. But she was not stuck. Nothing stands still. She just couldn't detect her own deeper currents, her trajectory, toward hope. She was advancing toward it, but she was walking backward, mistaking what was before her eyes for the ground beneath the backward stepping heel, choosing the lift and press of her step based on terrains already traversed.

Exhaustion pressed her to the mattress. Her body seemed to sink. As she drifted off, she became aware of a presence. Not one newly arrived but one just noticed. Margaret. Not a ghost, Tatum knew, but a phantom. A phantom limb. Not really there and yet part of her.

Tatum rolled to her side and opened her eyes. A slip of something on the other pillow caught her attention. She reached out and picked it up. She rolled to her back and squinted. Right there in her hand, it was Vincent.

35

Lee couldn't tell you his story because he couldn't see it. That is why he moved from face to face looking for it. The approval. The need. He required both. The need was necessary because he knew the approval was based on an illusion. But all this occurred beneath the veil of the subconscious. Unaware that he was so afflicted, Lee existed at the whim of physics.

The physicists say that reality takes shape at the pleasure of perception. Look into a teeming field of particles and they organize within the parameters of the stencils the one looking projects. *There it is*, one thinks, for it is obvious and solid. But the looker turns, and it shimmers away. Attention, alone, sustains it. Sustained him. Outside eyes turned upon him and he'd freeze frame, lit up in accordance to their hopes and fears. Was what they saw him, in part, at the least? Or was it merely bits and pieces parsed out from a grand whole, broken mirror images of other people's minds?

Alive, Margaret had an omnipresent eye on Lee. An eye *in* him, thinking him into being. When Lee didn't like what the eye saw, he found Corrina. Then he made the eye look at what Corrina saw. But when Margaret died, the eye closed. The notion of her ghost, though disembodied as the eye, offered no comfort. Ghosts don't tell stories. Ghosts are stories. Then, Corrina left. There had been no breakup. No big talk. Lee remembered something Corrina had told him early in their affair. "Single men take up too much energy," she had said. "I prefer to carry the light side of the load."

He had been comforted by it at the time.

Now, Lee listened to the low roll of the Atlantic and mistakenly drowned the wrong thoughts in alcohol. The part of his mind he dulled with Bloody Marys was the one that had it all figured out. The dulled part could've told you – had it not been dulled — that if you want to save your marriage, you must first save yourself . Had it not been for Corrina, he knew, it might've been him instead of Margaret. Dead. In order to save himself, he had lied to Margaret. True. But Lee found that most women didn't want to deal with the truth. They wanted to deal with their feelings. They wanted you to deal with their feelings too. It didn't matter what messed-up, imaginary nonsense their feelings were based on, they wanted you to *acknowledge* them.

Acknowledge them. Hell, Lee felt he was drowning in them. If Corrina hadn't sat down on the stool beside him in a bar on Rush Street, Margaret's feelings would've filled his ears and nostrils and lungs and dragged him down to rot at the bottom of a dark sea.

But Corrina did take that barstool, her hips wrapped in leather, her hair in long sheets of braids. The group she entered with simmered and sparkled. They dressed hipper. They laughed louder. They were a cluster of electricity at the end of the bar with Corrina sitting on the only available barstool, the one next to Lee's. She pushed several strands of braids behind her shoulder and twisted on her stool toward her empty glass. Lee was looking at her. So she looked back.

She gave her brows the slightest of lifts.

"Let me guess," she said, her voice the flavor of honey and cynicism, "your marriage sucks." A sneaky half-smile crept across her face.

Lee shape-shifted where he sat in the light of her flashing eyes and the sneaky half-smile. The colossal failure that was his marriage was a wry joke, an urbane fact over which witticisms were exchanged. When the bartender refilled Corrina's snifter with brandy, Lee caught his eye and tapped his stack of bills. They postponed introductions for the thrill of mystery and were clever with each other, throwing down truths like gauntlets.

"My wife wants to renegotiate our relationship," Lee told her. "As far as I can tell, 'renegotiating a relationship' means a woman telling a man how he needs to change."

Corrina leaned in, as though she were about to confide.

"Here's what I know," she said. "Men tend to think that when a woman tells him her feelings, she's accusing him of causing them." She picked up her snifter and raised it to Lee. "Thanks," she said.

The group she had arrived with was moving to a newly emptied table. Corrina waved good-bye to Lee and joined them.

Lee thought about her, and her friends, all the next week. He remembered being them, the best and brightest in a room. He had felt that way with Margaret once, as a couple. They ranked in a crowd. People were aware of them and not the other way around. Because he had felt it again with Corrina, that old simmering, he knew that it was not he who had been diminished by time. The problem was Margaret.

He hadn't gone looking for an affair. Nor had he leapt into one at the first hints of marital dissatisfaction. Lee told himself this, and it was true. But when he came upon it, the improved reflection, it drew him like a magnet. He took shape before it. Over the next week, he watched Margaret as she moved behind him in the bedroom mirror and as she made school lunches and loaded the dishwasher. He realized that even her expressions of pleasure had to squeeze their way through her mask of hurt and resentment. Margaret's face had become to him a constant accusation.

But then, approval from the needy is hard to come by, as their dissatisfaction is built into the neediness. It comes to be, in fact, that the needy's approval isn't worth much anyway as the value of approval lies in the source. Margaret had been discredited by her desperation, cultivated by Lee though it was, and now all he saw in her eyes was that he was not good enough.

Perhaps some cakes can be had and eaten too. But when it comes to wanting neediness and approval from the same person, both sides are out of luck.

Lee returned to the bar the next week, hoping to find Corrina, and himself. That was a year before Margaret got sick.

Living as the reflection in Margaret's eye had come to feel to Lee like a slow dying, which was why, looking back, he could see that he had been in a life-or-death situation. He chose life. The body ducks without thinking. The soul, he figured, does the same. It reflexively dodges bullets and reaches blindly for lifelines when drowning.

Corrina was that line, that life preserver floating on the surface. Lee told Corrina that if he hadn't met her, he thought it might have been him, and not Margaret, who would have gotten cancer. He thanked her for saving his life.

Corrina said that it was too bad Margaret couldn't find someone to save hers.

Lee's affair with Corrina did not make him feel like a louse. He felt like a good man who in order to be a good husband had to go re-find his goodness some place else. His affair with Corrina had not felt like the low and sneaky part of his life but the honest part. Lee didn't divorce Margaret. He never left. Technically, she did.

~

Now, from an Adirondack chair, Lee watched the Atlantic's crash and rumble, the tide moving in and out like breath. Bloody Marys kept the world slightly a blur but couldn't stop the dreams, dreams in which he would find himself floating just slightly off the ground, feet grabbing for the earth. The only escape was to waken. The dreams were with him in Florida right after Margaret's death. They were with him in Newark, and they were there for those two days in between — just two days that he had spent in his own home since parting paths with his daughter.

After the launch of the satellite office in Newark, Lee had been free to return home. But instead, he headed south to Cape May, where it was still off-season and quieter than he had anticipated. Since the dreams followed him anyway, they were not the reason for avoiding home. His two days in the house had been suffocating. Everything there, the furniture, the appliances, the very walls seemed to ask *where is she?* as though his connection to them was through Margaret and here they had been stuck with each other awkwardly, blown off by the intermediary each had depended upon. Lee didn't want to sell the house or give everything away. Nor did he want to be responsible for it. He didn't know how.

So it sat unoccupied. Almost.

Margaret was there. But she wasn't in her grave. A fact only Lee was aware of. She was in a box in their bedroom. Lee knew that Margaret wanted to be cremated, the logistics of decomposing too unseemly for her to stomach. But she didn't want to offend relatives and her Catholic heritage. She told him all this years ago before she was sick, before she was unhappy, back when such a conversation was innocent, macabre musings, a projecting of themselves into a harmless future too far away to worry about. But Margaret had not left Lee with instructions as to what to do with her next, after she was burned. Before leaving for Florida, he had placed her on the shelf beneath her nightstand, slid in between a Bible and a green leather book.

For those two days at the house, Lee did not sense Margaret's ghost watching him. No one was watching him. His calls to Corrina went unreturned. He gravitated to the box of ashes. He sat on what was once Margaret's side of the bed and looked down at the box. But it failed to look back. It was silent and self-contained. He reached down and pulled the green leather book from the shelf. Margaret had told him about the Book but had left out the nitty-gritty details. As far as Lee was concerned, it was nothing more than a type of family tree.

He flipped through it. He noted the strange, self-congratulatory tone. Maybe, he thought, it was something that made sense to women. He paused over his daughter's entry. Her birth date caught his eye. It was two days away.

Lee did not think of his daughter much. It had not been his habit. She had been well cared for by Margaret. He had no cause for worry. He provided the cash, and the two lived within the comfortable wing of protection it cast. The world the two shared was satisfying and complete. He paid the tab. And now, Rachael was in his wife's sister's care. Doing the right thing sometimes means finding the right person to do it. He probably hadn't brought it about as well as he might have, but the outcome was what mattered. Rachael was cared for. She was safe.

Yet, there on the edge of the bed during those two days, the terrifying lightness snaked in through his feet, climbed his legs, and reached up into his chest and shoulders. It was the warning, the feeling that came in the dream right before the force field lifted him.

Lee couldn't explain why Margaret's death had surprised him, but it had. Even after the fact, he walked through the next days like he was playing a role, testing a circumstance, sampling it, to see if it was to his taste. That was how he had been feeling when Tatum said to him, "You should probably check on Rachael." Tatum had been standing in his kitchen. They had been planning the funeral. She said the words, and then she picked up the phone to order Chinese food.

Checking on Rachael would not have occurred to him. But it was not because he didn't care. He had assumed, without even knowing he was assuming it, that Tatum had assumed such duties. The recognition that his daughter was uncared for unleashed adrenalin into his blood stream. It was the moment he realized that Margaret had made no arrangements for Rachael. It was the moment he realized that Tatum hadn't stepped up to the plate.

Fear. Embarrassment. Helplessness. They added up quickly. They were the anxiety. They were the adrenaline. But Lee had a different interpretation for his upset biochemistry. Lee interpreted the discomfort as insult. Insult was preferable to the insecurity that might overtake him on the way to his daughter's room. He climbed the stairs, indignant at what he considered Tatum's "order." He pushed on the half-opened bedroom door. His eyes slipped through the room. He didn't see Rachael, and he moved to back out, when he heard a rustling. A shifting.

So he took another step, deeper into the room. He saw little socked feet sticking out from where Rachael crouched between the wall and the dresser. More steps, a floor's creak, and her face appeared, her eyes lifted to him, large green pools, pulling at him with wordless, shapeless need. She was a black hole, and the force she exerted dismembered him where he stood.

His skin went first. Then, the organs. He was ripped apart, robbed of even the organizing intelligence that said the heart goes here, the arms go there. Perception did not shape him. It reached at him with greedy hands. Lee floated like a junkyard of parts. He unraveled among pink ruffles, unicorns, and glitter. So he wasn't even there, not really, when he lowered himself to a knee and placed a hand on Rachael's arm.

"You'll be okay," he said.

He didn't realize it, but in telling her "you'll be okay," he had let her know that she was on her own.

It made the sucking stop, but the need remained. This, Lee did know. Still, he stood and turned.

And there she was. Tatum. She had slipped into the bedroom and leaned against the wall near the door. He flushed, as though she could read his thoughts and knew that he knew he had stopped the sucking but not the need. A moment that had passed for him with discomfort, though not self-reproach, reframed itself through the lens that was Tatum. She had sent him to his daughter to watch him fail. Hatred flickered in his chest, and it was its own explanation.

The next day, Tatum stood beside him as the hired backhoe dug Margaret's phony grave. Her questions about Margaret being buried on the property were oddly specific. Did it take a permit? Were there laws governing family plots? It made him wonder if she knew that Margaret would acutally be cremated and she was testing him.

When the backhoe was done, Tatum was silenced by the product. She squatted down and fingered the dying grass beside the grave. It was a crisp autumn day, the trees swaying ever so slightly.

"That last call from Margaret," she had said, "I wish I knew if there had been something important she wanted to tell me, some final message."

Lee looked down. She was looking up, her eyes green pools like Rachael's, exerting a pull too, though not as strong. She was asking him a question, and he felt he knew the answer she sought.

Lee remembered the moment from his Adirondack chair in Cape May. Seagulls shrieked and landed not far from his chair, acting nonchalant, while piercing him with their sidelong glances as though if they pierced hard enough, a Cheeto or Cheerio might be extracted from his flesh. He shook the white pebble ice cubes in the bottom of his glass as the morning haze drifted. Standing there by the phony grave, it could've been so easy. He could have made up anything. He could have told her that Margaret wanted her to take care of Rachael. Her, and no one else. Her, above all others. Even himself. But he just couldn't give it to her.

Instead, he had pleaded overwhelment. His tears were real. Take Rachael, he asked of her. He asked for time. He knew it was the right thing. Right for him. Right for Rachael. Right for Tatum.

Of course, she had said yes. But she judged him for it and made it no secret.

He had left Tatum standing there beside the grave. He walked toward the house over the matted leaves, a strange mix of relief and fear making him unsteady as he crossed the yard. He lifted his eyes to the trees and noticed an empty bird feeder hanging on the dogwood near the house. How long had it been empty, he wondered? Since Margaret got sick? For years? He felt it again, the feeling that had started in his daughter's room the day before. The unraveling. The eye closing.

As Lee looked up at the tree and feeder, a sense of lightness had entered through his feet and traveled up his legs. To keep from floating up, he reached for things — the knob to his front door, the railing on the stairway inside as he raced up, the varnished wood surface of the door to Rachael's room as he pushed it open. When Rachael saw his face, her bottom lip set to quivering and then panicked tears began to fall. Lee sat on the bed and pulled her into his arms.

Four days later, he loaded her into Tatum's car and sent her west. He headed south.

Three months later, when he returned home for just two days, he had visited Margaret's ashes, but not her grave. The ashes hadn't looked back at him, but the green leather book had. When he stood from the side of the bed and left the room, he had unconsciously carried the Book along. When he took the birthday gift he had bought to the shippers, he also sent the Book of Rachaels.

෯

And now, he was alone, with no He to be. The eye had closed. Margaret was no longer inside his mind, watching him like God, present and silent. He had existed to her always. In his presence. In his absence. In love. In anger. In sorrow. In contempt. Clocks told her when he was leaving and when he was late to come home. Calendars told her when she needed to make sure the dry cleaning was picked up for his business trip. A ringing phone. Was it him? He was the sun. She orbited. He was the tree that fell, and she was the ears to hear. He had never really believed she would die. He thought that someone who wants something from you doesn't leave.

The seagulls gave up on him. The white waves of low tide crashed and were pulled back to sea, dragged by their heels, ruffled fingers clawing at the packed sand. Lee stood and headed up the beach to the restaurant's patio. Unfaithful husband. Part of his mind knew what it meant. It meant that he had been unfaithful to a role in order to be faithful to something that ran much deeper. But the part of his mind that knew this was softened by vodka. The part that was left didn't know what to know. He looked up into the washed out sky, but it gave him vertigo. He looked down, but the rolling granules of sand that tumbled forward with each step did the same.

He crossed the restaurant, his eyes taking a quick inventory of the few customers. He didn't know that he was looking for a woman. A face. Someone to look into him and see herself and mistake him for the self she had misplaced. Vanity didn't kill Narcissus. It was mistaking his beauty for that of another's.

Back in his room, Lee sat on the edge of the bed and called in for his messages. He listened to Tatum's voice, earnest but without edge. Her words made him remember the "hunkered-downness" of his daughter. The green pools of her eyes. The need. But the black hole that had dismembered him now felt more like gravity pulling him in, reassembling the pieces of a self that had fractured and broken. Tatum told him to try to see himself through Rachael's eyes.

He did, and he could. He was the mysterious stranger. He was her father. When he imagined her, he felt a push-pull coming from her. Enough pull to keep his feet on the ground. Enough push to keep him from sinking.

36

Geneva used her best lotion. She dressed in a cream-colored sweater and blue canvas pants and wore her flat, brown leather boots. A little eyeliner. Eyebrow pencil. A touch of rouge. Aging shrinks the range between how a woman looks at her best and how she looks at her worst. On the upside, it saves time. Geneva reached quickly the outer limit of how good she could look. There was no sense in pretending there was further to go.

She picked up the directions to John's and headed for her door. The last of his directions included unmarked roads and navigation by landmark as opposed to street name. She was curious about his word choice. He referred to his house as the "shack" on the left.

Shack. Was he being cute, and it really referred to a ranch estate? Was it indeed a "shack," and he would meet her in his long johns having just finished shaving over a water barrel? It crossed her mind that it might not be his home at all, but the shed he used to butcher his victims, middle-aged women in search of a last hurrah.

She hesitated at her front door but then returned to her desk. She wrote a note including the date, the time, and John's address — for the investigation, just in case.

Outside the city limits, the valley spread, subdivisions occasionally blemishing the expanse of ten- and twenty-acre lots. Horses stepped toward their barns, shaking out their manes, finished with the day's work of gracing the landscape and providing elegant foreground to the distant snow-capped Rockies. The drive from Geneva's front door to the last stretch of dirt and gravel that led to John's shack took thirty minutes. She approached from the west and noticed a structure on the right. It truly did look the size of a shed, too small to house a man of John's size. As she passed, she looked up into her rearview. On the other side of the small building was an outdoor grill with John standing behind its open lid. Ahead, the only building was a tall and narrow outhouse.

She hit the brakes and threw the car into reverse, rolling back slowly over the gravel. She turned into his drive. Psycho killer or no, Geneva liked the cut of his body against the sky.

John closed the grill and watched her walk from her car across the dust and prickly pear. His eyes sparked at her like he had been waiting for her for years, decades, always knowing that someday, she'd turn her wheels up his drive.

Geneva reached him and turned out her arms as if to say, *Here I am.*

John hung the meat fork on the grill. Behind him in the distance, the Continental Divide lumbered across the sky, snow-capped and purple in the dusk.

"It's a beautiful night," Geneva said.

"And it's all for free. Come on in," John said, motioning toward the shed.

The front door was open and constructed like one to a horse's stall — tall, wide, and split with an upper and a lower gate. Inside, there was one large room with north and south facing windows. A queen size bed and nightstand took up nearly a third of the room. The opposite corner included shelves, a sink, and refrigerator. The large wood stove had two burners and an oven compartment. The smell of potatoes leaked from the bubbling pot on top.

"You cook on that?" Geneva said.

"All the time."

Geneva took in the room. It was completely simple but not without modern conveniences — a refrigerator, a radio. Maybe not a microwave, but a toaster oven.

"How long have you been here?" she asked.

"I bought the land twelve years ago," he said. "There's twenty acres, total. I built this cook's shed and was going to live in it until I built my house."

"And lo and behold?" she said.

"Yep. Now it's Home Sweet."

"What did you run out of," Geneva asked, "money or will?"

"Neither, really," John said. "I just got a feeling I was pushing the river. I got as far as the slab," he said, pointing out the door toward a cluster of trees some two hundred yards away.

Geneva looked but couldn't really see it.

"Won't you sit?" he said, motioning to the table in the middle of the room. On it were two simple, but crystal, wine glasses and a good bottle of Shiraz. One of the glasses was a quarter full. John picked up the bottle and presented it like he was a wine steward.

"Please," Geneva said.

John poured her a glass and handed it to her. Then he lifted his own glass and extended it to her for a quick *chink*. After taking a sip, John put down his glass and picked up a towel and opened the lid of the pot on the stove.

"Can I help?" Geneva said, a reflex.

John turned in her direction and shook his head no with a small smile. He replaced the lid and excused himself to go check on the meat. Geneva let her eyes take a lap around the shack, rooting out the revealing details. Under the nightstand, there was a stack of books, a mix of Eastern religion, Louis L'Amour, and construction how-to's. A postcard on his fridge was of South Dakota's Black Hills. Behind the bed tacked to an exposed two-by-four was a photograph of a sunset that was likely taken right outside the door. Her eyes dropped to the bed. The quilt looked old and handmade, gingham squares bonded by ties of blue yarn. The bed was built high off the floor. If he comes in, she thought, takes my hand, and leads me to it, I'm going.

But best, she thought, not to be caught contemplating his bed. She turned her attention to the man, the rear view of him, standing at the grill. He held his body like a man with decades of physical labor under his belt. She could sense both its power and the creaks and glitches that caused him to lean into his right hip, his left shoulder pulled up slightly toward his ear.

John turned and returned to the shack, a platter of chops in one hand.

"I'm married," Geneva blurted. "He's in Parkview Home with Alzheimer's. He hasn't recognized me for seven years."

John stared at her, his face serious. He shifted his body weight to the side.

"So what you're telling me," he said, "is that if he finds out about us, it's okay, because he'll probably forget in pretty short order."

Geneva buried her face in her hands, pleasantly embarrassed.

"Pork chop?" he said.

Geneva nodded without looking up. John put the platter on the table and drained the pot of potatoes. He placed them in a bowl and put that on the table too. He retrieved the butter from the refrigerator and put a loaf of ciabatta on a cutting board.

"I'm sorry," Geneva said. "It's just, you know, full disclosure."

"Full disclosure?" he said, pulling plates from an open shelf.

"You know, marriages, diseases, outstanding warrants."

John placed silverware beside the plates and took a seat. He lifted the platter and extended it to her.

"Pick your pork chop."

Geneva looked them over and took a small one with burnt edges.

"Have you ever been married?" Geneva asked him, dropping it onto her plate. "Or rather, are you married and maybe she's locked up somewhere too?"

"No one in lock down," John said. "Nothing current."

"But ever?"

John shifted in his chair.

"Married the first one at nineteen," he said, "and divorced the last one at forty-two."

"And the grand total was?"

"Three."

John picked up his pork chop with his fingers and bit into it, ripping the meat off the bone.

"How do you do that?" Geneva asked.

"What?" he said, chewing.

"Get married over and over," she said. "I always thought that if I didn't make it in the one I had, I'd never do it again."

"So you'd blame the institution."

"Maybe," she said. "I think I'd blame myself, though, mostly. I'd be the one who couldn't do it."

"My parents were married for sixty-three years," John said, getting up and grabbing a couple of paper napkins off the top of his refrigerator. "They were happy. Maybe that's why I think it can be done. When it comes to what we can and can't do," he said, "I think it's a bad idea to look to evidence. There's never evidence that we can do something we haven't done yet."

"True," Geneva said. She smiled. "I like that. I like counterintuitive things that make sense."

"I thought you might."

John poured the rest of the Shiraz into their glasses. The next bottle, a cabernet, was already breathing on the table.

Geneva lifted her glass but didn't take a sip.

"Sometimes," she said, "I wonder if a husband or wife getting Alzheimer's is any different than any other change that makes you feel like you don't know them anymore."

"At least it's a change," John said. "I've always thought that you either have two people changing all the time, two people never changing, or you've got a problem."

"One changing and one not?"

"One changing and one not."

Geneva briefly wondered if her own problem was that Ralph had changed, and she was the one lagging behind. But it's not what she said.

"I think the problem with marriage," Geneva said, shifting the subject slightly, "one of them, anyway, is that when a woman gets married, she doesn't get to be irresistible anymore."

John made a face that indicated he might disagree. He reached for another pork chop.

"It's inevitable," she said. "Not because he falls out of love or thinks she's unattractive, it's simply that at some point, sometimes, he can take it or leave it. He's too tired, too irritable. Sometimes he just doesn't want to give her what she wants to prove he doesn't have to. It's inevitable. It's life. But that doesn't negate the loss."

"So because he may not find her irresistible all the time it means she's no longer irresistible?"

"Exactly," Geneva said. "If you're not irresistible all the time, it means sometimes you're resistible, thus, you're not irresistible."

John rolled the wine in his mouth and then swallowed.

"Sounds like math," he said. "What if a man other than her husband found her irresistible?"

"Well, unless she's going to cheat on her husband, it doesn't matter, because she won't be able to *experience* the irresistibility because he'll have to resist, see?"

"You think all women feel this way?" he said.

"I don't pretend to know what all women feel," she said.

"Well, I don't know if you're right," John said, "but it does make sense."

Something warm flickered in Geneva's chest and then spread throughout her body. *I don't know if you're right, but it does make sense.* It struck her as the most marvelous thing anyone had ever said to her.

Their plates were empty, and no one was reaching for more.

"How 'bout a fire?" John said.

Then, he stood and covered the food but left it on the table. Night was falling, deepening the purple of the mountains and turning the snow-capped peaks to pink icing. John tucked the wine bottle under his arm and picked up both their glasses. He motioned out toward a fire pit surrounded by a log and tree stumps.

Outside the shed, away from the stove, the air was cooler. They made small talk as they stepped across the prairie. Geneva thanked him for dinner. They agreed on a preference for pork over beef. They discussed sunsets, not any one in particular, and the herd of elk that passed through from time to time.

At the pit, they settled in, Geneva seating herself on a stump. John handed her a glass and placed his own on the stump beside her. He pulled matches from his hip pocket and lit the prepared paper and kindling.

"I think the problem with marriage," John said, returning to the subject, "is that if there's a lot of love, it's going to bring up a lot of scary stuff. The problem is, the amount of love it takes to bring the scary business up is only about half the amount you need to figure all the scary business out. You never know going in how much is in the well."

"I think a lot of people, most, maybe, never figure it out," Geneva said.

John added two larger logs to the fire and blew on the kindling. He picked up his wine glass and took a seat on the stump beside Geneva. The dry pine slowly took the flame.

"Not me," he said. "I can't just keep covering the same ol' ground."

"But don't you have to keep covering the same old ground until it breaks and you can move on?"

He looked out at her from under a heavy brow.

"Like maybe I've just quit too soon?" he said.

Geneva shrugged.

They were quiet as the fire kicked up, crackling, and finding momentum.

"I'm happy to be here with you," John said.

He leaned forward on his stump. He held his wine glass between the fingers of his upturned hands. He looked like an ancient creature, not so much old as from another time. Sitting there, Geneva had the sense that his fires were not for company only. She could imagine him alone, sitting on a stump, contemplating the orange glow traveling through the wood, snake eyes, opening and closing.

"Before he got the Alzheimer's," John said, "was it good?"

"Yes," Geneva said, but not firmly. "Ralph expected absolutely nothing of me, but that I be there, happy to see him when he showed up."

"Oh," John said. "He kept you."

"He set me free," Geneva corrected him. "He never tried to keep me from anything I wanted to do."

"As long as you were there when he got home."

"No," Geneva said. "It wasn't like that. It was more, 'whenever you're with me, no matter what, let it be enough.'"

"Don't want," John said.

"Don't want *more*," Geneva corrected him, "or different."

"Don't change."

"Kind of."

"And was that something you managed to do?"

Geneva looked at him. The firelight licked at his face.

"No," she said. "I did change. I pretended I didn't. But . . . " she looked away and shook her head. "If you feel you've changed on the inside, but on the outside pretend you haven't, which is the lie?"

"Good question."

Geneva smiled at him, but then her lips flattened in thought. She blinked. Then shrugged.

"Ralph didn't want to be pushed to do, think, or talk about anything he didn't want to do, think, or talk about," she said. "That's reasonable, though, isn't it? Nobody wants to do something they don't want to do. That's why we call it something we don't want to do."

"So he said go forth and do what *you* want."

"He did."

"As long as what you wanted was what he wanted."

Geneva half-laughed.

"I guess it was a lucky coincidence," she said, "that for a time, anyway, the two were the same."

John shifted on his stump.

"How 'bout this?" he said. "What do you want *me* to do?"

Geneva's brows drew together.

"He said 'do what you want,'" John said. "I'm saying, 'What do you want from me?' There are people to whom I doubt I could give anything they wanted. But you? I could. Not because you don't want much, but because anything you'd want would be good, something I'd want in myself too. Or for myself. I know I'm not omnipotent," he said, crossing a giant leg over his knee, "but my gut tells me I can grant any wish that it's in you to ask." He looked not at her but the fire. "I would trust what you want," he said.

His face was serious. He was no frat boy in a bar making movie promises that he lacked the self-knowledge to keep. Geneva knew that she, herself, had never been as certain about anything as John seemed to be of what he offered to her. She was attracted to the certainty, and she was attracted to the man, and she tried to force herself to distinguish between the two.

And, she wondered, what would she ask of him, if she were to take up his offer? He turned to face her just then, as though he had heard her thought and was waiting.

Would you kill for me? She could say it with a wicked flick of the brows, deflecting the weight of the moment and escaping her own discomfort. Or she could lift her glass in his direction. *Pour me some wine,* she could say, imperiously. But it seemed a sin to waste wishes out of fear they'd come true.

The fire snapped and spit up ash.

"Why?" she finally said.

"'Why' what?"

"Why do that for me? You don't even know me."

John lifted the bottle from beside his stump. Geneva extended her glass, and the neck of the bottle chinked against the rim.

"From the first time I saw you," he said, "I've been considering it. That afternoon in the coffee shop with your little friend, it wasn't the first time I saw you. I'd seen you in the Grounds before. Thinking. Staring. The idea grew inside me over time." He smiled sheepishly at her. "I'm not spontaneous."

John then reached down, picked up a nearby stick, and poked at the fire. He turned to face her again but rolled his head farther to see the sky. He pointed a finger upward, and Geneva's eyes followed. The moon hung above them silver, like a quarter tossed to the sky. Darkness pointed at Geneva's back, and warm light illuminated and warmed her face from the front. No stars fell. Geneva didn't wish. A log shifted, sending up a cloud of wood smoke and a spray of hot cinders.

Geneva watched the orange spray vanish in the night.

This is what it's like, she thought, *not to be alone.*

"I don't want you for a friend," John said. He reached over and placed his hand on hers.

Geneva looked to him. She didn't want him for a friend either. Nor had it ever been what she had wanted from Ralph. Friends don't stretch us, she thought, the way lovers do, or lead us to those inner cliffs that we must leap from alone, not knowing whether or not those that brung us will be there when we land.

John took his hand from the top of hers. He lifted the stick and poked at the fire. There was nothing more to say. John was there with a decision, and Geneva was there with a choice.

The fire kept its own counsel, burning down, singing softly to itself. They drank to the bottom of their glasses.

John walked Geneva to her car in the unsettled silence of indecision.

"You call me if you want to," he said.

Geneva turned when they reached her car door. He was taller than her by nearly a foot.

"Kiss me," she said, and he did. He smelled of flesh and wood smoke. His lips were cracked, but his flavor, sweet. Their mouths opened to each other's. The land around them stretched out wide, and it felt to Geneva like they were its warm center. Each cell in Geneva's body came to life, lit up by an illicit sense of grace, illicit because it was stolen, stolen from the beautiful and young, the crime witnessed by the moon.

John was the one who broke away.

"It would change who I am," Geneva said, a fact, not a complaint, nor a reason one way or the other.

Her chin dropped, and her body slumped. John stepped back. Geneva turned and slid into her car. She hesitated with the key at the ignition but then turned it over.

She backed onto the dark road, put the car into gear, and turned into red taillights in the night. But she didn't make it far — fifty yards? — before her foot shifted from the gas to the brake and the car rolled to a tentative stop. The road before her was empty, dark and narrow, barely wide enough for two cars to pass. The headlights lit up the dirt and gravel. What difference could it possibly make, she thought? She'd practically been declared a rapist as it was. Why not a cheater, or a whore, to boot?

She eased into reverse, looked over her shoulder, and gave the car the slightest bit of gas. She tried to shake the image in her mind of Ralph in his pajamas lying in his bed, his fragile mind sensing a frayed rope snapping as she traveled that one more irrevocable inch. Once snapped, she and Ralph would continue to drift apart, lost in space, pulled apart by separate forces. Even if she continued to visit, continued to make cassette tapes, and place flowers at his bed, he would be alone.

She couldn't do it. She pressed on the brake and shifted back into drive.

But driving forward meant going back. Geneva thought of the duplex. She thought of Tatum, hand wringing in the face of everything she wanted. She didn't want to be like Tatum, walking away from her desires. It was bad juju. It misinformed the powers that be.

She hit the brake, put the car into reverse again, and threw her arm over the back of the seat. The time for finding happiness in concepts was over, she thought. It was time to choose it in touch. This was her thought when she slammed on the brakes as the shadow stepped out into the center of the road.

John came around to the passenger side of the car and climbed in. They mauled each other like teenagers.

"Back this baby up," John said.

Geneva did.

Geneva's bra was stuffed into her purse. It was four a.m., and she felt thoroughly fucked. Turns out John was a horse. She didn't know her insides extended that far up. Another inch, and it would've been unpleasant, about size and nothing more, maneuverability lost to sheer bulk.

But it had been perfect. Glorious. The universe did not collapse as she thought it might, which wasn't to say that it didn't change everything. She could have never called his number. She could have never gone. Never moved to the fire. Never tasted his breath. But well enough isn't meant to be left alone. The effort to leave it alone is futile. Moments press on moments. One cell replaces another. We are re-created against our wills. How can the re-created self be held responsible for the choices made by a being who has since self-destructed?

The highway was her own. The valley lights ahead were a shimmering sea. She thought of what John had said to her, *What do you want me to do for you?* She thought maybe the question was the thing. Another's faith in what she wanted. Another's faith in her perception.

She turned down her side street and tried to block out any thoughts involving "next" — what this would mean in the light of day and what this would change. For now, the world twinkled, and her pelvis radiated. Time would unfold as it did. She would catch up to it later.

She parked in the garage. Voodoo joined her as she crossed the yard, trotting at her feet. Geneva entered through the back door and moved with slow pleasure down the hall to the front of the house. She dropped her purse on the desk. The answering machine blinked.

She hit the button. It was Parkview Homes. They needed her to call at the soonest possible moment.

Geneva picked up the phone and dialed, but she already knew that Ralph was dead.

37

Geneva rolled away from the sudden blast of light and covered her face
with the bed sheet. Geneva's friend, Helene, stood at the switch, a barn
jacket thrown on over her blouse and jean skirt.

"Let's go, Eva," she said.

Ralph was on Geneva's nightstand, cremated to dust.

"Get rid of him now," Helene said, "or you'll spend years trying to
figure out what to do with him."

Geneva turned over in her bed, rose to an elbow, and squinted in
Helene's direction. She shaded her eyes with her hand. The service had
been earlier that day. Vincent had arrived on Geneva's doorstep within
ten hours of her having called his mother, Helene, to tell her that
Ralph was dead. It took Helene another day and a half to arrive from
Ventura. Vincent and Tatum had dealt with the logistics of the service
while Helene served as muscle for Geneva. For the last few days, to get
to Geneva, you had to go through her.

"Where are the keys to that piece-of-shit car of yours?" Helene
said.

"It's not a piece of shit."

Helene flashed the lights on and off several times. Geneva watched
Helene's short, thick frame disappear and appear again.

"Get dressed," Helene said.

Vincent had been five inches tall on Tatum's pillow one morning and
sitting on her sofa the next. It made the paper doll seem like a voodoo
doll, a magic spell. She had always imagined Vincent running from her,
checking over his shoulder. How could it be that he was here, she wondered, looking at her sidelong, and knocking her out? How could that
be a one-way feeling? It felt so much like an in-between.

But it wasn't. It wasn't chemistry. Chemistry is about a combination of forces, not a one-way hunger. In nature, one-sided attraction is considered predatory. I-want-you-but-you-don't-want-me usually means you're lunch. Wanting to consume what doesn't want to be consumed — is that what unrequited love is?

No wonder he ran, Tatum thought. Wouldn't she? Or did she want to be consumed? Loved like a lion loves a gazelle — with hunger, with anticipation? Or would she run from such love too, as though running for life itself?

On the morning of Ralph's funeral, she, Rachael, and Vincent sat on the sofa choosing frames for the pictures that Helene had brought over. Rachael had not been included in the planning of her mother's funeral. But Vincent had invited her in to planning Ralph's, and her legs swung and kicked the side of the sofa as they worked. Vincent didn't talk to her like she was a little girl, which, ironically, brought it out in her. He explained cremation to her. He told her there were many ways to return to the earth.

Vincent dressed for the service in dark wash jeans, a crisp white shirt, bolo tie, and black sports jacket. Rachael wore a new dress, purple and black, and slightly more mature than she had worn in the past. Geneva didn't want a church, and so Tatum had arranged for the main floor and deck of a local bed-and-breakfast. Geneva and Helene had selected a black lacquer box for Ralph's ashes, which would be placed on a white tablecloth surrounded by pictures spanning the course of Ralph's life. Vincent would do the eulogy.

Tatum stood and left Rachael and Vincent to the framing job and went to stand on the side of the bathtub to see her whole outfit in the mirror above the sink. The new blazer was meant to be for work. But apparently, a funeral would be its debut. She adjusted the slate blue blouse's collar above the blazer's lapel. Her head was cut off in the reflection, but she could see the line of jacket, slacks, and shoes. She thought about Margaret and wearing her skirt at her funeral. Tatum knew she had looked terrible that day. The clothes were upscale, and yet somehow, she had managed to look dressed from boxes dropped off behind a Salvation Army.

She stepped down from the tub and realized why Margaret had crossed her mind. Vincent's and Rachael's voices spoke softly as they worked. They were talking about Margaret. Tatum stood still so she could hear.

"Does all this make you think of her?" Vincent asked Rachael.

"A little," she said.

"What was she like?"

"Pretty," Rachael said. "Nice. But she used to cry a lot."

Margaret used to cry a lot. Of course, she did. A strange guilt crept up in Tatum. She knew Margaret cried a lot. Why did she know and never admit it? Was it Lee who made her cry? Or something older, more ancient?

Or did the crying Rachael referred to come after the diagnosis?

Tatum didn't move but kept listening, either for sounds from the living room or coming up from the heating vent. Sometimes she could hear Paris moving around below. Paris was taking the night off to attend the funeral and reception, but largely, he had been making himself scarce while Vincent was around. It had bothered Tatum at first. Embarrassed her, really. She didn't want Vincent to think her boyfriend wasn't attentive. Silly, but true. Still, it had its advantages, the two of them, Paris and Vincent, not being together. The two times they'd all been together in the previous four days, Tatum had felt as though with each word and use of eye contact, she was choosing one above the other. Besides, she was enjoying Vincent's attention. She could tell she had risen in his esteem, was better in his eyes than she had been when he had left. Somehow, she had improved. She was flattered and insulted, both.

Paris did not seem to much impress Vincent. Either that, or he just didn't want to let on he might care. Tatum thought she did notice once, however, Vincent's eyes trying to penetrate him, trying to see what he was made of. If they were dogs, there might have been a scuffle, just to see who was whom.

Tatum had been embarrassed to find out about Ralph's death through Vincent. She may have been promoted in Vincent's eyes, but it was the opposite with Geneva. It's a dose of humiliation, finding out someone likes you less than you thought. Then Helene arrived. If Tatum and Helene were dogs — bitches, as they say — Tatum knew there would be no scuffle. As to who was alpha was clear.

Geneva held Ralph on her lap. Helene drove. They headed out on the strip toward the highway. Neon blinked. The bank's marquee flashed that it was just after midnight and forty degrees. Traffic signals issued commands to no one. Lights and shadows stretched and receded across the dashboard.

"I don't like that girl," Helene told Geneva.

"Rachael?"

"Not the little one, the aunt."

"Tatum?"

"The one Vincent used to see. That's a woman waiting to be rescued. Women like that are nothing but trouble."

"She's ,all right."

"Yeah, you think so, but you don't have sons. The boys want to ride in on white horses. They don't realize that for girls like that getting rescued is like heroin."

"Does Vincent like to ride in on a white horse?"

"Vincent rides *through* on a white horse."

"Well, then there's no need to worry, at least not for him," Geneva said. "Besides, she's seeing Paris." She placed her hands on each side of the black lacquer box. "I don't know what to do with him," she said, meaning Ralph. "It seems to me that the time to do something is when I know what to do."

"Nah-ah, no way," Helene said. "I'm not letting you think about this for another ten years."

"Well, I'm not going to dump him along side the road or leave him in the bathroom of a 7-11."

"You'll think of something."

Geneva looked sidelong at Helene leaning forward over the wheel as she drove. Helene had a tendency to ride the brake — she always had — and so she accelerated big and broke long, pressing with her wide foot stuffed into slip-on rubber sandals.

"In the end," Geneva said, "I lost my capacity to love him, you know. My great failure."

"I don't know what to tell you, Eva. I don't know if not loving a person means you *failed* to love him."

"That's my suspicion." Geneva looked out the passenger window at strip malls and the Chinese Buffet. "This is the problem with being smart," she said. "You know you're responsible for everything."

"Nah," Helene said. "Just because you create a stupid life doesn't mean you owe it anything."

Helene hit the blinker and merged onto the ramp. The sides of the highway opened up, uncluttered by commerce. Gradations of black and blue-black formed silhouettes against the sky. The moon and earth had just begun their monthly good-bye, and the moon looked over its shoulder as they parted ways. Helene pulled her purse from the floor at Geneva's feet and dug in it with one hand as she drove. She pulled out an old Sucrets tin and handed it to Geneva. Geneva tucked Ralph's ashes between her legs and opened the tin. Inside were three fat doobies.

"You know what I was thinking during the funeral?" Geneva said.

"What?"

Geneva took a joint from the tin. Helene passed her a lighter. Geneva spoke with the joint in one hand, the lighter in the other.

"I think, to Ralph, my life was my hobby."

"Isn't it?"

"Really?" Geneva said. "The cultivation of my soul is on par with collecting porcelain kitties?"

"You're fighting with a dead man," Helene said.

Geneva raised the joint to her lips and the lighter to the joint. She lit up and took a hit. She passed the joint to Helene and let the smoke out slowly.

"Speaking of the cultivation of my soul," she said, looking through the passenger window, "did I tell you I'm a whore?"

Paris wore khakis and a white dress shirt with the creases from the packaging still running down the front. He sat on the edge of his mattress. He had never aspired to much, he thought, and it seemed he had arrived. The presence of Vincent had rendered him invisible again. But it was a different kind of invisibility than before. It was not a cloak that served or politely allowed for the invisibility of others. In fact, it wasn't even his own invisibility. It had been cast upon him. He stood in a shadow.

So he hid. If he was to be invisible, he would at least be in the driver's seat. He deemed it not cowardice but the exercising of quiet dignity. He knew better, though. He knew he was no threat to Vincent, and that fact wasn't the problem. The problem was that the idea had crossed his mind, that the assessment had taken place at all. Since when did he want to be a threat?

But he was becoming someone else. He'd felt it happening for some time. His sense of duty had mutated. He had become a pair of sticky hands. Tatum and Rachael belonged to him. He belonged to Tatum and Rachael.

He looked up, hearing footsteps, male ones, he could tell, in the foyer above. He took a deep breath and rose from the mattress. There were no booths to wipe. No corn bread to make. There was a funeral to attend. Vincent was the man of the hour.

Paris climbed the basement steps and emerged through the door, but the image before him did not compute. A man at Tatum's door. Blond, not dark, hair. Not Vincent. The man looked at him then back to the door that was opening before him.

Lee. Tatum couldn't say his name. She couldn't say anything. Lee looked strung out, and it took her aback. Her eyes darted to Paris, who stood off to the side in the foyer. Rachael peeked from behind Tatum. She blinked, and her mouth opened. She ran to her father. He squatted. Her arms wrapped around his shoulders.

Tatum and Paris exchanged a look above the hug.

"Wow," Tatum said. "Come in. Come in."

Lee lifted Rachael, hiked her up, and stepped inside. Paris followed.

"Paris," Tatum said, "this is Lee, Rachael's dad. And this is Vincent," she said, gesturing behind her.

Vincent stepped forward, and Lee lowered Rachael to the floor. Vincent extended his hand.

"I'm sorry about your wife," Vincent said, holding Lee's hand and eye. Lee gave a short nod, acknowledging the expression of sympathy, but Tatum could also see the shadow of distrust crossing his face, perhaps unnerved by being known but not knowing. Then Vincent released Lee's hand and excused himself and knocked on the door across the hall before opening it.

"What are you doing here?" Tatum said, hoping there was the sound of pleasant surprise in her voice.

"I got your message," Lee said to Tatum. He took Rachael's hand and then took in the apartment. The furniture was a hodge-podge of on-clearance items and secondhand deals. It was not dirty. But by the standards of the affluent suburbs, the place was a dump.

Tatum took hold of her own wrist as though there were a watch on it.

"This is, this is such a surprise," she said, "but we're on our way to a funeral." Her eyes darted to Paris then back to Lee. "I guess, if you want, Rachael, you don't have to go."

Rachael sunk, face and body. This funeral was important to her. She'd helped plan it. It was under her control and a return to the scene of a crime.

"Or your dad can come with us," Tatum said. "Rachael's been a great help with planning it," she said to Lee.

Tatum looked at Paris and shrugged, unsure whether one brought guests to a funeral.

"That probably wouldn't be right," Lee said.

"It would be fine," Tatum said, "if you want to."

"I don't know," Lee said. He looked down at Rachael. Her eyes were pleading with Tatum, pleading that she plead on her behalf. "Do you want me to come?" Lee said to Rachael, pulling her eyes his way.

"I think," she said, looking at Tatum, "I think we should." Then her eyes shot upward to her father.

"Shoes then," Tatum said, and Rachael went off down the hall.

Once she was gone, Tatum turned to Lee. "How long you here for?"

Lee was looking down the hall, the way Rachael had gone.

"Long enough to figure out logistics, I guess," he said.

"The logistics of what?" Tatum said, her voice and stomach both dropping.

It was good California reefer, fragrant and fresh. Outside Geneva's window, the mountains seemed as if they were on a slow retreat from the highway, giant refugees crossing the prairie. Geneva felt like the car was a capsule moving through a space divorced of time. Without time, the car-capsule drove without seeming to make progress. Geneva told Helene about John, about the food and the fire, about the question he had asked — *what do you want me to do for you?* Geneva told Helene about the sex and John's giant dick.

"I got home," Geneva said, "and Ralph was dead."

"What came first?" Helene asked. "Ralph dying or the giant dick?"

"Technically," Geneva said, "Ralph died first. But those weren't the assumptions under which I was operating."

"So do you think you killed him?"

"No," Geneva snapped. "Do you?"

Helene shrugged, but she was just goading her.

"Speaking of giant dicks," Geneva mumbled, goading back. She turned and looked out the window and noticed, despite the sensation of having traveled nowhere, that they were approaching the exit off of which John lived. "He lives off this exit," she said.

Helene jerked the steering wheel and took the ramp.

"No, no, no," Geneva said.

"I want to see this shack of his."

"No. It's quiet out there. I don't want him to think I'm stalking him."

"Maybe he'll be flattered."

"Maybe he'll be frightened."

"He'll be asleep," Helene said.

"Go right," Geneva said at the top of the ramp.

It was darker still off the highway. Helene dug in her purse again as she drove and pulled out an old cassette tape.

"Remember this?" she said, handing it to Geneva.

Geneva took it from her. The ink on the label was faded, but Geneva recognized her own handwriting. It was probably twelve years old at least. The first song was "Almost Cut My Hair."

"I remember making this," Geneva said.

"Snap it in."

But Geneva didn't. She turned it one way and the other, trying to read it in the dashboard lights. She could make out Bowie and Ten Years After from the fading ink. She looked up from the tape and squinted.

"Take the next left."

Helene took the left off the paved road. The wheels snapped and popped on the gravel.

"What did your Big John have to say about Ralph dying?"

Geneva sighed.

"He asked if I wanted him at the funeral. I told him I needed to step back and do this."

"The funeral?"

"More than that, I think."

Though the eulogy was inside, Geneva wore big-ass sunglasses. She did it the way she wanted to, old school. She bypassed the hat but wore a black scarf wrapped like a headband, tying at the nape of her neck. She looked glamorous, very Yoko Ono. There was not a vacuum, but a space around her. Standing near her, you stood in it. She received you from another world.

In the parlor of the bed-and-breakfast, she sat in a red wingback closest to the table with Ralph's pictures and ashes. When she had arrived, the photographs had been arranged chronologically. "Mix these up," she had said to Helene, and the job had gotten done, though Helene hadn't done it herself. This arrangement was better. No progress and decline. Time, they say, is an illusion. And yet, it always manages to run out.

From behind her sunglasses, Geneva surveyed the room. Apparently, Rachael's father had appeared as though out from the mist. His face did not appeal to Geneva. His energy seemed to ride its surface rather than emerge from deeper inside. Beside him, Rachael seemed in a trance, called by a voice only she could hear. She seemed to move toward her father even though she was standing still.

Hope and fear. That's what Geneva detected in her. The two didn't mix well. Love-me/I'm-afraid-you-won't, mixed together, can taste like hate. Or love. And love. Either way, with the two, the level of devotion involved ran deep.

Geneva's eyes shifted to where Tatum stood behind Lee and Rachael. Geneva knew she had hit a soft spot in Tatum from which there might be no recovery. But what was there to do? Apologize for needing what she needed? Apologize for taking it? Tatum fidgeted. Slightly behind her was Paris, young among the men. He was sure of himself but not of Tatum. But he seemed to be mixing the two up.

Vincent came forward from the back of the room. He stood before the table. Only Geneva sat. Vincent spoke of death.

"We don't know Ralph's reasons," he said, "for hanging onto his body for so long. It's been a long good-bye."

He asked the group to bow their heads. Beginnings and endings often have fuzzy lines between them, Geneva thought. But this was death. It was supposed to be crisp and sharp to the point of discomfort, and yet, somehow, it did not seem so.

Behind Tatum, Paris stood listening to the tick of her mind as she worked up her arguments for Lee. She had shared her strategy with Paris. She would try to convince Lee to wait until school was over.

Then, summer. This was a whim. Tatum was certain of it. It would wear off. She just needed to buy some time.

"This can't be happening," she kept saying on the way to the service. Rachael had ridden to the funeral with her father in his rental car, following Tatum and Paris in hers.

"It's going to be okay," Paris said, and she had looked at him like he had lost his mind. Paris put a hand on Tatum's back as Vincent spoke, but she did not soften beneath it. At least Lee's arrival had diverted Tatum's attention away from Vincent. It was not a thought Paris was proud of. Besides, Lee was as likely to take Tatum from him as Vincent. If Lee took Rachael, Paris knew, Tatum might disappear too, into the loss, and push away whatever else there was to lose. Paris looked at Rachael from behind. She reminded him of a beautiful collie at the end of a leash as she stood at the end of Lee's hand. She knew who owned her. Paris remembered her small body against his in the car. Lee was a hole that could absorb them both, Rachael and Tatum, leaving him alone.

Rachael looked over her shoulder, perhaps feeling his eyes on her back. She and Paris locked eyes for a moment before she turned away, seemingly embarrassed.

Paris thought back to Lee's arrival at Tatum's door. He had felt like a bystander when Vincent stepped up to shake Lee's hand and had wished it was him, not Vincent, holding Lee's hand and eye.

However, the distance had allowed him to examine Lee more closely than he might have been able to close up. If his perception was correct, he had to hand it to Lee. Paris thought Lee could sense that the two other men present were not a team, that there were three of them, three men, each separate, merit and right distributing itself among them, and Lee doing the calculations, trying to work it out.

"Grief is love without the beloved," Vincent said. "Grief is love turned inside out. Nothing to be afraid of."

Paris mumbled Amen with the rest of them.

He stepped away from Tatum as the service broke up. Geneva stood and turned to face the room. Helene was at her side. Paris put out his hands as he approached her, and she placed her black-gloved hands in his.

"So that's the father?" Geneva said in a soft and measured tone.

Paris nodded.

"It's bad news?" she said.

Paris nodded again.

Geneva remembered Tatum standing in her living room asking if Geneva thought Rachael would be better off with Lee and whether she should call him. Yet, clearly, this situation was not of her own making. Tatum cocked the pistol, Geneva thought, and was now upset someone else was pulling the trigger.

"How do you feel?" Paris said.

Geneva looked off to the side from behind her dark glasses. She liked the way the question sounded in Paris's mouth. He meant it. He wanted to know. He had no assumptions. Geneva tried to be as honest as protocol allowed.

"I'm on a new planet," she said. "I suppose we all are. It must change a little, at least, every time someone dies."

The small group of guests retired to the porch and front yard. The giant lilac bushes surrounding the bed-and-breakfast had survived the hailstorm better than most and infused the gathering with a sticky, heady sweetness. Geneva sat on a settee on the porch beside Helene. Helene's hand rested on Geneva's knee. Geneva occasionally touched the blue, bad tattoo of a phoenix on the sun-spotted skin of the back of Helene's hand. A few people from the *Messenger* had come, and they expressed their condolences and then huddled together at the wine table. Two residents from the nursing home were parked in the sun in their wheel chairs, aides standing idly behind them. Geneva's neighbor, Ron, approached the settee. He told Geneva that if she needed anything, he was right next door. Vincent stood at his mother's shoulder, looking out at the lawn.

At the bottom of the porch steps, Tatum and Paris joined Lee and Rachael. An old-fashioned sleigh sat on the front lawn of the bed-and-breakfast with a solemn white wreath set up in the driver's seat.

"Can I climb on that?" Rachael asked Tatum, then blushed, and redirected her eyes to Lee.

Lee looked to Tatum and then quickly away.

"Looks like it," he said, and off she went.

Lee turned to follow. He watched her run, mount the runner on the sleigh, and then hoist herself into the seat. He had to admit, he wasn't sure if she had changed or whether he had never looked closely before. She looked different to him. No longer a subset of Margaret, but his, alone, she seemed, at once, both older and younger than he remembered.

"Lee."

He turned. Tatum had come up behind him.

"Lee," she said, and the reasoned arguments concocted during the service stuck in her throat and all she could say is, "what are you doing?"

Lee furrowed his brow.

"What are you going to do with a little kid?"

"Rachael?"

"That's the one."

Lee knew this might happen. He had considered it as he sat between flights. Tatum might judge him just as she had when he had asked her to take Rachael before. She didn't understand then, and she didn't understand now. He had decided he wouldn't negotiate. He didn't have to. His job was to do the right thing, not convince Tatum of its rightness.

"Thank you for all you've done," Lee said. "But you know as well as I do that she should be home now."

"As opposed to four days after her mother died."

"I did what was best for Rachael then," Lee said patiently, "and I'm going to do what's best for her now."

Tatum looked past Lee to Rachael, who stood on the sleigh beside the wreath of flowers, looking in their direction.

"I'm not sure you know the difference between what's best for you and what's best for her," Tatum said.

Lee stared at her coldly, then turned away.

"Just wait until school is out," Tatum said, changing her tone, pleading, "or after summer vacation. This isn't the sort of thing you do on impulse," Tatum said to his back.

Lee turned around slowly. His voice was exasperated.

"Why are you doing this?" he said, turning out his hands. "I haven't seen my daughter in six months." He said it like it was Tatum's fault. "This is our reunion. Our time. Why are you ruining it?"

"I . . . " Tatum said. "I'm not trying to ruin it."

"Well, you are," he said.

Paris came up behind Tatum and stopped short. He could feel the tension.

"I have no idea," Lee said, "how you could think she's better off with you than with me."

Tatum felt her face flush. She's better off with *us*, she wanted to say. With me, Geneva, and Paris. But she couldn't make promises on others' behalves, and she couldn't promise that she wouldn't drive them away. She might have already driven Geneva away. Words stuck in her throat.

Lee turned away from them and walked toward the sleigh. Tatum followed. Paris followed Tatum.

At the sleigh, Lee reached up and brought Rachael to the ground. Tatum could feel it coming. He was going to say something right now. Almost as though a bus were careening toward Rachael, Tatum wanted to rush in and shove her out of the path.

"I bet you're ready to come back home," Lee said.

Somehow, it was visible, the heat reaching up from inside Rachael's belly, turning her cheeks scarlet. Her eyes shot to Tatum. Rachael looked as she had at the water's edge. Busted. Found out. Would she start swinging? Tatum could see she would not. It would stay inside, a push-pull, a mix of desire and fear.

Lee felt the same push-pull as Rachael did. Desire and fear. But for him, the push-pull was soothing, the sensation of his feet touching the ground, but not sinking into it. There was no floating up, and there was no dragging down. Afraid to hold on and afraid to let go, Rachael's grip was one that offered a perfect equilibrium.

"Maybe we should all go," Tatum said, impulsively, and with false brightness.

Rachael looked to her father. Lee stared coldly at Tatum. He misunderstood her motives. He thought it was a power play, that she was trying to make him the bad guy in front of Rachael by forcing him to say no.

"Maybe that'll work up the road," Lee said.

Paris heard Tatum's blurted words. He had been invisible, listening to it all. But now, he had gone deaf. He stopped hearing the conversation and felt frozen to the spot, which was strange, because he was already moving down the front walk of the bed-and-breakfast, down the street. He wanted out of the khaki pants and the white shirt with the creases from the package. He wanted a white T-shirt and jeans. He wanted work boots, the diner's counter, and a poured cup of coffee to be enough. Paris wanted the sky at dusk and the sky before dawn and not this straight above light. Tatum was willing to leave, leave him and head off to the Midwest with Lee and Rachael. Paris knew that grief might consume Tatum in a way that she would become lost to him should Lee take Rachael away. He also knew that he might blow it with Tatum with his lies of omission and self-imposed curses. But he didn't know she would just walk away. He hated himself, and he hated all the lies. Not the ones of omission, but the ones he had told himself.

Hope had empty hands, empty as the hands of need, or longing. It was defined by the emptiness. That's what made it hope.

Away from the valley lights, the night was black and the sky packed with stars. Geneva's Saab crept up the road toward John's shack.

"Okay, that's close enough," Geneva said. She pointed at the dark silhouette of the building. "There it is. Now, let's turn around."

But Helene kept a light foot on the gas, rolling up the road. She pressed the brake as she pulled up beside the shack.

"Don't slow down," Geneva said. "Drive."

Helene gave the car some gas. Geneva watched the shack recede in the rearview mirror as they put distance between themselves and John's.

"It's a shack, all right," Helene said.

She kept driving, and the road started to climb. The tree line encroached, and the moon above now flashed in and out between the lodgepole and spruce. Helene slowed down.

"My night vision's shot," she said.

"That's a comfort."

With John's shack several miles behind them, Helene pulled over where the shale had broken free of the earth and spilled, carving a sort of stone waterfall into the side of the mountain. She killed the motor and silence asserted itself, there all along.

"What could I have done with my mind if I hadn't spent all that time trying to figure out my marriage?" Geneva said.

"Maybe you would've cured cancer."

"Probably not."

"The life that wasn't," Helene said. "You're bound to have one no matter what you do." She turned the key halfway to get just enough juice to roll down the window before realizing it wasn't electric. She shut the car back off and rolled down the window manually. The air came in smelling of earth and pine. "Well," she said, looking at Geneva. "What shall we do? We could ride up the road farther. Looks like it keeps climbing. We'll find the edge of something to pour him off of."

Geneva shook her head. "That doesn't sound right."

"Well, I have to go home day after tomorrow, and I don't want to leave you alone with that box."

"You know," Geneva said, "I want to do it when I feel good about it. Resolved. Right now, it feels like walking away from a failure."

"I thought you didn't believe in guilt."

"I don't. I believe in responsibility."

"So what responsibility are you living up to by carrying around that box of dust?"

Geneva stared straight ahead, hands flat on the top of the black box.

"I didn't succeed. I didn't do this right. I'm responsible to figure out how I could've done better. I don't mean I'm responsible to God or anything like that, just responsible to myself to do the best I can."

"But you haven't done anything for years — that's the problem. You want to do well at something you weren't doing."

"What wasn't I doing?"

"According to you, loving Ralph. You can't succeed at loving someone you don't love."

"But I did love him."

"Well, okay then."

An owl hooted, and Helene turned in the direction of the sound. She pointed with her thumb out the window.

"A sign?" she said.

Geneva felt the box in her hands. She wished she had the sudden impulse to leap from the car and climb a rock and speak into the night some final farewell, a request to Grandfather Owl to carry Ralph off on his sacred wings. But it didn't ring true.

"Drive," Geneva said. Helene sighed and turned the key. She started up the engine, rolled up the window, and turned the car around to go back the way they came. Geneva looked out the passenger window. She and Ralph both knew he loved her. They knew she loved him too but just wasn't good at it. He had been generous enough to allow her to keep trying to figure out how to do better.

Geneva's foot tapped agitatedly as they came back down the hill. They emerged from the trees into the open valley and traveled several yards when Geneva blurted, "Let me out." Helene looked at her but kept driving. "Let me out," Geneva said louder. Helene hit the brake. Geneva got out, taking Ralph with her. Helene watched through the windshield as Geneva hustled past the front bumper. The headlights illuminated the ditch and barbed wire stapled to fence posts. Geneva stopped up the road a bit but still in the headlights' glow. She put down the box at the edge of the road. She backed away from it, just a few steps.

Helene opened her car door and stood.

"I cannot think this now," Geneva said, without turning.

"Think what?"

"He didn't love me," Geneva said. "It wasn't me. It was him. I filled a slot for him. That's all. When I failed to fit snugly in the slot, he let me know, and I hopped to, shut up, rearranged myself, whatever it took to solve the 'problem.' I made myself palatable." Geneva looked back over her shoulder at Helene. "*Palatable*, for God's sake." They stood looking at each other in the night. "You knew," Geneva said.

"Uh-huh."

"But you didn't say it."

"I said it a million times," Helene said. "You couldn't hear."

Geneva put her hands on her hips and looked to the sky in exasperation. Stars winked.

"You're just mad at yourself," Helene said.

"Mad at myself."

"Yeah. For denying yourself. You wanted more. You talked yourself into less."

Geneva looked over her shoulder at her friend and then back around at the box. Geneva's body sank just slightly, as if sighing.

"I am not mad at myself for denying myself," Geneva said. "I'm mad at you for pointing it out."

Helene smiled.

Geneva stepped forward and picked up Ralph. She returned to the car. Helene swung back in and put it in gear.

"A man asking you what you want him to do might get old," Helene said as they drove past John's shack. "Isn't it hard enough figuring out what you want to do yourself?"

The group was too small for the tensions. Geneva tried to stay uninvolved behind her sunglasses. When it was near time to go, Rachael climbed the front porch steps to say her good-bye to Geneva.

"What a day for both of us," Geneva said to her.

Rachael pointed out to Geneva her father on the front lawn and told her he was taking her home. Helene stood from where she sat beside Geneva and walked inside as Geneva pushed the sunglasses down her nose, just enough to look over the top of them into Rachael's eyes. Vincent moved too, following his mother, but descending the front steps to where Tatum stood waiting for Rachael.

"Are you ready?" Geneva asked Rachael.

"I would like it if things stopped happening," Rachael said with a painful kind of laugh.

"Good things happen too," Geneva said, and Rachael gave her a sad "like when?" kind of smile.

Geneva pulled her in for a hug. "There's good out there," she said quietly into Rachael's ear, "and it's coming for you."

"What's going on?" Vincent asked Tatum, having seen from a distance the scene played out with Lee.

Tatum put on a good face.

"Rachael's dad wants to take her home. It's bittersweet, you know."

She looked up at him, and he looked down at her. He seemed to be taking in her words, comparing them to how things seemed. Tatum smiled and stepped away. She joined Rachael and Geneva on the porch. Geneva pushed her sunglasses back up her nose and looked to Tatum.

"Big changes," Geneva said.

Tatum nodded. She placed her hands on Rachael's shoulders.

"How are you doing?" Tatum said.

Geneva closed her eyes and nodded.

"We're right across the hall," Tatum said. But she knew as the words came out that it would only be her there across the hall. Rachael would be gone.

Rachael left the funeral with her father. He would drop her back at the duplex later. Tatum drove home and parked the Celica out front. She turned off the engine. She rested her forehead on the steering wheel. Paris. He had split. It was time to find out why.

Tatum got out of the car and headed inside. In the foyer, she rapped gently on the basement door. She knew Paris was down there — she could sense his presence — and when he didn't respond to the knock, she entered and went down the stairs anyway. She stepped slowly, craning her neck.

"Paris? Knock, knock."

She reached the bottom. Paris stood beside the mattress with a box at his feet.

"Where'd you go?"

"Here," he said, coldly.

"I'm going to try to talk Lee out of this," Tatum said, sitting at the edge of the mattress that had no sheet.

Paris said nothing.

"Do you think it's the right thing to do?" she asked.

"I don't think anything," he said, reaching for his pillow and shaking it from the case. "You know me."

Tatum realized then that his boxes had moved, the pile shifted toward the bottom of the steps.

"What are you doing?" Tatum said, abruptly knowing.

"I'm leaving, Tatum," he said. "Aren't you?"

"What are you talking about?"

"Aren't you going with Rachael back to Chicago?"

"I just wanted. . . I was just trying. . . Lee doesn't want me there." She tried to speak calmly. This was no big deal, a misunderstanding about to be fixed. "Didn't you hear him? He did some song and dance about sometime up the road."

Paris tossed the pillow onto the mattress and looked her squarely in the eye. She could see what was in there, the pain turned into anger.

"I don't mind being second to your," he closed his eyes and shook his head, "your sadness, or your fear." He reopened his eyes. "But you would leave me? You would just volunteer to walk away?"

"Paris," Tatum said, standing. "I couldn't have Rachael feeling pawned off again. She's a child. If she needed me . . ."

"You act like you were sacrificing yourself," Paris said, "but you were sacrificing me."

Tatum took a backward step.

"Is that what I was doing?" she said. "I didn't mean to. I'm sorry." She reached toward him but then pulled her fists to her forehead. "Paris, I'm sorry," she said. "I told you I'm no good at this."

"Yeah, Tatum," Paris said, "throw yourself on a sword. That's what I want."

Tatum looked up from her fists. Paris's face was stone.

"You don't love me anymore," she said flatly.

Paris searched the ceiling. He put his hands on his head like he was pulling out his hair.

"I have to leave you because I do love you," he said. "What you do with my love makes me crazy. I mean, it's like, *aarrgg*. It's like, you're stomping on it, and I'm like, hey, that's my love. You're so careless." He turned away from her. "Loving you doesn't feel very good, Tatum. Not knowing if at any second you're going to vanish off the face of the earth doesn't feel very good."

"That's how it is, Paris," Tatum said, with some anger. "People vanish off the face of the earth all the time. Get used to it. In fact, it seems exactly like what you're about to do."

"Look," Paris said, throwing up his hands, "forget it. It's all my fault. You're enough for me, but I'm not enough for you. You're all that matters to me." But even as the words fell from his lips, he thought of Linda, and Rachael, and the diner. He thought of his abandoned art supplies and he knew he was a liar. She wasn't all that mattered. Too much mattered. But the lie was out there and what did it matter now, anyway. "Go away, Tatum," he said, having nowhere to go away to himself.

Tatum stepped away from him. She bit her lower lip and then turned and climbed the stairs. She stopped halfway and looked over her shoulder but could only see Paris's jeans and boots. She continued up and returned to her apartment. She closed the door behind her, and the devil rose up in her living room, reminding her whose soul she was dealing with. Why can't it be different, she thought? Why not? Just one time.

She crossed the room and sunk into the orange chair. All this time, she had been getting on Geneva's nerves. She'd been breaking Paris's heart. All that time, Margaret had been crying. Dying.

And Rachael was leaving.

The tears inside stayed put as a familiar calm sunk in. A stillness. She was not traversing the scary turf of the new, where with each step you wondered if the ground would rise up to meet your falling foot. This landscape was predictable, flat and arid. For the first time in a long time, she knew what came next.

Helene and Geneva returned to the highway and drove until they saw a turn-off for state forest access. Helene pulled into an empty camp-ground, and they leaned against the hood of the car, smoking a joint. Helene thought they should climb the ridge before them, not too high, and release Ralph to the wind, although there was none.

"I know he was faithful," Geneva said. "He never cheated on me."

"Big deal," Helene said, quite stoned. "Vincent's father was faithful too. He reserved all his screwed up, private, intimate, abusive bullshit for me, and me alone."

"And you know," Geneva said, "he never said, *I love you*. He said, *you know I love you. Hey, Gen, you know I love you* — I found that confusing, like he was messing with my head. I don't think I like being told what I know."

"You know," Helene said, then laughed, "or maybe you don't — but it sounds to me like you really trusted him, enough to make you doubt yourself."

"That's exactly what happened," Geneva said, turning her wrist to pass the joint. "I could never figure out which to trust — myself or that voice that says I love you. I just figured the problem was me. He loved me. I didn't feel it." Geneva put her hands to the sides of her head as though trying to stifle voices inside. "I'm just tired of thinking about him," she said. "That was our relationship: Me thinking about him. Not talking to him, oh no, that didn't work. So I wasn't tired of talking to him. I wanted to talk to him more. I wasn't sick of having sex with him. I wanted more. More of everything. I never got tired of us because there was no us. Just me and," she jabbed her finger at her temple, "a him in my head. Maybe I didn't stop loving him, I just got tired of thinking about him. I *am* tired of thinking of him."

"So, let's go then," Helene said, pointing with her chin to the ridge and snubbing out the joint on the bumper.

"Yet, I have this sense of" — Geneva looked into the darkness before her — "incompletion. I don't know if I can move on without knowing I got the lesson."

"The lesson is to let go. C'mon."

"You're asking me to lie."

"No, I'm not."

"Yes, you are. You're asking me to do something symbolic, but there's no real thing for it to be a symbol of."

"Maybe if you do it, you'll have done it, and then it won't be a lie."

"I can't do it," Geneva said, taking the joint from Helene's hand. She relit what was left of it and took a hit. She held in the smoke, and she said it again. "I can't do it."

"Eva."

"Yeah."

"Ralph's a thought in your head you have to stop thinking."

Geneva stared forward into the dark and the night.

"I know," she said.

August

38

~

The basement of the Deluxe was not tidy like Geneva's. It required shoes at all times, not an ideal situation for Paris's feet. He had moved in after buying a new, used Impala from the want ads and a cot from the army/navy store. He joined a gym, where he showered but didn't exercise.

Despite its shortcomings, the basement of the Deluxe offered relief from the August heat and the layer of smoke choking the valley. Fire season always came on the tail of summer, but this was bigger. National news. The fires jumped highways and closed roads. In the valley, throats ached and eyes burned. Summer windows were closed. *Particulate*, it was called, and it was everywhere. Tiny floating filth. The elderly and asthmatic were warned to stay indoors.

Paris sat on his cot in the glow of a shadeless overhead bulb. He hadn't seen Tatum for nearly three months. The last time was at the diner two weeks after Ralph's funeral.

"I'm sorry," she had said.

She said it twenty times if she said it once.

"I failed you, I know. I'm sorry."

Paris worked as she spoke and didn't look up. He wiped the length of the counter's already clean surface.

"I told you I didn't know how to do this," she said, following him from the other side of the counter. "I told you I make a good friend but a lousy girlfriend."

Paris couldn't stand the sound of it. He stopped wiping and looked up.

"How's Rachael?" he said.

"Gone," Tatum said, her eyes tearing up and then swallowing the tears back down.

Paris looked away. She was who she was. She was afraid and had doubt. He wanted her to be brave and believe.

"I can't keep chasing you," he said, shaking his head. "I know you want me to love you, but you don't love me. You're always two steps out of reach."

"I'm not out of reach," Tatum said. "I'm right here. And don't tell me who I love. Maybe I'm not good at it, but that doesn't mean I don't feel it." Her lower lip started to quiver. "I thought you knew me," she said. "I thought it was okay. I thought maybe. . ." But it was all she had to say.

Then she was gone.

But Paris saw her everywhere. He suffered mirages and optical illusions. There were cases of mistaken identity in momentary flashes on sidewalks and in the diner's doorway.

Linda, on the other hand, he saw nowhere. He didn't ask the retards about her again. Still, he carried five hundred dollars in his pocket at work, just in case.

Work. It had been his refuge. It offered concrete tasks. Necessity and reason. But as of tonight, at 3 a.m., the Deluxe would officially close.

Paris climbed the stairs up to the kitchen for the last time. Love was no different than money or fame, he thought. Just another thing we're taught to chase and covet. Another thing the wise learn to be happy without.

Tatum spent the two weeks following Ralph's funeral fighting demons, and she thought she had won. She got up off the floor. She talked to herself. She got it all worked up in her head that everything was going to be okay. They would be okay, she and Paris. Because they loved each other. She drove to the Deluxe. She prostrated herself. She took all the blame. What more does anyone want?

She paced back and forth, following Paris on the opposite side of the counter. But he would barely look at her. Tatum reached and strained with her will and her energy trying to find a place in Paris that would receive it. Finally, she stopped in her tracks, realizing what she'd become again. A beggar. When it comes to love, it doesn't matter how nicely you ask for it, she knew. Once you're asking, you've already lost.

So what to do instead? Drink? Take pills? Punch walls?

Find Vincent?

Turns out, she didn't have to. He found her.

Tatum didn't sleep after that night at the diner, and she was out of coffee. At the Grounds the next morning, she ordered a large cup to go. Vincent tapped her on the shoulder. He had nothing but good news. He had received a six-thousand-dollar advance for a book and was in town staying at the Red Roof Inn while he worked on it. He asked how she was, and she decided to be good news too. She told him her story in happy endings — child reunited with father, she and Paris parting paths amicably. "Haven't seen much of Geneva," she told him. "You?" If Vincent sensed a different truth, he didn't ask.

Then, Tatum offered to look at his book. When they were together, she had always edited his articles and had even suggested placements for them. When his work took off, so did he. Tatum thought that people tend to discover they don't need you and that they don't love you right around the same time.

But that's how it came to be that they kept meeting, though never again at the coffee shop. Up until then, Tatum had been going there often, hoping to bump into Paris by accident. But she didn't want him to see her with Vincent. She didn't tell Geneva either. She was avoiding her, and so she wasn't sure whether Geneva was avoiding her too. Geneva seemed to be avoiding a lot of things. She hadn't bothered with the garden this summer, and that was unlike her. The perennials came up and barely survived.

Tatum turned into the Pie House's parking lot. She was meeting Vincent for lunch. Crossing the hot asphalt, she felt like she was in a movie, playing herself. But this self didn't crawl or care. *It doesn't matter* was her new mantra. Tra-la-la-la-la-la. She played it happy and turned on what there was of her charm. You wanna be loved, she thought, you gotta be lovable. She would get what there was to get from this life. A feeling, if not a fact.

Was there really any difference?

Inside, the air conditioning shocked her skin and gave her goose pimples. Vincent wore glasses to read now, but he pulled them off as Tatum slid into the booth. It was an endearing gesture she had become familiar with. She was attracted to him, yes, but she chalked it up to biology, nothing more. They would produce a healthy offspring. That's all. Not that anything had happened. Not yet. It was all business. Platonic, friendly. The past was a non-issue. It always is to the dumper. The dumpee pretends.

Tatum dropped chapters four through seven on the table.

"Interesting stuff," she said.

"But," he said.

"Not 'but,' my friend. 'And.'"

Vincent smiled. "And what?"

Tatum told him that she thought the intro kept dragging itself forward into the text. He needed to develop ideas at this point and trust he'd set the stage adequately. He nodded and took it in. Tatum spoke with authority but was outside her body. Extreme good looks are unnerving. It's hard to see with light in your eyes. It affected her tone of voice too, making it come up from under her words and not down upon them. Vincent exerted a pull. No doubt about it. Maybe it wasn't even toward him but just a general dismantling force. Perhaps it wasn't selfish genes or biology that drew her but the pull itself. It felt half like merging, half like being torn apart. Both held an attraction.

So she played with fire.

Why not? She knew the well-known fact that the only way to drown out the hum of one man is with another. She had never wanted to drown Vincent out, but Paris had come along and under the water Vincent went. Paris she wanted to drown out. She needed to. The loss was no companion. It was unbearable.

Paris. Rachael. Geneva. Margaret. They all were gone.

It doesn't matter, Tatum told herself.

Tra-la-la-la-la-la.

But there was something else gone too. Something Vincent didn't know about. Her breast. The time was coming, though. He wouldn't initiate sex, Tatum knew, but he wouldn't say no. The past was a non-issue. For the dumper. The dumpee pretends.

Sex with Vincent. It wouldn't be suicide. But it was the next best thing.

39

The Jackson 5 played on the stereo, distracting Geneva from the task at hand. Young Michael had the voice of an angel, Geneva thought, listening to him grind a note. How rare it was, she thought, to hear that kind of juice pumping out of such a little man.

The task from which she was distracted was the writing of her farewell column. She had resigned from the advice biz, and she wished to sum up her parting wisdom in a single sentence. But she was torn between two. Don't Look Back. Or, Look Forward.

The advantage of Don't Look Back, she thought, was that it at least gave a person some reference points to work with, somewhere concrete not to look. Look Forward had no such coordinates. Navigation was blind, taking place by feel alone. Don't Look Back took effort. Look Forward did not, and yet it was the more difficult of the two.

Geneva leaned on her kitchen counter hovering over her legal pad. She read the two statements again. Then she looked to Ralph sitting to her right in his black lacquer box.

"I like Look Forward," she told the dead man and then laughed at the irony.

The album ended. The needle lifted. The new silence of the duplex asserted itself at once. Rachael was long gone. Geneva had said goodbye to her in her living room with Lee and Tatum looking on.

"When you think of me," she had told Rachael, "think *I wonder when we'll see each other,* and I'll think the same."

And think of Rachael, Geneva did. Unlike with thoughts of Tatum, there was no accompanying tug or pull. Thoughts of Rachael would just appear like magic. A memory. A moment. Like she wasn't even really gone. It wasn't a haunting because it was pleasant. As promised, when it happened, Geneva would say the words. *I wonder when we'll see each other.*

She refused the word *again.*

There would be no more *agains*. History doesn't repeat itself, she thought. We repeat history. We re-create it at a loss for new ideas and take the raw material of the infinite and impose the same tired frames upon it.

Tilt the frame, Geneva thought, climbing up on her inner soapbox. Better yet, break it. Go a step further and change the person looking through it. And change, she was coming to suspect, always had to do with letting go.

She looked at the black lacquer box.

Helene hadn't believed that there was such a thing as a right moment. When it came to letting go, it was the doing it, she had said, that made the moment right. Maybe so. But even if there was no right moment, Geneva knew there was a right feeling. She was willing to wait for it.

And speaking of waiting. . . Her eyes slipped toward the clock. Ten minutes to go.

She had a rule: no thinking about John until she was on her way out the door to see him. She permitted herself to think about him for up to two hours after parting company too. She had two reasons for her mindfulness. First, she didn't want to transfer her preoccupation with Ralph to John, though it was tempting to live and relive a touch, a look, a word. Second, she also didn't want to turn John into an idea with which she had a complex relationship that he, the man, only dropped in on from time to time. She was having sex with John twice a week or so, but Geneva never slept over. Not yet.

Six more minutes.

Geneva abandoned her legal pad and went to spruce up.

In the bathroom, she washed her hands. She applied expensive moisturizer to her face, neck, and up her arms. In the bedroom, she dressed, choosing a black, gauze peasant blouse. *Don't* think of John, she thought. *Don't* Look Back. The *don'ts* don't work. They kept one in a holding pattern, caught in the gravitational field of the unwanted.

She looked at the clock.

Time.

Geneva grabbed her keys. She grabbed Ralph, too, as she liked to keep him on hand available to the convergence of the right time and right place.

It was early evening when she turned down the gravel road. The smoke from the fires was socked in like rain clouds, shrouding the mountaintops and sealing off the sky. But Geneva felt anything but claustrophobic. She was heading for the shack, and the anticipation was sweet.

Geneva reached John's driveway and pulled in beside his truck. She had been leaving Ralph in the car at John's, but today, she picked him up and carried him to John's door. Do different and different happens, right? John's door opened as she approached.

"Trying to keep the smoke out," he said, pulling the door closed behind her. Inside it was shadowy, the curtains and windows both closed. Fans were blowing from two sides of the room, circulating the stuffiness.

First, Geneva kissed him. Then she placed the box on his table. She stepped back, and they looked at it together.

"Let go, let go," she said. "Common advice, but no one ever lays out the mechanics of it."

"Open your hand?" John offered.

"You'd think," Geneva said, sitting down at his table. "But it's obviously more complicated. Do you think you have to know what you're hanging on to in order to let it go?"

John lowered his body into one of the plastic chairs. He put his hand before him in a fist, palm facing down. He opened it.

"Let go," he said. "Seems to me that whatever's in your hand is going to fall."

"I don't know," she said, shaking her head, unconvinced. "Just thinking 'let go' puts your attention on the fact you're hanging on. That alone might be the obstacle. Like just thinking about it, even letting it go, creates the gravitational pull that keeps it there."

John crossed his legs. The fans buzzed, chopping away at the air. She tapped her fingers on the table and then looked at John. A slow smile spread across his face. He had all the time she needed.

"Speaking of gravitational pulls," Geneva said.

She leaned in. He leaned in too. She placed a hand on the back of his head as they kissed.

"One sec," Geneva said, gently pushing him away. She picked up Ralph and carried him to just outside the door. She placed him on the ground beside the shack.

"One sec," she said again, this time to the box, and she slipped back inside.

40

Tatum and Vincent shared a platonic hug and parted paths outside the restaurant. From her car, Tatum watched him cross the street, heading back to his motel. She considered killing the engine and following him to his door. It beat going home to the unblinking light of her answering machine. Lee had told her he'd call by last week. Tatum had asked him if Rachael could visit before school started. There was another call Tatum hoped for too. A silent message and the soft click.

Stick to stalking Vincent, she told herself, as he slipped into his room. Sleeping with Vincent was the option she held in reserve. Her cyanide capsule.

She pulled out of the lot and drove home. Back at the duplex, she turned her key, and the click of the lock echoed. The whole place seemed hollow. It had been like this since Ralph's funeral. For a guy who never lived there, he sure seemed to clear the place out when he died. She dropped Vincent's next three chapters on the coffee table beside the small pile she'd assembled of odds and ends left behind by Rachael. Try as she might, she could dream up nothing from which to rescue Rachael, not one good reason to kidnap her and head for Mexico. Rachael was taking swimming lessons. Lee had gotten her a tutor so she wouldn't be behind in school come fall. Hard to justify taking a kid out on the lam for that.

Her eyes shot to the answering machine. No blink.

Good thing it didn't matter.

Okay, Tatum thought. Time to take some action. Pack Rachael's things. Ship them. Signal to her own subconscious that it was time to let go. She reached down and gathered up the pile left behind in the abrupt departure: Clothes from the hamper, now laundered and folded. Barrettes and books. The photo albums at which Tatum had never peeked. The glitch that had kept Tatum from shipping had been that such a thing required a box, and since getting rejected at the diner, the basement had been off-limits. The last thing she needed was to return to the scene of the crime and moon over the deserted mattress.

But it doesn't matter, she reminded herself. Not anymore. Tra-la-la-la-la-blah.

She carried Rachael's stuff to the kitchen counter and miscalculated putting it down.

"Crap," she said as the pile hit the floor. One of the albums fell open, face down, crumpling the pages on impact.

Paper dolls cut out from photographs littered the floor beneath it. They hadn't been pasted down. Tatum crouched down and shook the book to loosen whatever more of them there might be and then gathered them up onto the counter. There were two of Paris. Five Margarets. Four Genevas. Three Lees. Five Rachaels. Five Tatums. She pulled one of each from the pile and lined them up. Not one was still in her life.

Only Vincent was left.

Only Vincent was missing from the line of paper dolls. He was in Tatum's nightstand drawer.

She opened the photo album that the pictures had fallen from. How to put them back? She stared at the blank page. Could she fix it?

"Huh," Tatum said as a memory snuck up on her, one of staring at the blank space in another book asking the same question: *Can I fix it? Can I fix the Book of Rachaels?*

An idea was forming in her as to how to fix both.

At the top of the basement stairs, she threw the switch and began her descent. The empty boxes were in the far right-hand corner. She could pass the mattress without looking at it. Don't look at ghosts, and they won't see you. Isn't that how it works?

Just a corner of the mattress reached her peripheral vision as she passed. She located a sturdy, right-sized box for what she wanted. Then, she turned. She looked. Just real fast. As far as mattresses went, it was a sorry one.

"Go away," she said to the encroaching memories.

Vincent. Vincent. Sleep with Vincent, she thought heading for her stored belongings. Let go. Move on. She retrieved the Book she meant to defile. She meant to defile a lot of things. Then maybe she'd pack her own bags and put some miles between herself and the past.

She climbed the stairs back up to her apartment two at a time. This was her plan: Sleep with Vincent to get past Paris. Send Rachael her things and get past expecting her back. Then, turn her attention to moving. How far? She wasn't sure. But away. Away from Geneva. Outta here. Gone.

Tatum dropped the box and the green leather book beside the paper dolls. She retrieved Vincent from her nightstand and placed him in line with the others. Her plan was to paste the paper dolls where her entry in the Book of Rachael belonged. She'd paste in Margaret, herself, and Rachael. Lee, Paris, Vincent, and Geneva. She would write nothing. This would be her contribution to the legacy. The unfolding history of Rachaels would strike her like she was crystal, and she would scatter the ray.

She flipped through the pages determined and ready to execute her plan. But what she saw where she expected the blank space beneath her name stopped her.

Black ink. Her scar sucked into itself like fingernails pressing into one's palm. Her breast was silent, the scar of what was louder than the soft curve of present flesh. Tatum looked at the face and then looked away. It was complete. It was unnerving.

She reached to the page with a flat hand and crumpled it in her palm, tearing it from the spine as she did so. She dropped it on the counter. Paris had not turned away. He drew her eyes, and it was her. It was the lie of her. Or the truth of her. She didn't know which.

Paris drew her beautiful, and good.

Paris was gone, and he took that woman with him.

All the friggin' paper dolls were gone.

Except Vincent.

A body slamming into hers making her forget — that was what she needed.

Tatum grabbed her keys.

41

~

Paris emerged from the basement and into the kitchen of the diner. By tomorrow night, all the pots and pans would be sold, the kitchen equipment and the booths too. The place would be ransacked by second-hand buyers. He crossed the kitchen and pushed through the swinging door that led to the dining room. Jerry was behind the counter, folding a small wad of bills and easing them into his front pocket.

"Cash bonus," he said to Paris. "Guess this one's off the books." He jerked his head toward the casino. "Blair's got it when you want it."

Paris looked toward the casino. Pocketing the bonus would put a thousand bucks in his pants. He was already carrying, as he did every night, the five hundred he promised himself he'd give to Linda.

"What's next?" Jerry said, tucking a cigarette between his lips.

"Don't know," Paris said. "You?"

"Got a job at the Circle K."

Convenience store clerk. Paris could see it.

"Smoke bad out there?" Jerry said. He took the cigarette from his lips and tucked it behind his ear.

"I came up from the basement."

"Right."

It was a lot of conversation. It was a way of saying good-bye.

Jerry took a last look around and then raised a hand. He turned and took the walk out of the diner into the casino and through the orange-green flash of keno machines into sunlit haze.

Inside, Paris reassembled the newspaper on the counter. He helped himself to a bowl of clam chowder and ate it, scanning the empty dining room while he strategized over the evening's tasks.

The night would be slow. The clientele had dropped off as items disappeared from the menu, eighty-sixed with a black Magic Marker. There'd been minimum restocking. Paris finished his soup, drinking straight from the bowl. Back in the kitchen, he pulled his apron off of a nail. He did a final inventory of the cooler. Hamburger. Eggs. A bin of dry onions and a bin of soggy tomatoes. He knew there were french fries in the freezer. The bread was day old.

It was the end of a line.

"Good," Paris said, pulling the bin of tomatoes from the shelf. He soon would be back to having nothing to lose. There was penance to be paid for wanting more, and there was no more. Tatum had been right all along. Wanting more is really wanting something else.

Paris dumped the bin and watched the tomatoes slip into the garbage can. He would forget. He would forget all of it. The good as well as the bad. He knew how. There was work to do, and it was enough. There was hamburger, eggs, and day-old bread. It was enough too. He would make meatloaf.

Six p.m. turned to ten p.m. without a single customer. No one would know it, though, watching Paris's industry. Meatloaf and french fries, plates of it moved out from the kitchen and into the casino for Blair and every drunk and gambler who hovered or lurked. Paris kept an eye to the supply, though. He wanted to make sure the women got theirs.

When there was no one to feed, Paris worked on the cooler. He wiped down the metal shelves and then headed for the janitor's closet for the mop. He opened the door to the scene of his crime. It had been that next morning that he had gone to Tatum's, and she had shown him the scar. Look where it all had led. It made him glad that Linda hadn't returned. It was another sign that it was over.

Paris reached for the mop's handle and became unsteady. He thought he was panicking. The mop handle seemed to vibrate. Paris, himself, was trembling. A flash of wet heat came up behind his face. He reached for the wall.

Paris blamed himself for the loss of balance because he trusted that the ground beneath him was solid. That, at the least, was a thing he could count on.

But there is no "at the least." At the least, there is always nothing.

Paris was not shaking. It was the very earth.

Then, it stopped. Paris heard laughter and exclamations from the casino up front. Then, applause. The electricity in the air seemed elevated, the outpouring of adrenaline mingling with the tension shrugged off by the planet. The foundation upon which Paris stood was no longer the same. New cracks formed. Old channels sealed.

Before and after. Equilibrium returns, but we are not the same.

42

The fans oscillated, sending welcome breezes across John and Geneva's bodies as they rolled in the bed, one on top and then the other. It was not athletic but steady and peaceful, information exchanged with smiles, sighs, and backward rolling eyes. Afterward, they ate bread, cheese, and sliced pears. They opened the door to the west. Burning forests made for spectacular sunsets. Three different purples, orange, and blood red lay like ribbons across the sky. Geneva drove home glowing. She had come to love this stretch of highway regardless of the direction in which she drove. Her Doors cassette was cranked up. Love was calling her.

Love, she thought. It seeks a host. It wants us as much as we want it. At worst, we are parasites to each other, we and love, each destroying the other. At best, she thought, we seek each other out for mutual benefit. We co-evolve. Our relationships to one another are one thing, she thought. Our relationship to love quite another.

She arrived home and came in through the yard. Inside, she snapped her fingers as she settled in as though keeping beat with something slick and lounge-y. She wandered to her wall of albums, hips swaying before the selection. What was it her hips were hearing? Ray Charles? Tina Turner? She pulled a silver sleeve from the shelf. Drummers. Lots of them. Assembled by Mickey Hart.

"This will do," she said, going a different way. She slipped *Diga* onto the turntable. It had a percussion-driven instrumental of "Fire on the Mountain." Very apropos. But apropos, shmapropos. She went with the B-side instead. It was the better jam.

Geneva's hips rocked. Her eyes closed, and a smile played on her lips. The music was native all the way. Primitive. Speaking to the body, not the mind. She held up her hands, palms turned outward, and she led a parade of one through her living room. Her head bobbed. Her shoulders grabbed a shimmy then slid down her back. She turned her arms into snakes. Her body felt delicious, alive in the groove, grinding and stretching, working out the glitches, and shaking out the dead.

If this was love she was feeling, she thought, love was movement. Motion. Flow. Responsibility had clotted her love. The heart and the hearth are not the same. The Romans knew and kept their goddesses separate. Duty calls us. Love draws us. Duty tests our perseverance. Love tests our courage. You can value one. Or the other. You can value both. But they are not the same.

Geneva knew it would not be long now before the stars were right and the moment upon them, both her and Ralph, to let go of. . .

Geneva halted the parade and split paths with the music.

"Oops," she said.

Ralph. She had forgotten Ralph.

She made a sound that could pass for a single laugh, but her face was screwed up, her brows drawn together. She forgot Ralph. It was both a problem and a victory.

Could she leave him overnight tucked safely against the shack in the dust and smoke? Should she call John and ask him to bring Ralph inside?

It was 10 p.m. Late, but not too late. Geneva lifted the needle from the record and grabbed her keys. She would try to be quiet but suspected she would not go undetected. She headed out for the gravel road.

She turned off the asphalt highway and away from street lamps. Beyond her passenger window the mountains were dark whale backs surfacing above the earth. The forgetting was the sign, she knew. It was time. The letting go was here. She thought of what she had asked John earlier that day: *Do you need to know what you're holding on to in order to let it go?* The question now seemed irrelevant. John had been right. You just open your hand. What made it tricky, Geneva realized, was that when you opened your hand, you didn't get to decide what did and did not fall. To let go of anything, it seemed, you needed to be willing to let go of everything. On the bright side, there was nothing to fear since anything authentically yours can't go anywhere. Open your hand and your fingers don't fall off.

Geneva's heart blazed. Her vision seemed oddly clear. She felt fully attuned to the cosmic groove, otherwise known as the Tao. The flow. God. She drove through the night so in sync that, even on the bumpy road, she felt the car was gliding. The farther from the city and lights she drove, the deeper the stillness around her should have been. Yet,

Geneva sensed a vague stirring, a definite fluctuation in the frequency. She feared she was losing the cosmic thread. Something was wrong, unsettled. She glanced down at the car's controls, looking for red lights and warnings. She pressed the brakes and looked beyond her windshield. Everything started to shake.

Geneva threw the car into park and dove from it. It was a reflex. She stumbled into the road. She was disoriented for a moment in the wide darkness. There was nothing to hold onto. Nothing stood still.

And then, it was over.

In the middle of the road, Geneva stood with her adrenaline pumping. A single remaining stripe of indigo glowed above the mountain's curve. The stillness returned but had changed in quality.

It was an earthquake, she thought. Right? It wasn't personal. Was it?

She looked across the prairie. The mountains settled back in. Her headlights illuminated rocks and grass. Her car door hung open, and the motor ran. Geneva climbed back in and put the car in gear.

Somewhere, pressure had been released. Something, somewhere, let go. "God is Pressure." Geneva had read it once. And forgotten it. But the words had returned true. God is Pressure, the push of light. So you better let it flow. If God was indeed Pressure, it seemed to Geneva, holding on, holding on to anything, was to resist God.

Good luck with that, she thought.

She reached John's property and pulled toward the ditch outside the barbed wire fence. She stepped up his driveway, trying to keep her feet quiet on the gravel. At his door, she reached to the ground for the black lacquer box. Beside it, leaning against the shack, was a shovel she hadn't noticed there before.

Just then, the door opened. John squinted down at her.

"I forgot my husband," Geneva said.

"That's good," John said.

Geneva stood with the box.

"I know," she said. "I thought so too. There was just an earthquake, right?"

"A five-pointer plus, I'd guess," he said. "Rattled the dishes."

John raised his hand then, and Geneva saw he was holding an industrial-sized flashlight.

"Ready?" he said.

Geneva nodded. John grabbed the shovel.

"I know a good place," he said.

"Scattering him never felt right," Geneva said. "Burying him —
that's better."

They set out from the shack, past the fire pit, following the flashlight's pool of light. They walked for ten minutes in the sooty air
through a grove of aspen and into the open space beyond it. John
stopped and put down the flashlight.

"How's this?" he said.

Geneva looked around. In the darkness, she couldn't tell it from
any other spot.

"Good," she said, trusting him.

John jabbed the shovel into the ground. Geneva held the box while
he dug.

"Wish we'd get some rain," she said. "Wash out the valley."

"These fires are here 'til the snow flies," John said.

Soon John had dug a small trench. He stepped back and leaned
into a hip. His hands and chin rested on top of the long wooden handle. Geneva stepped forward. She undid the latch. She paused to see if
there were words. But she was done with words. That's what made it
time. She shook out the contents along the length of the trench, not
a scattering to the wind but a laying to rest under a sky that held the
transforming elements, earth turned to fire turned to air.

"You know," Geneva said, "I always figured if there were a heaven,
hell, and all those zones in between, that they were part of the big bang
too, and they'll get sucked back into nothing exactly when we do."

"Makes sense," John said.

Geneva thought they were the kindest of words.

"He said he loved me," Geneva said.

"What more could you ask for?" John said.

"For it to be real," Geneva said. She half-laughed, then sighed.
"Whether I was asking a lot, or a little, I have no idea."

John held his opinion.

"Think you'd ever sell this land?"

"No," John said. "I promise. He'll be okay here until he's not here
anymore."

"I wonder how long it takes."

"To disappear completely?" John asked.

"To become something else so completely that what you were is
gone."

John pushed the shovel into the pile of dirt he had dug out to make
the trench. He spread the dirt over Ralph's ashes.

"I want to become new," Geneva said. "But I get the feeling it entails forgetting who you've been. Do you think it's possible?"

"It's the Holy Grail," John said.

Geneva looked down into her hands. She laughed.

"Now I have to figure out what to do with this box."

43

Tatum spun into the lot of Vincent's motel. She took only one breath to collect herself then threw open the car door. She knew Vincent's room number, and she knew her mission. Overload the senses. Drown feelings. She would show him her scar and watch his face. He would struggle between backing off and pretending it didn't matter. He was not a superficial guy. That's not how he'd want to see himself.

A stage-three air alert had turned the night a dingy purple. Tatum stood in the eerie light outside Vincent's room. Her pulse raced. But before she could knock, the door opened. They both jumped, startled. Vincent looked surprised but not unhappy to see her.

"Vincent," Tatum said, "this has nothing to do with any expectations. I'm happy to edit your book no matter what. But I do want you. I want you."

A question mark on his face was followed by a soft smile.

"Wow," he said.

"Weren't expecting room service, were you?" Tatum said nervously. She looked at the ground.

Vincent lifted her chin. He moved his hand to her hip and kissed her. Tatum was surprised to feel her body brace.

The kiss was not long.

"I was just leaving," Vincent said. "I've got to meet someone." He motioned with his chin toward the restaurant across the street. "Half an hour, an hour at the most." He reached to her hair and took a strand of it between his finger and thumb. "Can you wait?"

"Okay."

"The manuscript is on the desk," he said, "if you need to amuse yourself. The TV has bad reception."

"All right," Tatum said.

Vincent stepped aside, and Tatum slipped into the room.

"I'll be back as soon as I can," he said. He hesitated before pulling the door closed behind him. "I'm glad you came."

"Well, you're welcome," Tatum said, and she winced as he closed the door.

You're welcome? She was such an idiot.

The motel room was rundown but not seedy. Tatum lowered herself onto the end of the bed almost as though she wasn't certain it would hold her. The air conditioner was off. It was the noise, Tatum knew, from her history with Vincent. Instead, the windows were open and traffic noises drifted in through the screens, as did the smoke. The room smelled dirty. The whole valley smelled dirty.

She surveyed the room. Tatum had to hand it to Vincent, letting her stay there alone, he must not have anything to hide. She stood and paced, examining what private details of Vincent's world might lay on the surface. A half-filled water glass. A comb on the dresser. Half a package of Rolaids. Her eyes drifted from the surfaces to the walls. Above the television set hung a mass-produced print of a landscape. Pine trees, a waterfall, and a little bridge crossing a creek. It was hideous. Tatum smiled. She'd been in a dozen motel rooms just like this. She had an affection for them and their crummy art.

But unlike those other rooms, she was not in this one for suicide. She was here for annihilation, the next best thing.

She walked to the desk and fingered the manuscript. She wasn't in the mood to read but knew Vincent would want her to say something when he got back. A few comments about his manuscript would stoke the fires. She picked it up and turned. Above the bed, she noticed a print similar to the one above the television set. She looked back and forth between the two. They were not similar. They were exactly the same.

"That's hilarious," she said aloud, but her spirits sank. It made her think of Paris. He'd toast the fact of it.

No, she thought. Not Paris. Vincent. She looked at the clock. Only ten minutes had passed. Self-annihilation better lends itself to spontaneity. Vincent was giving her too much time. Time to notice that the mattress was off the floor. Time to wonder how many women had made Vincent no-strings-attached offers of their bodies. Some people you have to love on their own terms. Their frailties and cruelties must remain unacknowledged. Then, there were people like her, crawling for love. A million sorrys, and it was never enough. What made some people worth more than others, she wondered? Why is a bone thrown from one person worth more than another giving everything she's got?

A grinding sound interrupted her thoughts. Wind hitting the building? She looked to the windows. Something wasn't right. Her mind tried to make sense of what it saw. Then, it clicked. She thought she heard a strong wind. But the curtains weren't moving.

The window was.

Earthquake.

Her mind formed the word, and it was over.

"Whoa," she said.

She looked back at the crummy artwork. One of the pictures had shifted, but they were still exactly the same.

The heat of the room snuck up on her. She looked at the worn bedspread, and it bored her to the point of claustrophobia. What made Vincent worth more than her, she thought? But the question dislodged a shard of hate, a shard not reserved for Vincent alone. When the people you love don't love you back, how can you help but hate them, at least a little?

Tatum dropped the manuscript onto the bed. She didn't leave a note. Her own thoughts were scaring her, and she had to get out. She left the room, nearly stumbling to her car. She barely remembered the ride, but there she was, parked outside the Deluxe. It was their last night open. Her last chance. She had no idea where Paris was living. She might never know again where to find him. Her fingers curled over the steering wheel. She bit her bottom lip. She wanted Paris to save her from her own thoughts. She didn't want to hate him. She wanted to love him.

But would he let her be the woman he had once loved? The one he had drawn in the picture?

She banged her head against the steering wheel. The problem wasn't who Paris would allow her to be. The problem was her and who she could be. She hadn't lived up to the image he had held of her. Was she any different now?

Tatum lifted her head and screamed at the windshield. No words, just a frustrated howl. She put the car in gear and peeled out. Back at the duplex, she stormed into her living room and stood there for a moment, not knowing what to do.

She didn't want to exist.

Her eyes darted through the room. There she was in the pillows. There she was in the ottoman. She lunged toward the sofa, yanking off the pillows and pitching them toward the door. She kicked over the ottoman. In the kitchen, she grabbed a box of plastic garbage bags and then marched to the linen closet. There, she pulled out the sheets and towels. She stuffed the bags. In her bedroom, she filled another bag with clothes and shoes. She tore apart her closet. She dared anything to matter enough to stop her.

Giant bag after giant bag landed at her front door. It wasn't suicide. It wasn't sleeping with Vincent. She could self-annihilate without self-destructing, she told herself. If she had nothing, she thought, she was one step closer to being nothing. Ground zero without the bomb. She loaded her Celica to capacity. It wasn't all she had, but it was all she could fit. In the foyer, she paused. It was nearly two in the morning, but she didn't care.

"Geneva," she yelled at Geneva's door. "Geneva."

But there was no answer. How could she not hear? Tatum imagined Geneva jamming her head under the pillow to drown out the sound of her voice. Tatum left the duplex, got into her packed car, and pulled away from the curb, heading for the Salvation Army.

Tatum drove the near empty streets past the marquees and strip malls. She parked behind the square, dark building. It wasn't the best of neighborhoods, but there was a floodlight above the Dumpster-sized drop box where people left their cast-offs. Let the poor rest their feet on her ottoman, she thought, tipping it over the bin's edge. Let the homeless wear her clothes, she thought, heave-ho-ing the garbage bags over the rim. Would Paris recognize her blue corduroy blouse on one of his midnight customers, she wondered? No. Tonight was the last night. He would never see the women again.

Tatum emptied her car and stood beside the drop box under the starless sky. Her apartment was torn apart. Her car was empty. The air was so packed with particulate that her lungs were fatigued by breathing itself. She looked for the moon and waited for the relief. The fix. She wasn't gone, but was she gone enough? Or should she have stayed in Vincent's room? Did she need a fistful of pills to get the job done?

The moon was nowhere. The moon was the one that was gone. Not her. It didn't seem quite fair. She turned a circle beside her car, her head thrown back and eyes turned upward.

The feeling she expected didn't come, the melancholy and heartbreak for a lost moon. One longs for what is gone, and Tatum knew that the moon could not be gone. It made her angry, not sad, that the moon wasn't there. She searched the overcast sky for the vague halo.

It was discomfort no matter how you sliced it, she thought. The discomfort of having. The discomfort of losing. The discomfort of fear.

The discomfort of courage. Maybe choosing one over the other wasn't so great a leap.

"I love you, Paris," she said, looking up into a moonless sky. "Okay?"

She got back into her car. She was going to the diner. She would drag Paris outside. She and Paris. They were going to find the damn moon.

44

The night was slow, as Paris had expected. It became clear he needn't worry that there would be meatloaf enough for the women. He collected the old menus and tossed them into the garbage can in the kitchen.

When 2 a.m. rolled around, the retarded women took their usual booth. Paris delivered piping hot plates straight from the microwave to their table. The women looked confused for a moment but then picked up their forks. Paris thought they might want soup too, for nostalgia's sake, so he brought them each a bowl. Only one other woman showed up that night, the alcoholic with the shake. Paris brought her food too, and they ate quietly while he cleared out the cabinets beneath the counter. He threw away unneeded cleaning supplies and carried stacks of dishes back into the kitchen. He found himself feeling almost good as he laid them out with the pots, pans, and cooking utensils ready for tomorrow's sale. He didn't know what the next day would bring or where he would go. West, he thought, maybe. It didn't matter. He was starting over. Soon he would be back to his old, invisible self. He would let people be and not expect anything to be other than it was. He would be one less pair of sticky hands.

A thud from the back of the kitchen interrupted his thoughts. He lifted his head and heard it again. Someone was banging on the back door. He walked toward the rear of the kitchen, craning his neck. He pushed the metal bar, and there she stood beneath the fire escapes in the purple night.

Linda.

"The 'tards said you wanted to see me," she said. She hugged her arms, though it wasn't cold. She looked down the alley then back at Paris.

So much for unsticky hands.

"You're closing tonight, huh?" she said, clearly nervous and unsure what he might want of her.

Paris stepped out and placed a brick kept nearby into the door to keep it ajar. He had thought it was all over, but here Linda was, so he reached into his pocket and pulled out the money.

"Here," he said. "I want you to have this."

Linda drew her brows together and looked at the bills.

"What's this?"

"To get out of town," Paris said. "I mean, if you need to, or want to." It occurred to him that that was his own plan as well. "I'm leaving too" he said. "If you need a ride, I can give you one," he blurted. "It's not about sex or anything," he added quickly, but the words felt awkward hanging in the air. "Just take the money," he said. "But you can have a ride too. If you want."

Linda looked from the money to his face. He knew that it would be difficult for her to believe he had no ulterior motive. He shouldn't have offered the ride.

"No blowjob is this good," she said.

"It's not about that," Paris said.

Linda took the money. She looked down the alley and then stepped toward Paris. She dropped to a knee and started in at his belt.

"No," Paris said, pulling her to her feet. "I just want to. . ."

But what he wanted was not to want.

Linda knew that Paris wasn't looking for sex. He was trying to make amends. She wasn't sure what he had done, whom he owed something to, and whether the debt was real or imagined. But she accepted what men might thrust upon her, surrogate for anger, love, or regret. Paris needed her to take the money and that much she would do. But she knew, too, that he wanted more. She knew something about wanting to be good, believing you are against all evidence, but knowing that you are not despite your best efforts. She felt sorry for Paris, but with this, she could not help him. She could accept the money but not the goodness. To accept the goodness would force her to open that space that receives and the price of that was just too great. To be open and grow empty again, it was a journey she had taken too many times. One trip was not worth the other. She stepped toward Paris and reached for his belt.

Linda pressed her mouth into his, and Paris found himself unable to pull away. It was the touch. The body heat. The place to disappear. Linda drowned out his goodness with a quick and firm caress of his balls. Paris drowned out Linda's name by closing his eyes. Linda backed against the Dumpster for support, dragging Paris forward with her. She pulled his dick out from his pants. She stroked it until it stiffened, undid her pants and pushed them down, and then shoved Paris inside of her.

Paris put his hands on the rim of the Dumpster behind her head. Linda's breath was in his ear. He drew back his head and fucked her. He fucked her for Tatum — that's how it felt — like it was, at last, what Tatum wanted, something sad and broken, and not his own desires. His eyes opened to a moonless sky, and he surrendered to oblivion. To thrust and sensation. He and Linda were both alone. Alone together. He looked to Linda's face, her profile against the black metal rim. She opened her eyes too. They landed on his for just a moment but then refocused over his shoulder.

"No," she cried.

Paris didn't know what hit him. All he knew was that he was on the ground, his pants at his thighs. His head screamed with pain. Linda screamed too and hiked up her pants. A swift kick landed in his stomach, and he rolled to his side, reaching for the sides of his jeans.

"Get out of here," Linda was yelling, and Paris wasn't sure to whom. He made it to his hands and knees and then up to his feet. But he was too late. Linda's husband had her by the back of the neck, and he dragged her into the kitchen, kicking out the brick, the door locking behind him. Paris heard Linda scream again.

Paris threw his body at the door. He pounded it. Then he turned and ran down the alley, slightly bent at the gut. He tried to holler "help," but it came out as only breath. He stumbled as he ran, one hand steadying himself on the brick backs of buildings. A drumbeat pounded inside of his head. Run. Then he heard a crash, a sound like an air conditioner hitting concrete from a three-story drop. A gunshot. He reached the corner and rounded the block. Street lamps cast soft pools of light on the empty sidewalks and lit up the floating particulate. Paris straightened his body as he ran. When he reached the Deluxe's door, he was pushed aside by two men racing out. Headlights from a car pulled up to the curb.

Paris burst through the door and moved swiftly through the casino, afraid of what he might find. But the casino was empty. As he approached the diner, he could see her, Linda, held by the hair by her husband. In his other hand, he held the gun. Blair lay on the threshold between the two rooms, holding his shoulder, the blood seeping out between his fingers. The retards were under the table holding each other, cheek to cheek, eyes slammed closed and crying like children.

White light exploded in Paris's head.

"Motherfucker," Paris said, breaking past the threshold.

Paris's blood ran cold. His boots could kick without mercy. His fists could pound one after the other. Don't stop. Don't stop until it's dead.

"Shoot me," Paris said, jabbing with his thumb at his own chest. "Shoot *me*, you motherfucker."

Paris didn't know he had blood running down his head and off his lip. He didn't know he had four inches on Linda's husband and that the veins of his biceps stood out blue and were pumped fat with adrenaline. He didn't know the force of his body walking the length between the booths and the counter was menace and threat and fearlessness, a single-focused rage and a self-disregard that made it so that no man could stop him. A gun might. Maybe a gun. Only a gun. Linda's husband's eyes were full of fear and feral threat, but they lost their focus on Paris for just a second, and in that second, Linda pushed at his ribs and spun, freeing herself just as Paris reached them and lunged for her husband's hand.

But the gun fired first.

45

෴

Geneva spent the night at John's for the first time. She dozed, rather than slept, which left her with a slightly buzzed, surreal feeling at six a.m. She sat up on the edge of the bed and stretched. John gently took her wrist, letting her slip from his calloused grasp as she rose. She smiled over her shoulder at him. As she drove home, she thought about the empty black lacquer box in the passenger seat. Perhaps someday she would fill it with Voodoo's ashes. Perhaps, it would be filled with her own. God wasn't pressure at all, she thought, driving in the diffused morning light. It just felt that way when you were holding on.

She parked in front of the duplex instead of in the garage. She would be going out later. She craved the new and decided a new sofa was the place to start. Tatum's car was not out front, she noticed. Out early, she wondered, or late?

The Russian sage bloomed in the haze. Geneva took her time heading up the walk. The plums, rose and orange, were beginning to drop from the tree. In the matter of a week, they would litter the front lawn. Given her neglect, Geneva was surprised anything at all had survived. As she took stock, she decided that when Tatum got home, she'd knock on her door and invite her on the shopping expedition. Together they could scheme a way to bring Rachael back, at least for a visit. They could put their rough patch behind them. Geneva opened the front door. She entered the foyer, and life turned into a different place.

Paris sat on the floor outside her door. He was bruised and stitched up. Part of his head was shaved, revealing the sutures. His eyes were wild, wet and red. He was a man betrayed by God.

"Oh, no," Geneva said, for whatever it was, it was real, and it was awful.

"Oh, no," she said again. She went to Paris and knelt before him. He needed to be held. He needed not to be touched.

"She's dead," he said.

"Tatum?" Geneva said, astonished.

Paris dropped his head into his hands.

Geneva assumed suicide. But then what had happened to Paris?

"What happened to you?" she said.

"She was shot," Paris said, and Geneva's breath stopped. "I went for his arm," he said, "but the gun went off first. I think. I don't know. Oh, fucking god. Oh, fucking god."

"Someone shot Tatum?" Geneva said.

His silence answered.

"At the diner?"

He nodded and shook.

"Oh, Paris," Geneva said. "The police came?"

His body convulsed, and his head managed to nod, yes.

Geneva reached for him, but he shrank from her grasp.

"C'mon," she said, pulling him up by the arm.

Paris allowed himself to be dragged inside, but he couldn't hold himself up for long. He dropped to his knees again inside the door. Geneva knelt down before him and put a hand to each side of his face.

"Who's got her?" Geneva said. "Where is she?"

"I don't know," Paris said. "The police came and an ambulance came. They took me," he said. "The police and the hospital."

Geneva placed a thumb at the side of each of his eyes and made him look at her.

"Paris, are you in any trouble?"

"No," he said, and he started to shake again.

Paris had told the police everything. Linda. The sex in the alley. Tatum. They broke up. She was his ex-girlfriend. The police asked why his ex-girlfriend would be coming to the diner at two o'clock in the morning.

Paris had sat on the examination table in the hospital unable to speak. He knew there could be only one reason Tatum had come. To say, *c'mere*. To call him closer, again. *I don't blame you, it's me*, she would say. *Let me try again. Teach me to love.*

There she would be, beautiful and alive, and meaning every word. She *was* there, behind his closed eyes as he sat on the gurney in his bloodstained T-shirt with his head throbbing. He could see her waiting for his answer.

And there he would be, fresh from the alley where he false-drowned in false feelings.

"I can't," he would have to tell her. "Don't you get it?" He would be unkind. "I can't teach you because I don't know how." And there they would be in their helplessness.

Her eyes would water to him. She'd drop to her knees on the other side of the counter, her heart in her hand. *Take it*, she would say and then brace for the blow. But he couldn't let her be there on her knees. He would climb across the counter and go to his knees too, so they both would be there, humbled, helpless, but together.

"Why do you think she'd be coming to the diner at two a.m.?" the officer repeated.

"We were still in love," Paris said.

Paris didn't know what happened to Linda or her husband. As soon as the gun fired, he knew there was someone in the diner behind him. There had been no expectation, only reflex, as he had whipped around. The bullet passed through Tatum's head. The thought was on her face. The heart in her hand. It was stopped in time.

His legs buckled as hers did. Paris went down as though the bullet had hit him, too. Then he crawled on his hands and knees, screaming. His head spun, and he was nauseous.

Feet stomped past him. Solid man strides in work boots. Linda, dragged past him in her discount huaraches. Tatum's blood was splattered on Blair's cheek and shirt. The retarded girls crawled out from under their table and came up behind Paris.

"I can call 911," the white one said, "because this is an emergency."

She went to the phone behind the counter, and the cross-eyed Indian one crouched behind Paris. She dropped her forehead to the nape of his neck. When the white one got back, she crouched by Paris too. Two more feet appeared, tennis shoes. Paris looked up. The alcoholic looked down. Her body twitched, and tears took jagged paths down leathered cheeks.

The recollection was like a baseball bat beating against the inside of his head. He grabbed the hair he still had, and he made pained animal sounds on Geneva's living room floor.

Geneva stood, taking Paris's wrists with her. She held his arms above his head. He sagged like a rag doll.

"Paris," Geneva said. "Have the police gone to her apartment?"

"I don't know," he said.

"I'm going over there," she said, "to get Rachael's number. Stay here."

Geneva released his arms and went to her kitchen. She pulled a black coffee mug from the shelf and dumped a number of keys onto her counter. She picked through them quickly, finding the right one. She paused at Paris again on her way out. She squatted in front of him.

"You will be okay, Paris."

"She's gone."

"She is. But Paris, look at me."

He lifted his broken face to her.

"You will be okay," she said again.

Geneva left Paris and turned the key in the door across the hall. She stepped into Tatum's apartment as though there were someone there to disturb. She paused and closed her eyes. Tatum was dead. It happens so fast. Our hearts shut to loved ones, and we expect them to be there waiting when we are ready to open them up again. It is a costly arrogance. Geneva collected herself. She'd been holding on for Paris's sake, and it wasn't time to break down yet.

She opened her eyes. It was then she took in the state of the apartment. It had been ransacked, but neatly so. The sofa remained. The chair and the plants too. But the odds and ends were gone. Geneva walked toward the kitchen. The cupboards were open and empty. On the surface of the counter was a smattering of cutouts from photographs, her own image among them. There were also two big books, photo albums, and a third book lying open and bound in green leather.

Geneva knew what the green book was, history carried like a cross. Beside the Book, a crumpled piece of paper caught Geneva's eye. A torn out page. Geneva uncrumpled it and smoothed it on the counter. Despite the wrinkles, the detail was astonishing. It was Tatum. Paris had drawn it. This she knew. A baby picture of Rachael and Rachael's name was absorbed into the drawing toward the bottom of the page. Geneva found it difficult to look at. Too personal. She wondered why it had been torn out but thought the more important question might be *when?*

She tucked the page back in the Book. No good could come from Paris seeing this and making bad meaning out of something they had no way of understanding. She stepped to the other side of the counter and slipped the Book into a drawer.

Cause and effect. It's useless to look.

Geneva turned her attention to the phone and saw a piece of paper tacked there. It said "Rachael," and a phone number was listed. Below the piece of paper, the answering machine blinked.

Geneva hit the button.

"Yeah, it's Lee. I think I can work this out for you," he said. "I can bring Rachael next week for five days. I have business in Colorado. I'll fly there from Montana."

Geneva heard the front door to the building open and footsteps in the foyer. She reached out and hit delete and then ripped the paper off the wall, cramming it into a pocket. There was a knock on the door she had left partially open. A rap, really, more so than a knock. A warning rather than a question.

The cop was a woman. It was sexist, Geneva knew, but she liked the girl ones even less than the boys.

"I'm Tatum's friend," Geneva said, before being asked a thing, "and I own this building. And I have power of attorney," she threw in, remembering it on the spot. Tatum had signed it over to her during chemo. "Where is she?"

"Coroner's office," the cop said. She had a long, blonde ponytail she was too old for and wore no makeup. "We need to contact next of kin. Do you know how we might reach them?"

"Yes."

"We'd appreciate it if you could share that."

The cop was behaving decently but was executing the standard hands-on-hips posture. She looked around the room. They always look around the room.

"I'll take care of it," Geneva said, pulling the cop's eyes to her.

"In situations like this, we like to send over an officer."

"They live in Illinois."

"You don't want to do this in a phone call," the officer said.

Geneva considered it. She didn't know all the details of the crime and doubted she could squeeze them out of the cop. She wouldn't be able to answer the inevitable questions. But she was concerned about Rachael and the manner in which the information reached her.

The hairs on Geneva's arms prickled. Irrational facts are facts nonetheless, and Geneva realized a big one. There wasn't time to artic- ulate it to herself fully, but she knew this was the plate. She was up to bat.

"Is there a way for me to know when the family has been contacted?" she said. "There's a child involved, and I need to know right away."

"Can't make promises," the cop said, "but I'll see what can be done."

Geneva steered the cop out of the apartment and into the hall. She provided her with Lee's name and relationship to Tatum. She read her the phone number off the piece of paper in her pocket. The officer left, and Geneva's door opened. Paris entered the hall. He looked terrible, his face destroyed by tears. He leaned in the doorframe of Tatum's apartment. His eyes narrowed, taking in the state of it.

"Was she moving?" Paris said.

"I don't know," Geneva said, coming up behind him. "We've been kind of disconnected since Ralph died. I've been disconnected."

Paris looked at her for a long moment and then back into the apartment.

"She has topless pictures," he said.

"She had me take them before the surgery," Geneva said. "She showed them to you?"

"No. I looked through her things once," he said. "I found them."

"Did you want them?"

"No," Paris said softly.

He walked in, eyes slipping slowly over what remained. At the kitchen counter, he pushed around the paper dolls with a finger.

"Rachael's pictures," he said.

"Where are you living, Paris?" Geneva said. "Where did you go?"

"It doesn't matter," Paris said.

"Do you need a place to stay?"

Paris shook his head.

"Stay," Geneva said.

Paris shook his head again. He pushed the cutouts farther apart. Tatum. Geneva. Himself. Vincent. Rachael and each of her parents. They lay there like puzzle pieces.

"For a moment," Paris said, "it seemed like everything was how it's supposed to be."

Geneva couldn't agree with him. She didn't believe in supposed-to-be.

"Tatum was an interesting woman," she said.

"I loved her," Paris said. He wiped his eyes with the back of his hand. "So why'd I walk away?"

He looked at Geneva over his shoulder. His eyes were bloodshot. Geneva shook her head. She didn't know why he walked away. She was asking herself the same question.

"Every time she said I'm sorry," Paris said, "I wanted to hate her."

"What was it that you wanted her to say instead?"

"I don't know," he said.

Neither did she, Geneva thought.

He turned back to face the counter.

"If I take this in," Paris said, "I'll never be able to forget."

Geneva stepped up behind him and placed her hands on his shoulders and rested her cheek on his back.

"You can think about it as little or as much as you want," she said. "But all you can ever change about any of it is how you see it. And even with that, you still end up stuck in time."

"So what do I do?"

Look forward, Geneva thought, but knew he was not ready, and that it was not yet time for the words.

46

Nobody wants to open his door to cops. All the inward guilts make one calculate in an instant, what have I done? And then, secondarily, who's dead? Lee stood with the police officer on his front step. The air was thick with summer heat. The sound of cicadas traveled across the landscape and gave the humidity the dimension of sound. The officer spoke in an official drone. All business. Even the "I'm sorry for your loss" was perfunctory, as devoid of emotion as a cashier's "Have a nice day." The cop handed Lee Geneva's phone number and told him she had asked to be contacted. The patrol car pulled away. The cicadas called out again.

Lee shoved his hands into his pockets. Tatum was dead. Margaret, first. Now, her sister. Then a morbid thought struck him. Such things came in threes, some people said. Was Rachael next? An image flashed through his mind. A dainty casket. Against his will his eyes were drawn to the grove where Margaret wasn't buried. The sight of it embarrassed him. It hadn't seemed wrong at the time.

He'd made some mistakes. Lee could see that now. At first, his reunion with Rachael had gone just as he'd dreamed. She had run to him. Blazed in his presence. But since arriving home, a tension had set in as if each were waiting, each unsure whether or not they were going to be enough for the other.

Lee blamed, in part, the house itself. The fact that Margaret wasn't there made it difficult to think of much else. It was why he had planned the trip to Montana. His plan was to drop Rachael with her aunt and go on to Denver for a job interview. He was hoping to move before the school year started.

The front door opened behind him, and Rachael's tutor stepped out, joining him on the front stoop. Lee listened to her but could not take in her report and pleasantries. Lee watched her drive away, delaying doing what had to be done.

What to say? Tatum was dead. Shot, for god's sake. He tried to remember how he had told Rachael about her mother's death. He had held her at Margaret's bedside. This, he remembered. But he had forgotten that no explanation had been necessary and that it had been Rachael who had told him.

He turned and went inside. The sudden soft chill of air conditioning gave rise to the small hairs on his neck and arms. He supposed there would be a funeral and wasn't sure what his role in the arrangements should be. Maybe this Geneva was managing it, he thought, fingering the piece of paper. He vaguely remembered her as Tatum's neighbor and the widow at the funeral he had attended. Funerals. Tatum's would be the third. That was the three. It was true that he didn't know one of the deceased, but he was there, so it counted. Three. Maybe the thing had run its course. Maybe he was lucky to be alive.

Not finding Rachael in the kitchen, he started up the stairs, dragging his hand along rail. Rachael didn't fill the house the way Margaret had. Nor did she turn a constant antenna to the ether, seeking out his presence.

With increasing unease, Lee moved toward Rachael's room. His legs felt unsure beneath him as a creeping realization made its way to his consciousness. With Tatum dead, his safety net was down. He was alone again. Alone with his daughter. When he reached the top of the steps, the phone rang, and Lee gratefully took the out. He bypassed Rachael's bedroom door, peering in and winking at her on route to his own bedroom, where he still did not sleep.

Lee answered the phone. A woman identified herself. Geneva. She reminded him of their meeting at Ralph's funeral. Have you heard about Tatum, she asked? He told her yes.

"How's Rachael doing?" Geneva said.

"The police just left," Lee said, lowering his voice. "I haven't told her, yet."

"Will you allow me to tell her?" Geneva said. "I knew Tatum better. I knew the two of them together."

Lee barely had time to weigh it before Geneva added, "Let me be the messenger. She'll need you to be there for her."

Lee sat on the side of the bed, looking into the hall through the open bedroom door. He was being rescued. He felt gratitude, and shame. He felt relief.

"That may be best," he said.

"Before I talk to Rachael," Geneva said, "one more thing. I know you were planning a trip here under better circumstances. I hope you'll still come for the service. If you do, I want you to know that Rachael is welcome to stay with me while you attend to your business in Colorado. It might be helpful to her. For closure."

Lee considered her words, and he didn't miss the careful intonation, the sell. She wanted Rachael to stay with her for a time. It would serve him too. He could still make the interview. He was about to say "yes" when Geneva continued.

"But here's the deal," she went on. "This has to be up to Rachael. If she doesn't want to come, I want her to have that choice."

Lee looked up. Rachael — small, with eyes filled with knowledge and dread — stood in the bedroom doorway.

"She's right here," Lee said to Geneva. "I'll put her on."

Lee covered the mouthpiece. He held out the phone.

"Geneva," he said.

Geneva's name sounded strange in his mouth. Rachael never spoke of Geneva. Or Paris. Or even her Aunt Tatum. She had the sense it was something she was supposed to pretend never was.

Rachael looked at her father and then the phone. Her eyes had been filled with knowledge and dread because Rachael already knew something was bad. She knew the feeling. The reason for the feeling would be the details coming like water to fill in the cracks.

She stepped forward and took the phone.

"Hello?" she said.

"Rachael," Geneva said, "I've missed you. I was thinking of you just yesterday and thought, just like we said we would, 'I wonder when we'll see each other.' But Rachael, I'm sorry, because I'm calling you with some sad news. It's about your Aunt Tatum."

"She's dead?" Rachael said.

"She's dead."

Rachael pictured her aunt, a fistful of pills in one hand, a cup of coffee in the other.

"Someone shot her," Geneva said.

"Someone shot her?"

"It wasn't on purpose. Someone was committing a crime, and she walked in on it."

Rachael imagined a scene like she had seen on television. A man in a ski mask walking into a convenience store. Aunt Tatum was in line with milk. It was a stick-up.

"Like at a store?" Rachael said.

"It was at the diner," Geneva said. "She went to see Paris. It was late at night."

"What about the women?" she said.

"What women?"

"The women who go there?"

"I don't know," Geneva said. "I don't know about any women."

Rachael had never been to the diner, but she remembered the story told in bed after she had gotten stitches. Paris was telling his story to Tatum, but Rachael had been there and his voice had reached her half-sleep and made the pictures unfold. The women she imagined had dirty faces. They lived in the riskier world of the night where soup was sucked from spoons and crackers were bitten gingerly.

What Geneva was telling her now appeared in her mind like it were a memory, a thing she had actually seen. Paris served the women soup. Tatum sat on a stool watching him. They exchanged shy and loving glances. Then a man burst in the door. He was going to kill Paris, but Tatum jumped in the way.

"I know you were planning on visiting next week," Geneva said. "Would you still like to come and stay with me for a couple of days? We could have a service for Tatum."

Rachael looked at her father, not knowing what she should want. A sad smile flickered across his face. Rachael thought about Geneva's living room, smaller than the bedroom she was standing in. Darker. She remembered lying on the sofa while Geneva rubbed her feet.

"If you don't want to, that's fine," Geneva said. "If you want to, that's fine. I've already asked your dad. He said either way is okay."

But Rachael knew that either way was not okay. Her eyes shot to her father, and she tried to gauge what he wanted her to do.

"I'll come," she said, taking a hopeful guess. Lee placed a hand on her shoulder.

"This isn't the way it will always be," Geneva told her. "This is it," she said. "You've got your dad. And you've got me," she said. "No more dying."

"Dad?"

Rachael was handing him the phone, but he did not see. He was staring down the hall, an idea formulating inside of him. Lee had sat on the bed as Rachael took in the facts. He would need to attend the service, he knew, before heading to Denver. He would let Geneva take the lead in the planning, he thought. He would pay for whatever needed paying for. He remembered the convoluted planning necessary for Margaret's funeral. The Catholic wake. The secret cremation. The burial that was a sham. And now, her ashes were stashed beneath the bed they sat upon.

"She wants to talk to you," Rachael said.

Lee snapped to and took the phone. He asked Rachael to excuse him. She left the room, and Lee put the phone to his ear. Before Geneva could speak he asked what arrangements had been made for the body.

"None yet," Geneva said, "but I can certainly . . ."

Lee cut her off.

"I'll take care of it," he said. "It's the least I can do."

The two agreed that Lee would deal with and pay for the cremation. Geneva would arrange the service. He and Rachael would arrive on Saturday. The service would be Sunday. He would take off for Denver on Monday and be back Thursday.

Lee hung up at his end but remained sitting on the bed. His chest filled with something warm. He called the feeling love, but it was, in fact, relief. Emotions, like other creatures of nature, sometimes use camouflage to pass for something other than what they are. Many feelings pretend to be love as it is the most effective disguise in the attempt to win you over and enlist you in their cause.

Geneva hung up and looked down at the Book before her. She turned another page or two and then flipped to where she had crammed the picture that Paris had drawn. She thought about the inevitable conclusions forming in Rachael's mind, the kind that can turn into self-fulfilling prophecies. What else was there for her to conclude but that everyone leaves? One way or another. They die. They pack you up and ship you off. *Don't count on anyone. Don't get too connected.* In a way, she knew, Rachael would be right. We run through each other's hands like water.

"But it's not what you think," Geneva said. Then she grimaced, knowing she meant something by it but not being sure what.

She closed the Book's cover. She turned away from it and wandered to the back of the apartment, peering into the rooms as she passed them. She wondered how much she should do, if anything, before Rachael arrived. At the rear of the apartment, she looked through the window in the back door. The dead have their secrets, she thought. They leave behind clues, but clues are different than messages. They were never meant for prying eyes. One thing did seem clear, however. The picture that Paris had drawn had upset her. The whole Book upset her.

"It's not what you think," she said again. It's not *personal*. That was what she meant. It was what she wanted Rachael to know.

Rachael had slipped down the hall back into her room. She did not look toward the window to where the trees outside were lit by sun, the leaves transparent and gold-trimmed. She did not look in the mirror either, not at the face. Not at Rachael. Or Mallory. She sat on her bed and tugged at the hem of her shirt. She looked to the space between her dresser and the wall where she had tucked herself in the aftermath of her mother's death.

Rachael.

But then the doorbell had rung. Her Aunt Tatum had come for her.

Mallory.

Rachael closed her eyes and pretended. In her mind, she pressed herself to Paris's chest as Tatum drove in a panic to Geneva's. Paris's heat wrapped around her. There was nothing her Aunt Tatum could do.

But drive.

47

~

Geneva opened Tatum's back door and stepped outside. The mid-morning sky above was gray. The air itself tasted gray. How could Tatum have done this, she thought, as she descended the steps? How could she do this to Rachael? Then Geneva stopped short, remembering again that it had not been suicide. Strange that she kept making the mistake.

From the patio, Geneva took in the tiered beds. Caretaking had not been the tenor of her summer. Not caretaking of the dianthus or foxglove. Not caretaking of Ralph or Tatum. Maybe that's why she kept thinking "suicide." Maybe she just wanted to blame Tatum and thereby throw herself clear of blame.

Tatum. Ralph. Two people in four months that Geneva had withdrawn her attention from and *zap,* they'd disappeared. It would be arrogance to think one controlled such things, yet in a way, Geneva thought, it might be so. We keep ideas alive by thinking them. We keep relationships alive by showing up. Geneva had stopped showing up. She had let them go, and now they were gone. Such was the risk in opening one's hand.

Geneva stepped off the patio and walked along the untended flowerbeds. Ralph. Tatum. Dead. Still, Geneva knew it would've been wrong for her to do other than what she had. Her love for each of them had eroded, pushed apart from itself like rock split by ice. Something else, something not-love, had seeped in. Resentment. Annoyance. It would have been wrong to hold them in her world with her heart unopened to them. So she had turned away. Not just in body, she had released them, too, from the hold her mind had upon them. Once she could hold them in a better place in her mind, she assumed her feet would follow, and she would come to behold them in her life once more.

But alas, there are no guarantees as to who will be there when you reach your newfound place, whether that place lies inside or outside your mind. Such are the risks, she thought, of following one's heart.

The heart points. The mind intends. The body moves. Heart. Mind. Body. Understanding their relationship to each other can be quite useful. The trick, however, is being able to tell one from the other.

Black leaves matted in the birdbath. Heart. Mind. Body. Three. A sacred triad. A sacred number. Not the number tragedies came in. That was a bum rap. Maybe the real meaning of the idea, Geneva thought, was that tragedy came in *three* — in the third dimension. Perhaps as we evolve as a species, she thought, and perceive in four dimensions, as opposed to three, we will understand tragedy differently. Perhaps from the fourth dimension, tragedy isn't tragedy at all.

Geneva felt the urge to smoke some weed and engage in some recreational contemplation of the number three. But she knew she would not. There was another impulse building inside of her, an intention that she preferred to experience from the neurochemistry of "straight." The intention involved Rachael. Geneva's heart had pointed.

She had known it standing in Tatum's apartment with the cop. Even if Rachael were happy where she was, secure with her father, Geneva felt she had to make the offer: live with me. There is always a place to go, she wanted Rachael to know. A number to call. There is no one source of anything. No one and final source of love.

Geneva's heart felt like a reservoir with slowly rising water, and yet, she questioned her intention. Did it matter that not a day had passed since burying Ralph and she was already considering taking on another creature in need and bringing new ghosts into her ken? Was this impulse to take in Rachael a healthy one? Was she backing away from what she claimed to want, John and intimacy and being truly known? She didn't know whether it was her mind or her heart that she didn't trust. Interest was different from love. So was obligation.

She put a palm to the sky to catch a stray flake of ash. She thought of Rachael. With interest. She thought of her and felt the nerve-ending pangs of responsibility. She felt the inner reservoir and the water she knew would overflow its banks.

She was a communist when it came to love, she realized. From each according to her ability, to each according to need.

Geneva knew what she had to do. For whatever answer Lee or Rachael might have, she had to make the offer. She blinked her eyes against the smoke and particulate and felt a pang in her stomach. She thought of John and what they might have had together, just the two of them. A world with few reasons outside of themselves. But could she really lose something she barely had, or be haunted by a life never experienced?

The pang started to reach upward toward her heart. She felt an oncoming tangle of feeling. But a sudden rustling in the hedge snapped her out of herself. Voodoo burst through the bushes and raced across the yard to the patio where he leapt onto a plastic chair. Geneva walked over to where he waited.

"You've got an opinion?" Geneva said.

Voodoo stretched his neck to meet her hand. Geneva stroked him from head to rear. He looked up to her with narrowed eyes.

A cat can teach you more than a ghost, he seemed to say.

A slow smile spread Geneva's lips.

On her patio on this smoky morning, there were no hungry might-have-beens. No black hole drawing her in. No sacrifice being made. She was moving of her own volition, and it was without obligation. Duty. Need. What had she been thinking? She was not assigning her love according to need. She loved. She stood in the state of it, and she was not alone. She loved Rachael because Rachael was there in its field. She loved John too. He was there. She knew it. She could feel it.

The answer was not Don't Look Back. It wasn't Look Forward, either.

Geneva bent down and kissed Voodoo's head.

"You're a genius," she said, though he already knew.

Geneva headed for her back steps. She had her last sentence. Her final column. She made it halfway up the stairs when a man's voice startled her. She turned around. He was standing outside of Tatum's back door. Vincent.

Geneva sighed and came back down her stairs. Vincent had come through Tatum's apartment. He wore his confusion and pointed with his thumb over his shoulder.

"What's going on?" he said.

"She's gone," Geneva said. "She's dead."

Vincent's mouth opened. He dropped backward slightly and leaned against the duplex.

"She was killed," Geneva said. She looked up at him from the bottom of Tatum's steps. "Shot. At the Deluxe."

"I just saw her last night," Vincent said. "I was on my way out. I was supposed to meet her back in my room," he said. "At my room," he said. "I was worried."

"Yeah?" Geneva said.

"She was working with me on my book." Vincent looked off to the side. "The Deluxe, huh."

"It wasn't personal," Geneva said, and Vincent looked back her way. "The shooting," she said. "It wasn't personal. She was shot by accident. Either the gun just went off or the bullet was meant for someone else. Maybe Paris."

"That guy."

"That guy."

Vincent looked down, seeming to do calculations. Geneva suspected, but wasn't sure, that his reunion with Tatum might have had to do with more than his book.

"What can I do?" he said, looking back up.

"Nothing."

Then Geneva looked at him long. She climbed the stairs and put a hand on each side of his face. She could still see in him the ten-year-old boy she once had known. His brown eyes darted back and forth, slightly restless, looking into hers. Geneva kissed him. Affectionately. Maternally. Love, she thought. *Stand there and see who shows up.* For her, Vincent always did. Every time.

"How 'bout keeping your distance from this," she said, letting her hands slide to his shoulders. "Leave the service to others. Let Paris and Rachael do this without you. Unless," she hesitated, "unless, there was more going on, and uh, you need to be there."

"I'm staying at the Red Roof Inn," Vincent said, "if you need me."

"In town long?"

"Hard to say."

Geneva wondered if she should offer him the apartment. But it was too soon, and Rachael was coming.

Vincent pushed himself off the wall. Geneva hooked her arm in his, and they walked back into Tatum's apartment together.

"You deal with a lot of spirits," Geneva said as they moved down the hall.

"Not really," Vincent said. "There are people who do, but I just deal with the dead."

"Well, let me ask you anyway," she said. "Who do you think has more to teach you, a cat or a ghost?"

"Depends on the ghost," Vincent said. "Depends on the cat. Why do you ask?" He turned to face her as they reached the front door.

"A theory," Geneva said. "My last column."

"You're retiring?"

Geneva nodded. Then she noticed Vincent squinting over her shoulder. She turned, following his gaze. Vincent stepped past her to the coffee table and picked up a stack of papers.

"My manuscript," he said.

Geneva was surprised she had not noticed it. She was glad Paris hadn't either. They both had been drawn past it to the kitchen counter and the cut-out paper dolls.

"Maybe you could take a look at it sometime," Vincent said.

"In a few weeks," Geneva said. She put a hand on his back as they entered the foyer.

"I'm really sorry," Vincent said at the front door.

"We all are."

"Call my mom," Vincent said, his way of trying to look after her.

"I do," Geneva said. "I will."

Vincent left, heading down the walk. Geneva watched him from the stoop. He was barely taller than Paris, but leaner. Tidier. Tighter. Geneva considered Vincent's distinctions. He did not deal with spirits. He didn't deal with the dying either. Vincent dealt with the dead, that moment in between the two that should be only a moment and yet so often managed to drag forward into time.

"Vincent," Geneva called to him.

He turned.

"The reason a cat can teach you more than a ghost," she said, "is because the cat's here. The ghost's not."

Vincent walked to his Chevy Trailer King. He had sucked in his lips and nodded in response to Geneva. He thought she was trying to tell him something, to let Tatum go. He climbed into the cab and turned the key. Geneva needn't worry, he thought. There was nothing he was holding on to. Nothing to let go of. It had not escaped him that Tatum had left his motel room, left him, to go to Paris. But it didn't change the fact that for him, death always opened a new pocket of space. He felt it every time he was called. He never discussed it with anyone, his awareness of the new space.

Death didn't bother Vincent because he didn't take it in. Instead, he stepped into it. He filled the empty space. It seemed to be what people wanted.

Geneva watched Vincent walk to his car. She considered that if Rachael came to live with her, Vincent would be in and out of Rachael's life because he was in and out of Geneva's. In Rachael's world, Geneva thought, men leave, but they come back. Women never leave, and yet they seem to disappear.

But not her.

"Twenty more years," she instructed the powers that be. That would get Rachael to almost thirty.

Vincent pulled away from the curb. Geneva turned back toward the duplex, wondering what to do about Tatum's apartment. Should she leave it for Rachael to see as it was? Only the largest items remained, and the plants, a footprint of the life that had passed through. Geneva walked to the kitchen counter and peeked into the box on its surface. Some clothes and hair do-dads. Rachael's things. Geneva picked up the green leather book also lying there to pack it with the rest but hesitated. She had been concerned about how the ripped up apartment would look to Rachael. What about the ripped out page?

Geneva opened the Book and withdrew it. She placed the two items, the book and the page, on the counter one under each hand. Why had Tatum ripped it out? Did it have something to do with going to see Paris? Was the picture somehow her suicide note?

It was not a suicide.

Geneva pursed her lips. She pushed the torn out page farther from the Book. They didn't belong together. Maybe that's what Tatum knew. It seemed to Geneva, however, that Tatum had crumpled the wrong item. The Book of Rachaels reminded her of Ralph's ashes. Something dead in need of a letting go. Geneva considered burying it just as she had buried Ralph's ashes the night before.

She left the torn-out page on the counter. She took the Book and made her way to the yard. Tatum had given her power of attorney. She entrusted her to pull the plug or not, if the time came. This Book wasn't even a life support system. It was a death support system. The time to pull the plug seemed to be now.

Geneva stepped outside. The sun didn't look well. It looked red, stepped on, and smeared behind a milky cataract. She held the Book against her chest and looked around to see if a spot jumped out at her. She would leave it to the gods, she decided, just as she had with Ralph.

If the right spot spoke to her, into the dirt it would go. If not, well, then its number wasn't quite up.

Her eye caught the gas grill. Another option. Death by fire?

"Geneva."

Her head whipped around.

Ron's head rose above the fading carragana bushes. His gray, thinning hair was as disheveled as usual.

"Saw a patrol car outside your house this morning," he said. "You all right?"

Geneva walked to the hedge.

"Tatum was killed last night," she said. "Shot at the Deluxe." It was the third telling in hours.

Ron closed his eyes and shook his head.

"Paris was working," Geneva said. "It's all too awful." She told him what she knew. "Rachael will be coming out with her father at the end of the week."

Ron's blue eyes were soft beneath his gray and wiry brows.

"You've had a rough couple of months, haven't you?" he said.

Geneva considered it. Rough? No. They'd been amazing. In a shack outside of town, her body had come as alive as her mind. The questions that had plagued her — did she love, could she love? — existed not behind her in time but elsewhere in space. They remained unanswered, but it didn't matter because they were no longer hers.

Rough? No. It had been a time of a slow letting go. Learning how to do it as she went along.

Ron misread Geneva's watering eyes. It wasn't grief. It was gratitude.

Geneva held the Book upright before her chest.

"I'm going to burn this," she said to Ron.

Ron's sympathy turned to confusion. He raised his chin and squinted.

"It was Tatum's," Geneva said. "It's a family history of sorts. It caused her nothing but grief."

Ron scratched at his beard.

"As a librarian," he said, "I can't condone this."

"I hate to contribute to this smoke, though," Geneva said, looking up.

"Book burning," Ron said seriously, shaking his head. "It's not a legacy I'd want to be a part of."

"This has nothing to do with legacy," Geneva said, pronouncing *legacy* with a hint of disgust. "Quite the opposite." Ron extended his hand, and Geneva handed him the Book over the top of the hedge. "Rachael's seen it," Geneva said as Ron flipped through. "Burning it just keeps it from being rammed down her throat. Family-wise, this stuff has become some sort of gospel. Burning it isn't about what it says. It's about what its very existence means."

"So, you're burning the gospel?" Ron said, without looking up.

"Bad book burners burn books because they're afraid of new ideas," Geneva said. "I'm a good book burner. I'm burning this book because I believe in new ideas." She reached across the hedge for the Book.

Ron surrendered it but wasn't buying her reasoning.

"Gotta do what I gotta do." Geneva sighed. She shrugged and turned away. She crossed the yard, returning to the patio where she opened the grill She picked up the long cylinder of matches.

"Stop," Ron called from the hedge. "Don't do this. Not in a gas grill. Come over here," he said. "Give it the dignity of burning in a Weber."

Geneva paused. A Weber. More cauldron-esque. Yes. She turned.

"All right," she said, and she returned to the hedge. She squeezed through where it was least dense. Ron had gone ahead. He stood on his patio where the squat, black Weber sat between a picnic table and several potted tomato plants.

Ron shook his head.

"Destroying knowledge," he said.

"It's not knowledge," Geneva said. "It's information."

"Information that might hold the key to answers that little girl goes looking for someday."

Geneva opened her mouth to speak, but Ron kept going.

"What came before helps us understand what's happening now."

"But who needs a map to where they're standing?" Geneva said.

"Geneva," Ron said, his eyes softening, "history's not the enemy. Knowing how you got to where you are shows you that the way things are is not that way by divine edict. There were reasons. Hows. Causes and effects. Maybe even lies. 'To understand something is to be delivered of it,'" he quoted. "Spinoza." Then Ron looked at the ground and rubbed his beard. "You're probably wanting to get on with your life, I suppose, losing Ralph and all," he said, "but where we've been, where we've come from — important stuff. Let Rachael have that."

"You've invited me here under false pretenses, haven't you?" Geneva said.

Ron cocked his head and lifted his bushy brows.

"Forward is forward," Geneva said. "Know where you want to go and go. Looking back just slows you down."

"But if you don't know your history," Ron said, "you're bound to repeat it. It may be a cliché, but clichés earn their status."

"Nah-ah," Geneva said. "History repeats itself because we keep thinking about it and keep talking about it. How can anything new happen?"

Ron frowned.

"Matches," Geneva said.

Ron pursed the lips tucked in his whiskers. He sighed and moved toward his back door. But Geneva had taken in his argument more than she had let on. She was questioning herself and her plans. Did the adage "Know Thyself" really require knowing a couple of generations' worth of knowing *thee*selves? Wasn't there something to be said for taking history out of the picture? Or was that impossible? She wasn't sure. She considered that maybe she should just pull out the pictures and destroy the text. Preserve content. Destroy context. Rachael did seem to like photographs. Or maybe she should save the Book, and someday they could examine it together, herself and Rachael, and talk about perspective and meaning.

But did it matter that the past could be seen from twenty angles? Wasn't it still just the past?

Ron emerged from his back door. Geneva wasn't sure what she was going to do.

"You can't change the course of history by burning a book," he said, reaching the Weber.

Geneva looked at him and decided.

"That right there," she said. "Just listen to what you're saying. The 'course of history' like it's a road that's already laid out. 'The course of history' like there's a *here* that necessarily leads to *there*. That there," she said, "is exactly the problem."

Geneva extended her hand for the matches.

Reluctantly, Ron handed them over. Defeated, he lifted the lid to the Weber.

Geneva opened the Book and ripped out several pages. Ron winced. She placed them on the grill. She tucked the Book beneath her arm and struck a match.

"This isn't history," she said, touching the flame to the corners of the pages. "This is a tuning fork, and what it attunes to is something that doesn't even exist anymore. It's a ghost. It's a distraction. This book is the great oppressor," she said.

"Viva la revolution," Ron sighed as the pages curled with dark edges, smoking and giving off a chemical stench. The smoke floated up, joining the effluvium of the surrounding raging fires. Spirits came together in the sky. Trees and grasses and woodland victims. Vapor tendrils touched. They spread out over the valley, unable to escape.

48

~

Geneva suggested that she and Rachael go across the hall to look for things to decorate the spot where they would bury Tatum's ashes. Geneva thought it best to have a concrete reason for going over there so that Rachael could gravitate naturally toward whatever she might want or need as keepsakes. They stood together in the doorway of Tatum's apartment. Lee had dropped Rachael off at Geneva's the night before as planned while he stayed in a hotel downtown. Not counting burning a generations-old family genealogy, Geneva left Tatum's apartment just as she'd found it.

"Like what kind of stuff should I look for?" Rachael asked.

"Oh, I don't know," Geneva said. "Jewelry. Anything pretty or something that makes you think of her."

They took several steps into the living room. Rachael's head turned, taking it all in.

"She died before she got the message from your dad," Geneva said. "She didn't know you were coming."

Rachael stepped into the apartment where she had lived for seven months. Unlike her mother's house, it was a world already gone, changed to something else. She stepped with her arms at her sides, reached toward nothing, and seemed not quite to know where to go. Geneva purposely moved toward the counter so that Rachael might meet her there.

"You've got some stuff over here," she said.

Rachael walked over and lifted her chin. Then she climbed onto a barstool and took a look at the cutouts. Geneva watched as Rachael stacked them into a pile, one on top of the other. She seemed to hesitate for just a moment over the cutout of Vincent. Geneva remembered Tatum telling her about the missing picture of him. Apparently, it had turned back up. But when? Before the ripped out page? After?

Once Rachael had the paper dolls in a tidy stack, she kneeled on the barstool and peeked into the box filled with old clothes, books, and barrettes. She looked them over without reaching in. Then she climbed back down.

"You okay?" Geneva said.

"Uh-huh."

"That's all you want?" Geneva said, thinking about the Book she had burned.

"Uh-huh."

"You want to check the bedrooms?"

"No, thank you."

Geneva understood. She even thought Rachael wise. There were no souvenirs here. Tatum herself had decided that there was a clean break to be made. Who were they to question her? Geneva placed a hand on Rachael's back and led her across the hall.

"Remember that man in the coffee shop?" Geneva said, back in her apartment. "The one who wrote something on your homework?"

"Kind of," Rachael said.

"Well, we've become good friends," Geneva said, heading for the kitchen. "He has lots of land. I told your father we can put your Aunt Tatum's ashes out there."

"And we'll leave it out there?" she said.

"We'll bury the ashes," Geneva said. "I buried Ralph out there too." She pulled a box of Ziploc bags from a drawer. She extended her hand for the paper dolls.

"Is it like a graveyard?" Rachael said, handing them over.

"It's a wonderful place," Geneva said. "A nice, quiet place."

Geneva slipped the cutouts into a plastic bag for safekeeping and handed them back to Rachael. Then they headed for the living room. Geneva sat in the wingback with the old deerskin throw. Rachael sat across from her on the sofa. She fingered the plastic bag in her lap.

"Remember when you told me I should get a more interesting sofa?" Geneva said. "I think you were right. Maybe we can do that while you're here."

"I also said you should get a TV." Rachael looked out from under her brow.

Geneva wagged a finger at her. She was glad to see that part of Rachael's spirit was intact. But then Rachael's face went solemn.

"Where's Paris?" she said.

"I don't know."

"Did he move out because of Vincent?"

"I'm not sure why he moved out," Geneva said.

"But he knows."

"He knows," Geneva said. "Remember? He was there."

"Was he upset?"

"He was very upset," Geneva said. "He loved her."

"Maybe he needed some time to be alone."

Just like Rachael's father said he did, Geneva thought.

Rachael rubbed the plastic bag between her fingers, fanning out the paper dolls within.

"What about Vincent?" she said. "Does he know?"

"He does."

"Is he going to talk at the funeral?"

"I asked him not to come," Geneva said. "I thought it would be nice to keep it intimate. I thought Paris would be here."

Rachael looked up from the bag.

"And he wouldn't want to be with Vincent."

"I had that feeling."

"At first, when you said she died," Rachael said, "I thought she killed herself."

"She didn't," Geneva said.

Rachael looked off to the side. Her legs dangled from the edge of the sofa.

"We might move," she said.

Geneva cocked her head.

"Who?"

"Me and my dad. He thinks it would help us."

"Help you what?"

"Be happy."

Geneva wanted to say it right then and there: come live with me. Protocol be damned and parental permission too. But she knew she had to wait. She intended to make Rachael the offer no matter what, no matter what Lee thought of it. He could put the kibosh on it, certainly, but Rachael was going to know it was out there. A place for her. With Geneva. And a place in Montana that was hers, solid and permanent.

That part had been John's doing. Geneva had been nervous to tell him of her intention to invite Rachael to live with her. God knows, she hadn't been excited at first at the prospect of a child in her life, and in that case, the child was just living across the hall. But she had to do what she had to do. Open her hand and let fall what may. Stand in love and see who stood with her.

She and John had been in bed listening to the night sounds, the owls and crickets. Geneva had taken a deep breath and then told him her plans. By the time she was done, both had their heads propped up on an elbow facing each other.

"I have to do this," Geneva said, "for whatever it turns out to be."

John puckered his lips. Then he rolled onto his back. He made a face like his neck was bothering him just a bit. Geneva continued to look at him. His eyes were closed. Then she nestled into the sheets too.

"Clans happen," he said.

Geneva took his hand beneath the covers.

The following morning, Geneva had opened her eyes to find John already awake, arm behind his head and gazing at the exposed beams above.

"We ought to give Rachael a couple of acres," he said. "That way, no matter what her father says, she knows she has something here that's hers."

Geneva eased herself into a sitting position, leaning back on her arms.

"We?" she said.

"Why not?"

Geneva stared at him. She adored his face. The strong jaw. The clear, blue eyes. She reached out and touched the morning stubble on his cheeks.

"Are you sure you want to do this?" she said.

John rolled his head in her direction, and she laughed. At herself.

Of course he was sure.

Geneva looked at Rachael where she sat on the sofa. *She has a place here*, she thought. She was excited to tell her.

"Being happy sounds like a good plan," she said.

The sky was solid, black and gray. Was it smoke or clouds above him? Lee couldn't tell. But because there seemed to be a pressure inside of it, an intent to fall rather than rise, Lee suspected rain, or even hail.

He bumped along the gravel road in his rental car, following Geneva's directions. The urn was in a box on the floor of the passenger's side and safe against the jostling. It held Margaret and Tatum both. He had shipped Margaret to the mortuary in Montana and had the two packed together. It seemed an elegant solution as to what to do with Margaret's ashes. Lee fully expected to get the job in Denver. Scattering Margaret here in Montana together with her sister would keep her closer. Since Geneva and Rachael seemed to have a relationship, Lee figured Rachael would be back. Her mother would not be far. Rachael could visit her, even if she didn't know it.

Lee looked out at the flat prairie and distant shrouded mountains. It was strange, he thought, how things turn out. It was as though all this was the reason he had not known what to do with Margaret's ashes, and the reason, too, that Rachael had gone to Montana with her aunt. Maybe his mistakes were not mistakes at all.

Lee pressed the brake as he passed a small hovel of a building. He looked into the rearview. He saw Geneva and a large, older man sitting in folding chairs on the western exposure. He backed up and pulled through the gate.

Geneva rose from her lawn chair and began her approach before Lee got the engine shut down. He lifted the urn out from the box on the floor and opened the car door.

"Rachael's collecting rocks," Geneva said, "to mark the site."

It seemed an abrupt greeting to Lee. The previous night, he had spent only fifteen minutes with her dropping off the half-asleep Rachael. The woman seemed different than when he had met her on his last trip. At that time she had sat behind big, black sunglasses and was flanked by Indians. She'd seemed remote, of another world. On the phone after Tatum had been killed, she was helpful. But when he looked at her now, standing with the shack and the man behind her, he sensed something different. He instinctively stiffened, slightly on the defense.

"I'd like to talk to you real quick," Geneva said, "if you don't mind. I'd also like to be frank. Rachael is welcome here anytime," Geneva said. "Long term. Short term. The door's open. I wasn't going to say anything until you got back from Denver but then thought that maybe having a few days to chew on it would be helpful."

Lee shifted the urn into the elbow of his right arm. He had chosen it over the phone. It seemed overly shiny juxtaposed to the surroundings, the shack and the dust.

"But," Geneva said, bringing her palms together as though in prayer and pressing her index fingers to her chin. "I'm not sure how to say this so I'm just going to say it. I wouldn't want her shuffled here against her will."

Lee's feelings of defensiveness reinforced themselves. The good feeling he had in the car seemed to form into one large drop that was slowly escaping him.

"I don't mean I'd be unwilling to help out when you needed someone to step in," Geneva went on. "I just meant, if she were to stay with me long term, it would have to be because she wanted it."

Lee looked beyond Geneva's shoulder toward the shack and the large man sitting there looking out at the land. Lee had an impulse to drop the urn into the dust, get back in the car, and hit the road out. To hell with all of them. He'd brought his daughter home, given her everything she could want, brought her to Montana for her aunt's funeral, and made sure her mother's ashes would be as nearby as possible. What was the great crime he had committed?

"Have I asked you for something?" he said coldly.

Geneva shook her head.

"No, you haven't," she said. "I'm sorry. But I know it didn't work out for you before, and that's why she was living with her aunt. I just wanted you to know that if it didn't work out again," she paused and sighed. "Actually," she said, "it doesn't matter to me if it's your choice or hers. She's welcome here."

"We're doing fine," Lee said crisply, his exterior remaining cool. He stepped around Geneva and shook his head as he walked. It was happening again. The judgment. It was an insult wrapped in an offer of help.

Rachael then appeared coming around the side of the shack carrying rocks in her folded up shirttail. Lee noticed her eyes flit from one adult face to the other. She gathered the rocks in her shirt closer to her belly and hurried toward him.

"I got some rocks . . . " she started, but her eyes got tangled on the urn tucked in his arm.

The large man stepped up behind Rachael, extending his hand to Lee over her head.

"I'm John," he said. "Good to meet you. Thanks for coming. We figured we'd have the service first, and then I'll make us all some supper, and we could sit with the evening for a while."

The man had broken the tension of the moment. Rachael slipped off to drop her rocks into a bucket and then went to Geneva's car to retrieve her Ziploc bag of paper dolls. She rejoined the group, and they started off — Rachael with her plastic bag, John carrying Rachael's bucket of rocks, and Lee carrying the urn. The sky above had a strange weight, loaded at once with smoke and moisture. John sidled up to Lee as the small group crossed the prairie. He told Lee of the work it took to put in a well and of his plans to build a permanent structure on the distant slab.

"There's twenty acres, total," he told Lee. "Eighteen pretty soon. We're giving a couple of acres to Rachael."

"What?" Rachael said from behind them.

"Two acres of this is going to be yours." He smiled over his shoulder. Geneva put a hand on Rachael's back. John looked back at Lee. "We're drawing up the papers," he said. "It'll be held in trust for her until she's twenty-one. Then it's hers to do with as she wishes."

"So then I'd come live here?" Rachael said.

"You could," Geneva said. "Or you could just let it sit here and be. You could sell it if you wanted to. It's yours."

Lee watched as Rachael's gait shifted. She took longer steps and hit the ground more solidly with the bottom of her foot, exploring the surface of the earth.

"It's a gift," John said to him, in a man-to-man sort of voice. "Something solid."

Lee saw nothing to distrust in the older man's eyes. There were no grounds on which to protest. In fact, he envied Rachael the gift. Not in terms of dollars or real estate, he envied what it meant. He knew what they were offering. They were offering something they did not believe he could.

They reached an open area and the freshly dug trench, a grave the size for a large baby doll. The mound of clay and cobble sat near by with a shovel dug in and standing straight at the ready. John put down the bucket of rocks. Geneva stepped up to Lee and reached for the urn.

"Do you mind?" she said.

Lee hesitated. It was Tatum. That's all Geneva knew. He handed her the urn. It was hers.

"Help me," Geneva said to Rachael and each took a side. Geneva opened the lid, and they shook out the ash along the trench. Lee wondered if Geneva noticed anything amiss about the volume of ashes. But she said nothing. When the urn was empty, Geneva placed it to the side. The four stood around the trench.

"I couldn't find Paris," Geneva said. Then she closed her eyes and sniffed suddenly. She touched the back of her hand to her face, held it there for a moment before letting it fall as she reopened her eyes.

"It is in your Aunt Tatum's name that we give you this land," John said to Rachael. "On her behalf."

Then he pulled the shovel from where it had been planted. He tossed the first spadeful over the ashes. The two sounds took turns, the thick *pith* as the spade dug into the mound, then the hush sound of clumps of dirt, sand, and small pebbles spraying over Tatum's ashes, filling the spaces between them and building the ground back skyward. When he was finished, Geneva went down to a knee. She pulled a rock from Rachael's bucket and started to outline the small trench. Rachael dropped to her knees to help.

Lee watched as rock by rock a rectangle took shape around the mound of dirt. It was Margaret's funeral at last. He felt a sinking from his throat to his chest, his organs migrating back to where they belonged. He didn't know it but he was being dislodged in time. He watched Geneva and Rachael working in silence. He wondered, given the choice, whom Rachael would choose? Whom did he want her to choose? He didn't want to know the answer. Not to either question.

Impulsively, he reached down into the bucket. He withdrew a single rock and placed it in line in the nearly completed rectangle. Geneva looked at him over her shoulder. Rachael turned away from the rocks to her plastic bag of cutouts. She pulled out one of herself, one of Geneva, Paris, her mother, and Tatum. She pulled out Vincent too. She placed Tatum in the center of the grave. Then with the other pictures she created a circle around her. Tatum's orbit. Lee watched her create the design, weighting each paper doll with a small stone.

Lee looked at the cutout of Margaret, his bride, and felt the weight of her disappointment. Then his eyes made their way around the circle. His own picture was not among them. He eyed the Ziploc. He was there inside.

"Rachael," he said. She looked up from her work.

"Geneva wants you to know you can come here any time and stay with her. You can even go to school here, if you want to."

Rachael was on her knees, looking over her shoulder. Behind her, Geneva bristled and shot him a look.

She put a hand on Rachael's shoulder. Rachael turned her head to face her.

"Rachael," she said. "We all want you to be happy. Be with your dad. Be with me. Or do both. Anything is okay. We all love you," she said, and she liked that the words had slipped from her. "*I* love you," she said. "I think you're super."

Rachael turned her face back to Lee and slowly rose to her feet. Lee looked into his daughter's face, vaguely knowing that now he was the pull, the dismantling force.

Then, Rachael turned her back to him.

"I think I should stay with my dad," she said to Geneva, backing into Lee's legs.

Geneva smiled and nodded firmly. "Let's all do a prayer," she said.

They gathered then, all four, on one side of the grave. Errant splotches of rain, big as spit, began to plop on the ground around them. The drops were cold and promising, but there was no need to run for cover. Not quite yet. John's arm slipped around Geneva's shoulder. Lee held tightly to Rachael's hand. Between the two men, Geneva and Rachael stood side by side.

Then, without thought nor eye contact, expectation nor obligation, Rachael's hand lifted up as Geneva's reached down. One action did not lead to the other. There was no cause and effect, just simultaneous reaching out — Rachael's hand up, Geneva's down. The hands clasped in the space between them. No one gripped too tight. Yet, they held firmly. On the prairie, surrounded by the fires and the promise of rain, they stood beside each other.

They stood together.

49

⮾

The ground appeared only as Paris's foot came down upon it. Above him, the valley was sealed. After he left the duplex that terrible day, he walked, forgetting he had a car and forgetting he had no home. A bird's broken wing on the sidewalk caught his eye, and he saw the ants carrying their dead. But they were far away from him. In another world. They minded their own business and didn't look back.

Paris was alone. He didn't know how it was that he hadn't realized it before. He was transparent. No outside. No in. Without edges, he was unable to touch the world.

His blind march led him to the concrete stairs that led beneath the barbershop. It wasn't until he reached the bottom that he realized he no longer lived there. It stopped him just for a moment. He reared back and kicked in the door.

The apartment smelled of work, dirt, and sawdust. Paris stepped in and walked along the stacked piles of boards. Buckets of nails and screws, different buckets for different sizes, lined up where he once would sit untying his boots. A stainless steel sink wrapped in heavy plastic sat beneath the window where the moonlight, both real and false, had poured through the rails above. Three hard hats were stacked beside his closet door.

Paris took a deep breath. He stifled a scream. He knew better than to kick the buckets.

He bent over and placed his hands on his knees.

Tatum was gone.

Tatum was gone, and God forgive him, part of him was glad.

It was an awful truth. Paris did love her. But he had drawn her in and then asked her to change. She had drawn him in too. But the place into which she had drawn him was not a place he wanted to stay. He had entered just to reach her. He thought it was a place they would leave together. He thought he could show her the way.

A creak cut through the noise in his head. He looked up from his knees. The closet door had popped just an inch. The wish to rip the door off its loose and squeaky hinges shot through him. He stood and took three strides to the door. He jerked it hard and, sure enough, tore out the top hinges. Inside, there they were. Untouched. The shoebox. The canvas.

Paris reached in and lifted the canvas by its top corners and backed it out into the room. He held it before him and pressed his forehead to its grainy surface. He spoke to a god he did not believe in.

"You win," he said.

He laid the canvas on the floor and returned to the closet. He went down on his knees and opened the shoebox. He withdrew the long, flat, interior box and retrieved a stick of charcoal that was smooth and cool in his hand. He left the closet and started in on the canvas. Paris worked. He worked on his hands and knees, without trying, no more than the wind tries to blow or fire tries to burn.

Linda came first. She emerged on the left side of the canvas, sitting profile on her heels, neck stretching and mouth opening as though to sing. She was holding something close to her heart. A hand. The kind you get dealt. Tatum stood, her back to Linda. Her body was twisted at the waist and shoulder. An arm covered her breast but not the scar.

Paris could not escape the thing he feared, and he did become each of them as he moved them through him and onto the canvas. He knew the hunger and want as he bent a limb and created light with shadows. But he found he could not draw them and hold onto to them at once. They moved through him not like spirits but like something pumped from his heart out through his hands.

Then, the birds came. On Tatum's knuckle. On Linda's shoulder. Some had just one wing. All were in some way broken. But their necks were thrown back and their beaks were open. Mute and singing, they were a chorus that sang of loneliness, unaware of all the subtle, winding harmonies, each believing its call was unreturned. Paris blended lines with his shirttail, his fingers, and the side of his hand. The image on the canvas hung like the smoke trapped in the sky.

Paris didn't try. As he pressed on, soon he didn't work either. Paris simply Paris-ed, just as wind blew and fire burned and love did its thing, seeking out willing hosts and looking for itself through their eyes.

Finally, he sat back on his knees. His hands were filthy. The canvas had the texture of skin.

He didn't hear the man come down the stairs and enter the apartment behind him.

"Hey, you," the man hollered, and Paris jumped and looked over his shoulder, eyes shot with blood, face bruised, and the side of his head shaved and sewn. But the man who had called to him was no longer looking at him but at the canvas.

Paris left. He took the canvas with him. He remembered his car and drove west. He didn't drive far.

He knew that the wanting was not the love.

Let go of the wanting and what do you have?

50

Time fills space unevenly. When Rachael would come to tell her story, she would exaggerate, stretching the seven months she had lived with her aunt into as much as two years. But her time in the valley did, in fact, end up extending beyond those seven months. Rachael returned to the valley every summer once her father remarried. For four years, Rachael had never let him out of her sight, worried he might float away. But when she was thirteen, beautiful, and boy crazy, she blinked.

Her father's marriage didn't devastate her, as her own attention was diverted as well. Boys on bikes rode past her house, back and forth. Later, they came by the carfuls. Geneva became Rachael's confidante, always believing in her, sometimes to Rachael's chagrin. Geneva had so much faith that everything was going Rachael's way that she never felt sorry for her. "I understand you're unhappy," she would say. "But it's hard to feel sorry for someone so fabulous."

In the throes of adolescent angst, Rachael once had thrown up her hands in the face of Geneva's persistent optimism.

"Everything isn't okay," she had insisted. "Sometimes things are hard or bad. You haven't always been happy."

"Yes, I have," Geneva said. Then her brow furrowed in thought. "Although it could be," she added, "that I just don't remember feeling any other way."

Rachael stayed with her and John part of every summer. Sometimes, they stayed at the house John built on the slab. Other times, they stayed in the duplex. Renters moved in and out of the apartment across the hall. Social misfits with good hearts, mostly.

After high school, Rachael went to the university two hours west of the valley. Not far. Only as far as Paris had gotten when he left with his canvas ten years earlier. When he first arrived, he had worked as a sous chef at a local hotel. Then his art took off. His first series was of a one-breasted woman. Thigh to cheek. Waist to eyes. Never the whole woman at once. The collection was bought up by lesbians and brave, bald, middle-aged women who used the word *empowerment*. When the National Breast Cancer Foundation in New York commissioned a work, Paris was made. Not rich, but able to make a living from his art. He lived in a modest bungalow he had bought with cash. It had great northern light.

His next series did as well as his first. It consisted of images of places unoccupied. Doorways. Empty stools. The images implied missing persons. Something in the rendering forced the eye to a thing not there. The empty space filled with the viewer's attention. They were bought up quickly. Paris wasn't sure how he felt about the series. He worried they did the world a disservice.

Rachael's freshman year, Paris had a show at one of the local galleries during a community art walk. He had celebrity in the local art scene, and his show was packed. Paris accepted compliments and congratulations with sincere modesty. Invisibility had become harder to come by. The only place to disappear was into the work. But then, in a way, that's how it always had been.

The well-heeled of the community shook his hand. Red dots went up beside canvas after canvas. One well-wisher would step away from him only to be replaced by another. In an open moment, through a gap in the crowd, two young girls no more than nineteen appeared. One had dark green eyes and long brown hair. She wore an olive suede coat and a black cap.

"Do you remember me?" she said hesitantly, lifting her brow.

Paris's heart missed a beat, and his insides seemed to flood with warm water.

Tatum.

"Rachael," he said.

She smiled and slipped a strand of hair behind her ear.

"Well, I go by Mallory now," she said. She swung a backpack around to her front. She unzipped it and withdrew a file folder. She opened it and handed Paris a piece of paper with a ragged edge.

"Geneva gave it to me," she said. "Remember Geneva?"

Paris recognized the picture. He had drawn it in the basement of the duplex in the back of Tatum's Book.

"Geneva," Paris said, looking up from the picture. "How is she?"

"Great," Mallory said, rolling her eyes. "She's always great. Will you sign it?" she said and dug in her bag for a pen, "now that you're famous and all."

Her friend giggled. Mallory handed Paris the pen. Paris pressed the paper to his knee. As he signed it, Mallory spoke to her friend.

"See this scar," she said, pulling back her hair. "I fell in this lake. Paris and my aunt took me to the hospital. He held me super tight in the back seat of the car. Do you remember that?" she said to Paris.

He handed back the paper and pen. She kept asking him, *do you remember?* Paris looked into the eyes that reflected light. Bits of amber were illuminated within the green murk. Mallory cocked her head. Paris could barely detect the scent of her. There seemed to be a sound just out of range too. Paris felt the urge to follow her home and sit on her stoop. Chase the promise of the thing only sensed. But the impulse was just itself. It moved through him. It was not his.

"I remember," he said, and Mallory smiled. They were awkward for a moment then loosely embraced.

Geneva got the twenty years she had ordered from the gods. When she and John both had died, Mallory was entrusted with half of John's land, Geneva's duplex, and both of their ashes bundled as one. Mallory did not bury them. She released them to the wind. Her boyfriend of the time was with her and stood at her side on a windy afternoon in April on John's prairie while the ash was carried off in gusts. As she stood there, Mallory remembered Geneva telling her that life's journey was like the walk of the Russian dolls, but in reverse, emerging not from the larger to the smaller but the other way around. When you realize you're bigger than the self you've known, Geneva told her, you'll feel pressure. You'll think you have to struggle. But pressure is a lie.

As the ashes blended with prairie dust, Mallory knew that John and Geneva had taken the walk. They'd moved from the smaller to the larger, let go and let pressure turn to flow.

Mallory — Rachael — learned early of impermanence. Some might say, too early. But time refined the lesson. She learned that shifting sands were the way of life. Space is open, not empty. Loss is movement. She grew to be a woman too detached for many men's taste. She suffered too little and failed to suffer on others' behalf. It wasn't on purpose. It wasn't that she couldn't see that there is fear as well as love. Pain as well as courage. Redemption and mistakes. Snakes and beauty.

But it all slipped past her like someone else's dream because she knew the thing she didn't know that she knew. Yet it operated beneath her skin as both compass and antennae. The thing she knew didn't save her soul, as it wasn't a soul in need of saving. But the thing she knew did save her time. She rarely got distracted. She knew.

There is good.

The End

About the Author

K.M. Cholewa is from Chicago. She writes in Helena, Montana where she lives with a large, black dog. *Shaking Out the Dead* is her first novel.